KAHAWA

BY DONALD E. WESTLAKE

NOVELS
Humans • Sacred Monster • A Likely Story
Kahawa • Brothers Keepers • I Gave at the Office
Adios, Scheherazade • Up Your Banners

COMIC CRIME NOVELS
Baby, Would I Lie? • Trust Me on This • High Adventure
Castle in the Air • Enough • Dancing Aztecs • Two Much
Help I Am Being Held Prisoner
Cops and Robbers • Somebody Owes Me Money
Who Stole Sassi Manoon? • God Save the Mark
The Spy in the Ointment • The Busy Body
The Fugitive Pigeon

THE DORTMUNDER SERIES
Don't Ask • Drowned Hopes • Good Behavior
Why Me • Nobody's Perfect
Jimmy the Kid • Bank Shot • The Hot Rock

CRIME NOVELS
Pity Him Afterwards • Killy • 361
Killing Time • The Mercenaries

JUVENILE
Philip

WESTERN
Gangway (with Brian Garfield)

REPORTAGE
Under an English Heaven

SHORT STORIES
Tomorrow's Crimes • Levine
The Curious Facts Preceding My Execution
and Other Fictions

ANTHOLOGY
Once Against the Law (coedited with William Tenn)

DONALD E. WESTLAKE
KAHAWA

THE MYSTERIOUS PRESS

Published by Warner Books

A Time Warner Company

Mysterious Press books are published by Warner Books, Inc.,
1271 Avenue of the Americas, New York, NY 10020.

A Time Warner Company

The Mysterious Press name and logo are registered trademarks of Warner Books, Inc.

Printed in the United States of America

First Warner printing: April 1995

10   9   8   7   6   5   4   3   2   1

Library of Congress Cataloging-in-Publication Data

Westlake, Donald E.
   Kahawa / Donald E. Westlake.
      p.   cm.
   ISBN 0-89296-533-9
   I. Title.
PS3573.E9K3   1995
813'.54—dc20
                                                                94-38983
                                                                  CIP

GRATITUDE

My gratitude goes, first and foremost, to Dean Fraser, who shared his experience and expertise to a wonderful degree. Les Alexander created the necessary environments with unflagging optimism, and Rich Barber, Knox Burger, and Gary Salt usefully shared their enthusiasm and professionalism.

I can best express my gratitude to some individuals by not spelling out their names. My friend T.E.M. of the railway (who introduced me to M. F. Hill's *The Permanent Way*) was patient, helpful, and amusing. J.M. of the Coffee Board provided tea and information. In Grosvenor Square, R.B. was charming and insightful, while C.M. provided anecdotes and a lovely copper nugget.

Back home, Brian Garfield, Gloria Hoye, and Justin Scott made fine suggestions along the way, and Walter Kisly built a bridge just when it was most needed. As for Abby . . . she knows; she knows.

INTRODUCTION: 1995

I was in Los Angeles, meeting with some other people on some other business entirely, and when I got back to the hotel, there was a message from Les Alexander, in New York. I had known Les as a friend for some years, and while we had talked about working together on something or other, it had never happened. At that time, he was a book packager and sometime television producer; he is now a film producer. I was and am a novelist with a minor in screenwriting.

When I returned Les's call, he was boyishly excited. He had a true story, he said, that would make the basis for a great novel. I told him, as I tell everyone in such circumstances, "I'll listen, but I won't give you an answer today. I'll call you tomorrow. I don't want to make a mistake and be locked into something I don't really want to do, or locked out of something it turns out I *did* want to do."

"Fair enough," he said. "A group of white mercenaries, in Uganda, while it was under Idi Amin, stole a railroad train a mile long, full of coffee, and made it disappear."

"Forget the twenty-four hours," I said. "I'll do it."

So it began as a caper. I've written capers, before and since, both serious (novels about a professional thief named Parker, written under the pseudonym Richard Stark) and comic (the Dortmunder series), so I feel I know a bit about the form. (It probably says something discreditable about me that I put the serious work under a pseudonym and the comic under my own name.)

One thing I know about the caper is that it helps if the job is outrageous in one way or another. Once, for instance, before the government started paying by check, Parker stole the entire payroll from a United States Air Force base. Dortmunder, not to be outdone, has made off with a complete bank, temporarily housed in a mobile home.

And what could be more outrageous than to steal a mile-long train from the dread Idi Amin, and *make it disappear?* This is going to be fun, I thought.

Then I started the research. Please permit me at this point to say a strong word against research. I hate it. My feeling is, the whole point of going into the fiction racket was so I could make it all up. We get enough facts in real life; that's the way I see it.

Unfortunately, that's not the way anybody else sees it. If you get a fact wrong in a novel, I have found, people will write you letters full of the most grating kinds of sarcasm and superiority. Of course, not all facts are equally holy among readers. Should you get a detail about a gun or a car wrong, the weight of mail will drive the postman into the sidewalk, but if you get the population of Altoona, Pa., wrong, you probably won't hear from many people at all; three or four. So if I were to write a novel set in Uganda during the reign of Idi Amin Dada, and if I cared about the health of my mailperson, I had to do some research.

And here's the other thing I hate about research. Once I actually start it, I get lost in it. Research is my own personal Sargasso Sea. It's exactly like entering one of our civilization's mental attics, a quotation book or thesaurus or large dictionary, looking for just *one* thing, and being found in there three days later by search parties, seated on the dusty floor, intently reading.

That's what happened this time. I had current events to research (Idi Amin, and how he got where he got, and what it meant) as well as history (the European exploration/invasion of Central Africa, and what followed), so there was much to get lost in. The end was reached when I found myself halfway through a one-thousand-two-hundred-page book called *The Permanent Way*, by M. F. Hill, which was the official history of the building of the railroad upon which my coffee train would travel half a century later. "That's it," I said. "This is ridiculous. As soon as I finish the other six hundred pages of this book, I'm going to work."

The Permanent Way, and other books, were interesting and useful, but one book, called *Uganda Holocaust*, by Dan Wooding and Ray Barnett, published by Zondervan, changed both me and the novel I was going to write; for the better, I think.

It seems that some Christian evangelical sects set great store by "giving witness," which is to say, speaking about and airing and publicizing great works of charity or martyrdom or goodness, done in Christ's name. It also seems that Idi Amin's primary goal during his years in power was to eliminate Christianity from Uganda, a large if unworthy task, since Uganda's sixteen million people were seventy-five percent Christian. Amini's onslaught resulted in over five hundred thousand Christian martyrs, people who went to their deaths not because they were political or rebellious or dangerous, but only because they were professed Christians. This was the largest and most extensive Christian martyrdom since Rome before Constantine. How's that for a distinction?

The instant Amin was driven from Uganda, Wooding and Barnett flew in with tape recorders to take witness from the survivors, and published the results in *Uganda Holocaust*, a book that not only made me horribly familiar with the inner workings of the State Research Bureau, but also changed the character of the story I would tell. As I told my wife at the time, "I can't dance on all those graves."

So it was still a caper, but now it was something else as well, something more and, I think, deeper. My own emotions of pity and rage and contempt were entwined with the story, though I knew better than to let them take over. But they were there, spicing the stew.

And altering the book in more ways than one. As you know, in our country "sexandviolence" is one word, and piously we recoil from its depiction; sure. In *Kahawa*, though, both sex and violence had to play a stronger part than usual in my novels, because the material demanded it. I would never throw in what is called *gratuitous* sexandviolence, because I have too much respect for story. If a word, one single word, distracts the reader from the story I'm trying to tell, out with it. Since both sex and violence can be distracting, I usually depict them sparingly, trying mostly to get my effects by allusion and implication. Not so in *Kahawa*; the book demanded a stronger approach.

Of course, when it was published, I got complaining letters, and their general tenor was, "I've always liked your books, and so has my teenage son/daughter, but how can I show him/her this book with all this graphic sex in it?" Five hundred thousand dead; bodies hacked and mutilated and tortured and debased and destroyed; corridors running with blood; and nobody complained about the violence. They complained about the sex. Ah, such wee, sleekit, cow'rin, tim'rous beasties.

My research was not limited to books; my wife and I also went to Kenya, and to London, to see some of the locations and talk with some of the people. (We did not go into Uganda, merely looked at it across Lake Victoria, since this was 1980, Amin was barely three years out of power, and Uganda was still in a state of anarchy. Trips to Uganda at that time were mostly one way.)

Accompanying us on the trip was the person who had originally told Les Alexander the story, which he had knowledge of because of his connection with the pilots who were supposed to fly the coffee shipment from Entebbe. This person has been in many interesting places at interesting times, and was an education in himself, though not quite perhaps as solid as an education from books. Later, when he learned that I was writing an introductory note of gratitude to those who had helped me put the book together, he phoned to ask a favor: Would I mind thanking him under a pseudonym? (He mentioned the name he would prefer.) He didn't want his own name in print, but he did like the idea of being thanked for his part in the enterprise.

So I thanked one person under an alias; is that the strangest part of the story? Maybe.

About that title. *Kahawa*. It is the word for coffee in Swahili. It leads to the slang word for coffee in some parts of Europe: "kawa." (In Polish, "kawa" is the regular word for coffee.) The original is the Arabic "qahwa" or the Hebrew "kavah," and really it's all the same word, virtually around the world. A *c* or *k* or *q* at the beginning, a *w* or *v* or *f* in the middle. Kahawa is coffee. Unfortunately, it's a little obscure to be a title.

The problem was, the change in the book as I got into my research. Originally, I was going to call it *Coffee to Go*; a fun title for a fun caper. After a while, that title just slunk off in embarrassment. Then I found myself toying with pomposities like *Time of the Hero*, but my feeling is, if the title is too boring to read all the way through, it might keep readers from trying the novel. So *Kahawa* it is.

The original publisher of *Kahawa*, in 1982, was in the midst of an upheaval. My original editor was let go before publication, to be replaced by an oil painting of an editor; pleasant, even comforting, to look at, but not much help in the trenches. The publisher moved by fits and starts—more fits than starts, actually—and though the book received good reviews, no one at the publishing house seemed able to figure out how to suggest that anybody might enjoy reading it. So it didn't do well.

My current publisher is not suffering upheavals, my current editor is lively and professional, and when it was suggested that *Kahawa* might be given a second chance at life, I was both astonished and very pleased. I've made minor changes in the text, nothing substantive, and agreed to write this introduction, and here we are, by golly, airborne again.

By coincidence, I ran into that oil painting at a party a few months ago. He said, "Are you writing any more African adventure novels?"

"No," I said, "but Warner is going to put out *Kahawa* again, in hardcover."

His jaw dropped. *"Why?"* he asked. (This is what we have to put up with, sometimes.)

"I think they like it," I said.

I hope you do, too.

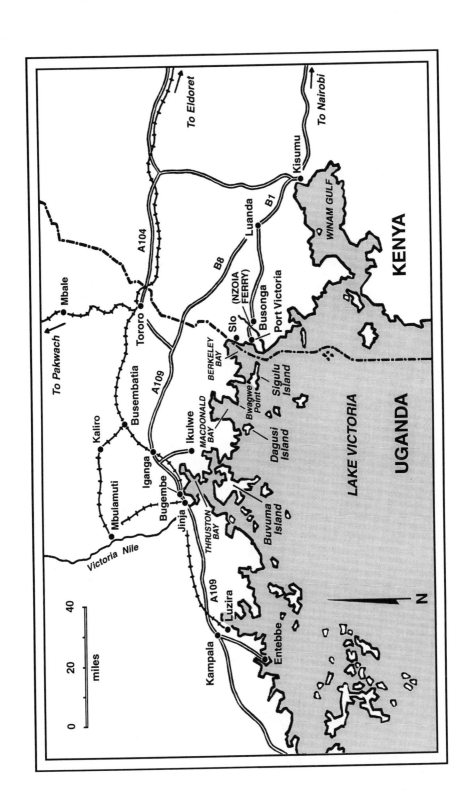

KAHAWA

PROLOGUE

Each ant emerged from the skull bearing an infinitesimal portion of brain. The double thread of ants shuttling between corpse and nest crossed at a diagonal the human trail beside which the murdered woman had been thrown. As a shadow crossed the morning sun, a dozen ants became crushed beneath the leathery bare feet of six men plodding down the trail from the Nawambwa road toward the lake, each bearing a sixty-kilogram sack of coffee on his head, none of the scrawny men weighing much more than sixty kilos himself. The surviving ants continued their portage, undisturbed. So did the men.

Farther downslope, the trail ended in a tangle of foliage at the edge of Macdonald Bay, with Lake Victoria visible beyond Bwagwe Point. The six men dropped their coffee sacks and sprawled beside them for a short rest, using the sacks as pillows. Two smoked cigarettes; three chewed sugarcane stalks; one scratched insect bites around his missing toe.

A helicopter flap-flapped by, very loudly, and the men became utterly still, looking up through the screen of leaves and branches as the big olive-green chopper went by, like a bus wearing a beanie. It was the same sort as the large helicopters used by the Americans to deliver troops to battle in Vietnam, but the markings showed it belonged to the Army of Uganda. Three black men in American-style combat uniforms crouched in the broad doorway in the chopper's side, peering down at the lake.

The six coffee smugglers, invisible beside the trail, watched and listened without reaction until the helicopter chuff-chuffed away across the sky, westward toward Buvuma Island. Then they all talked at once, with nervous enthusiasm, agreeing the helicopter had been a good omen. Having just searched this area, it was unlikely to return for some time. And how lucky they themselves hadn't arrived twenty minutes earlier; by now, they would have been visible and helpless on the open water.

Since luck was with them, they should seize the moment. Their two canoes were dragged out of hiding—the rifles safe within, the ancient, untrustworthy outboard motors still attached at the rear of each boat—and were pushed into the water. The sacks of coffee were loaded, the men arranged themselves three in each canoe, and they proceeded slowly out across the bay, southward, the motors stinking, the low morning sun in the eastern sky stretching their shadows across the calm water.

Forty minutes later they had progressed fifteen miles, heading east now toward the narrow strait between the mainland and Sigulu Island and thence to Berkeley Bay. The border between Uganda and Kenya— a line seen only on maps—bisected Berkeley Bay, and not far beyond lay the tiny, unimportant town of Port Victoria, their intended land-fall. A much shorter route for smuggling lay directly across Berkeley Bay from Majanji or Lugala on the Uganda side, but the shore there was heavily patrolled this year. And because so many floodlight-bearing helicopters prowled the border at night, the risky daytime passage had become safer.

All six men heard the chuff-chuff at once, over the nasal sputter of the outboard motors, and looking over their shoulders they saw the giant thing sailing toward them through the sky, like something on wires attached to God's fingers. There was no escape this time; they'd been seen, the helicopter was floating in a circle around them, its open doorway filled with pointing men.

It was guns they were pointing, and then firing. The smugglers had been prepared for arrest, for some brutality, possibly for torture, but they had not been prepared to become target practice in a great bathtub. Two of them dragged old Enfield rifles up from the canoe bottoms and returned the fire.

The soldiers, not expecting armed resistance, had flown too low and too close, the better to score hits on their fish in the barrel. Instead of which, two men in the helicopter doorway staggered back into the darkness within, and a third dropped like a full sack out into the air, falling beside his rifle down into the water. The helicopter, as though God had been startled at His play, jerked upward into the sky and tore away northwestward, toward land.

The men in the canoes were now terrified. The helicopter would soon be back, possibly with others. There wasn't time to reach that invisible line in the water and the dubious safety of Kenya. To their left was the shoreline of Uganda, low dark folds of hills, but they were in great fear of returning there. Directly ahead mounded Sigulu Island, ten miles long and a mile or two wide and covered with thick brush, but the soldiers would expect them to hide there and would have hours and hours of daylight for the search. To the right, a cluster of tiny brushy islands lay like suede buttons on the water; after a quick conference the six agreed to make for one of these. They ripped open the sacks and dumped the coffee into the lake, both to lighten the boats and to make it possible to deny that they were the coffee smugglers; but they kept the sacks, because they were poor men and thrifty.

They chose an island at random, pulled the canoes well up from the water's edge, and covered both their boats and themselves with layers of brush. But they were men who had never been in the sky, and were unaware of the clear lines the canoes had made in the mud and the brush, arrow shafts leading from the water directly to their hearts. When the helicopter did return within the hour and, after only the slightest hesitation, landed on the island of their hiding place, they could only believe it was devilry.

The officer in the helicopter was extremely angry. When the six men were found and lined up in front of him, he beat their faces with his fists and lashed their arms with a piece of brush. They had killed one of his men and wounded two others; it was a personal humiliation, an official disgrace, a blow to his hopes for military advancement. It was a blot on his copybook.

The six men denied that they were smugglers, which only enraged the officer more. He kicked their legs with his U.S. Army boots, while a uniformed man with an expressionless white face watched from the helicopter doorway. And when the empty coffee sacks were found, the officer turned cold and dangerous in his fury. He ordered the six men to lie on the ground on their bellies. He ordered his soldiers to pour gasoline onto the coffee sacks, and to spread one sack on each prone man. Then he personally set the fires. The flames in sunlight seemed to dance in midair, lightly, inoffensively, while the tan burlap darkened to match the stenciled black Swahili word *Kahawa*.

The men writhed and screamed beneath their burning blankets, and the rancid smoke rose into the clear sky as the white man in the helicopter doorway lit his cigar.

The soldiers broke up the canoes with small hatchets, and then boarded the helicopter and were flown away, through the drifting smoke.

This occurred early in March of 1977. It was reported in the London *Times* on April 5.

PART ONE

1

Lew Brady picked up the two-hundred-thirty-pound man, turned him over like a sack of potatoes, and flipped him onto the mattress. The other two attackers stood around blinking, openmouthed, not moving forward. "What's the matter with you birds?" Lew demanded. He grabbed one by his unzipped leather jacket, spun him, yanked the jacket shoulders so the garment came halfway down the man's arms to hold him like a straitjacket, then shoved him into the other guy. They stumbled together, tripped over the edge of the mattress, and fell on the two-hundred-thirty-pound man.

Lew stood with hands on hips, frowning down at the muddle of men. "I don't know," he said. "Maybe you clowns should just join the union."

One of the other men in the room said, "Mr. Brady, that's not fair. You're trained, and we're not."

"Training *you* idiots is what it's all about."

The three men on the mattress were beginning to take out their frustrations on one another, with fists and elbows. "Hold it, there, hold it." Lew leaned down to pull them apart. "*I'll* tell you when to fight."

They straggled to their feet, and Lew herded them over with the rest of the class: sixteen brawny adult males, all standing around looking sheepish and sullen, like a football team at the end of a winless season. "Line up," Lew told them. "Face the mirror."

This large top-floor space in a ramshackle low office building on the outskirts of Valdez, Alaska, was intended to be a rehearsal hall. Several ballet classes met here, as did a Yoga society. One long wall was mirrored. A piano stood in one corner and a cluster of folding chairs in another. Half a dozen ratty mattresses were scattered on the floor. Wide windows gave a view of the used-car lot across the way.

During Lew's first four months up here in Valdez, while he was learning to pronounce it "Val—*deez*" like a native, it had seemed there were no jobs at all here for a man of his profession. But then he'd met Alan Kampolska, who owned a small local trucking operation and was being harassed by union "organizers" attracted by the pipeline construction. Kampolska's drivers were big and tough, but they didn't know how to handle themselves against goon squads.

Which was where Lew came in, with his experience as a Green Beret and a mercenary in Africa. Kampolska had offered to hire him to teach his boys how to conduct the war against the union thugs. Lew, bored and frustrated, had agreed. But it was slow hard work, not at all like training recruits in an army.

The main problem was mental attitude. In most self-defense classes it's the instructor's job to build self-confidence by a long string of small victories; but these guys were brawlers and sluggers, men who could handle themselves in tough situations, and the problem was they were suddenly facing an enemy too mean and too organized for them. Their reaction was a kind of aggrieved bewilderment, a belief that they were already defeated. So Lew had switched from the ortho-dox method of ego boosting to an unorthodox program of kicking the shit out of them. If he couldn't build them up to self-confidence, maybe he could knock them down to self-respect. (And he was also, of course, working off some of his own irritable frustration.)

Now, with the sixteen in a glum row facing the mirror, Lew marched back and forth like the top sergeant he had frequently been. "Look at yourselves," he ordered. "You're a crowd of big, tough, no-nonsense sons of bitches, you look like you could hunt bear with a baseball bat, but you walk in here and all of a sudden you're a goddam bunch of ballet dancers."

The man who'd complained before complained again. "You're a trained professional, that's why."

Lew shook his head. "Tell me the truth," he said, making it a general question. "You want to throw in the towel, just give up and join the union?"

"No," they said. "Shit, no," some of them said. "Fuck the union," some others said.

Which was good spirit, but not quite good enough. Lew sighed, and went over to stand directly in front of the complainer, a tall and rangy white man named Bill, who sported several tattoos and a straw cowboy hat. Looking him in the eye, Lew said, "Bill, if we met in a bar and got into an argument, what would you do?"

Bill had the sullen look of a man who expects to be hurting in a few seconds. "Throw a punch at you, I guess," he muttered.

"And what would I do?"

"Grab my fist, twist it around behind my back, and run me into the wall."

"You've seen me do that."

"I sure have," Bill said. The others all chuckled. They loved to see one another get thrown around.

Lew said, "Bill, can you see in your mind that move I make?"

"Sure I can. I *dream* it."

"Then *do* it."

Bill massively frowned. "I dunno. I—"

"I'm giving you more warning," Lew told him, "than you'll get on the street. I am about to throw a punch. You'll either do the move, or you will become punched in the face."

"Jesus," Bill said, and Lew punched him in the face. Bill sat down on the floor, everybody laughed, and Lew sighed.

He turned to another of the men, but what he would have said was drowned out by the sudden roar of a low-flying plane skimming past, barely above the building roof. Everybody in the room instinctively ducked his head and hunched his shoulders until the roar faded. Then Lew saw his students exchange an amused and knowing glance, and he shook his head.

As they all knew, he was living with a pilot named Ellen Gillespie, who worked for the pipeline construction company. She always buzzed him on her return flight so he could drive out to the airport and pick her up.

Which made it seem like he was pussy-whipped or something— that's what these clowns were grinning about—but it wasn't like that at all. Ellen was Grade A; they fit together terrifically; everything was or should be fine. *Would* be fine if he would line up a real job somewhere.

Okay. The plane's roar had faded, and he had another few minutes before leaving for the airport. Standing close to his next victim, a very broad-shouldered black man named Woody, Lew said, "Okay, Woody. You know the move?"

"Yes, sir, I do." There was a gleam in Woody's eye; he was really going to try for it this time. Lew hoped the man would succeed, to give the entire class a lift. He also hoped the wall he was run into wouldn't be the one with the mirror.

"You're about to get punched," he said, reared back his fist, and felt a sharp pain in his shin. "Ow," he said, his concentration broken, and Woody punched him smartly in the eye. *Then* Lew threw his own punch; Woody plucked his fist out of the air, spun him, twisted his arm up his back, and ran him into the side wall.

Suddenly older and a *lot* more tired, Lew picked himself off the floor as his students yelled and cheered and clapped Woody on the back. The son of a bitch had kicked him in the shin!

When the celebrations and congratulations at last died down, Lew said, "There. That's what I'm talking about. Woody, you're the first guy here to figure it out. The rest of you guys think it over, and I'll see you tomorrow."

He stood ramrod-stiff while his class trailed out, chatting and chuckling and offering to buy Woody any number of beers. Then, alone at last, he permitted himself to groan and to rub the various parts that hurt.

"Something," he muttered, massaging himself and limping over to his outer clothing on one of the folding chairs. "Something else," he mumbled into the musky wool of a sweater he was pulling over his head. "Something has to happen."

2

Baron Chase, a man so steeped in his own villainy that the evidences of his evil now only amused him, paced the hotel-room floor like a pirate captain on his quarterdeck. "I am talking," he said, "about stealing a train."

"You must forgive my English," Mazar Balim requested. He spoke better English than most men of any nationality. "You are suggesting the holding up of a train? Pursuant to its robbery?" A well-off merchant of fifty-three, he sat on the bed, round body and short legs, like Humpty Dumpty, blinking up at Chase.

"I am suggesting *stealing* a train," Baron Chase said, smiling around his cigar, "pursuant to its rape." Secure in his power, giving Balim a moment to think, he paused in his pacing to look out the narrow slatted window with its view of the alley leading to Standard Street, where a rag-dressed woman now walked in the bright sunlight, balancing on her head a rusted five-gallon drum filled with bits of wood and metal.

In taking this modest room in the rear of the New Stanley Hotel, away from the conversational chatter of the Thorntree Café and the traffic noise of Kimathi Street, Chase had registered as James Martin, U.S. citizen, of Akron, Ohio, representing the Monogram Bicycle Tire Company of that city, and furnishing a passport, American Express card, and other documents in support of this identity. However, he dared not meet with Balim in either the first-floor cocktail lounge or the outdoor café, as "James Martin" would normally have done, but was forced to discuss the scheme with him here in this claustrophobic room, with its one comfortable armchair that Chase scorned, while Balim sat like a fat obedient boy on the edge of the bed, watching with round-eyed patience.

There are several first-rate hotels in Nairobi, but none of the others would have done. The Hilton and the Intercontinental cater to the package tourists, mostly American but also European, while the Norfolk caters to Britons in whom the spirit of the Raj still lives, as well as to those Scandinavians and Germans who like to pretend they're English. In the bars and restaurants of those hotels the customers' faces are all white. Only in the New Stanley, the businessman's hotel, the politicians' and journalists' hotel, are the customers—and their visitors—a mixture of white and black and Asian.

But even here Chase had to be wary. There was too much danger, in any public place, of his being recognized by a reporter or a civil servant as not James Martin of the bicycle tires at all but Baron Chase, of Canadian birth but now of Ugandan citizenship, an official in the government of Uganda and special adviser to Idi Amin himself. His presence here in Nairobi, in discussion with an ex-Ugandan Asian businessman, would be bound to cause questions; and if the questions were to reach the ears of Amin, it would be too late for answers.

"Where is this train?"

Turning from the window, withdrawing from his mouth the cigar he'd brought from Kampala, Chase allowed himself to look both surprised and amused. "*Where* is it? Don't you want to know what it carries?"

"Not necessarily," Balim said. "I am a businessman, Mr. Chase, which is a very small and cautious form of thief. I am prepared to remain small and cautious the rest of my days. I had enough of drama in 'seventy-two."

Five years before, in 1972, Amin had driven from Uganda the sixty thousand native-born residents and citizens of Asian heritage, forcing them to leave behind all their holdings and personal possessions except for cash to the equivalent of one hundred dollars U.S. Balim had been among those deported; because his mercantile trade had previously expanded into Kenya, he had been luckier than most.

"That was before my time," Chase said. "I had nothing to do with that."

Balim shrugged. "You would have," he said. "It doesn't matter."

"I was in Angola in 'seventy-two," Chase said. "Working for one faction or another."

"Or even two at a time," Balim suggested.

"It carries coffee," Chase said. His grayish pocked cheeks grew gaunt when he drew on the cigar. "Current market value, about three million pounds U.K."

"Six million dollars." Balim nodded. "A train full of coffee. The border between Uganda and Kenya is closed."

"Of course."

"This is Ugandan coffee."

"There will be an airlift," Chase told him, "operating out of Entebbe. It's being laid on by a British-Swiss consortium, selling our coffee to the Brazilians to make up for their shortfall."

"My knowledge of the world does not extend to South America," Balim said. "I apologize for that. Why would Brazil have a shortfall in coffee?"

"Frost hit the crop."

Balim sighed. "God's diarrhea falls with equal justice everywhere."

"The train will cross the northern uplands," Chase told him, "stopping at each plantation to pick up the crop. By the time it reaches Tororo it'll be full. Then it travels the main line west to Entebbe."

Balim patted his soft palms against his round knees. His eyes were bright as he looked at Chase. He said, "And somewhere along this line, between Tororo and Entebbe, something happens."

"The train never reaches Jinja," Chase said.

"Ah, Jinja." For a moment, Balim looked nostalgic. "A lovely town, Jinja. A friend of mine once had a weekend farm near there. Fruit trees. Gone now, I expect. What happens to this train before it reaches Jinja?"

"You steal it."

"Ho-ho," Balim said, laughing only with his mouth. "I do not, Mr. Chase. No, no, Mazar Balim is not a cowboy or a commando."

"Mazar Balim," Chase told him, "is a leader of men. You have employees."

"Clerks. Accountants. Drivers. Warehousemen."

"Frank Lanigan."

Balim stopped, frowning, gazing past Chase toward the narrow open window. Street noises came faintly. Finally he said, "Frank Lanigan did not discuss this with you."

Chase had returned the cigar to the corner of his mouth, and now he smiled around it, showing yellowed teeth. "You sound very sure of yourself. You believe Frank Lanigan wouldn't talk to me without reporting it to you?"

"Frank wouldn't willingly talk to you at all," Balim said. "Frank doesn't like you."

A little puff of cigar smoke obscured Chase's face; when the haze dissipated, he was calm and smiling. "Frank would like to steal a train."

Balim nodded his agreement. "There is that about him," he said. "A certain boyishness."

"I've known Frank for twenty years," Chase said. "Since Katanga. He's stupid, but he gets the job done."

"But what is your interest in this particular job, this train theft?"

Chase smiled. "Money."

"Doesn't Idi Amin pay you well?"

"Very well. In Ugandan shillings, very few of which I can get out of the country."

"Ah."

"I'll tell you frankly, Mr. Balim," Chase said, with the intensity of a man who speaks frankly very seldom, "Idi Amin is running out his string."

Balim showed surprise. "Who is there to overthrow him?"

"The world," Chase said. "When you kill an archbishop, the righteous shall rise up and smite you."

Anglican Archbishop Janani Luwum had only recently been murdered. Balim said, "You don't think that will blow over?"

"There's too much to blow over," Chase said. "He's getting crazier. He could even turn on me one of these days."

"An uncomfortable position."

"I'm forty-nine," Chase said. "When I signed on with Tshombe in Katanga, I was a kid in my twenties. My joints were never stiff, I could go without sleep for days, and no matter how many people died around me I knew I was immortal."

"Visions of retirement," Balim said with a sly smile. "The rose garden. Even the memoirs, perhaps?"

"I want more out of all this than memories," Chase said, an underground savagery surfacing for an instant. "I've been in this fucking continent half my life. I want to take something away with me when I go."

Balim shifted slightly on the bed, as though he found Chase's nakedness socially discomfiting. "I can see," he said, in deliberately businesslike and uninflected tones, "that I am the correct man for you to approach."

"That's right." Balim's calm had restored Chase's own equilibrium. He said, "I'm in a position to set the thing up. You have the merchant contacts in Kenya to move the coffee back into legitimate channels. You can finance Frank Lanigan in pulling the caper. You can arrange to bank my share for me in Switzerland. And you have a motive even stronger than money for getting involved."

Balim's surprise this time was certainly genuine. "I have? A motive stronger than money? What could this possibly be?"

"Revenge," Chase told him. "Most of those coffee plantations used to belong to your brother Asians."

"Who stole them from the departing whites in nineteen sixty-two," Balim pointed out.

Chase gestured irritably with the cigar; white ash fell on the rug. "The point is," he said, "Amin stole them in 'seventy-two, when he kicked you people out. It's Amin's coffee. It's Amin's personal money. You can kick him one up the ass."

"Well, well." Balim rose from the bed, adjusting his neat round trousers. "You realize I can't give you an answer immediately."

"The train runs in three months."

"You give me much to think about," Balim said. "Including the idea that you find me sufficiently trustworthy to bank your profits for you."

Chase removed the cigar from his teeth, so that his smile looked like the grin of a wolf. "You don't travel light, my friend," he said. "You're a man of homes and shops and warehouses. You know very well, if you double-crossed me, how easy it would be for me to find you."

"I see," Balim said. "Spoken by a man who believes revenge is more important than money. I do see. We shall talk again, quite soon."

3

Frank Lanigan steered the Land-Rover down Highway A1 toward
Kisumu and home. A heavy-jawed, big-boned, ham-handed man of
forty-two, Frank drove as though the vehicle were a reluctant mule,
shoving the gearshift this way and that, pounding the pedals with his
booted feet, mauling the steering wheel, grunting every time the
potholed roadway bounced him in the air to thud him down again
onto the springless bucket seat. The Land-Rover's roof had, over the
last eighty miles of bad road, mashed his wide-brimmed campaign
hat down over his eyebrows and against his ears, adding a headache
to all his other body aches and general dirtiness and disrepair. Kisumu
couldn't arrive any too soon.

Frank had been away for three days up at Eldoret, where the provincial inspector for the Department of Weights and Measures was refus-
ing to stay bribed. It was Frank Lanigan's least favorite type of
occupation, that; give him a fight, a war, even a ditch to dig—he'd
choose any of them over diplomacy. And particularly diplomacy with
a greedy minor official.

In the passenger seat, the scruffy black called Charlie hung on with
one hand, bounced around like a paddleball at the end of a string,
smiled vaguely, chewed sugarcane, and spat on the floor between his
feet. And sometimes on his feet. "Spit out the window, man!" Frank
yelled.

"Dust," Charlie explained with perfect equanimity. Frank wasn't
sure whether he'd never seen Charlie stoned or never seen him straight;
all he knew for sure was he wished he'd never seen him at all. Charlie
was a dirty, irresponsible, smelly, untrustworthy son of a bitch. Unlike
the Luo, the local tribe in this part of Kenya, a serious and hardworking
(if somewhat simple) people, Charlie was a bright tricky Kikuyu from
the Mau Range, the tribe that had made Mau Mau famous. A Britisher,
Sir Gerald Portal, had said it best back in 1893: "The only way in

which to deal with Kikuyu people, whether singly or in masses, was to shoot at sight."

It was too late to shoot Charlie at sight; Frank had been sighting him for nearly three years now, and familiarity had bred a kind of uneasy truce between them, in which neither made any effort to hide his disdain for the other.

And in fact Charlie did have his uses. Mr. Balim had instructed Frank to bring the little bastard along to Eldoret as interpreter and general assistant, and as usual Mr. Balim had been right. It was Charlie, snuffling around among the local *wananchi*, who'd found the source of the provincial inspector's instability: a woman, of course, reckless and greedy and discontent. And it was Charlie who last night had gone to the woman and threatened her with a knife, promising it would *not* kill her. This morning the inspector had abruptly seen the light, and now Frank could come back to Kisumu, report to Mr. Balim, and then go home, have a wash, have a White Cap beer (or maybe two), have a steak on his own screened patio, bed down with a couple of the maids for company, and ease the aches and knots out of his system.

There was a level railway crossing right at the city line, and damn if the barrier didn't come down, red lights idiotically blinking, just as Frank reached the rotten thing. He squealed the vehicle to a stop, then sat perspiring in the sunlight while the dust of his passage leisurely overtook him. Charlie negligently spat down his own shirt-front. "Christ give me strength," Frank said.

Stopping beyond the tracks, facing this way, chrome glittering painfully, was a gleaming dark-blue Mercedes-Benz 300 sedan, the vehicle of choice of the native-born winners in this part of the world. The chauffeur, capped and jacketed in black, half his face hidden behind huge dark sunglasses, sat stolid and unmoving at the wheel, dreaming perhaps of his own Mercedes and chauffeur farther down the road of the future. Behind him, the passenger or passengers were obscured in darkness; possibly a government official, or a successful contractor with government connections, or an even more successful smuggler, or an elaborately coiffed woman belonging to one of the above. (Given that many of the central African tribal names featured the formal "Wa" plural prefix—Wakamba, Wa-Kwavi, Wateita, Wa-

Nyika, even Wa-Kikuyu—and given these winners' invariable symbol of triumph in the Mercedes-Benz, the natives used an ironic tribal name for these detribalized successes: the Wa-Benzi. It was a deadly insult to call a Wa-Benzi that to his face. Not that he'd attack you with a knife or his fists; no, he'd wait and destroy you later, in some indirect white man's way.)

The train, when it at last appeared, was a freight, very slow-moving, pulled by a Garratt steam locomotive. Beyond the trundling freight cars, Kisumu hunkered in the hot sun, a seedy, sand-colored, low-lying commercial town, as ugly and as functional as a prison outhouse, a scruffy equatorial port like dozens of others around the world's waist, except that instead of facing an ocean it faced a lake, Victoria, the world's second largest, the size of Scotland, the source of the Nile, girdled by Uganda and Kenya and Tanzania. Serviced by the railroad from the east and by any number of freight boats from the west, Kisumu was the conduit for an awful lot of wealth, absolutely none of which showed.

As the rusty green caboose at last slid by, and the barriers began to lift, Charlie abruptly uncoiled himself out of his seat and out of the Land-Rover, saying, "Good-bye."

"Good-bye?" Frank watched with chronic irritation as Charlie sauntered away southward along the tracks, taking his own unfathomable direction. His shirt had once been white. His trousers, baggy-assed and too big in the waist and cut off now just below the knee, had once been black and probably the property of some up-country missionary or mortician. His legs, splaying out when he walked, looked as though they were full of doorknobs. "The thing I'd like to know," Frank said aloud—he'd been talking to himself for several years now, and as yet had found no cause to disagree nor end the conversation—"is why, if he wasn't going across the track, he sat in this bloody car for ten minutes until the train went by."

There was no answer. There was never an answer with Charlie. Frank shook his head, and the car behind him honked in impatience as the Mercedes-Benz came by. In the backseat were two Wa-Benzi, serious self-important men in suits and ties, discussing white papers in an ecru manila envelope. Frank wrestled the Land-Rover's gearshift into first, stomped the accelerator, and jolted across the railroad track.

* * *

The heart of Mr. Balim's enterprises, now that his holdings in Kampala and Luzira had been confiscated by Idi Amin, was a pair of long, low, rambling, concrete-block, stucco-faced buildings on Kisiani Street. They contained storefronts, offices, and warehouse space, as well as a broad yard area in the rear, and one and a half of them were colored a faded patchy blue, using paint Mr. Balim had once brokered but not been paid for. The paint had run out, leaving the right side and rear of one of the buildings the normal Kisumu color of pale sun-washed tan.

Fighting the wheel with both hands and both knees, Frank steered the Land-Rover through a tight turn into the narrow driveway between the two buildings. The side walls bore the scars of his earlier moments of impatience, but this time as it happened he hit nothing, and continued on to slam the vehicle into its normal parking space by the electrified fence at the rear of the property.

Walking toward the right-hand building, the one containing the offices, Frank passed two overall-clad employees hunkered by a rusty outboard motor, pointing at it with oilcans and screwdrivers and muttering together in Luo. Off to the left, another employee enthusiastically changed a truck tire with the assistance of a sledgehammer. Another pair of employees sprawled at their ease against the rear wall, awaiting the emergency best suited to their talents. Frank tried to spit into the sand to express his feelings about all these people, but his mouth was too dry; he contented himself with a disgusted look and went on inside.

Isaac Otera, at his desk in Balim's outer office, also looked disgusted, and was speaking with weary patience to somebody on the phone. "We have a policy about that," he said, obviously not for the first time. "We do not pay for goods we have never seen." Frank, with a small wave, started to walk on through to Balim's office, but Isaac waggled his hand in negative fashion while he kept explaining to the phone.

No? Frank looked at the closed door; was Balim in there with someone else? He couldn't ask Isaac until the phone call was done, so he went out again to the soft-drink machine in the hall and bought two 7UPs. One he poured on his head; the other he drank. Then he went back and sat on the bench opposite Isaac and rubbed his nose with the back of his hand; it tickled after the 7UP.

Isaac must be dealing with somebody in the government; otherwise, he wouldn't be putting up with it this long. But that was all right; being patient with government officials was what Isaac had been born for.

Like Balim himself, Isaac Otera was a refugee Ugandan. A member of the Langi tribe from the northern part of the country, he had been well educated at Makerere University and had started in government service with the Uganda Land Commission some twelve years ago, at the age of twenty-two. He was a natural Wa-Benzi, a tall and handsome, intelligent and educated man with a respectful liking for Northern culture, and in a rational world he would still be what he had been three years ago: some sort of assistant undersecretary somewhere in the bureaucracy, not yet the possessor of a Mercedes, but at least owning a Ford Cortina.

But Idi Amin's Uganda was the reverse of a rational world. The Langi were one of the two tribes Amin hated most, and against whom he had assembled death lists thousands of names long. Three years ago, driving homeward toward Kampala one evening after an unexpectedly long conference in Jinja, Isaac had had a blowout in the Ford Cortina. With some difficulty he had found a garageman to help him with the repairs, and a phone to call home to tell his wife and two daughters that he'd be late. He hadn't been alarmed when there was no answer, since phone service was chancy at best and he'd assumed their phone was out of order. When finally he'd reached home, three hours late, the lights were all on but the house was apparently empty. Isaac had walked through the rooms, calling their names, until he'd seen the smear of blood on the basement doorknob. It had not been possible for him to touch that doorknob, to open the door and see what lay behind it. Taking what money he could find, and two sweaters, he had gone out into the fields behind the house and waited. Sometime after midnight two cars had stopped outside and several men had emerged to enter the house through both the front and rear doors. After a while, a lot of shooting had sounded from in there: machine-gun fire and pistol shots. Several of the lamps were shot out. Then the men had driven away again, leaving the remaining lights burning, and Isaac had crept off, making his way to the house of a friend, who had driven him before dawn to Tororo and the Kenyan border.

Now Isaac was Mazar Balim's inside man, just as Frank was his outside man. While Frank dealt with bribery and thievery and occasional rough stuff from thugs who saw profit in intimidating an Asian merchant, Isaac talked to bureaucrats from the government and the railway and the airline, he conferred with the representatives of American and European companies offering goods for sale, he dealt with taxes and tariffs and import restrictions. Set a bureaucrat to catch a bureaucrat; old Balim knew what he was doing, every time.

The phone conversation never actually ended; as with most such dealings, it merely faded away into vague suggestions and possibilities. As usual, Isaac outwaited his opponent, and there was just a glint of combative triumph in his eye when at last he cradled the receiver and said, "You're dusty."

"I stink," Frank said accurately, and gestured at the door. "Who's in there with the boss?"

"No one. Mr. Balim isn't here."

"Not here?" Frank got restlessly to his feet, hitching his belt around his sweat-soaked waist. "Where is he?"

"Flew to Nairobi this morning. I expect him—"

The door opened and an employee stuck his black head in and said something fast to Isaac, who spoke equally quickly back. The employee disappeared, and Isaac said to Frank, "He's coming in now."

"Is that what he said?" It rankled with Frank that after a hundred years of hanging out with Englishmen these natives were still determined to talk Swahili. It wasn't as though Swahili were their native tongue; they all had tribal languages, hundreds of them throughout eastern and central Africa. Swahili wasn't even a proper language at all, when you stopped to think about it. The very word *Swahili* came from the Arabic word *Sawahil*, meaning "coast." When the Arabs had founded their trading cities at Zanzibar and Mombasa and elsewhere on the east African coast in the seventh century, and inter-married with the several Bantu tribes they'd found living there, this bastard tongue had emerged, using Bantu syntax and a combination of tribal and Arabic vocabularies. The Arab slave caravans had carried this African Yiddish a thousand miles westward across the continent in their bloody man-harvests, so that even today when a Nandi, for instance, wanted to converse with an Acholi, it was always in that damn Swahili.

Frank had been kicking around Africa for nearly twenty years, ever since Katanga, and he had made it a point of honor to resist learning Swahili. He knew enough to take himself successfully through a parade ground or a battle—"More ammunition here," "Keep your fucking head down," "Whose foot is that?"—but no more. Let the Bantus learn damn English, like civilized people.

Mazar Balim came in, looking rumpled but not upset. "The road from the airport continues to deteriorate," he said. "Soon we shall not be able to ship light bulbs."

"Or beer," said Isaac.

Frank, unable to repress his curiosity, said, "How was Nairobi?"

"Very excited about itself. Isaac, anything of import?"

"Nothing that can't wait."

"Good. Frank, come in. You look very dusty; have you been home?"

"Not yet."

Frank followed Balim into a small, crowded but comfortable room in which the windows were all blocked by filing cabinets, except the one tumorous with an air conditioner, which Balim turned on at once. "Our friend in Eldoret is our friend again, I presume," he said, edging through the clutter to sit in the old wooden swivel chair behind the desk. The two scarves thrown over the chair were so threadbare they had virtually no color left.

Shutting the office door, dropping like an abandoned novel into the brown vinyl chair facing the desk, Frank said, "All fixed," and went on to give an account of the fixing that was totally unfair to Charlie. At the end of which, Balim nodded and said, "That's good. I knew you and Charlie would handle it."

"Mm," Frank said.

"There is another matter," Balim said. "What do you think of coffee smuggling out of Uganda?"

"Profitable." The 7UP in his hair, drying in the air conditioner's draft, was making his head itch. "Dangerous," he went on. "Not a long-term business."

"Agreed." Balim smiled as though a bright pupil had once again showed his promise. "But as an extremely profitable one-time operation, what then?"

"Depends on the circumstances. You've got something, huh?"

"Depends on the circumstances," Balim said. "I would like you to study the situation."

"Sure."

Balim touched papers on his desk, not as though he were looking for anything in particular but more as though to reassure himself as to his identity and strength. "This task," he said, "will undoubtedly consume very much of your time."

"For how long?"

"Three months, perhaps longer. Would you know someone you could hire, on a temporary basis, to take over some of your duties?"

"A merc?"

"A white man, yes." Obviously enjoying the irony of the phrase, Balim added heavily, "An old African hand."

"There aren't that many wars going on right now," Frank said. "I'll call around, come up with somebody."

"Somebody you trust."

"Come on," Frank said, grinning. "Think again."

"I do beg your pardon." Balim performed his own kind of grin. "I meant, of course, someone you know how *much* you can trust."

"Can do."

As Frank got to his feet, stretching out the tightnesses in his joints, scratching the 7UP crystals on his head, Balim said, "You might be interested in who has brought us this opportunity."

"Someone I know?"

"An old friend." Then Balim corrected himself, raising one finger. "No, I'm in error again. An old acquaintance."

"Who?"

"Baron Chase."

Frank stopped scratching, the itchy 7UP forgotten. "*That* son of a bitch? You want to deal with *Baron Chase?*"

"That's why," Balim said, "I'll be wanting your undivided attention in the days ahead."

"You'll need more than me," Frank told him. "You'll need a special angel from God. Chase would melt his grandmother down for the silver in her hair."

"I do believe you," Balim said, shrugging, "but I am driven by my poor merchant's greed. He has offered us a railroad train, a freight train, a complete train filled with very valuable coffee. I want that coffee, and so I must deal with Baron Chase. But only with you, Frank, always at my side." Balim smiled, waggling a finger. "Which is why it is so important," he said, "that you find just the right person to be your assistant. Choose carefully, Frank."

4

Out at Valdez International Airport, Lew Brady sat in a five-year-old Chevrolet Impala and felt the heater's dry air destroy the interior of his nose while he watched Ellen Gillespie taxi the Cherokee to its pad. Although it was nearly April, Lew still thought of the climate as wintry. "I'm freezing to death here," he muttered. "These Alaskans are crazy."

It didn't help when Ellen came out of the plane in khaki slacks and a short-sleeved lavender blouse. She came smiling and waving across the stubby new grass, a tall and slender woman with short dark-blond hair and a long angular face that combined beauty with efficiency in a way that left Lew helpless with desire.

Ellen was twenty-eight, daughter of a commercial pilot who'd taught her to fly when she was still in her teens. She was licensed for multiengine jets, but she didn't want to spend years apprenticing as navigator and engineer, and her youth and sex limited her to jobs for which she was overqualified: commuter services in Florida, skywriting in California, even dragging a sunburn-treatment message through the blue summer haze over Fire Island.

She'd been on that last stint when they'd met. Lew, after six and a half years on the African continent, involved in wars from Chad in the north to Angola in the south, Ethiopia in the east to Biafra in the west, had suddenly run out of Dark Continent conflicts and had accepted a job offer half the world away, in the Caribbean, training anti-insurgency forces on one of the smaller islands there.

The most sensible travel route had been via Amsterdam and New York, and it was in New York that he'd been intercepted by a message: his employer government had just been overthrown, before he could arrive and train anybody to defend it.

Out of work again, Lew had gotten in touch with a pilot he'd known in Africa, a man now working for a commuter airline between New York City and the Hamptons, operating out of Flushing Airport in Queens. At that airport, Lew had first seen this beautiful woman pilot, back from her day's sunburn chores, and he had been immediately hooked.

Her manner at the start was cool but friendly. Gradually she became less cool, and then more friendly, and finally Lew moved in with her for the rest of that summer. And in the fall, when Ellen was offered the job here in Alaska, they'd agreed he would come along.

"Hello, lover," she said now as she slid into the car and kissed his lips; comfortably, not passionately. Then, as he put the car in gear, she switched off the heater and opened her window. He'd known she would do that. "Spring," she said, with marked satisfaction.

He steered in a long curve toward the gate in the chain link fence. "Nice flight?"

"So-so." She looked out her open window, elbow resting on the sill, short nails tap-tapping the plastic of the door. She was often like this after flying, a little nervous, vibrant, edgy, hyperactive. He had learned with disappointment that it was a bad time sexually; she was distracted by the sky. She said, "The same trees get boring, eventually."

"Nothing to deliver?" Her primary job was to carry papers, blueprints, instructions up to the field offices where the pipeline was being laid; sometimes there was a reply, and they'd detour past the construction company's Valdez office to drop it off.

But not today. "No, we can go home."

The guard at the airport was an old friend by now; he waved at Lew, who waved back.

Ellen said, "How's the class?"

"Improving, finally."

"I thought so. You're starting a nice shiner. What else did you do today?"

"Made some calls. Talked to some people."

"Any luck?"

"Dim possibilities. Not really."

They were passing a construction site; yellow earthmovers crawled on a churned-up corner lot behind a sign featuring a future bank. Ellen looked at it, then said, "Remember what you said when we came up here?"

He did. " 'There must be plenty of work,' " he quoted, " 'for an able-bodied man in Alaska.' "

"You're making yourself old, Lew," she told him. "Sitting around, waiting. Playing with truck drivers. You aren't a house pet."

"I could operate a bulldozer," he said, voice flat, not as though he were making a serious suggestion. "I could tend bar. Repossess automobiles. Drive a truck for the pipeline."

"Lew," she said gently, "Alaska isn't going to war."

"Somebody is."

*　*　*

The phone was ringing when they parked beside the trailer they called home. "Jesus!" Lew cried, and ran. He pounded into the bedroom, to their only phone, shedding clothes, already certain, and when Ellen came in a minute later he was grinning so broadly he looked as though he meant to eat the phone. "Frank," he was saying, as a believer who sees a vision might say, "It's the Mother of God."

Ellen sat on the bed and Lew paced, jamming the receiver against his ear and mouth, holding the cradle in his other hand. "God, yes, Frank," he said. He barely understood Frank's words, didn't at all understand what job he was being offered, and couldn't have cared less. Frank Lanigan—good old Frank Lanigan, from Angola and Portuguese Guinea and Ethiopia—Frank Lanigan was offering him a *job*, a piece of work. In *Africa*.

Then he noticed Ellen sitting there, and he interrupted Frank to say, "One thing. There's one thing."

"What's that?" The voice came thousands of miles to sound clear and uninflected in Lew's ear.

"I've sort of doubled up with somebody else," Lew said. "A pilot. You got work for both of us?"

"A pilot? Lew, I don't think so. This isn't the kind of job—"

"She travels with me," Lew insisted. "I'm sorry, Frank, but that's the way it is." And he waved the phone cradle at Ellen, to wipe away her troubled expression, to reassure her it would be all right.

"Lew, I could ask some— Did you say *she*?"

"That's right."

"Oh. That makes it different. She gotta be a pilot?"

Exultation made Lew savage. "Hold it," he said, and cupped the mouthpiece while saying to Ellen, "It doesn't have to be pilot, does it? It could be any job for an able-bodied woman, right?"

She laughed, calling him a bastard. He grinned at the phone and said, "Sorry, Frank. It has to be pilot."

"We'll work something out," Frank said.

They spent a few more minutes discussing the transportation details, while Lew grinned without interruption at Ellen seated on the bed. Then he said good-bye and slapped together the halves of the phone. "Don't get up," he said.

5

Ellen's first sight of Frank Lanigan, in the main waiting room at Wilson Airport, in Nairobi, reminded her just why it was she found Lew Brady so precious. Lanigan was like most of the men Ellen had met in these outlandish global crannies: hairy, sweaty, an overgrown boy, a blunt roughneck with an inflated opinion of his own courage and prowess. Lew, living in the same world, was stronger and braver than any of them, *and he didn't know it*. How could she help but treasure him?

Proudly Lew made the introductions, as though he'd invented each of them especially for the pleasure of the other. Frank Lanigan took Ellen's hand in his hammy fist and leaned toward her a connoisseur's smile, saying, "Lew always could pick 'em."

Already I'm a *them*, Ellen thought. "Nice to meet you," she said, with her boring-party smile. *Cold bitch*, said Frank Lanigan's eyes, behind the welcoming heartiness. *That's right*, her eyes said back as she withdrew her hand from his, and her smile could have iced an entire bucket of daiquiris.

Frank looked away from it at the two battered flight bags beside them on the floor, saying, "This all your luggage?"

"We travel light," Lew told him.

"A woman who travels light," Frank said. "Will wonders never cease?"

Oh, you bastard, Ellen thought. She watched with some amusement as Frank tried to figure out which bag was hers—so he could carry it, of course, the eager overgrown Boy Scout approach—then grabbed one at random. The right one, as it happened. Lew picked up his own bag and Frank said, "This way," adding to Ellen as they started off, "We're putting you right to work."

"Oh, yes?"

Ellen had been so doubtful about this whole deal that she hadn't actually quit her job in Alaska, but had merely asked for and received two weeks off without pay. If the African adventure came out badly, she could always turn right around and go back. She still rated the normal courtesy airline discount for flights and hotels, so she wasn't risking much in coming all this way with only the vaguest promise of a job once she got here. But now perhaps the job was real?

"You're our pilot," Frank told her over his shoulder as he led the way toward the exit, shoving aside the dozens of raggedy-dressed black men offering taxis. "No taxi!" he bellowed, and pushed through the door into the blinding sunlight of Africa.

Lew had been only one of the reasons Ellen had agreed to this iffy voyage. Africa was the other. She had worked in both North and South America as well as in Southeast Asia, she had seen Japan and parts of Europe as a tourist, but the entire African continent was new to her. She was fascinated by the thought of it, a fascination only slightly dampened by the cholera and yellow-fever and typhus shots they'd had to take before departure, and the supply of malaria pills they were supposed to take—one every Tuesday—not only during their entire stay in Africa but for two full months thereafter. It was beginning to seem that Africa was not only as exotic but also as hospitable to the human race as Mercury or Jupiter.

Her first ground-level view was disappointing. Flat dry scruffy fields under a huge baking sun. The taxis, small and rusty but with gleaming windows, were clustered helter-skelter near the terminal exit, drivers and hangers-on sitting on the fenders and hoods. The airport buildings, low and hot-looking, reminded her of smaller islands in the Caribbean.

"This way," Frank shouted. Swinging Ellen's flight bag at an importuning cabman, he marched off around the side of the building.

Ellen glanced at Lew, to see him smiling and beaming and gawking around as though he thought he was home. He loves this awful place, she thought, and her heart sank.

There was a brief business of showing documents at a gate in a chain link fence, and then they started off across the scrubby ground toward a double row of tied-down planes to one side of the main east-west runway.

Ellen walked close beside Lew, saying to him too softly for Frank to hear, "Does he expect me to fly something?"

"Beats me," Lew said. "Maybe so."

In the last sixty hours, they had flown by commercial airliner from Alaska to Seattle, and from there to New York, where they'd had a three-hour layover before the overnight Alitalia flight to Rome. In Rome they'd taken a hotel room near the airport for the day, followed by the final overnight flight to Nairobi, arriving at eight in the morning. They had crossed thirteen time zones and had spent twenty-three hours in the air. And now was Ellen expected to fly a plane she'd never operated before over land she'd never seen before in a country and a continent and with an air-traffic system that were all new to her?

She considered saying something to Lew, but hesitated. She hesitated, as she hated to admit to herself, partly because she was afraid any objection would be treated as special pleading, but it was also because she wanted to see just what Frank Lanigan had in mind.

"We're here ahead of the rains," Lew said.

She looked skyward, seeing only a few scattered high thin clouds. "Rains?"

"They're due the end of March." He grinned and said, "First drought, then flood."

"There are better systems."

They were about halfway to the planes when Frank, up ahead, suddenly let out a roar of rage, dropped Ellen's bag onto the brown grass, and raced heavily away like an aroused bull toward a twin-engine Fairchild painted white with orange trim. Unlike the others parked here, it was not tied down. Lew and Ellen looked at one another, shrugged, and kept on walking. Ellen picked up her bag on the way.

Meantime, Frank was roughly yanking somebody out of the Fairchild, so roughly that the man tumbled onto the ground, landing on his shoulder and rolling forward under the wing. Frank ran around the length of the wing, like a dog playing a game, and reached the man again as he pulled himself to his feet between the port engine and the fuselage.

By this time, Ellen and Lew were close enough to hear what Frank was yelling. "What are you doing in that plane? I said to clear out of here!"

The man mumbled something, and Frank raised a threatening hand. "You got your money! That's all you get!" Watching, Ellen thought Frank was putting on the anger, that he was much more in control of himself than he pretended.

"It's only *my* gear," the man said, in a north-of-England accent. He was thin, perhaps forty, moustached, with blotchy red skin and heavy bags under watery eyes. He had been drinking, and had shaved himself recently but erratically. His voice contained a whining he was obviously trying his best to conceal. "I only took what was mine," he said.

Ellen and Lew had arrived at the plane. Lew said, "Frank? A problem?"

"Watch this bird," Frank told him, "while I see what he was up to."

"Personal possessions!" the man cried, as Frank went away around the wing again, apparently unwilling to risk his dignity by stooping low and scuttling under it.

Ellen, looking at the man, was surprised when he suddenly met her gaze and his expression turned sarcastic, his weak mouth trying for a sardonic smile. "So you're the *pilot*," he said, with heavy emphasis. "Frank's new tramp."

Lew dropped his flight bag, moved his left foot forward, and hit the man in the face with a straight overhand right. The man staggered back, his head banging the fuselage, and fell to the ground, not unconscious but stunned.

"Lew!" Ellen said.

He turned to her, saw the anger in her eyes, and immediately stepped back, embarrassed, opening his hands out of their fists. "I'm sorry," he said. "I'm not awake."

Twice in their early days together, Lew had hit men under the mistaken impression he was defending her, reacting to provocation as he thought she would want him to react. Since he remained permanently unaware that the patronizing assumptions of a Frank Lanigan were a thousand times more offensive than any angry name-calling, he was hardly the protector of choice, even if she felt the need for such a medieval thing. She'd thought that argument had been resolved months ago, but now she saw that, if you got Lew Brady tired enough, jet-lagged enough, disoriented enough, the old incorrect basic responses were still alive and well and living in the middle of his wooden head. "I'll fight my own battles, Lew," she said.

"I know. I know. I'm sorry."

The man had struggled to his feet, patting his nose and mouth with the back of his hand as though dabbing for blood. "Oh, you'll have a good time," he said to Ellen, his anger undiminished. "Yes, you will."

"You aren't hurt," she told him.

He put his hand down at his side, almost standing at a kind of attention, apparently remembering the dignity he'd earlier been striving for. "I can tell your kind," he said. "You're as bad as they are. You can all rot in hell together."

Frank had come back around the wing, this time carrying a clearglass pint whisky bottle, about a third full. Extending it to the man, he said, "Here's your personal possessions."

The man snatched the bottle, tucking it inside his shirt. "Thanks for nothing," he said, and strode swiftly away toward the airport gate, walking with unnatural rigidity, to prove to them his sobriety in case they were watching.

Lew said, "What was that all about?"

"Didn't recognize him, did you?" Frank said. "Timmins. Flew cargo when we worked for the Front. Angola."

"Doesn't ring a bell," Lew said. "What's his problem now?"

"He was our pilot." Frank grinned at Ellen. "You're taking his place."

Ellen looked after the departing stick figure. "That's why he was so upset?"

"Still surprised, that's all," Frank said, and shrugged. "Let's stow your goods." He took Ellen's flight bag from her hand.

Ellen said, "Surprise? Why surprise?"

Frank led the way around the wing once more and toward the cargo door aft on the fuselage. "I just fired him about twenty minutes ago."

"Twenty minutes!"

He paused in unlocking the cargo door to grin at her. "I wanted him to fly me and the plane down here, didn't I?"

Ellen looked again after the previous pilot, but he had gone through the gate and disappeared. "Not much notice," she said. "And no severance pay either, I suppose."

"I can see you've got a soft heart," Frank said. "But don't worry about Roger, he shouldn't be a pilot anymore at all."

"He drinks too much," she suggested.

"He drinks at the wrong time." Frank slammed the cargo door and moved forward to open the passenger door and tilt the front seat forward. "I'll ride in the front to show the way. Lew, you get in back."

"Right."

While Lew climbed aboard, Frank gave Ellen a quizzical grin, saying, "I hope you know how to fly this thing."

"At least I don't drink," she told him. "Not at the wrong time."

Frank laughed, clipped the front seat into place, and climbed up into the copilot's seat. Ellen followed, and took a moment to familiarize herself with the instrument layout. She had never in fact flown this exact model before, but it wasn't much more complicated than getting behind the wheel of a strange automobile.

Frank said, "We've filed a flight plan to Kisumu. Charts oughta be in your door pocket there."

"In a minute." She found the control checklist in the pocket and studied it, then pulled half a dozen aerial charts from the pocket. They were old and flimsy, marked here and there with a variety of pens and pencils in several colors, and most of them were starting to tear at the fold lines. She found Nairobi on one, and asked, "Which way do we head?"

"West-northwest."

"To Kisumu, you said?"

That was on the next chart westward. Very high ground, the Mau Escarpment, nosed down into the direct line between Nairobi and Kisumu, but by heading directly west she could skirt the southern edge of the mountains. There was a small airfield shown at Ewaso Ngiro, eighty miles out, another at Mara River, forty miles farther on. From there she would turn north-northwest, passing between the airports at Kisii and Kericho as the land sloped gradually downward toward the shores of Lake Victoria, three hundred miles away. The airport at Kisumu, at the inmost point of Winam Gulf, was, surprisingly, marked for international flights. But of course the countries here were so small that international travel meant something very different from what it did in the States. Again she was reminded of the Caribbean.

Frank said, "Everything okay?"

"Just fine." Unclipping the earphones from the stick, she put them on and spoke to the control tower. Meantime, Lew leaned forward in his seat to start a conversation with Frank. Catching a word here and there, Ellen understood they were gossiping about old friends: where are they now, what have you heard from So-and-So. Except that with men it wasn't called gossip.

She started the port and then the starboard engine, ran through the items on the checklist, and rolled out of the line of parked planes toward the asphalt taxiway. The wind was fairly strong and out of the west, so she drove to the east end of the runway, waited while a British Airways VC-10 took off and a Kenya Air DC-9 landed, checked again with the tower, then lifted into the air.

She loved it. This part she always loved: the lifting, the soaring, the sudden diminution of the Earth slowly turning beneath her. The plane responded well, and already her hands and eyes moved automatically among the switches and indicators. Sliding the right earphone back onto her hair so she could hear conversation in the plane while still listening to the radio through her left ear, she settled more comfortably in the seat and watched the brown land slowly unroll beneath her.

"That's the new airport," Frank said, yelling over the engine drone, pointing ahead and to the left. "Supposed to be done next year." He grinned at her. "Guess its name."

She looked down at the white-and-tan construction scars, seeing that the new airport would be something like three times the size of the old one. "Its name?"

"Jomo Kenyatta!" Frank shouted. "President of the country! Heap big chief!" Laughing, he gestured upward with his thumb, as though the president of the country were in Heaven, or seated on some fishbone cloud.

Lew leaned forward, his forearms on Ellen's and Frank's seat backs, his head just visible between them. He said, "Tell me more about the job, Frank. Guerrillas, is it?"

"Kind of." Frank seemed still amused by Jomo Kenyatta. "In a kind of a way it's guerrillas."

"Going in against Uganda?"

"It's a raid," Frank said.

"Just one raid?"

"Ah, but what a raid." Frank's big happy manly smile encompassed them both. "We're taking a train, Lew. We're putting the arm on a whole train."

"A train? Not a passenger train."

"No no no," Frank said, waving his arms around in a negative gesture too large for the confined space inside the plane.

"Hostages," Lew said, shaking his head. "I don't like that kind of thing."

"Don't worry, Lew," Frank told him. "This is clean as anything. You'll love it."

"A goods train," Lew suggested. "Weapons."

"Coffee," Frank said.

Glancing over at Frank, Ellen suddenly understood that something was wrong. Lew hadn't been hired for the job he had expected. It was something entirely different.

She saw that Lew had also guessed that, and was trying not to know it. His forearms rested on the seat backs; his curled hands hung down between the seats; his face was stretched forward above his hands. Now, gently cuffing himself on the bottom of the jaw with his half-clenched fist, an unconscious nervous gesture, he said, "Coffee, Frank? I don't get it."

"Six million dollars," Frank told him. "A huge motherfucking coffee train. Oh," he said to Ellen. "Excuse me."

"Blow it out your ass," she said, looking downward toward the ground.

Lew said, "Frank, what's going on? Is this a Ugandan guerrilla operation, or what is it?"

"It's a little different," Frank said. "Our bunch isn't exactly guerrillas."

"But Amin," Lew said. "There's *got* to be anti-Amin forces somewhere."

"Down in Tanzania. Nyerere keeps 'em in cakes and cookies, but they're mostly all fucked up."

Ellen glanced at Frank and found him grinning at her. He winked with the eye Lew couldn't see.

Lew was saying, "In that case, who are *we?*"

"A couple white boys working for some people gonna steal six million dollars from Idi Amin."

"It's his personal coffee?"

"Everything in that fucking country is his personal property."

The tower was directing Ellen farther north, away from east-west air traffic. The usual urban sprawl spread out below her: Nairobi, capital of Kenya, business center of East Africa. The slums were bright colored and crowded, while richer homes lazed on the hillsides amid greenery. A railway line crossed their path, north to south, glinting in the sun like an ornamental chain. Frank said, "There's your railway now. Eighth fucking wonder of the world."

Ellen said, "Why does it shine like that?"

"The ties aren't wood. They're steel."

"Steel?"

"Seventy pounds apiece, two thousand per mile, seven hundred miles from the coast of Kampala." He reeled this off with apparent satisfaction, as though he'd personally carried and placed every steel tie himself.

Ellen said, "But why steel?"

"They tried wooden ties," Frank told her. "The British, when they built the line around the turn of the century. But the ants ate them, and the floods rotted them, and the natives stole them for firewood. So they used steel. Indian coolies did the work, and sometimes in the sun the steel ties burned the skin off their hands."

The glittering chain had fallen behind them, and now the tower permitted Ellen to steer southwestward to her intended route over the Kedong Valley. She said, "You seem to know a lot about it."

"I learn things," he said. "I don't just sit around pulling my pecker all day."

Lew said quietly, "Frank, talk to Ellen the way you talk to me."

Frank gave him a surprised look, as though he hadn't expected a challenge from this quarter. Ellen considered the situation and decided the assistance fell within the range of the acceptable, so she said nothing but merely concentrated on her flying.

After a moment, Frank nodded at Ellen and said to Lew less aggressively, "We'll get used to each other."

"Sure you will," Lew said.

"I'm a reader," Frank explained, talking now directly to Ellen. "I like history."

The tone of voice meant he was trying to make amends. Ellen cooperated. "African history?"

"Mostly. I like to read about the fuckups of those who came before me. It's nice to know I'm not the first damn fool to run around this continent."

Ellen smiled, surprising herself. "I can see how it might help."

"Every day in every way." He shifted, making himself more comfortable, then went on in a more casual, storytelling style. "Those coolies worked their asses off," he said. "Lions ate them, mosquitoes gave them malaria, drought robbed them of food and water, floods tore out the tracks they'd just put down, they caught dysentery and yaws and diseases they never heard of before, native tribes hit them with clubs and spears and poison darts, their British overseers objected to their sex lives, and every once in a while when conditions were really muddy a locomotive would fall on them. But they kept going, for almost ten years, and they built the fucking railroad. And do you know what it was all for?"

"No, I don't," Ellen said.

"To keep Uganda in the British imperial sphere of influence." Frank grinned. "How's that for a joke?"

*　*　*

On the ground of Kisumu, a ragamuffin black man whom Frank called Charlie tied the plane down while Frank went away to make a phone call. Ellen and Lew stood near the plane, watching Charlie, who appeared to be drunk or stoned but who in his slow and distracted manner was nevertheless doing the job right, and Ellen said, "Do you want to turn around?"

Lew frowned at her, about to become irritable. "What do you mean?"

"You don't like this."

"I don't even know what it is yet."

"You know it isn't what you expected."

"Let's wait and see. Frank's a good man." But he couldn't keep the doubt out of his voice.

Frank came rolling back toward them, with a strong but loose-jointed gait, as though all the screws and dowels in his body needed tightening. "We'll just drop in and see Mr. Balim," he said, "then I'll take you to your house."

"Fine," Lew said.

Frank turned and shouted, "Aren't you finished, you stupid bastard?"

"Slow," Charlie said, slurring the word.

"I know you're slow. Pick up these bags and come along."

Frank led the way, followed by Ellen and Lew, with Charlie bringing up the rear, carrying both bags. Ellen looked back at him, and Charlie smiled at her, drooling down his chin. Ellen faced front again.

Their immediate destination was a tall and filthy Land-Rover with a patched canvas top. The yellow license plate with black numbers was dented in three or four places, as though somebody had been using it for target practice, like signs on country roads in the States. While Charlie heaved the luggage into the storage well in the rear,

Frank said, "You two ride in back. Charlie's turned this front seat into an outhouse."

Lew and Ellen clambered into the vehicle, and the instant she touched the hard and uncomfortable seat a wave of exhaustion poured over her so severe that she thought for a second she might be sick. Instead, her eyes watered and she yawned hugely, bending forward, her brow touching the top of the front seat.

Lew said, "Ellen? You okay?"

"Just tired." The heaviness of the humid air pressed in on her.

"Won't be much longer."

"Good."

Adrenaline and curiosity had kept her alert and active this long, through the endless traveling from Alaska, and then the three-hour piloting job from Nairobi, but all at once it was catching up with her. She yawned again, behind her cupped hands, so hugely her jaw hinges ached.

Charlie and Frank took their places in front. As Frank started the rackety engine, Lew said, "Frank, we're both kind of tired."

"Fifteen minutes," Frank promised. "We'll stop in for one word with Mr. Balim—he just wants to say hello, shake your hand—then I'll drive you right to the house."

The Land-Rover jounced forward. Ellen watched Frank's shoulders and back moving in great effortful bunched thrusts, the way the man in the carnival wrestles with the alligator. They bounced and skidded away from the airport and out onto a narrow blacktop road cluttered with huge slow-moving trucks. Frank slalomed among them.

Lew said, "Frank, tell me about Balim."

"Asian. Born and raised in Uganda, thrown out. Merchant. Probably rich, I don't know. I work for him."

"Doing what?"

"Twist arms, break heads, kick asses."

Charlie giggled.

Lew said, "Balim isn't political?"

Frank laughed. "Balim thinks politics is a dirty word."

"Do you?"

Frank grinned over his shoulder, then looked out at the road again. "I think it's a funny word, Lew. Since when did you get political?"

Lew jounced around in the backseat, gnawing his thumb knuckle, looking worried. "I've always been on *somebody's* side," he muttered, but not loudly enough for Frank to hear.

Charlie turned, smiled beatifically at them both, and said, "Can you tell me why it is that politics makes strange bedfellows? Can you tell me what it is, 'strange bedfellows'?"

Surprised, Ellen said, "You speak very good English!"

He beamed at her. "So do you," he said.

*   *   *

Mr. Balim said, "Did you like my plane?"

"Very much." Ellen was surprised at how quickly she was warming to this little round man.

He had been waiting for them in front of what was apparently his place of business, a low long scruffy building of an oddly washed out blue, as though it had been here for a thousand years. Seeing him, Frank had yelled, "There he is right there!" and made a violent U-turn in the teeth of oncoming buses and motorcycles. Charlie had chittered something happy-sounding, like a toucan, but when Frank skewed to a halt, Charlie had at once slithered out of sight, as though he were a stowaway.

And the little round man with the round head, the large soft brown eyes, the hesitant smile, the delicate plump hands, had introduced himself, bowing from the waist. "Mazar Balim. So happy to make your acquaintance."

Now, introductions over, the plane mentioned and admired, Balim said, "You must both be very tired from your journey, though I must say you don't look it. Frank, how do your friends look so fresh after such a trek?"

"Fever," Frank suggested.

"Very possibly so. Go home," he told them, smiling. "Rest. Eat. Sleep. Make love. Do not see me again until you are wasting away from boredom."

Lew said, "There's an order I won't have any trouble following. Nice to meet you."

"And you. Both of you."

Ellen tried to say something polite, but a yawn overtook her. Balim laughed, and when the yawn was finished, so did Ellen. She waved to him, unwilling to try to speak again, and allowed Lew to lead her back into the Land-Rover.

The five-minute drive was a blur. She had no real sense of her surroundings, and was aware only that they stopped in front of a small low house of tan stucco. Inside, she had a sense of hard surfaces and cheap furniture and primary colors. Frank, talking heartily, carried their flight bags in and showed them the bedroom and went away, slamming the front door. "No more," Ellen said, and pulled off her clothing as she approached the bed, and lost consciousness as she was drawing back the sheet.

*   *   *

It was dark. Ellen came awake slowly, out of confused dreams and heavy sleep. She was perspiring; the sheets and pillowcase were wet. She turned in the too-soft bed, grunting, and felt the hard, angular body of Lew beside her, slick with sweat. She knew him wonderfully well, in darkness or in light. She ran her hand down his hot damp belly, felt the wet tangle of hair, felt his cock half-erect.

"Mp," he said when she touched him, and moved in a way that said he wasn't completely asleep. She grasped his cock and as it rose from slumber he reached awkwardly for her, his questing hand bumping into her nipple. He clutched her breast, and his foul-breathed mouth invaded hers. "Oh, God," she tried to say, but it was muffled by his tongue.

Through the contortions she held on to his cock. She loved it, she filled her mouth with it and then she filled her cunt with it. They were so wet that, as they fucked, their stomachs made suction noises, poppings and fartings that eventually made Lew mutter, "Shit. Enough of this." He grabbed her leg and turned her over without losing contact. Knees and shoulders and cheek on the bed, holding her breasts with both hands, she opened her mouth and gasped into the pillow as he pounded her from behind. Another orgasm. "Who's counting," she mumbled into the pillow, and ground her ass backward into his belly.

"What?"

"Shut up and fuck!"

"Oh, you smart cunt." He slapped the right cheek of her ass, which did nothing for her but make her mad.

"Just *fuck!*" she yelled, and reached back to slap his thigh just as hard.

"Damn damn damn damndamndamn *damn* KEE-*RIST!*"

But then they couldn't find tissues or towels or anything at all. Rolling around on the swampy bed in the humid night, his come tickling her legs, she said, "Where in God's name *are* we?"

"Africa," he said.

"Jesus Christ," she said.

6

It was Sir Denis Lambsmith's first visit to Kampala. He faced it with the same thrill of anticipatory horror with which at the age of six he would greet the arrival of the magician at a friend's birthday party: Can he really do magic? Will he choose *me* to hold the hat, the birdcage, the scarlet scarf? Will something dreadful happen, at last, *this* time?

There was almost no passenger air traffic in and out of Uganda anymore, but Entebbe International Airport was maintained as though for the imminent arrival of thousands, perhaps millions, of tourists. Waiting areas and rest rooms were kept immaculately clean. The duty-free shop stood uselessly open; the stout girl on duty listlessly took the quiz in a two-month-old copy of the British *Cosmopolitan*. Next door the gift shop was also open, tended by an arthritic old man who slept with his cheek pressed against the cash register. Behind him, colonies of insects had taken up housekeeping in the stuffed lions and giraffes.

Mr. Onorga, the Uganda Coffee Commission man, met Sir Denis at immigration and led him out to a waiting chauffeur-driven black Mercedes. Riding in the backseat with Sir Denis, Onorga seemed glum, distracted, like a man with family worries. Conversation was limited to weather and scenery. Sir Denis, a tall white-haired man of sixty-one, with the stoop-shouldered quasi-humble stance of the British aristocrat, was bursting with questions about Idi Amin—Is he really as dreadful as they say? As imposing? As brutal? Will he choose *me?*—but of course politesse forbade such curiosity, without at least some opening indication from the host that gossip was in order. But Mr. Onorga's gloom blanketed all.

Daringly, Sir Denis did offer one opening himself, when Mr. Onorga asked, "How is Brazil?"

"Improving," Sir Denis said. "We rather think the worst excesses may be over. Changes of government are trying times; still, life settles into its wonted way soon enough."

Which was an opening Mr. Onorga could have driven an Army truck through, had he desired; but he merely nodded, gloomy in his satisfaction, and asked if Sir Denis had ever been to the United States.

"Several times," Sir Denis said, irked, and looked out the car window at a poverty-stricken city: ragged people, boarded-up shop-fronts, shriveled-leg polio victims scuttling across the crumbling sidewalks on their hands and rumps. Among them, the few healthy and well-dressed people seemed to be written in italics. Many of these latter were dressed in the same odd style as the driver of their car: wide-leg trousers, flashy cheap shirts, shoes with built-up heels, very dark sunglasses. When one of these came along, the other pedestrians seemed to make a point of getting out of his way.

Much more beautiful was the Nile Mansions Hotel, a sprawling luxury establishment built on the same grounds as the International Conference Center. A short and skinny bellboy took the luggage, as Mr. Onorga conducted Sir Denis across the lobby to register.

Some electricity in the air, some awareness that everyone else's awareness was directed to a certain spot, caused Sir Denis to look away to the side, toward a long, cool-looking cocktail lounge flanked by a bar. The dozen or so people in there were sitting very still, speaking fitfully to one another, as Mr. Onorga had spoken in the car. And at the far end of the lounge, at a table by himself, sat a massive man in an ill-fitting gray safari suit, who was gazing with heavy eyes toward the lobby. His hand was closed negligently around a glass, and as Sir Denis watched, he lifted the glass and drank. Immediately, the other customers in the lounge also drank, hurriedly, gratefully. The glasses returned to the tables, and the massive man's eyes shifted, not seeming to focus on anything in particular.

It's Idi Amin! Sir Denis blinked in astonishment and apprehension, while a most irrelevant memory surfaced in his brain. Back in the 1940s, during the war, he had been seconded for nearly two years to the U.S. Navy, in Washington, D.C., in connection with the transatlantic convoys running the U-boat blockade. His family had been with him, and one Christmastime he had taken his daughter, Anne, then three, to see Santa Claus at Garfinckel's. That stout figure, all red and white, had been the center of attention on his throne at the end of the room, exuding a benign—and of course inaccurate— aura of power: the power to give, to answer prayers, to provide happi- ness. Here in Uganda, was this not the other side of the same coin, this heavy figure all black and gray?

Anne, Sir Denis remembered, had been afraid of Santa Claus, had cried and refused to approach him. She had had her Christmas presents, anyway.

Formalities at the registration desk were brief. And why not? He was, after all, Sir Denis Lambsmith of the International Coffee Board, here to complete negotiations for the sale and shipment of a very large portion of Uganda's next coffee crop to the Brazilians. As such, he represented a strong—perhaps an overwhelming—figure of impor- tance in the Ugandan economy. Reminding himself of this, trying to ignore the weight of those heavy eyes on his shoulder and arm, Sir Denis signed the registration card, accepted the three messages waiting for him, gravely shook hands with Mr. Onorga, as gravely thanked him for his courtesy and kindness, and followed the bellboy toward his room.

* * *

The three messages were from: Captain Baron Chase, signing himself "Deputy Chief of Protocol," welcoming Sir Denis to Uganda and inviting him to a reception with President for Life Idi Amin Dada in the president's suite, 202, at five this afternoon; from his daughter, Anne, now thirty-eight and married to a banker in the City, asking him, should he return through London on his way back to Brazil, to call her and to bring her an African woven rush bag; and from Carlo Velhez, of the Brazilian Coffee Institute, saying he was in Room 417.

Having unpacked and showered and made shorthand notations about the day thus far in his diary—seventeen volumes of this dull stuffy material in crabbed private code were now stored in London and Sussex and São Paulo—Sir Denis phoned Velhez and invited him to the room for a pre-reception conference.

Whisky and safe water were already in the room. Sir Denis downed a short neat whisky, and had the glass washed and dried and back on the tray atop the dresser before the small economical rapping at the door introduced the small economical person of Carlo Velhez, a tiny dapper man incongruously kitted out with a great flowering bandit's moustache. In Brazil, Sir Denis and Velhez were matter-of-fact with one another, not close socially or personally, indifferent to one another's presence or absence; here, in the usual manner of travelers meeting far from home, they were nearly brothers, reacting with honest pleasure to the encounter.

"Come in, come in."

"You're looking well."

"Pleasant flight?"

"Odd place, this."

They then sat down with light whisky-and-waters to discuss the purpose of their being here, speaking together in Portuguese, which infuriated the State Research Bureau men in their basement listening post.

"There is some question of money," Velhez said.

"But the price was determined last month."

Velhez nodded, manicured fingers toying with his alarming moustache. "Nevertheless," he said, "the price continues to rise in the commodity markets."

Outrage at human inconstancy had long since faded in Sir Denis to pragmatic weariness; one dealt with the human race not as it should be but as it was. Still, he pointed out the obvious: "The agreed-on price is the agreed-on price. If the market went down, would the Ugandans expect to receive less?"

"They have been given that argument," Velhez said drily. "But in fact I think this is only a negotiating step."

Sir Denis observed the pale liquid in the bottom of his glass. "Of course. They don't want more money, they want something else. Some change in the shipping arrangements?"

"No. We—that is, the consortium—are still to provide eight

planes to transship the coffee to the steamers at Djibouti." Velhez smiled sadly beneath the moustache. "What they want is a larger percentage in advance."

"How much?"

"One third."

Looking and feeling astonished, Sir Denis said, "Twelve million dollars? In advance?"

"I have it from Baron Chase himself," Velhez said. "That's what they'll want, and they won't back down from it. In fact, they'd prefer the suggestion to come from us."

"Baron Chase. Captain Baron Chase." Sir Denis crossed the room to pick up his messages from the bedside table. "Deputy Chief of Protocol," he read, and looked at Velhez. "Who is this chap?"

"Canadian. Working—"

"A white man?"

The Velhez moustache quivered in amusement. "Exactly so. He may have taken up Ugandan citizenship."

"Captain," Sir Denis repeated. "Captain of what?"

"Apparently, Amin wanted him to call himself General," Velhez explained, "but Chase has a finer sense of the ridiculous than Amin, and they compromised at Captain."

"What does he do? Is he important?"

Velhez shrugged. "With one-man rule, it's hard to say who is or is not important. But Amin has two or three of these whites to advise him, to smooth the way for him internationally, to act for him where his own Nubians would make a botch of things. Chase is ubiquitous."

"I must have a word with him, then," Sir Denis said. "One third in advance. What if, after all, the rains come inopportunely and ruin the crop? What if this government falls? Governments have been known to fall."

"So has rain," Velhez agreed. "So has frost, as we both well know."

Sir Denis frowned. "Has Bogotá been informed?" He was referring to the Bogotá Group, the OPEC of coffee, a combine of eight Western Hemisphere producers: Mexico, Brazil, Venezuela, Colombia, El Salvador, Costa Rica, Honduras, and Guatemala. They had approved the original deal.

But Velhez merely shrugged, saying, "It doesn't concern them, so long as the final price doesn't change."

"Well, I don't believe," Sir Denis said slowly, "that Emil Grossbarger will stand for it."

At that, Velhez looked doubly worried, as well he might. Although the actual coffee sale was being conducted between governments— sold by the official Uganda Coffee Commission and bought by the quasi-governmental Brazilian Coffee Institute—there was an inevitable middleman, in this case a venture capital group from London and Zurich headed by a Swiss named Emil Grossbarger. The shipping of the coffee, its delivery to the Brazilians' customers, and the collection and disbursement of moneys, would be in the charge of this private consortium, which had both the capital and the clout in the international financial community to guarantee delivery and honesty. If the Grossbarger group were to bow out now, if Brazil had to start all over and negotiate for coffee elsewhere to fulfill its commitments, the price would certainly be higher, the availability of sufficient product would be very much in doubt, and Brazil might well find itself going into the next coffee season with its new crop already committed to past debts. "Don't you think," Velhez asked, unable to hide his anxiety, "you could talk to Grossbarger? Persuade him?"

"I'm not certain it would be honorable to make the attempt," Sir Denis said somewhat primly. "Grossbarger came to the ICB because we are known to be neutral in such matters."

The ICB, the International Coffee Board, was a London-based organization supported by the coffee industry and endorsed by the governments of both the producer and the consumer nations, with the task of dispassionately overseeing the international coffee trade. Sir Denis, an expert with the ICB for the last seventeen years, a man who moved massive shipments of coffee around the world in a great endless obscure game of Go, and whose special relationship was with the Bogotá Group and particularly the Brazilian Coffee Institute, had at Emil Grossbarger's personal request handled the negotiations among the various parties to the current sale. So far he had done the work in London or São Paulo, but now that the pact was about to be signed he had come here to Kampala for the final formalities.

Where an immediate snag had appeared. The agreement, as Sir

Denis very well remembered, was for an initial payment of one tenth, or approximately three and a half million dollars U.S., of which the Brazilians and the Grossbarger group would each put up half. Now, at the last minute, this down payment was to be very nearly quadrupled. After pausing to give himself and Velhez another pair of drinks— and allow Velhez to recapture his composure—Sir Denis said, "Emil Grossbarger is simply not a man to toy with."

"I'm sure," Velhez said, "something can be done. There's certainly goodwill on all sides."

"One third?"

"Uganda, I understand, has foreign-exchange problems." Velhez tried to shrug away Uganda's political mess. "The closing of borders and so on. One can understand their position."

"I have difficulty," Sir Denis said, "understanding the position of any principal who reneges on an already completed negotiation."

Looking more and more worried, Velhez said, "But you'll speak with them?"

Knowing he meant the consortium, Sir Denis said, "They aren't politicians, Carlo, they're businessmen. They've already committed themselves to an initial outlay of well over one and a half million U.S. dollars. Not counting the cost of transport, warehousing and all the rest."

"But you'll speak with them."

Sir Denis sighed. His practiced mind had already reached the compromise that all parties would be able to live with. The task now was to get them all to accept it. Laying the groundwork, he said, "Carlo, you know I'll do my best."

"Something can be worked out," Velhez said, as though uttering a prayer.

"To be frank with you," Sir Denis said, not being at all frank, "I think it very unlikely Grossbarger will move at all."

Startled, almost angry, Velhez cried, "The profit remains the same!"

"But the initial risk increases. There are other investments these same men can make, severally or together. Also, there's the loss of income from the additional capital being tied up."

"I realize that." Velhez blew in agitation through his bandit moustache. "But we've come this far."

"It's possible," Sir Denis said, noticing how suddenly alert Velhez became, "that I'll be able to bring them up a bit. But certainly not to fifty percent of the new demand. Not to six million dollars."

"Perhaps forty-five, forty—"

"No, Carlo. These people are going to be very angry when I talk to them, and neither you nor I can blame them."

"Of course," Velhez said. "But it's not *our* fault. Surely they'll understand that."

"I doubt they'll much care whose fault it is," Sir Denis pointed out. "I am willing, Carlo, to urge the Grossbarger group to increase their advance payment to two million U.S."

"Two! Out of twelve!"

"If I were to ask for more," Sir Denis said, "they'd hand me my hat at once. I'm not at all sure but what they'll do so, anyway. However, we can but try."

"Two million," Velhez repeated, his expression dazed. "Ten million from us."

"What I'll *also* do," Sir Denis went on, "is have a word with the chaps here. Captain Chase, or whoever it might be. Perhaps we can bring them down a bit."

"I don't know about that," Velhez said. The wind was well and truly out of his sails; even his moustache sagged.

"Well, we'll speak with them," Sir Denis said. "We may have a beneficial effect. And what I'll suggest to you now, just between ourselves—"

Velhez sat up. "Yes? Yes?"

"When I speak to our friends in London and Zurich," Sir Denis told him, "I won't talk in terms of percentages. I'll put the idea of raising their ante to two million in the best possible light, and with luck they'll agree. Then, whatever concession you and I can obtain from the people here will benefit exclusively your share of the obligation."

Sir Denis Lambsmith's great talent lay not in finding brilliant solutions to knotty problems but in finding brilliant ways to describe and present the messy pedestrian solutions that were usually the best of a bad lot of options. Velhez, having five minutes ago believed that his new liability was to be a mere six million, now became happy and relieved to hear that whatever relief from ten million he could wangle for himself he wouldn't have to share with his partners. "That's wonderful," he said. "It's possible, I suppose, possible we could talk them down to a quarter rather than a third. In that case, with two million from our other friends, our own cost would be no more than seven million."

"Let's not be premature," Sir Denis warned. "There are still many people to be brought on board."

"You're right." Velhez stood in a sudden hurry, moustache aquiver. "I must phone São Paulo."

"I have some telephoning of my own," Sir Denis said, also rising. "I'll see you at the reception."

"At the reception," Velhez replied. "Good luck to us both."

* * *

Suite 202 was guarded by sloppy-looking soldiers in British-style uniforms and berets. Inside, in a room awkwardly combining traditional English and modern Danish furniture with Arab carpets and wall hangings, there was a fairly large and motley crowd. The white faces belonged mostly to businessmen, British or American, German or Scandinavian, plus a sprinkling of diplomats from those foreign embassies still open in Kampala: Arab, mainly, but also the French and a few others. The blacks present were of three sorts: slender cold-faced men in military uniform; male and female civil-service types in suits and party frocks, providing the underlay of cocktail-party chit-chat; and beetle-browed, angry-eyed men in safari suits or loud shirts, many wearing large dark sunglasses, most of them standing with side-thrust hip and one arm reaching behind their backs to clutch the other elbow. It was a childlike posture, but it made Sir Denis think of evil children, as though the hand gripping the elbow were a last restraint from some thoroughly vicious act.

Sir Denis was later arriving than he'd wanted to be, having been held on the phone for quite some time, principally with the consortium's de facto leader in Zurich, Emil Grossbarger. Still, he assumed his hosts were bugging his telephone and would understand why he was late.

As he entered the large central room of the suite—the party seemed to flow also into rooms to left and right—Carlo Velhez approached with a tall and somewhat heavyset white man. Both were carrying drinks. Carlo's expression was hectic, his frantic eyes almost distracting attention from his luxurious moustache, while the other man had a lidded look, like a snake on a sunny rock. *Baron Chase*, Sir Denis told himself.

"Sir Denis Lambsmith," Carlo Velhez said in his thickly accented English, his voice quivering with suppressed emotion, "may I present Captain Baron Chase."

"Delighted," they both said, and Sir Denis extended his hand, which Baron Chase took but did not return. Instead, continuing to hold Sir Denis's hand, Chase said, "We must get you a drink."

"Thank you, I—"

Still gripping him by the hand—an experience Sir Denis found horrible—Chase turned half away, lifting his free arm in a signal. "Can't have our guest of honor without a glass in his hand." In his speech, Chase affected a jaded homosexual style that he probably thought of as upper-class. His accent was homogenized midlantic.

A servant—short, skinny, young, apprehensive, foul-smelling— pressed rapidly through the crowd to Chase's side. Sir Denis, while ordering a gin-and-tonic, was not at all surprised to see the man who had been his driver from the airport standing against the wall with two similarly dressed fellows, all frowning and glowering alike. Like the Tontons Macoute in Haiti, the "secret" police in this country were blatant about their existence.

At last, a drink having been ordered, Chase permitted Sir Denis to reclaim his hand, saying, "Your friend Carlo has been telling me his troubles, and I've been telling him mine."

Meaning that Carlo had not managed to whittle down the new demand; thus Carlo's frantic expression. Sir Denis amiably said, "I did hear something about an attempt to reopen the negotiation."

"Oh, really?" Chase frowned in apparent puzzlement. "On what basis?"

"Perhaps I was mistaken," Sir Denis said. "Something about a larger payment in advance."

"Oh, the restructuring!" Chase laughed, shaking his head. "That's not a— Here's your drink."

"Thank you."

The foul-smelling boy went away. Sir Denis sipped gin with a hint of tonic and too much lemon. Chase said, "There's no renegotiation, Sir Denis. May I call you Sir Denis?"

"Of course." And why not? Sir Denis would know he was being spoken to with formal correctness, and the Canadian would believe they were on an informal footing; another diplomatic triumph.

"A restructuring of the payment schedule, Sir Denis," said Chase, relishing his new formal informality, "is hardly a renegotiation. But that's not your concern. Do come along and meet the president."

A coldness ran up Sir Denis's spine, to become a thrill of dread raising the hairs on the back of his neck. He restrained a shiver, saying, "I'd be delighted."

"We'll talk later," Carlo said to Sir Denis, his expression that of a man too polite to mention that he was drowning.

Holding Sir Denis gently but persistently by the elbow—could this man never keep his hands to himself?—Baron Chase steered him past conversations in several languages and through the connecting door to the next room on the right, where a dozen or so people stood in the awkward poses of bad statuary, facing the family group which dominated the center of the room.

The sudden need to laugh only intensified Sir Denis's dread. Idi Amin wore a camouflage uniform, several sizes too small, the meandering swaths of greens and browns stretched tight across his huge torso and thick thighs, so that at first glance he looked like an aerial photograph of rolling countryside, emphasized by the bulging jacket pockets just below the putative waist. The string of medals on his chest—so many they overlapped, like magazines on a coffee table— might be the region's principal town. But what to make of that brooding mammoth black olive of a head, with its wide dissatisfied mouth and heavy disbelieving eyes?

To Amin's right stood a young and beautiful light-complected black woman, very tall and slender, in some sort of native costume involving many yards of wrapped colorful cloth. Her hair, in the local style of the very rich, had been braided and twisted into arches and figure eights rising a foot from her head like a modern sculpture in wrought iron. The young woman was very happy, smiling as though she believed this to be her own birthday party.

Flanking the adults were two children, each a kind of echo. The little girl beside the young woman—probably six or seven years of age—had a simpler and more traditional hairdo but wore a similar costume. The boy of about ten, pressing shyly against Amin's left leg, wore an exact replica of his father's camouflage uniform. Both children were beautiful, with large brown eyes and solemn expressions.

The guiding hand on his elbow forgotten, Sir Denis allowed Chase to pilot him across the room. All else disappeared, and Sir Denis watched those black eyes watch him approach.

"President Amin Dada," Baron Chase said, releasing the elbow at last, "may I present Sir Denis Lambsmith?"

A broad smile bisected Amin's face. Sir Denis, having expected any smile from this creature to be ferocious, was astonished at how boyish Idi Amin could look, despite his size, his ugliness, his reputation. Shaking Sir Denis's hand in his own big but gentle paw, Amin said, "Foreign exchange," and laughed.

"Delighted to meet you, Your Excellency," Sir Denis said.

"Foreign exchange," Idi Amin said again, as though the phrase were Sir Denis's name, or a password, or a joke known only to them. Then he laughed some more, and patted Sir Denis's shoulder, and turned away to signal to one of the nonentities at the side.

The man who hustled forward was neat but shabby, intelligent looking but worried, tall but bent with anxiety, unquestionably Negroid but with an aquiline nose and pointed chin. Circling behind Amin and the woman and the two children, this fellow took up a position beyond the little boy—who was gazing with perfect solemn curiosity up at Sir Denis—and apparently awaited instructions.

Which came rapidly, in a quick rattle of words from Amin. The language was breathy and sharp-toned, with clicks and glottal stops and frequent harsh joinings. Swahili. The new man listened, nodding, and when Amin had stopped he turned to Sir Denis and said, "The President for Life says he is most happy to have you here in our beautiful country. He hopes you will take the opportunity while you are here to travel about and see some of our most famous scenery. And he is glad that you will take the interest in us to help us with our problem with foreign exchange."

Sir Denis listened to all this in some astonishment, then said directly to Amin, "Your Excellency, it was my understanding that you speak English."

The translator was about to render this into Swahili, but Amin answered it first, in that language. The translator told Sir Denis, "The President for Life says he has some very poor English, good only for the barracks ground. With a person as important as yourself, the President for Life considers it necessary that the language is, umm—"

"Pre-zeis," said Idi Amin.

The translator blinked and swallowed, as though he'd been threatened. "That the language is precise," he said.

"But surely," Sir Denis said, again speaking directly to Amin, "this is a social situation. None of us will try for hard bargaining here, I hope."

Amin smiled again, this time the look having something of that ferocity Sir Denis had been anticipating. Another rattle of Swahili, like hail on a tin roof, was translated: "All the bargaining is over. The President for Life is happy that the Brazilians and the International Coffee Board have found Ugandan coffee tasteful." More Swahili, then: "And the price of our tasteful coffee acceptable."

"The coffee and the price are both excellent," said Sir Denis, essaying a small smile in the direction of Amin.

More Swahili: "The President for Life is happy that the Brazilians and your own, um, leaders are—"

"Print-zi-pals," said Idi Amin.

"Your own principals," the translator hurriedly said, "are agreeable to the very small and modest advance payment of one third."

"I had not believed," Sir Denis said carefully, "that the discussion on that point was finished."

"All finished!" Amin said, laughing out loud, thumping his palm in satisfaction against his stomach, making a single muffled drumbeat. Other people in the room, who could not have heard the conversation, nor have understood it if they'd heard it, found a reason to laugh. Amin reverted to Swahili, and the translator delivered the translation: "We are here now, in great friendship and joy, to sign many papers."

One of the more useful tools of diplomacy was the tactful display of annoyance. Speaking now to the translator, Sir Denis said, "Would you tell the President for Life how happy I am that this problem has been resolved? I wasn't before this aware of its resolution."

Idi Amin laughed again and spoke in Swahili. The translator looked very unhappy and remained silent. Idi Amin lowered an eye to glance at him. The translator said to Sir Denis, "The President for Life says, his cock is bigger than yours."

"Oh," said Sir Denis, at a loss for the first time in his adult life. "Well, yes, I see. Perhaps so."

"Foreign exchange," Idi Amin said, and leaned forward in the friendliest way to pat Sir Denis's arm. "Very happy," Idi Amin said.

Sir Denis, in the hot humiliating fire storm the world had now become, once more felt Baron Chase's hand on his elbow. With one final statement to Amin, he allowed himself to be led away.

Afterward, in his hotel room, writing up his notes of the meeting, he couldn't remember for the life of him what that last thing had been that he had said to Idi Amin. Somehow, he doubted it had been adequate.

7

That morning Mazar Balim closeted himself in his office with Isaac Otera for an hour to discuss various details of business. Isaac had brought to Balim's commercial affairs a bureaucratic love of files and paperwork it had never known before. At first Balim had been made uneasy by this massive tidying, and had complained, "Isaac, when some government eventually hangs me, they will use all these papers of yours as their only evidence." But eventually he'd grown used to it, and now he was even pleased at how thoroughly his business was known by this nonmember of his family, this non-Asian, this in fact black Ugandan.

They were interrupted at one point by Frank, who was told by Balim through Isaac to wait. Then they continued, one careful neatly labeled manila folder at a time, until all lake and railroad shipping, all warehousing, all sales and purchases, all payments and collections, had been taken under consideration and discussed. Then at last Balim smiled his round shy winning lovely (completely deceitful) smile and said, "Thank you, Isaac. Would you tell Frank to come in?"

"A moment, sir," Isaac said, surprisingly enough. Instead of rising, he continued to sit on the wooden chair beside the desk, knees together, all the manila folders in a neat stack on his lap. "May I speak?" he asked.

"Of course," Balim said, his smile turning politely quizzical.

"You have not discussed with me this new operation," Isaac said.

Balim nodded agreement, his face showing nothing.

"You have not asked me to open a file, to check anyone's references, to do a cost estimate, to arrange warehousing, transportation—"

"Yes, yes," Balim said. "The point is taken."

"In sum," Isaac said, with his own small functionary's smile, "it is to be presumed that I know nothing about the operation at all."

"I would never presume that, Isaac."

"If I understand the situation correctly," Isaac went on, "the centerpiece of the operation will be the theft of a large amount of coffee inside Uganda and its smuggling into Kenya."

"I take it," Balim said, "that your source of information is Charlie."

Isaac ignored that. He said, "I appreciate your delicacy in not involving me in an illegal and quite probably violent act. You have naturally taken it for granted that, since I am an active Christian, and since my background is in government affairs, I would prefer to have nothing to do with such an activity."

"You do me honor by the suggestion," Balim said.

"However," Isaac told him, gently yet firmly, "in some ways this operation is similar to any complex business undertaking. There will be partners and employees—the two Americans who arrived yesterday, for instance—who must be vetted and their positions made clear. There will be questions of transportation, perhaps of lodging. Sooner or later the coffee itself must reenter normal business channels, and must do so armed with appropriate paperwork."

Balim watched him, bright-eyed, and softly said, "Are you volunteering, Isaac?"

"One cannot, of course, volunteer for what is already one's job." The tiny smile again came and went. "But there is another point to consider."

Balim waited, nodding slightly, hands folded on his plump lap.

"I still have contacts within Uganda," Isaac said. A sudden harshness always came into his voice when he spoke of his native land, the only indication of the complexity of the emotions he forced himself to conceal. "The economy is collapsing," he went on. "It might be fair to say it has already collapsed. The expulsion of the Asians had a lot to do with that, of course—"

"Then there is justice, after all," Balim murmured.

"But there's also," Isaac said, "the financial ignorance of Amin and his Nubians. They're doing worse than living on capital; they're living on the bank itself."

"Nicely put."

"Coffee is their life preserver." Isaac leaned forward, his stifled agitation causing him to ruffle the folders on his lap, so they were no longer perfectly aligned. "The people starve, but Amin buys whisky and cars and new uniforms, and coffee pays for it."

"No doubt."

"I am not a hero," Isaac said, the tension fading from his face. He sat back, realigned the folders, seemed to sigh through all his body. "I am not the lone man with a rifle," he said, looking down at his dark hands on the pale folders, "who slips across the border and hunts down the tyrant. To avenge his—his family."

"Isaac," Balim said softly, leaning forward as though he might touch Isaac's hand.

"I am a bureaucrat," Isaac said, not looking up. "I am a paper shuffler."

"Isaac, you are a man. Every man has his purpose."

Now Isaac did look up. The eyes in his dark face were always a bit red around the pupils, but now they were more so. "Every sack of coffee that is stolen from Amin," he said, "shortens his time. The more coffee is stolen and smuggled out of the country, the sooner he'll run out of money to keep his Nubians drunk and himself in new medals. I hope that train carries every coffee bean from the entire crop."

"May God hear your words," Balim said, gently smiling.

"You'll need me," Isaac told him. "Not, of course, to hold up the train."

"Of course."

"Shall I open a file?"

"Yes."

"What shall I label it?"

Balim thought. " 'Coffee Break,' " he said. "Tell Frank to come in now."

Isaac smiled and got to his feet. At the door, holding the stack of manila folders, he turned back and said, "Thank you, Mr. Balim."

"Thank *you*, Isaac."

Isaac went out and Frank came in, boots thudding the floor, khaki whipcord trousers rustling, pressed cotton shirt neatly buttoned and sleeves rolled up to his biceps. " 'Morning, Mr. Balim," he said, and dropped backward into the armchair.

"My first impression of your friends," Balim said, "was a good one."

"I wanted to talk about that," Frank said. "About the way we handle Lew Brady."

"Handle?"

"He wasn't the first fella I called," Frank said. "To tell the truth, he wasn't even the tenth."

"Oh, no?"

Frank scratched his head with a rasping sound. "I don't know what's happening to everybody. People I know, they're all dead or disappeared or retired. *Retired*—can you figure that?"

"People get older," Balim suggested.

"Those guys? Dan Davis? Rusty Kirsch? Bruno Mannfelder?" Shaking his head, Frank said, "More and more, they're all getting like Roger Timmins."

The reference to their previous pilot made Balim's eyebrows rise. He said, "How did Mr. Timmins take it?"

"Badly. Complained. Anyway, the point is, I finally got Lew, and at least he isn't over the hill or gone to drink or retired or dead."

"But?"

"But we gotta handle him," Frank said. "The thing is, Lew's what you call an idealist."

"Oh, yes?"

"He don't think he is," Frank explained. "He thinks he's a mercenary, like anybody else. But when the chips are down, he likes the idea he's doing some good in this world."

"I see."

"So when you talk to him," Frank suggested, "try to push the political side a little bit, see what I mean? How what we're really doing is give Amin one in the eye. He'll go for that."

"Ah," said Balim. His smile turned sadly downward. "I'll tell you the best thing, Frank. You have your friend Lew talk to Isaac."

"Oh, yeah?"

"Absolutely," Balim said. It was the saddest smile in the world. "Every man has his purpose."

8

In London, Sir Denis stayed at the Inn On the Park, which actually stood a short block away from Hyde Park, though it was true that, while eating breakfast by the window in his high-floor room, he could look over the tops of the intervening buildings to see the broad green vista of the park, with the Serpentine, the equestrians along Rotten Row, the short fat Arab women in their black shrouds of cheap cloth and their black plastic domino masks, and the stripped corpselike mammoth logs of the ancient elms stricken by blight and cut down in a panicky effort to save the remaining healthy trees.

After breakfast, Sir Denis walked through the Grosvenor domain, past the American Embassy at Grosvenor Square, and over to the Coffee Board headquarters on Warren Street, just south of Oxford Street. The two men he met there were named Bennett and Cleveland, and the discussion centered on the character and prospects of Idi Amin.

"You've seen him," Bennett said. "What's your reading?"

"An erratic man," Sir Denis said. "I don't doubt he could be dangerous."

"He has already been dangerous," Cleveland said drily.

Bennett said, "Did you talk much while you were there with a chap named Onorga?"

"From the Uganda Coffee Commission," Sir Denis said. "Yes, he met me at the airport. A dour fellow."

"What did he tell you?"

"Nothing. He barely opened his mouth."

Bennett and Cleveland looked meaningfully at one another. Cleveland said, "Puts paid to Onorga, if you ask me."

Sir Denis frowned from one to the other, then concentrated on Bennett, the more serious of the two. "What's wrong?"

"Onorga was our man on the scene."

Sir Denis was astonished. "But he didn't say a word!"

"Afraid to," Cleveland suggested. "Knew they were onto him."

Sir Denis said, "Why do you think there's trouble?"

"He hasn't radioed," Bennett said, "since you left Kampala."

Sir Denis knew that somewhere within this building was assembled a highly complex and expensive communications system, but he had never concerned himself with its function. It was true that coffee was grown on almost every continent and consumed in every nation, and it was also true that a vast amount of money changed hands over coffee. (Last year the United States alone had paid over two and a half billion dollars for the coffee it had imported.)

The International Coffee Board controlled not the product itself but its movement through the commodity markets in the financial centers of the world. Sir Denis was a part of the overt expression of that control. He had always been aware that a covert section also existed, but he preferred to know little or nothing about it and to believe that under normal circumstances it was neither needed nor employed.

But here it was, and gloomy little Mr. Onorga was a part of it. Sir Denis said, "You think he was fired?"

"We think he's dead," Bennett said.

"If he's lucky," Cleveland added.

"Dead?"

Sir Denis kept waiting for them to laugh, to say they'd been pulling his leg. But Bennett merely shrugged and said, "He was a spy, if you like."

"An industrial spy, then, at the very worst," Sir Denis said, finding himself becoming indignant. "And not even that, if he was merely reporting to the Board. You don't kill a man for a thing like that."

"We don't," Cleveland agreed. "Idi Amin does."

"Have there been inquiries?"

"When the archbishop was murdered two months ago," Bennett said, "there were any number of inquiries. There are still inquiries. The archbishop was rather a more important man—"

"Prominent," corrected Cleveland.

"It's all the same," Bennett told him, and turned back to Sir Denis. "The answers to the inquiries about the archbishop have been almost flippant in their disregard for facts. If we were to inquire after Onorga, they'd merely laugh at us."

"Poor devil," Sir Denis said. "No wonder he seemed so morose. There's no objection, I hope, to my asking after him myself on my return down there? Merely in a friendly way, asking after the fellow I'd met the last time."

"You may do," Cleveland said, "if you're that keen to waste your time."

Bennett said, "Our problem at the moment is, we do need very much to recruit someone else."

"Not easy," Cleveland added, "under the circumstance."

"Nor kind to the recruit, either," Sir Denis pointed out. "Always assuming you're successful."

"If anyone does take on the job—" Bennett started, and Cleveland interpolated, "—which is unlikely."

Bennett nodded at him, faintly showing impatience. "Of course," he said. "But if someone does agree to have a go, he won't be ignorant of the danger."

Cleveland laughed. "Hardly," he said.

Bennett leaned closer to Sir Denis. "Did you meet anyone else there? Anyone who might be useful?"

"I met very few of the locals. Principally Onorga, in fact."

Cleveland said, "When you go back, you might just keep an eye out."

"Yes, of course."

"Given a head of government as unstable as Idi Amin," Bennett said, "we would feel very much more content had we a listening post on the ground."

"I can see that," Sir Denis said. "I'll do what I can."

For the rest of the meeting they discussed the changed circumstances of the sale, now that Uganda was demanding a third down rather than a tenth. The Brazilians were suffering but would find the money, and Sir Denis could report that the Grossbarger group had accepted with fairly good grace their own small increase in the required front money.

"In fact," Sir Denis said, "I'm having lunch with Emil Grossbarger today."

"He's in London?"

"Just for a few days, apparently. So far, he doesn't seem particularly worried about the deal."

"Perhaps," Cleveland said, "he doesn't yet understand the situation."

*   *   *

Emil Grossbarger was a large heavy shambling man of nearly eighty, with long unkempt white hair and big-knuckled hands. Arthritis and old age had conspired against him, so that now he had to move with the aid of a walker, but when seated he looked as powerful as he had always been, his meaty shoulders and barrel chest forming the proper base for his large outthrust head. He had a long pointed nose, deep-set pale-blue eyes that glared through unobtrusive gold-rimmed glasses, and a broad sensuous mouth that mirrored his emotions with fluid constant movement, now laughing, now frowning, now snarling as though to bite.

They would lunch together at the club they shared, the Special Services, just behind Harrods. The club was open to present and past members of the intelligence services of the NATO countries and their immediate families. Sir Denis, during his Washington stint in World War II, had been a spy for British Intelligence, learning as much as he could about the discrepancies between what the United States told its allies it meant to do and what it actually meant to do. In the same war, Emil Grossbarger had been of fairly high rank in German Military Intelligence, until he became one of the few plotters in the July 1944 attack on Hitler to escape with his life. He'd made it to Switzerland just ahead of the Gestapo, had become a Swiss citizen shortly after the war, had gone to work for a Swiss bank in its security department—counterintelligence, actually, protecting the identities of depositors—and had soon become a financial force himself. Today he could command almost unlimited funds for whatever prospects attracted his attention.

The Special Services was the only club in the world to which both Sir Denis Lambsmith and Emil Grossbarger were likely to belong. The club's NATO referent meant that both sides of World War II were unusually well represented among the members present at any one time in the small but neat orange-brick building on Herbert Crescent. The conversations that took place over sole and hock in this dining room, between former enemies, would have raised eyebrows among those who still believe the history of the world is the struggle between good and evil.

Grossbarger had brought a guest with him, a shrunken old man with whom he had been speaking in German before Sir Denis arrived, apologizing for being late. The walk had taken a bit longer than he'd expected.

"Sink nossing of it," Grossbarger ordered him. "*All* my valks take longer zan expected. Ziss is Reinhard Neudorf, Sir Denis Lambsmitt."

Shaking hands, seating himself at the table, unconsciously patting the snowy linen, Sir Denis said, "Neudorf? The name seems familiar."

"I was naughty during the war," the old man said, with an unrepentant sly smile. His English was much better than Grossbarger's, and he used it in an insinuating way, as though he could be much more unholy in this tongue than in his native German.

"Nuremberg," Sir Denis suggested, the memory very hazy.

"They sentenced me to eight years in prison."

"He served sree," Grossbarger said, his mobile mouth laughing. "Zey needed him, so zey released him."

"I am an engineer," Neudorf said. "I build very good dams, with or without bodies."

"An excellent engineer," Grossbarger insisted, and leaned forward in mock confidentiality to add, "Ve vere just discussing ze Fourth Reich."

"Very soon," Neudorf explained, deadpan, "National Socialism will accomplish its long-awaited return."

"Heil whoever," agreed Grossbarger, "und *march*. Ze swastika on ze rise!"

"However," Neudorf said with a faint shrug, "the time never seems quite perfect."

"Ve have very many brilliant soldiers, all around ze world, merely awaiting ze call." Grossbarger's eyes flashed; his mouth gobbled at the comedy.

"Unfortunately, at any given moment," Neudorf said, "most of them are in hospital."

"And ze rest," Grossbarger added in satisfaction, fondly patting the walker that stood beside his chair like a misplaced bit of tubular balcony railing, "are like me."

"But we haven't abandoned hope," Neudorf explained. "For what could be more terrifying and undefeatable than a dedicated band of crippled old men with a dream?"

Grossbarger laughed so loudly and enthusiastically he nearly toppled off his chair, and had to clutch at the walker for support. Neudorf watched him, smiling faintly, then shook his head and said to Sir Denis, "Please excuse me for one moment."

"Certainly."

Sir Denis watched Neudorf move away from the table. Apparently he had recently lost a great deal of weight. His clothing hung tentlike on him, and the two main tendons in the back of his neck stood out like iron rods holding up his head.

Grossbarger had finished laughing, and now he leaned forward again, much more seriously, to say, "I hope you vere not offended."

"Not at all," Sir Denis said, though he wasn't sure whether the joke had been offensive or not.

"He is dying," Grossbarger explained, waving a big gnarled hand after Neudorf. "He likes zese jokes, so I indulge him. And I let it continue in front of you because you are a man of ze world."

An intended compliment, then. Responding to it indirectly, Sir Denis said, "Years ago, in the United States, I was told a bit of American slang. 'The elevens are up.' In fact, the American Navy officer who told it to me was referring to President Roosevelt at the time."

"Ze eleffens are up?"

"The tendons at the back of the neck," Sir Denis explained. "When they stand out like that, the man is dying."

Grossbarger looked thoughtful, his mouth chewing the information. "A more cold-blooded phrase zan I would have antizipated from zat nation," he decided, then shrugged it away. "However, ze characteristic of Reinhard's illness is such zat he vill frequently be leaving us to enter ze toilet. Ve can discuss business matters during zose intervals." Turning to the hovering waiter, he said, "I hope you vill not be offended if I do not choose one of your no doubt excellent English vines. But I vould prefer a Moselle, ze Bernkasteler Doktor. You know ze one I mean."

The waiter acknowledged that he did. He distributed the Xeroxed sheets of today's menu and left. Grossbarger shook his head at Sir Denis, saying, "One of ze few dry Moselles left. Zey add too much sugar now. For ze American taste, I am afraid. Ze export market." Fatalistically, he shrugged.

"I find myself more and more moving to the Italians," Sir Denis agreed. "Though we have some surprisingly good wines in South America, mostly from Argentina."

With another burst of laughter, Grossbarger slapped the table and cried, "Grown by our co-conspirators, of course! I must tell Neudorf!"

"He's returning."

Grossbarger tapped the side of his nose. "Business later."

* * *

The next time Neudorf left was between the quiche and the sole. Sir Denis immediately described his experiences in Kampala, and Grossbarger listened intently, asking one or two quick questions. He seemed untroubled by the increased down payment. At the finish he said, "Ze nub of ze ting is Amin himself, of course. I vould like to understand him better."

Sir Denis astonished himself by answering, "He said the most extraordinary thing to me." Until this moment, he had believed he would never tell that to anyone, but somehow the anecdote belonged to Emil Grossbarger and Sir Denis found himself obediently delivering it, like a dog bringing his master the morning paper.

Grossbarger at once understood that this was the gravy. Eyes quickening, mouth moving, he said, "Oh, yes. Vat did he say?"

"I had allowed my irritation to show. Because of the sudden change in the terms. And he said, through his translator, 'My cock is bigger than yours.' "

Grossbarger roared with laughter, punching his chair arms with his big fists, ignoring the diners who glanced reprovingly from other tables. "Oh, my goodness!" he cried. "Oh, how awful zat must have been for you!"

"It was, rather."

"I sink I love ziss fellow," Grossbarger said, nodding, his mind working inside the joke.

"Whom do you love?" Neudorf asked, returning, lowering himself with obvious pain into his chair.

"Idi Amin," Grossbarger told him.

"Ah, yes, the madman of Kampala." Neudorf turned his sly gaze to Sir Denis, saying, "We're thinking of declaring him an Aryan. There are one or two problems, of course."

The sole arrived then, and Sir Denis was amused at how naturally the waiter rested his tray on Grossbarger's walker. Discussion slowed while the food was eaten, but midway through, Neudorf had to leave again and Grossbarger said, "You met a man named Baron Chase?"

"Yes, I did."

"Describe him."

"Canadian. Ugandan citizenship, I believe. A nasty piece of work, I suspect. Very close to Amin."

"He has been in touch viss me." Grossbarger watched the last of the second bottle of Moselle poured by the waiter into the three glasses, then went on, "Indirectly. He suggests zat ve might make a *deal*. I do not know vat he can possibly have in mind, but ven you return you vill contact him on my behalf."

Technically, Sir Denis could only represent the International Coffee Board in this transaction, but since the Board's only purpose was to assure a reasonable level of honesty and consistency in these large-scale coffee deals, it was not at all unusual for one side or the other to employ him at some particularly delicate stage of the operation. He possessed four qualities unlikely to be found anywhere else: he was knowledgeable, trustworthy, dispassionate, and discreet.

"I'll be happy to," he said. "Is it a bribe, do you think? To assure a smoothness of the flow?"

But Grossbarger shook his head, poking at his remaining fish. "It doesn't have zat feeling. Ve are already paying *chai* to a number of minor officials zere. Zat's vat zey call it in east Africa, you know."

"*Chai?*"

"It is Swahili for 'tea.' I had my research people look it up."

"A bribe is tea," Sir Denis said, frowning. "I don't follow the derivation."

"Ven you vant somesing from ze government," Grossbarger explained, "you invite ze official concerned to join you in ze shop across ze street from ze government building for a cup of tea vile you discuss ze situation."

"*Chai,*" Neudorf said, seating himself again at the table. "You two are planning a bribe. There'll be none of that in the Fourth Reich."

Grossbarger raised his glass in cheerful mockery. "To ze honest and simple Aryan," he said. "And to ze blitzkrieg of ze dreaming old men."

9

The shower stall was a concrete-block closet painted a blurry pink, with a mildewed white plastic curtain and a gray cement floor featuring the rusty beauty spot of the drain. Light oozed fitfully through a fixed Lucite panel in the ceiling. The water, which came from a concrete cistern on the roof and was heated by the sun, was a lukewarm trickle in which Lew found it almost impossible to rinse. Elephant Soap was the brand, and it lathered wonderfully, which was a pity.

He finally gave up, stepped out to the other part of the bathroom, and finished with a cloth dipped in the cold water of the sink. Then, shaved and clean and shivering, he padded wet and naked to the kitchen, where he found Ellen, dressed in tan slacks and a *Chorus Line* T-shirt, drinking bottled Coke with a small dapper young Asian in a Mondrian silk shirt. The Asian stood, smiling at Lew's nakedness, his black-olive eyes dancing with mischief. He said, "And you will be Lew Brady."

"I not only will be," Lew said, shaking water drops off his fingertips in case this was someone he should shake hands with, "I already am."

"Coke?" asked Ellen, also amused. "This is Mr. Balim's son."

"Bathar Balim, at your service." He was a few years younger than Lew, and he bowed to emphasize the difference. "I am here with the car," he said.

"Yes," Lew told Ellen, then said to Bathar Balim, "I'm not quite ready."

"No hurry."

The refrigerator was small and very rusty, both within and without. Ellen took a Coke from it—it seemed to be filled to capacity with nothing but bottles of Coca-Cola and White Cap beer—opened it, and handed it to Lew, who pointed at the elaborate watch on Bathar's slender wrist, saying, "Could you tell me the time? Our watches stopped."

"Seven minutes past one. Do you need the date?"

"No, thanks." *And not the barometric pressure, either.* Lew carried the Coke and the information to the bedroom, where he set his own watch and put on his clothes.

They had awakened several times, separately or together, in the filtered daylight of the bedroom, but none of the attempts at consciousness had taken until at last Ellen had pounded his hip with her fist, crying out, "We have to get *up!*"

So they'd gotten up. In the kitchen—small, cheaply outfitted, with a light-green tile floor—there had been a note on the Formica-and-chrome table: "Lew. Phone 40126 when you're ready. Frank."

The phone had eventually been found in the living room—rickety red Danish sofa, massive Victorian armchair, a white-elephant sale of mismatched tables and lamps—and when Lew had dialed the number, a crisp male voice had answered in Swahili.

"Frank Lanigan," Lew said.

"Mr. Brady?"

"Yes."

"This is Isaac Otera, Mr. Balim's assistant."

"Hello."

"Shall I send a car for you now?"

"Give us half an hour."

"Of course."

But half an hour hadn't been quite long enough, not with the soap problem in the shower. Dressed, Lew filled his pockets: wallet,

Zippo lighter, three-inch spring-action knife, sunglasses, leather folder containing passport and driver's licenses and inoculation record and (false) Interpol membership card, Swiss Army knife, ball-point pen, pocket flashlight with a twenty-dollar bill wrapped around the two triple-A batteries. Finishing the Coke, he walked back to the kitchen, where Ellen was laughing warmly at something Bathar Balim had said. The Asian turned his smiling bland face when Lew entered. "All ready?"

"All ready."

Lew put the empty bottle on the table, but Ellen at once picked it up, saying, "Bathar says this is our house now." The small garbage can had a foot pedal—operated lid, which squeaked when she opened it to throw the bottle away.

"Home sweet home," Bathar said, smiling at Lew.

Lew bared his teeth back. "I'll have to put up my hunting prints," he said.

* * *

Outside the house, the humid heat was a surprise. A white haze veiled the sky but did nothing to cut the glare of the sun. The house, a low yellow pillbox on a dirt street lined with similar structures, was surrounded by hard-baked dry earth in which only a few sawtooth weeds could grow. This section wasn't a neighborhood but an encampment; there was no sense anywhere that anyone thought of this place as home. The two tiny black children playing with toy airplanes in the dirt several houses away seemed to be merely idling away the time until the moving van should arrive.

The car was a white Nissan safari van, rather cleaner than Frank's Land-Rover. Ellen rode beside Bathar, Lew behind her. Bathar was as fast a driver as Frank, but much smoother. He seemed to be saying, If anyone could lead a camel through the eye of a needle, it would be me. Lew kept track of the turnings, surprised that his mind contained absolutely no memory of the initial drive here with Frank.

At Balim's blue headquarters, Bathar smiled at Ellen and said, "Nice to meet you both."

"You, too," said Lew.

Smiling, Bathar drove away, as Frank came out the front door, grinning like a Derby winner and saying, "Had your beauty sleep?"

Lew was feeling generally irritable. Trying for the light touch, he said, "Don't we look it?"

"She does. Come on inside."

Inside was a cluttered warehouse, piled with cartons, crates, mounds of machinery parts. Because the windows were so dirty and the stacks of goods so messily high, the light was very dim, which gave a first false impression that it must be cooler here than in the glare outside. In fact, it was just as humid and possibly more hot and certainly stuffier. A few blacks, seated on the floor, playing some sort of card game, moved with the slow economy appropriate to the climate.

But not Frank. He strode through it all as though the place were in the Arctic. "The offices are back here."

Frank opened the door and led them into another world, a much more European or American world, with neat office furniture, a Kenya Railways calendar on the wall beside a color photograph of President Jomo Kenyatta, and a crisply proper black man at the desk wearing a dark-gray suit, white shirt, narrow light-gray tie.

Frank made the introductions: "Isaac Otera, Ellen Gillespie, Lew Brady."

"We met on the phone," Lew said, shaking the man's hand.

Isaac Otera looked puzzled for just a second, then vaguely disapproving. "I have never heard that locution before," he said pedantically. "Is it an Americanism?"

Surprised, Lew said, "I guess it is."

Frank said, "Isaac'll fill you in. Ellen, come along."

"Where?" Lew immediately asked, and just as immediately regretted it. He avoided Ellen's eyes.

"To talk with her boss," Frank said. To Ellen he said, "You'll like it in here. Air conditioning."

Frank and Ellen disappeared through the inner doorway, and Isaac gestured to the wooden chair beside his desk. "Sit down."

Lew sat, and Isaac opened his lower-right-hand desk drawer, taking from it a camera—a Cavalier SLR II, made in East Germany—putting it on the desk, saying, "Frank says you are familiar with cameras."

"I can take a picture. I don't win prizes."

"Good." From the same drawer came a white legal-size envelope. Isaac shook its contents out onto the desktop: a set of keys, several papers. Pushing the items one at a time toward Lew, he said, "There's a yellow Honda Civic parked in the back, rented from Hertz. Keys, rental contract. You have an international driver's license?"

"Sure."

"Good. This is your confirmed reservation for three nights starting tonight at the International Hotel in Kampala."

"I'm going to Kampala?"

"No."

From the drawer Isaac now took a road map and opened it to the section he wanted, then placed it on the desk in front of Lew. It was a map of Kenya, but the left quarter—the part Isaac was showing him—also included some of Lake Victoria and some of Uganda and even, at the lower left corner, some of Tanzania. Kenya's share of the lake frontage was very minor indeed.

"We are here," Isaac said, touching with his square-nailed fingertip the farthest eastern point on the lake. Not even the lake itself, but an extension from it called Winam Gulf.

Reading the name *Kisumu* below the fingertip, Lew nodded and said, "Okay."

The finger moved up across the top of the lake. "Jinja," Isaac said.

"Wait a second."

Lew leaned over the map to familiarize himself with at least the basic layout. From Kisumu it was probably seventy to eighty miles north along the shore to the Uganda border at the northeast corner of the lake. Then, turning west and running along the northern coast of the lake, it was perhaps another seventy miles to Jinja, which Isaac had started to point at, and fifty miles beyond that to Kampala, the capital of Uganda, on the shore at the very farthest left extreme of the map. "Okay," Lew said.

Isaac's finger again touched Jinja. "Until nineteen thirty-one," he said, "the railway from the coast terminated here. Then the bridge was built over the Nile."

Surprised, Lew said, "The Nile?"

"This is the Nile." Isaac's finger slid along a slender blue line snaking northward from Jinja, flanked by the red lines of highways, the yellow lines of minor roads, the black lines of railways. "This is where it starts from the lake."

"The source of the Nile." Lew found himself grinning. In his years in Africa he'd been all around this territory, but never exactly here. And while he didn't have Frank's love of history, he was at least aware of the search for the source of the Nile as having been the great Quest of the nineteenth century, civilized man's last major trek into the unknown before the turn to space. Explorer after explorer had died or returned broken with disease in the effort to trace the Nile to its source. And now it was merely a spot on a map, called Jinja, with a railroad.

Apparently Isaac was following Lew's train of thought. Drily he said, "We always knew where it was."

"You probably should have kept the secret."

"We tried to." But pedantry took over again, and Isaac went back to his earlier, humorless manner, saying, "In any event, when the railway crossed the Nile in nineteen thirty-one, it made obsolete some equipment that had been used there earlier when Jinja was the end of the line. Some of that equipment is still in existence. We have a report on it, but so far we have no photos or reliable eyewitnesses."

"A report? From somebody in Uganda?"

Isaac frowned. He placed his palm on the map, fingers splayed, and looked earnestly at Lew. "Forgive me if I am blunt, Mr. Brady," he said.

"Go ahead."

"I am not a thief," Isaac said. "Nor is Mr. Balim. If the purpose of this exercise were to steal cotton from Tanzania or copper from Zaire, I would have nothing to do with it."

Lew watched him carefully. "What is it, then?"

"A blow against Idi Amin." A sudden grating quality rasped in Isaac's voice as he spoke the name, and a hardness came into his face, as though he combined in himself both the flint and the steel.

Lew smiled, suddenly feeling at home. Appearances had been wrong. This man wasn't an office clerk, he was a partisan!

Misunderstanding the smile, Isaac said, "Not everyone is motivated merely by money."

"Oh, I know," Lew agreed. "Believe me, I know that. Frank just led me to—"

"Frank does what he does for his own reasons."

"He led me to believe those were everybody's reasons."

Isaac shrugged. "He can't be expected to describe what he doesn't understand."

"True."

"But what about you? I'd assumed you were like Frank."

"I can always make a living," Lew told him. "I'd rather do something interesting."

Isaac gave him a long scrutiny. Lew sat unmoving under that gaze, at attention, like a dog being patted by his master's friend. Finally Isaac smiled and said, "I'm surprised Frank had the wit to select you." Unfolding a piece of poor-quality, thick typewriter paper and handing it over, he said, "Read this."

Lew looked at words printed with ball-point pen in a large and somewhat naive hand. Without introduction, without signature, it read:

EAST AFRICAN RAILWAYS MAINTENANCE DEPOT NUMBER 4—
IGANGA

AN ENGINE SHED AND TURNTABLE. WATERING FACILITIES USED TO DRAW WATER UP FROM THE GORGE (THRUSTON BAY) VIA AN OLD PETROL ENGINE-DRIVEN PUMP (COVENTRY CLIMAX). ENTIRE FACILITY CHOKED WITH VEGETATION.

TURNTABLE CONSTRUCTED IN THE FORM OF A WOODEN PLATFORM ON A-SHAPE STEEL GIRDER FRAME ROTATING IN A SINGLE-GROOVE TRACK ON LARGE CASTER-TYPE WHEELS. TURNED MANUALLY.

20′ TRACK BEYOND TURNTABLE TOWARD GORGE, SAFETY BUFFER AT END STILL IN PLACE.

ORIGINAL CONNECTING SECTION TO MAIN LINE REMOVED WORLD WAR TWO FOR USE ELSEWHERE ON LINE, DUE TO SHORTAGE OF MATÉRIEL. SPUR TRACK STILL IN PLACE BEGINNING 12′ FROM MAIN LINE. INVISIBLE FROM MAIN LINE DUE TO VEGETATION.

AMPLE SUPPLIES OF RAIL (BUT NO SLEEPERS) PILED UP BESIDE ENGINE SHED.

OLD SERVICE ROAD FROM HIGHWAY STILL PASSABLE FOR 4-WHEEL-DRIVE VEHICLES. RUNS TO LAKE.

Lew finished, nodded, and put the sheet of paper on the desk. "That's the report from inside Uganda."

"Part of it. Do read it again—I'd rather you didn't take it with you."

Smiling at all the implications in that, Lew obediently picked the paper up and read it again.

He was partway through the third reading when the inner door opened and Ellen and Frank came out, Ellen laughing at something. "I certainly won't," she said to whoever was still inside—presumably Balim—and came toward Lew, bright-eyed, cheerful, saying, "Hi. How you doing?"

"Going for a ride in a car-car," he told her. "How about you?"

"Going for a ride in a plane-plane."

"Up up and away," Frank said, with his carnivore's grin.

"Have fun," Lew told them. The smile made his jaw ache.

They left, and Isaac said mildly, "You're wrinkling that paper."

* * *

The sun was bright on the hood of the little yellow car. Lew drove slowly, squinting behind his sunglasses, keeping an eye on the odometer. Eleven kilometers since the turnoff at Iganga, and counting.

The trip so far had been uneventful. He'd started from Kisumu at two-thirty, after lunch with Isaac Otera, during which Isaac had told him several Idi Amin horror stories, including (with some reluctance) the details of his own flight from the country. It was clear to Lew by now that Frank was merely being his usual cynical self when he'd claimed this was no more than a simple civilian robbery. Balim and Otera were both Ugandan exiles, driven from their homes by Amin. Otera was in fact a former government official. What was being planned here was every bit as political as an IRA bank robbery in Belfast.

It had taken nearly two hours on the truck-choked main road to reach the border at Busia. Most of the other traffic had turned off before then, however, and his was the only car visible in either direction when he reached the border, which was officially closed. But the closure primarily affected goods shipments and the nationals of the two countries involved; white tourists with money to spend were not turned away.

Once in Uganda, with the road almost completely to himself, he had taken barely more than an hour to reach Iganga, and eleven kilometers beyond. The afternoon sun was very high and hot in the sky ahead. The fields and forests all around had the brown, attenuated, thinned-out look that all of Africa gets just before the long rains.

Twelve kilometers; this was where Isaac had said the old road would be. Slowing to a crawl, Lew studied the verge beside him. Being in a former British colony, he was driving on the left, in a car with the steering wheel on the right, so he had to look across the shiny hood at the brown grass, the faded weeds, the drooping brush and trees.

Yes? A spot, wide enough for a truck to pass through, where there were no trees. Lew stopped and looked out the left-side window. The cleared swath was plain, though heavily overgrown. It had the vaguely cathedral look of all untended paths dimmed by overarching trees. This was the place.

Before turning, Lew glanced in the rearview mirror: nothing. He looked ahead and saw the glint of sunlight on chrome far away. He shifted back into Park, prepared to wait for the car to pass. Taking a map out from the under-dash compartment to explain why he'd stopped, he opened it and studied the lines and the names.

The car approached swiftly, then more slowly, and Lew had just registered the fact that it was not one car but two—identical new and shiny black Toyotas—when they both abruptly swerved toward him across the road.

He thought they meant to crash him, and ducked instinctively away, but the one Toyota shuddered to a stop directly in front while the other passed close on his right and angled to a stop, filling the rearview mirror.

"Oh, I am a goddam fool," Lew said aloud, and dropped the map. He could drive neither forward nor back. Even if he managed the tight turn into the old abandoned road, it would lead nowhere, and the Honda Civic wouldn't take him far along it. And there was no point in getting out to run.

Men were piling out of both Toyotas. They wore extremely dark sunglasses, garish shirts, bell-bottom slacks, platform shoes. Spreading out, they approached the car.

10

Ellen liked Mazar Balim more and more. Unlike his son, unlike Frank Lanigan, unlike most of the men she'd met, he wasn't interested in going to bed with her. But at the same time he clearly did like her, and she was happy to respond to that.

The meeting went this way: Frank said, "Ellen, come along," and Lew said, "Where?" and Frank said, "To talk with her boss," and Ellen knew that Lew would sooner or later drive her into a serious reaction against that sort of thing. Seeing Lew avoid her eyes, she knew he knew it, too. And she went into the next office with Frank.

Mazar Balim rose from behind his cluttered desk, in his small, cluttered, air-conditioned office. "Ah, Miss Gillespie," he said. "Do sit in that chair. It receives the benefit of the cool air without the draft."

"Thank you," she said, and sat in the minimal but comfortable green vinyl-covered chair directly in front of the desk, aware of Frank's dropping backward as though he'd been shot into the battered armchair against the wall.

Balim said, "It is a wonderful thing to me that I have been born in an age where a woman may be beautiful without shame and at the same time useful without shame. You have flown many planes in many strange parts of the world."

"But never before in Africa," she said, still smiling at the baroque compliment.

Balim waved his hand. "The air is the same. And now that you are here, let me admit to you boldly that you have been summoned somewhat under false pretenses."

The smile curdled on Ellen's lips. She had feared this from the beginning, that the so-called job would turn out to be merely a placebo to satisfy Lew's demands, that Lew was the only one they really wanted or needed here. And yet the plane did exist, and there had been a previous pilot whom she'd replaced.

"The long rains," Balim said, "will begin any day now. They tend to be very heavy and almost continuous. Most of the time for the next two months it will not be practical for you to fly my plane."

"I see."

"So we must work you very hard from now till the rains begin," Balim said, with his sweet smile. "And then again we shall work you very hard when the rains come to an end."

"I've flown in bad weather," Ellen pointed out. "Alaska isn't sunny all the time."

Balim smiled. "Still," he said, "I think you will find our long rains impressive, and you shall fly in them only when absolutely necessary. Now, as to where you shall fly, and for what purpose, let me assure you that I am a much more important and powerful man than I seem." This was said with such a self-deprecatory grin that Ellen didn't feel the need for a polite contradiction. Balim went on. "My merchant interests extend across Kenya so far as Mombasa, and also into Tanzania, and from time to time require my personal attention. Frequently I must go to Nairobi or Dar es Salaam or Tanga or even Lindi to deal with customs officials or traders or perhaps customers. Also Frank often must deal with problems at a great remove from here. Finally, there are at times small and delicate shipments which require special handling."

"He means ivory," Frank said, grinning, in the periphery of Ellen's vision.

"I was about to mention ivory," Balim said, looking faintly nettled. "There is no longer any overt trade in ivory in Kenya," he explained. "Concerns of a humanitarian and conservationist nature have brought an end to the slaughter of elephants, which we all can only applaud."

"Mama Ngina," Frank said, laughing, as though he were deliberately teasing his employer.

"It is true," Balim said (Ellen couldn't tell now if he was annoyed or amused), "that the sale of art objects previously made of ivory from elephants slaughtered in the unenlightened days of yesteryear has also been banned, and that whatever ivory the government can find has been impounded, and that rumors have drawn a connection between Mama Ngina and the warehouses in which these confiscated treasures are stored."

Ellen said, "Who is Mama Ngina?"

"Forgive me," Balim said. "I forget that my part of the world is a mere unimportant corner. Mama Ngina is the first lady of Kenya. The wife of Jomo Kenyatta."

Ellen said, "It's illegal to own ivory in Kenya?"

"It is illegal to own it for a commercial purpose," Balim told her. "Or to sell it."

"You want me to deliver ivory for you?"

"Oh, my dear lady, no!" Balim seemed truly shocked at the idea. "I would never offer to place you in such jeopardy. And certainly not at the salary I am paying you."

Ellen laughed despite herself. "I was thinking the same thing." She was to be paid seven hundred dollars a week plus expenses; six hundred of it to be deposited directly into her bank in San Francisco.

"You are a pilot," Balim insisted. "You are not responsible for what your passengers may be carrying on their persons. Nor, if your passengers experience legal difficulty, will that difficulty extend to yourself."

"You're sure of that."

"I guarantee it."

"It's all right, Ellen," Frank said, as though he and she were old comrades and she would know she could trust his word. "This whole ivory scam stinks so much the government wants it kept just as quiet as we do. If I'm stopped, and I've got a little ivory statue in my ditty bag, all they'll do is confiscate it and tell me don't do it again."

"With a Kenyan national," Balim said drily, "there might be a bit more difficulty. But not with whites."

"Besides," Frank said, "there isn't that much ivory to trade anymore."

"Unfortunately," Balim agreed. "In fact, the goods you will transport are much more likely to be mundane matters indeed. Medicine, for instance, or industrial diamonds, or merely great thick clumps of documents."

"I'm used to all of those," Ellen said. "When do I start?"

Frank said, "Today."

"Good. Where am I going?"

"Today's a little different," Frank said. "Today we'll just take a joyride. Do a little sightseeing."

"Where?"

"Uganda," Frank said.

* * *

"I'll just stop by my place for the cameras," Frank said. He had thrown a couple of filthy blankets over the filthy passenger seat so Ellen could sit there, saying, "If Charlie were an American Indian, his name would be Running Sore."

Ellen laughed, but said nothing, and looked with envy at the little yellow car that Frank had pointed out as Lew's transportation for today.

He started the engine, and she watched the exertions with which he forced the Land-Rover to do his bidding. Did all things for him require that much effort?

Frank's place was a neat stucco cottage on the fringe of town. A low openwork concrete wall bordered the property and was nearly obscured by a profusion of flowers. "Beautiful," Ellen said.

"It's a great country for flowers," Frank agreed.

Getting out of the Land-Rover, Ellen walked along the front wall, looking at the colors. "That's a delphinium. Is that jasmine?" She pointed to a thorny bush with hard-looking leaves and starfish-shaped white flowers.

Frank had walked along behind her. "No," he said. "But it smells like it. In Swahili it's *mtanda-mboo*. You can make a pretty good jelly out of the fruit. See that one?" He was pointing at a tall knobby shrub with clusters of dry-looking orangy-yellow flowers. "In Swahili it's *utupa*. A very tricky plant. You can get a tough poison out of the leaves, and the antidote for it out of the roots."

"Really?"

"Honest injun. The Masai use little doses of the poison for a laxative. The Luo dip the flowers in water—that makes it holy water—and sprinkle it around the house to keep off the evil spirits. Come on in; we just sprinkled this place yesterday."

Whitewashed rocks neatly flanked the packed-earth walk to the front door. "Bibi!" Frank yelled, opening the stained wood door. "Eddah!"

The entrance led directly into a wide shallow front room, filled with cool-looking sunlight. Ellen looked around at bare white plaster walls, stone floor, heavy rustic furniture, everything extremely neat and tidy, two vases at opposite ends of the room filled with a mixture of the flowers from out front.

A short giggling black girl in her twenties entered from the rear, swathed in the native style in bright-colored cloth. Her hair was done up in more cloth in a tall gaudy knob on her head, looking like a model of the Guggenheim Museum covered with graffiti. "Eddah gone," she told Frank, nodding and giggling as though it were a great satisfactory joke. "Gone store."

"Bibi, Ellen," Frank said offhandedly, and told Bibi, "Make sandwiches. Beer. Picnic."

The idea delighted her. Her teeth were large and crooked and very white; her eyes were filled with laughter; she kept nodding and nodding her whole body as though each moment of life increased her ecstasy. "Okay yes," she said. "Double-quick."

"Good sandwiches, now," Frank warned her, and held out his big hand in a threat to spank. "Good thick sandwiches."

"Yes, yes," she assured him, laughing at the idea that she could do anything less than totally please him. Patting the air, laughing, throwing some of her laughter and quick sparkling glances in Ellen's direction, she hurried from the room.

"Come take a look at the place," Frank said.

This of course was the seduction scene. Knowing there wouldn't be calm between them until Frank had been allowed to do his mating dance, Ellen said, "Sure," and went with him to see the place.

It was some sort of adolescent clubhouse dream: the counselor's hut in the Boy Scout camp, plus pinups. The entire house was neat and sparkling, which was clearly not Frank's style, but within the tidiness he had made his presence felt.

The kitchen, in which merry Bibi sawed away at bread with a serrated knife, was modern and tended heavily to brushed chrome. The dishware was all orange plastic, and one cabinet shelf was filled with jars of dry roasted peanuts. A small white plastic radio quietly played reggae-sounding music, as though for its own enjoyment. Visible through an aluminum screen door was a small kitchen garden, and beyond it, a wire enclosure containing chickens.

Frank opened the refrigerator, which was of course full of beer, and took out two bottles, but Ellen said, "Too early for me; I just got up. Besides, I'm supposed to fly. You don't want me to drink at the wrong time, remember?"

"You win," he said, grinning, meaning that round but not the fight. "Seven-Up or Coke?"

"Coke."

The hall, which had a few attractive unframed batik pieces on the walls, led one way to the maid's quarters and the other to Frank's bedroom, which was dominated by a king-size bed covered with a scarlet spread, on which a medium-size brownish dog of no particular breed lolled at his content. "Goddamit, George," Frank yelled, "get the fuck off that bed!"

George, midway between boredom and cowed sullenness, slowly rose, yawned, stepped down to the floor, and slunk from the room. Ellen said, "Washington?"

"Patton."

"Of course," she said, laughing at him. So the second round was his.

There were Playmate centerfolds on the white walls, of course, plus a poster of two ducks screwing in midair over the caption "Fly United." The female demurely smiled, while the male showed a devilish leer. That must be the way they want to see themselves, she thought. And the way they want to see us. "Which way do your windows face?"

Windows were in two walls, lightly curtained. Pointing, Frank said, "East and north."

"So you get the morning sun."

"But not too much."

Rush rugs partly covered the gleaming floor. There was no closet, but in a large old armoire hung his bush jackets and trousers, all laundered to a fare-thee-well. The small bathroom, seen through a partly open door, was less attractive than the rest but had been so thickly painted with white enamel and so determinedly scrubbed so often that it too managed a look of Spartan simplicity and dignity. An air conditioner, not turned on, was built into the wall below one of the north-facing windows. "Do you use that much?"

"Only when I work up a sweat."

Wrong technique. That was for girls you met in bars. "The house seems nice and cool without it," she said, nicely and coolly.

"It's the thick walls. Are you Lew's exclusive property?"

She laughed, in pleasure and surprise. "Very good!" she said, and actually clapped her hands together when she turned to congratulate him. "*That* puts me on the defensive!"

He found it impossible to hide his annoyance; maybe he wasn't even trying. "I just want to know how to behave," he said. "If Lew owns you, that's it."

Something happened now that wasn't his fault, though it was hard not to hold him responsible, anyway. As so often in a situation like this, without any overt threat from the man, she was reminded of her comparative physical frailty. If he wanted, right now, he could knock her out, he could strangle her, he in fact and in truth could do whatever he wanted with her. She would struggle, of course, but eventually he would win.

Sometime ago she had learned various self-defense measures, just because of the recurrent moments like this, but she doubted they would be much of a surprise to somebody like Frank. So she stood in this room saying no to him, and she would go on saying no to him, but in a far corner of her brain she was afraid of him; she knew it was ultimately his choice whether or not he took her no for an answer.

Neither her expression nor her intentions changed, but in the back of her mind the fear lived, sending out little tendrils through her thoughts like the red lines from a gangrenous wound. "You know who owns me, Frank," she said, trying neither to show the fear nor to blame him for it. "*I* own me, the way you own this house. And if I ever decide to give you a tour, I'll let you know."

Frank laughed, visibly relaxing. *Had* she been in danger? "That's okay, then," he said. "I'll be around. And I'll remind you every once in a while."

"I'm sure you will," she said.

* * *

She did have a beer after all, with the sandwiches, in the plane, flying over Lake Victoria. The sandwiches, on thick slices of darkish white bread, were like housed salads, the basic ham or chicken engulfed in pepper slices, pieces of cheese, lettuce, tomato, very thin radish slices, bits of herbs. It was messy eating, juice and tomato shreds falling into the paper napkins on their laps, the plane caring for itself in the easy updrafts over the lake. The White Cap beer was pleasantly sharp, dangerously gassy, the perfect accompaniment.

While they ate, Frank told her odd bits from his reading of African history. "The Baganda," he said, "they're the main tribe in Uganda, they were the most civilized blacks in Africa before the white men came. They had a king, called the kabaka, and a court, and a whole civilized social structure. But they were already crazy."

"In what way?"

"When the first Englishman arrived—his name was Speke—he met with a kabaka called Mutesa, and gave him gifts, the way the white men always did. Give you some cloth and beads and shit, and then take your country."

Ellen laughed, her mouth full of sandwich.

"Anyway," Frank said, "Speke showed Mutesa the first firearms he ever saw in his life. Mutesa had him shoot some cows. Then Speke gave Mutesa a carbine, and Mutesa—he was on his throne, in court—he gave the carbine to a page and told him to go outside and shoot somebody and let him know how it worked."

Ellen stared. "You're making this up."

Shaking his head, Frank said, "The page went out, Speke heard a *bang*, the page came back and said it worked just fine, the fellow was lying out there dead."

Ellen kept trying to read hoax in Frank's face, but it simply wasn't there. She said, "But who did he kill?"

"Nobody knows. It didn't matter. Listen, if you don't believe me, you look it up. Speke wrote about it in a book. *Journal of the Discovery of the Source of the Nile.*"

"That's the most awful thing I ever heard."

"They haven't changed much since," Frank said in gloomy satisfaction.

Finished with lunch, Ellen circled low over the lake while Frank dropped the paper bag of their garbage. Then she turned north, toward the lowering dark coast of Uganda.

Flying along, relaxed from the beer and from the successful conclusion of the bedroom scene, she said, "You worked it this way on purpose, didn't you? Separating Lew and me."

"Sure," he said, comfortable and self-assured. "But we really do need both. The man on the ground to look up close at what's there. And the aerial surveillance to know what the enemy will be able to see when the time comes."

The enemy. Despite himself, Frank couldn't help but view this as a military maneuver. Ellen smiled to herself and flew northward while, beside her, Frank studied the charts. "There's Dagusi Island," he said, pointing ahead and slightly to the right. "Stay to the right of it; we'll go over Macdonald Bay. That's where the road ends."

Uganda sloped sharply upward from the lake, heavily forested, unlike the brown scrubland along the Kenyan coast. Macdonald Bay was an irregularly shaped pocket of restless water, glinting and glistening.

Frank had dragged up from the rear seats the khaki canvas bag with his cameras, one of which he selected, screwing a lens on. "The road should be somewhere along the left shore," he said. "It won't be much; it hasn't been used for years."

"Is that it?"

A faint scar of brown scratched westward from the water's edge, disappearing almost at once into the trees. "Good eyes," Frank said, looking through the camera's viewfinder. "Get down on the deck, let's take a—"

A jet buzzed them, crossing their route from left to right, going very fast. It was all so sudden and so close that Ellen automatically pulled up, then had to retrim, while the afterimage cleared in her brain. A fighter, with camouflage paint. "What was that?"

"MiG," Frank said, sounding grim but not yet scared. He held the cameras in his lap. "Ugandan Air Force."

"What's he doing?" She craned forward to look all over the sky but couldn't see him.

"Well, we're in his airspace. Coming back at three-o'clock level."

Once again the jet whooshed by, this time more slowly, arcing lazily away at the last instant as Frank gave a big hearty wave and smile out his window. In addition to its registration numbers, the plane had a symbol on the side of the fuselage: a flag shape divided diagonally from bottom left to top right. The upper triangle was green, the lower an orangy-red.

"He's making me nervous," Ellen said. "I'm going back over the lake."

But halfway through her turn, the jet appeared again, sailing by. It was so much faster than they were—and couldn't slow to their speed without risking burnout—that it was hard to get a clear picture, but she had the impression the pilot had waved this time on the way by. For confirmation, the jet waggled its wings once it was out in front, then lifted into the sky, hurrying away, due west.

"He says we're okay," Frank said. "Just tourists flying around."

"I was afraid we were the ones he was supposed to shoot to see if his guns worked."

Frank laughed, and Ellen completed the three-hundred-sixty-degree turn, coming in over Macdonald Bay again, this time much lower. The scar was now clearly a road, but it still disappeared under the thick dark-green trees.

"Head northwest," Frank said, taking pictures.

Below them, the forest was impenetrable, nothing but the thick-leafed branches. Frank lowered the camera. "Thruston Bay over there," he said, pointing ahead and to the left. "The turntable should be between us and it."

Traveling very slowly, just clearing the treetops, she turned toward Thruston Bay. "Wait," she said, throttling back, then had to rev up.

"What was it?"

"I thought I saw something shine."

They were over the bay. Ellen made a tight turn in the sky and headed back over the trees. Frank said, "When you get where you saw it, turn left."

That would be inland, away from the lake. "Right."

She saw no glint this time, was not in fact absolutely sure where she'd seen it before. When she felt she must be past it, she turned left, and very soon they crossed a railway: a single pair of tracks and the gleaming line of metal sleepers.

"We've gone too far," Frank said. "The turntable's between the railroad and the lake."

Ellen started another turn, the sweep taking them over the highway just north of the track. Down there, three cars were stopped in an odd relationship, like a chinese ideogram: two black cars at angles to a yellow car between them. A group of men stood in the middle of the road around a lone man.

Ellen stared. "The car—that's Lew!"

"Holy shit," Frank said.

One of the men hit the man in the middle with an object of some kind, a stick or pipe or gun barrel. The man fell, and two of the men kicked him, and he curled up like a leech when salt is poured on it.

Frantic, staring around at the unforgiving forest, Ellen cried, "Where can we land? Where can we land?"

"Are you crazy? This is Uganda! Get back to Kisumu, fast!"

Two of the men had looked up, were pointing at the plane. One hurried toward a black car; to radio someone?

Ellen accelerated into the turn, climbing higher into the empty comfortless sky. "We'll get to Balim," Frank was saying. "He'll know what to do." He'd undone his seat belt to turn and put the camera bag on the backseat.

Bracing herself, Ellen abruptly pulled back on the stick, and the plane dropped fifty feet like a stone before she accelerated again. She'd been ready for it, but Frank hadn't. He was thrown violently up against the metal top and flung just as violently down again. *"Jesus!"* he yelled, scrabbling for something to hold on to. "Watch it!"

"I am watching it, Frank," she said, and her tone of voice made him stare at her in sudden alarm. The airspeed indicator kept climbing. Not looking at him, she said, "You sent Lew over there today so you could fuck me."

"It should have been safe!" He was hurriedly trying to get his seat belt snapped. "I told you, we needed both—"

This time she sideslipped, cracking his head smartly against his side window. He yelled, and she said, "Don't argue with me, Frank. I could kill you up here, and you don't dare touch me because I'm the pilot. You want another taste?"

"No! Jesus Christ," he said, trying to hold his head and at the same time brace himself for any conceivable shift in speed and direction. "What's it *for?*"

"I want Lew back," she told him. "And I want you to know how serious I am, Frank."

"Don't do it again!"

She didn't. "I want him back."

"You'll get him," Frank promised, grim and sullen and abashed. "You'll get him. And welcome to him."

11

Like Rome, Kampala is built on seven hills, and is in fact named after one of them, *Kampala* meaning "Hill of the Impala," that graceful harmless antelope of the long curved horns, a peaceful herbivore. Another of these hills is called Nakasero, and on its crest sat the Presidential Lodge, one of many residences the restless, discontented Amin maintained throughout Uganda. In rustic luxury, the Lodge nestled amid mango and gum trees, bougainvillea vines, frangipani, and hibiscus. By day the sweet-smelling groves rang with the laughter of Idi Amin's children; he had at least twenty-five, by five wives.

Down the hill, farther down the hill, within sight of the windows of the Lodge, was a large lovely open park, a green, four hundred yards wide. On one side of it stood All Saints Church, the See of Anglican Archbishop Janani Luwum, who had been murdered personally by Idi Amin on February 17, 1977. Opposite stood the French Embassy and, next to that, a three-story pink building surrounded by barbed wire. This was the State Research Bureau, in an office of which Amin had shot the archbishop in the face, then had phoned one of his useful white men to say, "I've lost my temper. I've shot the archbishop. Do something."

Lew was semiconscious, in the trunk of one of the Toyotas, when the two cars drove in at the front gate of the State Research Bureau. He felt fevered, delirious, but was conscious enough to know he was in the worst trouble of his life. He didn't know, and wouldn't have been cheered to hear, that someone had once said of the State Research

Bureau at Nakasero, "When you go in there, the question is not when or if you will come out. The only question left is when the pain will stop."

They opened the trunk of the Toyota and pulled him out by his ankles and elbows and hair, letting him fall to the ground and then kicking him for his clumsiness, yelling, "Up! Get up!" in Nubian dialect. Lew curled into a ball, protecting his head and torso, his back shielded by the Toyota, until they stopped kicking him and grabbed his arms to jerk him to his feet. Swimmingly in the glare of the sunlight he saw the green beyond the barbed wire, and what appeared to be the mirage of a cathedral far away. Parked next to the barbed wire, one side dented, was a bus in which, two months ago, a group of hospital nurses had been coming back to Kampala after a dance at Makerere University; State Research Bureau men had stopped it, driven it here, and beat and raped the nurses through the night, releasing them in the morning. There had been no retribution.

Lew was hustled into the building, where a harsh-looking man in Army uniform sat at a reception desk. A Colt .45 was on the desk, easy to his right hand. Lew, blinking, trying to rid his eyes and mind of fuzziness and spots of deadness, looked at that automatic on the desk and licked his puffy lips, tasting blood. But even if he were fully conscious, with all his coordination, grabbing for that gun would be a very stupid move.

"Name?"

"Lew—" He coughed and cleared his throat and tried again. "Lewis Brady."

He saw the man write it down in a long ledger, the dark parody of a hotel register. The book was thick, the open page in the middle, a dozen names already listed before Lew's. Reading upside down, blinking and blinking, Lew saw that there were two headings at the top of the page: NAME and CHARGE. Under CHARGE, after his name, he watched the Army man write "Not specified." Almost all the other entries on the page said the same thing.

"Valuables."

He gave them everything, but they wanted more than everything and made that clear by hitting him on the sides and the back of the head with gun butts. They wanted his shoes and belt, and when he turned them over he was taken up a flight of stairs to a long wide corridor and told to sit there on a wooden bench. All but two of the men went away, the remaining pair leaning against the opposite wall, frowning at Lew with great intensity, as though their hostility were the only thing they clearly understood.

The half hour on the bench was a very good time; if it was supposed to be a psychological ploy to increase his nervousness, it had quite the opposite effect. Lew began to think again, to recover a bit from the beatings, and to observe the area around himself. He was in a long bare corridor lined with office doors, perhaps a third of them open. From within one office toward the far end came the halting sound of amateurish typing. At intervals along the walls were large notices: SILENCE. Here and there between the demands for silence were hung framed printed slogans and sayings; the one Lew could read said NO WISDOM IS GREATER THAN KINDNESS. THOSE WHO BUILD THEIR SUCCESS ON OTHERS MISFORTUNES ARE NEVER SUCCESSFUL. It was signed "Mjr Farouk Minawa."

The least encouraging thing about the corridor was the thick bloodstains along the wall above the bench, just at the height of Lew's head. Clearly, it was a habit here to beat the heads of seated prisoners against the concrete walls. An abrupt and messy death. Or possibly merely a fractured skull and irreparable brain damage. Lew sat braced to defend himself should either of those men across the way decide to play the game on him; even though he knew resistance was hopeless.

A strange thing about the two men guarding him: the nail on the little finger of each hand was over an inch long, curved and sharp and yellowish-gray, like the talon of a hawk.

After thirty minutes, two new men appeared from down the corridor and said to Lew, "Come with us." Lew got to his feet, his former guards went away, and he walked between these new men down the corridor to the end and into a large office marked HEAD OF TECHNICAL OPERATIONS, where a thick-faced uniformed man sat at a large table piled with an assortment of junk.

This was Major Farouk Minawa, commander of the State Research Bureau and author of the homilies framed in the corridor. It was Minawa, a Nubian Muslim, who along with the Ugandan Chief of Protocol, Captain Nasur Ondoga, on July 5, 1976, at nine in the morning, went to Mulago Hospital, yanked Mrs. Dora Bloch (the only unrescued Israeli hostage) from her bed, dragged her screaming down three flights of stairs while staff and patients stood by in helpless shock, threw her into a car, drove her twenty miles from Kampala on the road toward Jinja, pulled her from the car, shot her by the roadside, and tried unsuccessfully to burn the body. (The white hair didn't burn, and was the first clue to her identity.)

There were also three other Research Bureau men in the room, in their uniforms of bright shirts, platform shoes, bell-bottom trousers, dark sunglasses. One of these sprawled on a sofa to one side, drinking a bottle of soda. There were two other sofas, both empty, while the other two Research Bureau men prowled the room like big cats in a zoo. The two who had brought Lew in walked over to one of the empty sofas and sat side by side there, casually, crossing their legs, looking around, as though waiting for a bus. Everyone in the room but Minawa had the long nail extending from the little finger of each hand.

Minawa pointed at the carpeted floor in front of Lew. "Sit down."

"On the floor?"

"Sit down!" Minawa fairly bounced in his chair with his sudden rage.

Sensing movement behind him from one of the roving men, Lew dropped quickly to the floor, bringing his knees up, folding his arms around them. Minawa glared across his messy desk, but when he next spoke, his voice was once more calm. "What did the CIA order you to do in Uganda?"

"The CIA?" In his bewilderment, Lew had one millisecond of joy, in which this would turn out to be somebody's error and he would simply be released with apologies; but the fantasy didn't last.

There were rifles, pistols, automatic guns stacked and stuffed under the sofas. One of the seated men took out a knife and studied the blade with great concentration.

"The CIA! The CIA!" Minawa pounded the tabletop. "You think we're *stupid* here? You think we're *niggers?*"

"I have nothing to do with the CIA," Lew said.

"You are an American."

"That doesn't mean—"

"Your name is Lewis Brady."

"Yes, it is."

"Call me 'sir'!"

"Yes, sir, my name is Lewis Brady." To have refused the demand would have invited another beating. It wasn't fear that kept Lew from wanting another beating, but the knowledge that he would need to be in the best possible physical and emotional shape for whatever came next; there would clearly be beatings enough without his requesting extra portions.

"In nineteen seventy-four," Minawa said, referring to a sheet of paper on the table before him, "you were assigned by the CIA to the repressive government of Ethiopia."

"No, sir," Lew said. "Ethiopia hired me as an instructor. That had nothing to do with the CIA or any—"

"In nineteen seventy-five," Minawa interrupted, "the CIA transferred you to the Angolan National Union. You won't deny *that* was a CIA operation."

"If it was," Lew said, "I didn't know it."

The man lying on the sofa said, "You think you'll kill us, but we can see you."

"We have *lists*," Minawa said. "When you crossed the border, we looked at the list."

"What list would I be on?"

One of the roaming men, behind Lew at that moment, kicked him painfully in the ribs. "You will call the major 'sir.' "

"I beg your pardon." The kick made breathing difficult, but Lew tried not to show that. These creatures were more beasts than men, and would be attracted to weakness or fear. He said, "Sir, would you tell me what list my name was on?"

"Mercenaries," Minawa said, "that our friends have identified as CIA."

"What friends? Sir."

"*Our* friends!" Minawa's sudden displays of rage were metronomic, seeming to arise at specified intervals regardless of provocation.

"We have many friends," the man on the sofa said. "And you have no friends at all."

"The holy rebels of Chad learned the truth about you," Minawa said, "and that was when you fled to Ethiopia."

"Chad?" Briefly Lew had been involved in a rebellion in Chad, back in 1974, but why would—? And then it came clear. "Holy rebels" indeed; that was the rebellion financed by Libya. And wasn't Colonel Gaddafi of Libya very tight with Idi Amin? "Libya," Lew said.

They didn't like it that he had seen through their mystery. The man on the sofa looked up at the ceiling as though no longer taking part in the conversation, and Minawa busily moved things around on his messy table, glowering and moving his lips.

Lew said, "Major, I can only assure you I have never been an employee of the CIA in my life."

Still gazing at the ceiling, the man on the sofa said, as though reasonably explaining some simple concept to a dull child, "We will kill you before you can kill us. We have to protect ourselves; that is justice."

"I am a tourist," Lew said. "I have hotel reser—"

Minawa pounded his palm flat against the table top. "You are not a tourist! You are a mercenary soldier, a provocateur, an agent of the CIA!"

"No, sir, I'm—"

"If you lie," Minawa said, pointing a blunt finger, "it will go very badly for you. We already know everything. You will write a paper. You will write what the CIA told you to do in Kampala. You will write the names of the people you were supposed to contact in Uganda."

"Sir, I can only tell you this is a mistake. I have no—"

"You refuse to write the paper?"

There was nothing to say. Lew looked at the angry thick face of Major Minawa until one of the prowling men came over and stood in front of him, blocking Minawa from sight. The man calmly rapped his knuckles hard on top of Lew's head. Lew winced but made no other move. The man rapped again, harder, and when Lew still showed no reaction he became enraged and pounded his fist down onto Lew's head the way Minawa had just a moment ago pounded the table top. Pain jolted through Lew's head, spread behind his eyes, swelled in all the muscles of his neck. If the man did that again, he would surely cause damage. Lew unclenched his hands from around his knees, preparing to kick, but Minawa said something in Nubian and the other man made a disgusted sound, slapped Lew across the face in a halfhearted way, and moved to the side.

Minawa said, "You will write the paper."

"I would if I could, Major," Lew told him, "but there's nothing for me to say."

The man on the sofa said, *"Kalasi?"*

"No," said Minawa. "Not yet." To Lew he said, "Stand up." Lew did so, and Minawa said, "Come over here. Open your pants. Put your cock on the table."

Lew stared at him. "Do what?"

Both prowling men now rushed over to hit and kick at him until he did as he'd been ordered. He stood there, humiliated, in pain, trousers open and penis a tiny helpless fish on the edge of the table, and he felt a fear very unlike the fear of death.

Minawa picked up a rusty—no, bloodstained—bayonet from the clutter on the table. He tapped it gently on the table near Lew's shrinking member. He said, "You will write the paper."

"Major," Lew said, his mouth and throat completely dry, "Major, I'd write anything you wanted me to write. You know that. But if you say put down names of contacts in Uganda, I'll have to make them up. There *are* no contacts in Uganda."

Everyone in the room waited to see if Minawa would become angry. Minawa himself seemed to wait with the same sense of suspense. Finally he nodded and put down the bayonet and said, "The names are more important. You'll give them to me later. You think you won't, but you will."

Laughing softly, the man on the sofa said, "You'll tell us the thousand names of God. You'll beg us to listen."

"Close your trousers," Minawa said, expressing contempt, as though Lew had been guilty of a social breach. Then he spoke in Nubian.

The two men who'd brought Lew in here got up from the sofa, one of them gesturing for Lew to go to the door. Lew turned, and found the man who'd hit him on the head standing there, blocking his way. Smiling at him, the man lifted his hand and extended his pinky with the long fingernail toward Lew's left eye. The tip of the nail nearly touched the eyeball. Lew looked at him, unblinking, thinking, If you put that in my eye, I'll rip your Adam's apple out before they can stop me.

The man's smile faltered, as though he found himself less funny than he'd expected. Or as if he'd seen something he didn't like in Lew's expression. He lowered the hand and spoke in Nubian past Lew to Minawa. They all laughed, which gave the man back his self-confidence; grinning, he stepped to one side and gestured elaborately for Lew to exit.

* * *

There was singing some distance ahead, a hymn being sung by many voices. Lew and his guards descended several flights of stairs, down into the earth under the State Research Bureau building, and the ragged but determined chorus of male voices grew steadily louder. The melody was "What a Friend We Have in Jesus," but the words were Swahili.

Sunlight was far away now, the corridors and stairwells lit by harsh fluorescents too widely separated, so that the areas of glare led to pockets of shadow. The floors and walls were stained as though rivers of blood had flowed through here, and afterward had been imperfectly cleaned. Under Lew's shoeless feet the steps were cold.

And then they reached a closed metal door with a ventilator opening near the top; it was from behind there that the singing came.

A soldier with a machine pistol had been sitting on a wooden stool beside the door. Lew's escort spoke to him, and he stood, putting the machine pistol on the stool while he unlocked the door. At the sounds of the unlocking the singing within faded away into an expectant, perhaps horrified, silence.

The soldier pulled open the door, and a most incredible stench poured out, with the force of a physical punch to the stomach. A compound of rot, of human feces, of blood, of filthy unwashed bodies and filthy clothing, of urine and spoilage and death and fear. Lew stepped back against the opposite wall, appalled, and his two escorts laughed at him.

At first the interior was merely a sort of writhing darkness, the mouth and throat of some hideous monster exhaling that stench, but then the soldier hit a light switch beside the doorway and a fluorescent ceiling light came on in there, and the look of the place was even worse than the smell.

When the Yugoslavs had constructed this building for the Ugandan government, they'd included a tunnel leading from its basement to

Amin's Lodge, so he would have an escape route if ever he were besieged on his hilltop, and so he could in privacy come from the Lodge to the State Research Bureau to participate in the torture and murder here. (He liked, while wearing a gas mask, to club people to death with the butts of two pistols.) But the tunnel had turned out not to be the most practical route between the buildings, so the Lodge end had been sealed off and now the tunnel was used as a kind of holding pen for Research Bureau victims.

The tunnel was six feet high and five feet wide, and full of men. They were all black; some were half-naked; some wore rags and the torn remnants of clothing; all were barefoot. There were over a hundred in there, sitting or crouching on the floor, their backs against the wall, receding into the semidarkness beyond the fluorescent's reach. Many of them were bloodstained, many had fresh wounds on their heads or chests or arms, and all of them blinked and moved in the sudden light, slack-jawed and moronic-looking.

A man near the door chattered in a fast panicky Swahili at the soldier, while pointing at someone or something farther back in the tunnel—perhaps the rusty trash barrel in the middle of the floor there.

No, it was about one of the other prisoners. The soldier replied, and there was a brief discussion, during which Lew adjusted his mind to this horror and gave his guards no more reason to laugh. Then two of the men in there stood up, picked up another man by the ankles and arms and, crouching under the low ceiling, carried him out and laid him on the floor in the corridor. He was dead. At some time recently, the hinge of his jaw had been broken and left unattended; the jagged-edged protrusion of white bone, blood-smeared, just under his ear, was as vivid as a scream against his black skin.

Lew was pushed forward. He crossed the threshold and stood there under the fluorescent, looking at the astonishment on all those faces as they stared back: a white man, in *their* Hell. Then the door clanged shut and the light went out.

In the dark he could hear them murmuring around him. The smell in here was violent in its intensity, and made more so by the darkness; it made him want to vomit, but at the same time was so thoroughly foul that it dried his mouth and throat and made vomiting impossible.

Lew wasn't quite sure what to do—if he took a step, he'd probably walk on somebody—but then a hand touched his shin and a voice low to his right said, "Sit here. There's room."

Lew crouched, touched bodies, touched the cold rough wall where they had moved over to give him space. He sat, put his back against the wall, started to stretch his legs, and bumped them into someone else. "Sorry."

"Put your legs over mine," said the man across the way. "Later, we'll reverse."

"Thank you."

The man beside him, the one who had touched his shin and spoken to him, now said, "Have courage, brother. God will watch over you."

There was some dim light from the ventilator slot in the door. By its light, Lew could see that the man was portly, gray-bearded, probably the wrong side of fifty. He wore a torn white shirt and black trousers, and he had recent cuts around his eyes and on the bridge of his nose, as though he'd been hit while wearing glasses. He said, "I am Bishop Michael Kibudu."

"Lew Brady. Bishop?"

"Of the Evangelical Baptist Mission. My church is in Bugembe."

"How long have you been here?"

"Two months. I don't believe there has ever been a white man in here before. Not in *here*. Would it be improper for me to ask what unlucky chance brought you to this place?"

"They got it into their heads I'm connected with the CIA."

"Ah. They accused the archbishop of being in the employ of the CIA."

"The one they killed? Is this some kind of religious persecution or something?"

Bishop Kibudu smiled, a sweet sad incongruous expression. "Something like that," he said. "May I ask, are you saved?"

Had that particular question ever been asked in more ridiculous circumstances? "I don't think so," said Lew.

12

Frank took a swallow of 7UP, then carefully poured gin into the bottle and gently swirled it. He tasted again, nodded in satisfaction, and carried the bottle into Balim's office, where Balim himself was on the phone, while to one side Isaac Otera and Bathar (who was known to everyone except his father as Young Mr. Balim) looked worried and useless as they watched Ellen pace back and forth in front of the desk, her expression full of storm clouds. "Here," Frank said, and extended the bottle.

She glared at him, at his hand, at the 7UP. "What's this?"

"Got gin in it. Calm you down."

"I don't want to calm down, you prick," she said, and turned away to glare instead at Balim, talking slowly and insinuatingly and gently into the telephone.

Frank threw a mutinous look at the back of her head and downed the spiked 7UP himself. She was going too far, that's all, and his sense of guilt was finally giving way to anger. They were doing what they could, weren't they?

Drawing the conversation to a close, Balim extravagantly thanked the person he'd been talking to and with apparent reluctance hung up. He said to Ellen, "Now we must wait, the most difficult part of all."

"It's been hours." Even Frank could see it was only her anger that kept her from falling apart; still, she shouldn't go on calling him names in front of everybody.

"Patience is our only friend, at this point," Balim said.

"He could already be dead."

"Please," Balim said, rising heavily from behind the desk, "put that much out of your mind. I have been told that a shipment of black Toyotas was received from Japan in Uganda within the last year, all consigned to the government. So these are not kidnappers or bandits." He had come around the desk while talking, and now he tenderly touched Ellen's forearm with his fingertips, as a faith healer might, as though to encourage a flow of his own strength and assurance into her. "They have taken Lew into custody, that is all."

"But we don't know what they'll do to him."

Frank said, "They'll question him. It's some kind of mix-up; they think he's somebody else. They could even figure it out for themselves and let him go." He didn't himself quite believe any of this.

Ellen gave him a look of utter contempt, but at least she didn't call him a prick. She said to Balim, "I want to call the American Embassy."

Not again, Frank thought, we've been through all that. But Balim was patience itself. He said, "Ellen, I know my concern for our friend pales beside yours, but believe me, my concern is real, and if the American Embassy could help us I would phone them first. *First.*"

"Of course they'll help. He's an American citizen."

"The American Embassy in Uganda is closed. Shall an American chargé d'affaires in Nairobi phone the French Embassy in Kampala and ask a chargé d'affaires there to make what would surely be a routine inquiry for a wandering American believed to be in Ugandan custody?"

"Why not?"

"Who is this American? the Ugandan authorities would ask themselves. Who is he that diplomats ask after him? And soon they will learn he has a long career as a mercenary soldier in Africa."

"The same with the American Embassy in Nairobi," Frank said, "not to mention the Kenyan government. What's our connection with this guy Brady? What are we all up to? See what I mean?"

Even as he finished his statement, Frank saw by the warning looks from the others that he'd made some sort of tactical error, but he didn't know what it was until Ellen turned to glare at him, saying, "So that's the point, is it? This *deal* you're all in on. We'll try everything we can to get Lew back, just so it doesn't endanger the *deal*."

Fortunately for Frank, Balim himself answered, saying, "Ellen, no, certainly not! Frank made his point badly, but his intention was a good one, I assure you."

Frank didn't much care for Balim's talking about him that way, even just as a psychological ploy with Ellen; nor did he care at all for Ellen's sneer of contempt when she said to Balim, "A good intention, from Frank?"

Isaac Otera suddenly said, "You call it a deal. Maybe it is."

Everybody turned in astonishment to look at Isaac, who wore the tight-clenched expression of the public speaker struck by stage fright but determined to go on. Blinking, hands closed into fists at his side, he said, "Maybe it's something else. But whatever it is, if it comes out that Lew is in Uganda to help set up a coffee-smuggling operation, you'll never see him again."

"That's right," Balim said.

With a huge smile, feeling a great weight lift off his chest, Frank pointed at Isaac and said, "That's what I meant! That's the whole thing!"

Isaac took a hesitant step toward Ellen, saying, "The truth is, even though Lew was arrested because of some mistake, *he has something to hide.* Whatever we do to rescue him, we mustn't risk giving away his secret."

"Good God," Ellen said faintly.

Balim said, "I am attempting now to get in touch with a gentleman high up in the Ugandan government. It may take—"

"Father, dear Father," Young Mr. Balim said, "tell her the whole truth. She deserves it."

Frank glowered, thinking, *He's after her, the slimy little wog,* but the elder Balim nodded, accepting his son's reproof. "The habit of secrecy," he said, "is at times too strong in me. Ellen, our associate inside Uganda in the coffee transaction is a white man named Baron Chase, who is very high up in the government there. One of Amin's most trusted assistants."

"A white man?"

"Frank has known him for years."

"A snake in the grass," Frank said.

"But even a snake in the grass," Young Mr. Balim said, smiling comfortably at Frank, "can have its uses."

"I bet it can," Frank told him.

Balim Senior said to Ellen, "I can't call Baron Chase directly. What I have done is send messages to him through two separate intermediaries, that he should get in touch with me at once, on a matter of the utmost urgency. Those two gentlemen are both now on their way to Uganda. If one of them experiences difficulty—"

"Or cold feet," said Young Mr. Balim.

"I think more highly of my friends than does my son," Balim said, giving Ellen a rueful smile. (Frank saw that she faintly responded to the smile; Balim could do anything, when he set his mind to it.) "Still," Balim added, "if for any reason one of my couriers fails, the other must surely succeed. Then Baron Chase will phone me, I will explain the problem, and he will arrange for Lew's release."

Still clearly dubious, Ellen said, "You make it sound almost easy."

"It almost is. You go home now," Balim said, patting Ellen's shoulder, "and I'll call—"

"No," she said. "I'll wait here."

"Ellen, I promise I'll call you the minute—"

"Where should I go?" she demanded, astonishing Frank by suddenly flaring up at *Balim*. "Back to that little house by myself? Or to your guest room, or Frank's living room? I'm better here."

"But if the call comes late at night, when I'm at home?"

She looked at the telephone on his desk. "Wouldn't it be the same number there?"

Balim laughed, again patting her shoulder, saying, "You win."

"If the phone rings, I'll pick up, but I won't speak. I'll just listen. No matter what he says, I won't say a word."

"I believe you," Balim said. "You can stay."

* * *

The pail contained two sandwiches that Bibi had made, four bottles of White Cap beer, two glasses, napkins, a small bag of homemade cookies. Frank looked in the pail, smiled, and was pleased. Putting its top on, he smacked the giggling Bibi on the rump and carried the pail out to the Land-Rover.

It was nearly eleven at night. The streetlights of Kisumu are dim and widely spaced. There isn't much by way of nightlife, not out on the streets. Frank kicked the Land-Rover past houses that were mostly dark, or with a wan light showing pink through cloth-covered windows, and parked at last in front of Balim's buildings. Two of the guards—ramshackle ragged men for whom hard hats and Sam Browne belts served as uniforms—lounged near the door on upturned wooden boxes; they made some small effort to look alert when Frank appeared, but didn't go so far as to stand. The other guards would be around back, from where the possibility of theft was naturally greater.

The dog that patrolled inside this building at night was named Hakma. A big barrel-chested unamiable brute, he had once been described by Frank as half German shepherd and half gorilla. "Yeah, Hakma, hello, you know who I am, you fucking beast," Frank said, standing still just within the door while the dog—much more conscientious than the human guards—sniffed his body first, and only then, having recognized the pass-smell, turned his attention to the good aromas from the pail. "That's not for you, fucker," Frank said, pushed the dog away, and headed for the offices.

The door between Isaac's and Balim's offices was ajar. The light was on in there, and voices sounded. Massively frowning, holding the pail up in front of himself with both hands on the handle as if it were an offering, Frank tiptoed across the dim outer room and looked through the doorway.

The kid! Son of a bitch bastard, it was Young Punk Balim in there with Ellen, grinning like the rat he was, telling stories, chuckling away. A wicker picnic basket was on the floor; a small gaily printed cloth now covered a third of Balim's desk, and on it were plates and stemmed glasses. What were they eating? Cold chicken, cheese, fruit. Gritting his teeth, Frank watched the rotten bastard pick up a bottle of white wine to refill their glasses. "It may be my provincial background," he was saying, oily punk, "but I have always found theater in the West End somehow too slick. Did you have that sense?"

"I know what you mean," Ellen said. She was completely at her ease. Frank wanted to go in there and make her feel guilty, ask her how she could just *picnic* like this with Lew in God knows what trouble. Of course, he'd have to hide his own pail of sandwiches.

Reluctantly, in utter silence, he retraced his steps, shutting Isaac's outer door behind himself and calling Hakma several uncomplimentary names on the way out.

It would be a loss of face in front of Bibi and Eddah to return this soon, and with the picnic uneaten. Feeling badly used, Frank drove southeast out of town and found a place to park where he could look out over the moonlit gulf. Forty miles away, too far to see from here, Winam Gulf opened into Lake Victoria, itself two hundred miles wide and two hundred fifty miles long. In all that vast expanse, with the moon shining down and the calm water rippling like a purring cat, there was not one place where Frank Lanigan would not feel unhappy.

"If that's her taste—" he muttered, and opened the pail. He ate both sandwiches, drank two of the bottles of beer, skipped the cookies one by one across the calm water, drove home to the darkened house, kicked George off the bed, and slept like a log.

13

It was a beautiful young black woman in a bright-colored print dress who met Sir Denis Lambsmith this time at the strangely empty Entebbe Airport. Her dark-cinnamon skin glowed with innocent health, but there was something seductive in her broad smile and the eager glisten of her eyes. "I'm delighted to meet you, Sir Denis," she said, shaking his hand, her own hand small and slender and firm. "I am Patricia Kamin, of the Ministry of Development."

Sir Denis, despite the fact that he was immediately taken by this attractive young woman, couldn't resist the temptation to ask, "What's happened to Mr. Onorga?"

She looked prettily confused for a second; then the sunny sexy smile broke out once more and she said, "Oh, the man from the Coffee Commission! I believe he was transferred. You're in my hands now."

"Then I'm delighted," Sir Denis said, smiling down upon her from his greater height and age and sex and race.

"You have your luggage? The car is this way."

It was a black Toyota, which Patricia Kamin drove herself. No secret police this time; how pleasant. Beside her in the front seat, Sir Denis took pleasure in the movement of her knees and her sleek legs as she angled the car out of the empty parking lot and around the sweeping circle to the main road. All airports in former British possessions are toy versions of Heathrow, no matter how redundant the roundabouts.

"How is London?" she asked, once they were on the road toward Kampala.

"Drizzly."

She laughed, a musical sound, and said, 'Still full of foreigners?"

He looked at her, surprised, not quite sure how to answer, not at all sure who she thought *she* was. "Foreigners?"

"When I was there over Christmas, the city was full of Norwegians and Danes and Frenchmen and I don't know who all."

"Oh, yes. Shopping."

"That's it," she agreed. "You couldn't get *near* Harrods. I did my shopping on Oxford Street."

"I imagine that was also full."

"It was. I'll never understand international finance," she said, flashing him another smile. "I met the nicest Swede, and he kept explaining to me over and over how he was saving money by coming all the way to London to do his Christmas shopping, but it simply never made sense. And the hotel he was in! A shower *really* big enough for two!"

Sir Denis drove himself from sexual thoughts with pompous statements. "I think we'll find normality returning," he said, "once the North Sea oil starts to flow."

"No more of those headlines? 'Pound Soars,' 'Pound Plummets'? That's all the papers said, every day I was there. You could get positively giddy."

"Newspapers," Sir Denis said, with a wry smile and shake of the head.

"Did you ever hear," she asked him, "the description of who reads which London papers?"

"No, I don't believe I have."

Frowning ahead at the road, her expression that of an earnest student, she said, "The *Times* is read by the people who run the country, the *Observer* by the people who *think* they run the country, the *Guardian* by the people who think they ought to run the country, the *Express* by the people who think the country ought to be run the way it used to be run, the *Telegraph* by the people who think it still is, and the

Sun is read by people who don't care who runs the country, just so she has big tits."

His heightened sexual awareness at her use of that ultimate word almost—but not quite—overpowered Sir Denis's polite response: the chuckle, the nod, and, "Very good. Very accurate."

"I have cousins in Fulham," she said. "They keep me up-to-date."

So they chatted, and Sir Denis learned that Patricia Kamin had been for a while an attaché at the Ugandan Embassy in London, that her cousins had left Uganda at independence in 1962, and that she herself seemed unusually sophisticated on the question of national allegiance. Sir Denis at one point asked, "You don't find it . . . difficult to work with the current government?"

She shrugged. "Why? At bottom, all governments are the same bureaucracy. If you learn how to do an acceptable job while letting your boss take all the credit, you can work for any government in the world."

He laughed again, and saw that they were driving up a wooded hill, though still in the middle of the city. "Where are we going?"

"The Presidential Lodge. Since this is a more informal occasion than last time, President Amin wants you to be his guest in his home."

That should have been flattering; but instead was frightening. Trying to hide his real fear with the display of a false trepidation, Sir Denis said, "I hardly think I deserve such an honor."

"British modesty," she said, quite openly laughing at him. "The rest of the world will never get the hang of it."

"Not at all modest," he said modestly, unable to keep from a modest simper.

Her own simper was downright suggestive. "I bet you have no reason to be modest at all," she said.

* * *

His room was spacious and bright, but erratically furnished with too many contrasting items; Europe, Africa, and Arabia clashed in the pictures and tapestries and ornate mirrors, in the unusually tall king-size bed covered with a gaudy cotton throw, in the wooden rocking chair painted a refreshingly straightforward white, in the cheap-looking frosted-glass light fixture in the middle of the ceiling. Heavy dark-green draperies were open at one end of the room, revealing glass sliding doors and a small concrete-railed terrace, on which stood two chrome-and-plastic lawn chairs.

Showered, changed, fortified with a whisky from his flask washed down with water from the bottle on the dresser, Sir Denis stepped out onto the terrace and looked at the hillside before him, dappled with bright swaths of color over pockets of darkness, alive with the late-afternoon songs of birds. Below, through the foliage, he could see the green, the church, the tall pink building. Idly, he wondered what that was.

Something made him turn, and the sight of a person in his room, through the glass doors, startled him so thoroughly that he grasped the concrete rail for support. But then, heart still pounding, he recognized the man as Baron Chase, and the expression on his face as a smile. Sir Denis made as though to reenter the room, but Chase came forward, gesturing to him to stay where he was.

Sir Denis had earlier pulled the glass door almost completely closed behind himself. Now Chase slid it open, stepped out onto the terrace, and said, "Forgive me, Sir Denis, I hope I didn't startle you."

"Not at all."

"I knocked, but I'm afraid you couldn't hear me out here."

"Not to worry."

Chase slid the door shut. "I've learned since our last meeting," he said, as though casually, "we have a mutual friend."

"Oh?"

"Emil," Chase said, with a faint knowing smile.

Sir Denis had been so appalled at the idea that he and a man like Chase could have acquaintances—hardly friends—in common that it took him several embarrassing seconds to realize Chase meant Emil Grossbarger, who at lunch in London had said Chase wanted to make some sort of obscure deal. Then, even more embarrassingly, in his surprise he started to blurt the name out: "Emil Gross—!"

"*Yes,*" Chase said, so quickly and with such intensity and such a sudden feral glare that Sir Denis blinked and clamped his teeth shut. That had been a look at the *real* Baron Chase.

Who immediately dove out of sight again, like a submarine. His surface placid, Chase gazed out over the hillside, saying, "A beautiful city, Kampala. Probably the loveliest in the empire. What Saigon was for the French."

"It's fortunate in its setting."

"If in nothing else," Chase said wryly.

"I was wondering," Sir Denis said. "What's that pink building down there?"

"State Research Bureau," Chase said, without inflection.

"What's that?"

"Statistical section. You know, red tape."

"Ah. Red tape in a pink building, how appropriate."

"Isn't it? Care for a walk on the grounds?"

Having understood—though belatedly—that Chase had spoken so indirectly about Emil Grossbarger because he expected that even on this terrace the bugging equipment might still pick up their words, Sir Denis now further understood that a walk on the grounds was the way to avoid eavesdroppers, so he immediately said, "Delighted."

"Good. Come along, then."

* * *

There were paths among the twisted branches, the great glossy leaves, the brazenly colorful and sweet-smelling flowers. Chase and Sir Denis strolled along, incongruously once or twice passing soldiers in field uniform and armed with machine pistols, for whom, apparently, the color of their skins was bona fide enough. Sir Denis waited for Chase to mention Emil Grossbarger, but for a long time the man merely chatted inconsequential things: air travel, the climate in London and in Uganda, the current trade problems between Uganda and Kenya. Knowing that Sir Denis now domiciled permanently in São Paulo, Chase also questioned him rather closely about Brazil, explaining he was thinking about various parts of the world in which he might "retire." "Parts of the world other than Africa," he said at one point, with his characteristic self-mocking smile.

Having already played the fool once today, on the terrace, Sir Denis refused to bring up the topic of Emil Grossbarger himself. His companion apart, the walk on the hillside was extremely pleasant, in this area too wild to be a park but too tame to be jungle. From time to time the pink building downslope was visible through the branches and blooms, its windows sparkling in the sun. The air was soft-scented and delicious, the light clear without glare, the rich earth underfoot

padded with the mulch of centuries. The pink building formed a
fanciful backdrop to a lovely soothing setting.

Chase said, "I understand you've met Patricia Kamin."

"What? Oh, yes, she drove me in from the airport."

"A bright girl," Chase said. "Very good at her job, I believe."

"I was impressed by her."

"One of your liberated women, I understand," Chase went on.
"Sexually, if you know what I mean."

Feigning mere polite interest, heart suddenly beating, the memory
of Patricia's mention of the Swede and the hotel shower suddenly
engorged in his head, Sir Denis said, "Oh, really?"

"I'm told she's quite the bedroom acrobat. I wouldn't know, myself."

"You surprise me," Sir Denis said, heartily hating him.

"I don't shit where I eat."

The crudity of the phrase, mixing with the overstimulation of
the subject matter, shut Sir Denis down completely, gave him no
response at all, and made him unready for Chase's abrupt change
of subject:

"Grossbarger says you'll talk for him."

"Well— Yes, I suppose so."

"You work a lot of sides of the street, eh?"

Sir Denis wanted to slap that knowing smile right off Chase's
mouth. "Not at all," he said.

"You work for the Coffee Board, you negotiate with the Brazilians
for the benefit of Grossbarger and with Grossbarger for the benefit of
the Brazilians, you negotiate with us for both of them, and now you're
the go-between on a private arrangement between Grossbarger and
me. I call that more than one side of the street."

"I don't," Sir Denis said with utmost stiffness. "I have no personal
stake in this matter at all."

"You aren't here for your health," Chase snapped. He seemed angry,
that subterranean violence threatening to surface again, as though Sir
Denis in insisting on his own legitimacy somehow threatened that of
Chase.

Sir Denis explained, "I am here representing the International Coffee
Board. I am their employee, and they are the only ones who will pay
me any money as a result of this transaction."

"My, our skirts are clean."

"I don't know about yours," Sir Denis said, "but mine certainly are." And he was fully aware just how ludicrous it was to engage in this sort of silly contretemps in the middle of this lush flower-filled tame jungle, surrounded by birdsong, watched over by the sun-glinting windows of the pink building.

But perhaps the argument was over. Sir Denis's last protestation might have done the trick; Chase now looked at him in a brooding way, as though considering the possible truth of what he'd been told. Tentatively, he said, "You transmit bribes."

"Of course I do." Sir Denis added, "I wouldn't be a bit surprised if, before this transaction is done, I'll be transmitting *you* a bribe."

Chase ignored that deliberate insult; when involved in contemplation of his own advantage, Chase was clearly capable of ignoring any and all extraneous provocations. He said, "If your skirts are so clean—"

"Oh, come," Sir Denis said, truly weary of this line of argument. "Just because a lot of naive American congressmen can't accommodate themselves to the reality of this world doesn't mean *I* have to be lectured on bribery by the likes of *you*."

"American—" Chase seemed honestly bewildered by the reference, then abruptly laughed and said, "Oh, the Lockheed business. Yes, I catch your drift."

"I would not bribe you to kill a man," Sir Denis said, "that goes without saying. Nor to commit armed robbery."

"Pity," Chase murmured.

"But there are many parts of the world," Sir Denis went on, "and I believe this is one of them, where the individuals in the pipeline must be given separate acknowledgment of their existence and importance."

"Oh, well said!" cried Chase, laughing out loud, obviously delighted, holding no grudges at all.

Trying to get the discussion back on a rational and emotion-free track, Sir Denis said, "Emil Grossbarger suggested to me that it wasn't a bribe you were after."

"He did, did he? What did he suggest I *was* after?"

"He didn't know."

The two men strolled along the winding paths, the soft earth humped with the twisted dark shapes of exposed roots. There was barbed wire around the pink building; how odd.

Sir Denis kept expecting Chase to continue, to say what it was he wanted from Emil Grossbarger, but Chase had all at once fallen into a kind of blue funk. Sir Denis glanced from time to time at the man's profile, but he remained deep in thought. From the unusual gauntness of his face, he was sucking on or biting his cheeks.

At last, at a junction of two paths, Chase said, "Well, I suppose we ought to go back. Dinner won't be long."

"But—Emil Grossbarger?"

Chase gave him a blank, meaningless smile. "We'll talk again later," he said.

* * *

The Presidential Lodge was a magpie's nest, a pack rat's lair. It was as though Idi Amin were on the mailing list of every gimcrack mail-order supply house in the world. *Two* wall barometers in one room. Fine Arab tapestries shared wall space with prints of ducks in flight. The furniture was of all styles, all gradations of taste, and there was far too much of it. A large avocado-colored refrigerator stood absurdly in a corner of the formal dining room; from time to time a white-coated waiter brought from it for the assembled guests beer or ice water or white wine.

Idi Amin sat at the head of the table, smiling, expansive, heavy, seeming to be performing some African touring company version of Big Daddy in *Cat on a Hot Tin Roof*.

In addition to Sir Denis, at Amin's right hand, there were nearly a dozen other guests, including Patricia Kamin diagonally across the way, Baron Chase toward the other end of the table, and at Amin's left the wife Sir Denis had not exactly met the last time he'd been in Uganda. Nor did he exactly meet her this time; though she smiled politely at him when they all went in to dinner, Amin never did introduce her.

The others present included a very nervous middle-aged American white couple, owners of a small air-charter service based at Entebbe and apparently dependent now for their livelihood not on the long-gone tourists but on the scraps from the government table. There was also another of Amin's white advisers, an Englishman named Bob Astles with a brushy moustache and a hearty beefeater manner; he was apparently a bit closer to the Amin ear than was Baron Chase; at least he was at dinner, being just beyond the unnamed wife and just before Patricia Kamin.

To Sir Denis's right was a German woman, Hilda Becker, who represented the German manufacturer that had recently delivered several new diesel engines to Kenya Railways; apparently Amin was negotiating with her for similar diesels for Uganda Railways, which unlike the rest of the rail lines of Africa was still run almost exclusively by steam.

Sir Denis would have liked to talk with the German woman, but Amin monopolized him throughout dinner. Gone was the nonsense of translated Swahili; Amin spoke a good and colloquial English, though with quite a pronounced accent: "But the Brazilians will be happy," for instance, came out "But-a dah Brah-zilians will-ah be hop-pee." In that slow heavy voice from deep within that barrel chest, with the words forming one by one like bricks and linked by extra syllables, there was an impression of great power, surprisingly lightened by Amin's laugh and his clear appreciation of the ridiculous. It was as though Henry Kissinger at his most ponderous had been crossed with Muhammad Ali at his most butterfly-and-bee.

Unfortunately, the ponderous side was much more evident than the playful. Sir Denis, to his astonishment, midway through the meal found himself the one-man audience to an Idi Amin lecture on hygiene. "Dis-ah continent," Amin told him, leaning toward him, lifting one finger from the table to emphasize the point, "dis-ah continent is not ah good place to be dirty. No, is not. You got-ah dah"—and he held thumb and forefinger close together to emphasize their smallness— "bugs. Not like-ah Europe. It's a cold-ah country, you see. Europe is a cold-ah country. Not-ah so good for dah bugs." Then he laughed, the hearty boom, and said, "Not-ah so good for dah people, needer."

Sir Denis might have responded to that, with some dinner-table jest, but Amin became at once serious again, and the lecture swept on, undiminished. "But-ah in Africa, you got-ah to be *very* careful about how clean-ah you are. You got-ah to look under dah finger-nails"—he pointed at his own horny square amber nails on his thick-fingered brown-skinned hand—"you got-ah to look in your hair"— he tapped a middle finger against his great coconut skull—"and you got-ah to look very careful at-ah your private parts." This time he pointed at Sir Denis.

"Actually," Sir Denis said, determined to waylay the conversation and take it off to some more pleasant clime, "even in Europe—"

"*And*-ah your clodes," Amin told him. "Your under-ah-clodes and-ah your shoes and-ah all-ah your clodes. It's-ah very important for-ah dah African to keep-ah himself clean. Dis is-ah *why* when dah European come, dey brought-ah dah epidemic."

"Yes, I take your point," Sir Denis said, speaking much more quickly than normal, "but I don't think—"

"Now-ah dah Nile," Amin said, leaning closer, as though about to impart an extremely important secret, known to few, "dah Nile is *very* dangerous for-ah dah water. Also dah crocodile"—here he interrupted himself to chuckle, but swooped back to the lecture before Sir Denis could make use of the opportunity—"but more-ah dan even dah crocodile you got-ah dah microbe. You know-ah dah microbe?"

"Yes, of course, I—"

"It can make-ah you very sick," Amin said. "In-ah dah stomach, and out-ah dah ass."

It went on like that.

*   *   *

After dinner, in a rustic unfinished-looking room—rather like the lounge in a small unsuccessful family hotel in the mountains—there was entertainment. Amin, showing another side of his personality, stood by the Ping-Pong table and described with vast enjoyment an epic game of table tennis between himself and a young Ugandan Air Force colonel. Amin mimed the great sweeping forehands and intricate little sneaky shots, his mobile face ranging from comic triumph to comic despair. He gave a running commentary—a quite funny running commentary—mixed with quotes from himself and from the colonel. He imitated the colonel as a very upright, very British, very old-school-tie sort of young chap, and he imitated himself as a clumsy but game bear. At the end, when all hope seemed lost, the bear delivered a series of massive backhand smashes—"A *high*-drogen bomb! *Boom!*" Amin cried, and lashed his arm around as though to demolish the wall—and the bear won.

Sir Denis was surprised to find himself laughing, along with the rest of the guests. The man could truly be quite funny, quite charming and personable. The only reminder that this wasn't the total Amin was the fact that the American couple with the government-dependent airline laughed much too loudly and too long, and twice they even led applause. The odor of their panic was a subtle but effective antidote to Amin's playful charm.

After the recitative, music. A band dressed irrelevantly in Mexican-style outfits—sombreros, small bullfighter jackets, black trousers with intricate silver designs down the seams—stood at one end of the room with horns and guitars and played tinkly popular music accompanied by the rattling of a lot of gourds.

Amin started the dancing, his first partner being Patricia Kamin and the second his wife. Sir Denis watched Patricia, small and graceful in the arms of big lumbering Amin, and then he looked away.

There was a bar at the opposite end of the room. Sir Denis went there and asked for a brandy. They had none, so he took gin-and-tonic, and was turning away when Baron Chase came over, saying, "Wait for me. Beer," he told the barman, accepted it, and strolled with Sir Denis down the side of the room.

The obedient American couple were now dancing, awkwardly, their elbows sticking out. Bob Astles danced with the German woman. Chase said quietly, "If I heard you right this afternoon, you're a neutral."

They were moving closer to the band, and it was hard to hear Chase over the trumpet and saxophones, which was undoubtedly the man's idea. Sticking close to him, Sir Denis said, "I'm not sure I take your meaning."

"You have no stake in this," Chase said. "You don't have opinions. You just do what you're told."

"I suppose that's a fair description."

"You don't carry tales."

"I'm afraid you have me at a disadvantage. I don't understand the statement." Amin was dancing now with his wife; Patricia was at the bar.

"I mean," Chase said, frowning at the trumpet player, "if you found out the Brazilians were cheating Grossbarger, just as a for instance, you wouldn't squeal to Grossbarger. You're neutral."

"Oh, I see." Sir Denis thought hard about that. "I'm not sure that's right," he said. "Morally neutral? I wouldn't want to do anything to destroy a fair and equitable negotiation, but if one party were engaged in fraud, wouldn't it be my obligation to bring that into the open?"

Chase suddenly smiled, as though that were the answer he'd been waiting for, all along. "Fine," he said. "We're all safe with you, our secrets are safe, our prospects are safe, as long as we're all good boys."

"An odd way to look at it."

"Oh, very good!" Chase cried, but now he meant something else. He was looking across the room, and now he started to applaud. So did the American couple. The band hurriedly finished their number.

Amin was coming forward, grinning and nodding, carrying in one hand a small accordionlike instrument. A band member dragged over a folding chair from the side wall. Amin nodded his thanks, sat down in front of the band facing the audience, and called out, "Now you goin tah hear sometin! Now you goin tah dance!" He thumped out the rhythm with his right foot and started to play a bouncy little tune. Raggedly at first, but then more professionally, the band gave him accompaniment.

Patricia was standing beside Sir Denis; tapping his arm, she said, "Care to dance?"

"I'd love to. I am a bit rusty."

"We'll lubricate you."

He put his glass on a side table next to hers, and they joined most of the other guests in the middle of the floor. He wasn't quite sure whether he was doing a waltz or a polka or a fox-trot, but it didn't seem to matter; high spirits had taken over, and from an extremely unpromising beginning, an actual party was coming to life. Also, it was delicious to feel the slender athletic body of Patricia Kamin in his arms.

Amin played two tunes, then played both of them again, then stopped. Patricia smiled at Sir Denis, told him how well he danced, said she would love to squire him to a dance someday in London, and when Amin stopped playing she said, "It must be very lonely for you, spending so much time far from home."

He didn't have a home, not since the death of Alicia, but that didn't seem the right topic for conversation at the moment, so he merely said, "Well, I have my work. I do enjoy that."

"Still. They gave you the pretty room, didn't they? The one with the great big bed?"

"That's right."

"I get lonely, too, sometimes," she said, astonishing him. "If I get lonely later tonight, may I come see you?"

"But of course," he said, flabbergasted.

"Till then." Her smile, so warm and friendly and yet at the same time so loose and seductive, beamed on him like a golden light. She touched the tip of his chin and left the room, picking up her drink on the way by.

I'm sixty-one, Sir Denis thought, but he was only astonished by his luck; he didn't doubt the luck.

Across the room, Amin was showing the American wife how to play his musical instrument, which he called a melodeon. Her husband was displaying so much fear and humiliation that Sir Denis couldn't bear to look at him.

Baron Chase came over, and clearly he had at last made some sort of decision. "I have something for you to tell our mutual friend," he said, again speaking under the party sounds: the melodeon and Amin's booming voice and the slightly hysterical laughter.

"Of course," Sir Denis said.

"Tell him," Chase said, "that I am very interested in making a personal business deal with him, one that's very much in his interest."

"Certainly."

"However," Chase said, and was interrupted by a white-coated servant. Chase gave the man an irritable frown, but stepped away to listen to him. Sir Denis couldn't hear what the servant said, but he heard Chase say, "Now? What could be so urgent at this time of night?"

The servant obviously pleaded ignorance, but with a further explanation, to which Chase replied testily, "Then he can go right back to Kenya."

The servant waited, unsure whether he was to stay or go, or what message he was to deliver. Chase was very annoyed, but also fatalistic; at last he sighed and said, "All right, if I must." Turning back to Sir Denis, he said, "Tell our friend I can't discuss the details with neutrals. He must send me somebody of his own." Then he was gone.

* * *

Lights gleamed in the windows of the pink building. Sir Denis, on the point of closing the green draperies over the glass wall facing the terrace, looked down through the tame jungle and saw the office lights on, and was amused: the bureaucrats of the State Research Bureau never sleep. He closed the drapes.

He was wearing a maroon silk robe, one of his oldest possessions. He had left the party almost immediately after Patricia, had showered in the small rusty bathroom adjoining this room, and now he was waiting, jagged with anticipation.

He waited more than an hour. After two failed attempts at putting down tonight's activities for his journal, he merely paced the room, fretting, his mind full of worries. Would she actually come? Had he been right in thinking the invitation a sexual one? Would he be able to perform acceptably?

The knock on the door was so gentle he barely heard it. Then he stood for several seconds, merely staring at the door. Don't be a fool, he told himself, and corrected it at once: Don't be an *old* fool. You're sixty-one, you are rich in years and wisdom and the things of this world. There is nothing vital at stake in this room tonight, nothing for you to be afraid of. At the very worst, you'll make a fool of yourself in the eyes—and perhaps the arms—of a woman young enough to be your granddaughter, and if that does happen, you won't be the first sixty-one-year-old ever to be in that position.

There. Feeling better, more secure, even laughing at himself a bit, Sir Denis finally opened the door.

She was dressed as she had been at the party, which made him instantly believe he'd misunderstood the whole thing, but even as he was trying to phrase the apology for his own informal garb, she smiled that lascivious smile and said, "Oh, I love this room. And I love that big bed." And he knew it was all right.

Closing the door, turning the switch to lock it, he said, "I'm delighted you're here."

"So am I." Putting down the small bottle of wine she'd brought, she put her hands on both sides of his head, drew his face down to hers, and kissed his mouth.

*   *   *

Over the years, Sir Denis had read in books or heard in stories about women who were tigresses in bed, but he had never known one from personal experience.

A tigress can be a frightening thing, even when she is loving you. Patricia, long tawny body, strong breasts, supple legs, ravenous belly, was the tigress, and he was the veldt on which she prowled, insatiable, hungry, demanding.

He had never in his life tasted a woman's genitals, but she would not be denied. Against his mouth she ground herself, insisting on his tongue and his teeth, pulling his hair, while his nose filled with her juices and he found himself laughing into that mask of bone and flesh. He wanted to do more; he wanted to do things he'd never heard of. And he did.

When his climax came he was spread-eagled on his back on the huge bed, she straddling him, her hard hands pressing his bony shoulders down, her sleek belly pumping as he lunged upward into her, crying out, gasping, craving that wonderful warm grotto, cave painting with his semen on its yielding walls.

He thought then that he was finished, and had nearly fallen asleep when she came out of the bathroom to insist they shower together. The tigress still prowled.

In the warm water she soaped his body, then arched and preened and laughed as he soaped hers. They tickled and played and she rubbed against him, but when he saw her smile change again to that intense look he said, "Oh, my dear, I'm not as young as I used to be. I couldn't possibly do that again tonight."

"Oh, yes, you could," she said.

She dried his body with the rough-textured towels, pinkening his flesh and making him wince away, saying, "Gently. Gently."

"Not gently," she said.

Still, for a long time he remained unready, no matter how she crawled on him on the bed, how she engulfed him. She had to no effect taken him into her mouth, and he was about to apologize once more and suggest they sleep for now, start over in the morning, when all at once she shoved a finger deep into his rectum. "Ow!" he yelled, shocked and hurt, and she pulled it halfway out and rammed it in again.

It *hurt*! He tried to arch away from it, but that merely pushed him against her mouth, the tongue and teeth and lips working on him like busy mice at a sack of grain, and suddenly it seemed as though

a steel rod were running painfully through his body from the tip of
that probing finger directly into his cock. It stirred, it swelled, it
stood, aching and vibrating but absolutely solid, and she laughed in
triumph.

"Take it *out!*"

"No!" she shouted, jabbing him with real savagery. "Put it *in!*"
she demanded, and raped him, first in this position, then that, but
always with the damnable finger there, urging him on. Deep inside
one another, they clawed and tangled on the bed, Sir Denis biting
hard at her shoulders and breasts, trying to draw blood from her
buttocks with his nails, even at one point clutching her by the throat
and strangling her while pumping away below with the desperation
of the driven beast.

He thought he was dying; he thought he'd exploded, had a stroke,
had a heart attack, was already dead. There had never been an orgasm
like it, something beyond pleasure, even beyond pain, extending into
some alternative universe of inside-out wrenching unreality. It was
like being thrown into flames, or into ice water. Pain lanced up from
his scrotum and out the tip of his cock, and even *she* screamed from
it, grinding down, pressing for more, insisting on every last drop of
agony, while he thrashed on the bed, his muscles knotting, his bones
shattering, his empty tortured belly draining out of him and into her.

And this time the tigress was satisfied. While he panted, sweat
running on his body, she stretched like a well-fed cat. Then, laughing,
lightly slapping his cheek, she tripped away to the bathroom, and
when she came back, she poured out two small glasses of sweet thick
local wine from the bottle she'd brought. She cut his with water from
the bathroom sink, saying, "No Englishman likes this without water."

It was still too sweet, but he was in too much rapture to deny her
anything. In this bed tonight she had made him a thirty-year-old,
and his aching, quivering, trembling body was in seventh heaven.
The combination of gratitude, delight, and lust with which he looked
at her could fairly be called love. He drank the wine.

Neither of them was immediately ready for sleep. With the room
illuminated only faintly by the bathroom light through the slightly
open door, they sat side by side on the bed, backs against the wall,
sipping the wine, and she asked him about his work. He told her

about Grossbarger and the Brazilians. He told her about his confusing conversations with Baron Chase. He told her more things and then more, and was surprised to hear himself, but still he went on answering her questions, sipping the wine. And when the wine was finished, she said, "Now you sleep."

"Oh, yes." He lay flat on the bed, then rolled half over to kiss the inside of her thigh. "Thank you, Patricia," he said.

"My pleasure." She ruffled his thin white hair, and very soon he fell asleep.

She was still awake an hour later, when the scratching sounded at the door. He heard it, in the deepest part of his sleeping brain, but didn't wake up. Nor did he do anything but shift position slightly when she slid out of bed, crossed the room naked, unlocked the door, and opened it for Idi Amin to enter.

He was beaming, grinning from ear to ear. Nodding over at the sleeping man, he whispered in Swahili, "He talked a lot. That's good."

"I enjoyed it," she whispered.

Amin snuffed the musky air. "Lot of fucking going on in here."

"You know me," she whispered, grinning.

"Get ready for it," he said.

She knelt on the floor, legs spread, head and shoulders down, round smooth rump high. Amin opened his trousers and knelt between her ankles and shoved himself into her. Clamping his hands on her buttocks, he moved her back and forth like a machine he was operating. He grunted from time to time, and she moaned into the carpet.

On the bed, Sir Denis slept, frowning, uncomfortable. He dreamed of large dogs eating dark chunks of meat among boulders. They frightened him, and yet he was above them, merely an observer.

In the morning, he awoke alone.

14

The stench never got better. Lew had expected to grow used to it, but every intake of breath brought the same revolting shock, those fumes spreading through the brain with a message of despair: No one in such a place as this should ever hope for comfort or happiness again.

And yet, many of the men in here—perhaps even a majority—seemed not to have abandoned hope entirely. Low-voiced conversations took place; there was the intermittent singing of hymns; now and again there was even an instant of wry laughter. Whenever a man, driven by the imperatives of his body, was forced to use the trash barrel, he invariably apologized for the addition he was now making to the general stink. "We are mostly Christians here," Bishop Kibudu said by way of explanation, and he meant people who were active and fervent in their religion.

That Idi Amin's repression, which began as tyranny's usual weapon of terror against political dissent, ended finally as massive religious persecution was partly an accident of history, partly a result of Amin's own ignorance, as the Bishop explained. Amin had been put into power in 1971 with the help of the British and the Israelis, neither of whom had any idea what sort of monster they were spawning. All the British knew was that Amin's predecessor, Milton Obote, appeared to be leaning too far to the left; the Marxist rather than the Labour left. And all the Israelis cared about was the rebellion then going on in southern Sudan, the nation lying between Egypt and Uganda; with a friendly government in Uganda, Israel could give covert assistance to the Sudanese rebellion, thus tying up thousands of Egyptian troops who might otherwise be turned against Israel.

Amin had always been a soldier, caring only for that, with no active interest in religion. He came from the Muslim north of Uganda but had never claimed to be a Muslim. In talking with ministers and priests he had expressed interest in Christianity but had never followed through. When he visited Israel shortly after taking power, he had many nice things to say about Judaism.

But that was also the trip when he asked the Israelis to help him attack the Tanzanian port city of Tanga in order to give his landlocked country a corridor to the Indian Ocean. He also asked for a lot of money, but was vague about how he intended to spend it. And in that same period he asked the British to give him a fleet of jet bombers, explaining he wanted to use them to bomb South Africa.

Just as the British and the Israelis were both saying no to Amin—a bit belatedly—he happened to meet Colonel Muammar al-Gaddafi, the fool who runs Libya. Gaddafi, a Marxist Muslim, explained to Amin that the Israelis were really Jews, who are no good, and that the British were capitalists, and therefore also no good. He further explained that Libya had millions of dollars in oil wealth, to be spent to advance the cause of radical Islamic Marxism around the world. "But that's me!" Amin told him, suddenly discovering his deep religious feelings, and he went on to explain to Gaddafi that Uganda was a Muslim nation with only a splinter of Christians left, and that he—Idi Amin Dada himself—had set as his primary task the complete Islamization of his country.

It's a mark of Gaddafi's grip on reality that he believed this guff. Uganda in fact is the most thoroughly Christianized nation in Africa, having been the target of European missionaries for nearly a hundred years. In 1972, when Amin was telling Gaddafi that the country was ninety-five percent Muslim and only five percent Christian, it was in truth eighty-five percent Christian, and six percent Muslim. (The final nine percent still clung to the old tribal animist creeds; a favorite rock or tree.)

Gaddafi began to give Idi Amin money; pots of money. And weapons. And a country house for himself and his family in Libya. And whatever else Amin wanted.

And Amin, for his part, began to give Gaddafi results. He turned against Britain and Israel, saying "Hitler was right about the Jews, because the Israelis are not working in the interest of the people of the world, and that is why they burned the Israelis alive with gas in the soil of Germany." He banned twenty-nine Christian sects. Entire congregations were arrested, imprisoned, beaten, sometimes murdered en masse. The Salvation Army was banned. White ministers were usually left alone, but black ministers were tortured and killed. Of the five hundred thousand people eventually murdered by Amin's government with the help of Gaddafi's money, over half went to their deaths believing themselves to be Christian martyrs.

Bishop Kibudu explained some of this to Lew, as the hours went on. In a place of such horror, calm conversation seemed to help, to keep the brain from exploding. The bishop described the church he and his parishioners had built at Bugembe, a suburb of Jinja. In return, Lew described Alaska to the bishop, who had never been to the Western Hemisphere. The bishop told church anecdotes involving weddings, the visits of foreign clergymen, comical mix-ups at picnics. Lew told cleaned-up mercenary anecdotes: travel on rafts on the Congo River, rifles shipped with the wrong-caliber bullets. And every second of every minute of every hour was intolerable.

And of course there were the lice. The tunnel was filled with lice, living on the wounded bodies, inside the filthy clothing. Lew felt them crawl on him, and at first he fought back, but they came in the thousands, inside his pants, inside his shirt. He scratched when they bit him, but whenever he put his hand under his shirt it was as though his skin were moving. With all his will, he tried to pretend they weren't there.

From time to time the door was opened, the glaring fluorescent light was turned on, and a minidrama was played out. Three times, additional men were pushed in, always bleeding from fresh cuts and scrapes and puncture wounds. Twice, certain men's names were called and they went out. Those times, the stillness in the fetid tunnel took on a new quality, a communal gathering together, because those men were going to their death.

"John Emiru. Nahum Tomugwang. Godfrey Okulut."

Each man, tattered, encrusted with blood, struggled to his feet and climbed over all the other legs to the doorway. Each man was hand-cuffed, his hands in front of his body. Quiet good-byes were said by the men still seated on the tunnel floor. The handcuffed men nodded, keeping their heads down. The door shut. The light went out. Bishop Kibudu said, "They will soon see God."

"There are many ways to die here," said a man across the way.

"They don't like to use bullets, that's too expensive. They may strangle you with wire. They may cut you through with swords. They may beat you with tire irons."

"Sledgehammers," said another man. "When they take out the men one at a time, it's for the sledgehammer."

Lew scratched his bites and licked his dry lips. "Why one at a time?"

"Well, two at first," said the man. He had the manner of a fussy teacher, perhaps at the high-school level. "Two men are taken out. One is handed a sledgehammer and told if he will beat the other man to death he will be set free. So he does it, and then another man is brought out and given the sledgehammer and told *he* will be set free if he kills the second man. And so on."

"It is Satan's work," Bishop Kibudu said. "To try to make the sin of murder a man's final act before he goes to God's judgment. These people have given themselves over to the Prince of Darkness."

Each time the door opened, someone called to the guard to ask what time it was. The stupidity of that, here where time no longer mattered, finally prompted Lew to comment to the bishop, "He sounds as though he's got an appointment somewhere."

"It's for the history," the bishop said.

"History?"

"This will come to an end. There will be survivors. Each one of us records in his mind as much as he can of what goes on here. At two in the morning of March twenty-eighth, nineteen seventy-seven, this person and that person were taken away. When this is over, the survivors will write down what they know. They shall bear witness for the rest of us."

"And if there are no survivors?"

"God survives. God's history lasts. God's justice is final."

The light came on, the door opened, and the soldier was there, with two other soldiers, both carrying rifles with bayonets attached.

"What time is it?"

"Three-thirty in the morning. Lewis Brady."

"God be with you," the bishop said.

* * *

It is sometimes possible to defeat handcuffs. If, when the cuffs are being attached, one tenses one's forearms and thumbs and fingers just *so*, the wrists expand slightly and the cuffs are likely to be attached one notch looser than otherwise. That's the first step.

It seemed to Lew the first step had worked; when he relaxed, the cuffs didn't feel particularly tight.

The soldiers with the bayoneted rifles apparently spoke no English. They jabbered together in some other tongue—not Swahili—and directed Lew with gestures and shoves. They would be going back the way he had come.

Along the way, on the right, was an open door leading to a fairly large concrete cell. The three men who had been taken away an hour ago were in there, on their hands and knees, scrubbing the cell with their cuffs still on. At first it looked as though a fifty-gallon drum of chocolate syrup had burst in there, but then Lew realized it was blood. Thick on the walls, lying in three-inch-deep puddles on the floor. A warm sick fragrance flowed out the open door. The kneeling men were themselves now covered with the blood as they soaked rags in it and squeezed out the rags over buckets. Lew staggered, feeling nausea and vertigo, but the soldiers shoved him on, and the vision of that cell was left behind.

Lew continued to totter and to slump, giving the impression that he was very weak, and while slumped he greased his hands with the sweat from his chest and neck.

To remove the handcuff, you fold the base of the thumb in as tight to the palm of your hand as you can get it, at the same time folding the little finger in from the other side. You push the cuff upward along the hand, screwing it back and forth. You spit on your hand to increase the lubrication. There's a spot where the bone at the base of the thumb and the bottom knuckle of the little finger conspire against you, but you keep twisting, feeling the flesh tear, feeling the sting of sweat and saliva in new cuts. But once you're past that point, the handcuff is off.

At the foot of a flight of stairs, with the soldiers behind him, Lew fell forward onto the steps. Head lowered, looking past his body, he could see their feet as they came up to chivvy him onward. It was the left cuff that was loose, so when he sprang up turning from the steps he lashed his right hand around, the dangled cuff smashing into one soldier's face. The man screamed, dropping the rifle, falling back against the wall, and Lew kicked out at the other soldier's groin.

But number two was already backpedaling, aiming the rifle. He seemed uncertain what to do, had probably been ordered to bring Lew along without too much violence; they still wanted to question him about the CIA.

Before the soldier could make a decision, Lew jumped him, lunging forward, then ducked to the side as the man brandished his rifle. Lew's right arm thrust forward beside the rifle, the loose cuff sliding onto the bayonet, scraping along it to the hilt like a perfect throw in a ring-toss game. Lew flung his arm upward, and the rifle twisted out of the soldier's hand and fell to the ground. Lew kicked him in the face as he reached for the weapon, grabbed it himself, turned, and as the other soldier came groggily away from the wall Lew ran him through with the bayonet. He heard the blade grate and break against the concrete wall.

The other soldier tried to run, back down the corridor. Lew caught him in three steps, folded his arms around the man's head, and snapped his neck. He let the body drop, then looked from one soldier to the other. Both dead. Good.

When in action, when plying his trade, there was a thing that took over in Lew, a welding of mind and body as complete and as efficient as that in a concert pianist on a stage or a basketball player on the court. At other times he might have opinions about war, about destruction, about killing, but when he was in it, the opinions ceased to exist. He was a craftsman of death, and he was good at his craft.

The rifles were their only weapons. In their pockets were some Ugandan shillings and some matches, all of which he took. Also the key to the handcuffs.

Without the cuffs, carrying the rifle with the unbroken bayonet, still shoeless, Lew hurried up the stairs.

At the top, the corridor turned to the right. Looking around the corner, Lew saw a guard seated on a bench, gazing at a comic book, apparently half-asleep. He was possibly thirty feet away.

A shot would attract attention, even in here. Lew detached the bayonet, leaned the rifle against the wall, and held the bayonet against his right forearm, its hilt in the cupped palm of his hand. Then, his manner confident and decisive, he strode around the corner and directly toward the guard.

He had thought it out this way: either his presence in this building as a prisoner was generally known, or it was not. Did every paltry soldier know every detail of the events here? There was a good chance that a white skin and a self-confident manner would carry the day.

They did. The guard looked up, mildly curious, and then mildly surprised to see the strange white face, and then horribly astonished when Lew stabbed him through the throat.

Back to pick up the rifle. With rifle in his left hand and the bayonet in his right—blade cleaned on the dead guard's sleeve—he hurried forward, retracing his steps from yesterday afternoon.

Two men in uniform came out of a room ahead of him, failed to see him, and strolled away down the corridor, one of them lighting a cigarette for the other. Lew killed them both, one with the bayonet and the other with his hands, then went back to the room they'd come out of. It was a plain small office, empty although the light had been left on. Bound copies of *The Economist* filled a low bookcase under the windows; before Amin, the State Research Bureau had really been a statistical section.

The casement window wouldn't open all the way until he broke the mechanism. Then he could look down and see that he was on the first floor, but with a fairly long ten-foot drop to packed brown earth. Floodlights glared out there, but they were concentrated on the parking areas and the barbed-wire fence, leaving the building walls in semidarkness.

Up the hill, through the trees, shone the lights of some sort of villa.

Lew dropped the rifle first, then jumped, carrying the bayonet. He lost it when he landed and rolled, but found both weapons and moved around the building, staying close to the wall.

Barbed-wire fence. A guarded front gate. But parked in front of the building was a black Mercedes-Benz, and pacing impatiently beside it was a tall white man in Ugandan Army uniform. A *white* man in Ugandan Army uniform!

Lew was too cheered by his good luck to question it. In that uniform, in that car, with his white face, surely he could get through the gate and away.

Again the rifle was left behind, this time with the bayonet beside it: he wanted no blood on that uniform. He moved through the shadows, crouching, stopping, easing on. The man paced back and forth, his range from just ahead of the Mercedes to two paces behind it. That was where Lew would get him; behind the car.

The man completed a circuit. He turned. Lew came up like a panther out of a tree, his arms reaching for the man's head, closing, twisting.

"Lew Brady!"

His victim shouted it, and that half-strangled cry saved the man's life. An inch from death, he hung there from Lew's arms while Lew listened to the echo of his own name.

Still holding on, feeling the man taut but not struggling in his grip, Lew eased himself back, breathed deeply, moved slowly out of that killing mode in which he'd been operating. It was hard not to kill this man; it was very hard. Still holding him, still wanting to finish the move, he whispered in his ear, *"Who are you?"*

"Baron Chase! I'm here to get you out!"

Baron Chase. Frank had talked about him; Balim had mentioned him. His arm aching from the incomplete action, Lew released the man and stepped back as Chase turned, holding his throat, leaning back against the rear fender of the Mercedes for support. "My God," he said, his voice very hoarse. "You're damn good."

"Explain yourself." Lew had no interest in chitchat.

"Balim sent me word. I put on this uniform and came down to get you out." Then Chase looked more closely at Lew, frowning at his eyes. "You haven't hurt anybody, have you?"

Lew laughed at him.

15

When the second call came, at four-fifteen in the morning, Ellen and Young Mr. Balim—whom she now called Bathar—were playing Parcheesi at the elder Balim's desk. Bathar, having just rolled doubles twice in a row, had captured two of Ellen's pieces, and she, very involved in the game, said, "I need some good news now." And the phone rang.

Bathar sat smiling fondly at her as she picked up the receiver and listened to the conversation. It was Baron Chase again, the same man who had called the first time, when Ellen had listened to Balim describe the problem with a wonderful slippery economy. This call, the conversation was even shorter.

"Package recovered," Chase said to Balim, who had picked up his extension at home.

"Any damage?"

Ellen stopped breathing, waiting for the answer.

"Not to the *package*." That had been said with some sort of inexplicable bitter twist. But then, more normally, Chase said, "I'll ship it back to you in the morning."

"Very good. Your help is appreciated."

In the room, Bathar said, "You're smiling."

Ellen hung up while the two men were saying their farewells. "He's all right," she said.

"I could tell."

"He'll be back tomorrow."

Bathar got to his feet. "Shall I drive you home?"

"Don't you want to finish the game?"

"No." Bathar seemed amused by something. "I don't think I was going to win, anyway."

She was so absorbed in the idea of Lew that it wasn't until the next day that she caught his meaning.

* * *

The sky was heavy with clouds in the morning, great dirty pillows and blankets piled up and falling about, some moored in their places while, above or below, thinner layers scudded along in full sail.

Frank picked her up at the house—she'd slept fitfully, awakened early, breakfasted on crackers and Coke—and drove her out to the airport. He seemed bad-tempered this morning, but she hardly noticed; she was just grateful he wasn't making any of his heavy-handed passes.

As they turned in at the airport entrance, he finally said something that attracted her attention by making the reason for his sulkiness clear. "You and Young Mr. Balim have a good time last night?"

Oh, for Heaven's sake. Laughing at him, treating him like a pet, some shambling Saint Bernard dog, she said, "Wonderful. The *positions* he knows."

"Very funny," Frank said, and drop-kicked the Land-Rover into a parking space, where he beat it to death with his elbows.

A private charter plane was to bring Lew to Kisumu from Entebbe, but of course communication at these small airports was minimal at best, so there was no telling when he'd arrive. Ellen paced back and forth in front of the building, looking up at the cloud herds ranging over the sky, and after a few minutes Frank brought her a bottle of White Cap beer.

"I thought you were mad at me," she said.

"I am." But a self-conscious grin lurked behind his crossness. "But I figured it out," he said, "and you wouldn't be screwing anybody while Lew was in a jam."

"Thanks for the vote of confidence."

"Back in nineteen oh five," Frank said, wiping the bottle mouth on his palm and taking a swig of beer, "the British provincial commissioner banned women from living in Kisumu."

"Why?"

"They had too many plagues here already."

"I see."

He laughed heartily, delighted with his sally. Then, having apparently evened some sort of score and satisfied himself, he said, "No, but that's just about right. This whole place used to be swamp before the British cleared it. And the gulf is so long and narrow, there isn't much water circulation in from the main body of the lake, so what you had here was stagnant water plus swamps. So that meant malaria, dysentery, blackwater fever, bubonic plague—"

"Lovely," she said.

"Sleeping sickness used to wipe out a lot of them," Frank said, with some evidence of survivor's satisfaction. "And when the British were here, it seemed like thinking about the diseases was sometimes as bad as catching them. They had plenty of suicides, people who couldn't take the suspense anymore, wondering which sickness would get them. That's why for a while they banned women."

"They should have banned everybody."

"They almost did. One of the provincial commissioners here then, a guy named John Ainsworth, he said, 'Kisumu is not a place for a melancholy man.' "

"Did he say who it *was* for?"

"Jokers and jollies, I guess. Same as today."

"Jolly Rogers, you mean."

"That, too. Is this our plane?"

It came in from the north, a twin-engine Cessna inching along under the clouds like a fly walking on a ceiling. The breeze at ground level, damp and warm, came out of the west over the lake, so the small plane turned away to its left before reaching them and spiraled down some invisible banister in the sky, touching the ground far away at the eastern end of the runway.

Ellen and Frank walked out across the field, the dead grass crackling under their feet. The plane approached, throttling back; it passed them, went on to the other end of the runway, turned off onto the taxiway, and slowly trundled back, wing tips gently bouncing. On both doors was a stylized drawing of a leaping impala and the name "Uganda Skytours."

"There he is!" Ellen pointed at Lew, identifiable in the copilot's seat. He and the pilot were the only ones aboard. Ellen waved, then felt silly about it, then waved again, defiantly.

Both men climbed down from the plane once it had come to a stop. The pilot was middle-aged and white and very worried-looking. He carried a manila envelope.

Lew looked a mess. His clothes were torn and filthy, and his face showed recent bruises and cuts that had been given no more than hasty first aid. His look was drawn, as though he hadn't slept much, but more than that, he looked as though he were thinking hard about something, like an inventor just before the breakthrough.

Ellen went to him, feeling oddly awkward, as though they were strangers. Touching his arm, she said, "Lew?"

He looked at her from miles away, then grinned and said, "I *am* in Heaven." But the light touch was forced.

So was hers. "Welcome to cloud nine," she said.

He gazed at her as though his mind had gone blank, then abruptly pulled her close, wrapping his arms tightly around her, bending her back, his face pushed into the angle of her throat, the lines of his body pressed against her. "Jesus *Christ*," he said, his lips moving against her skin, "but you feel good."

"Ahhh," she said, closing her eyes, going limp, feeling him hold her. "So do you, so do you, so do you."

The fretful pilot said, "Frank Lanigan?"

"That's me."

"Envelope for you. For somebody named Balim." He had an American accent.

"Right."

"I have to get back," the pilot said. "I can't be— My wife is— I want to beat the rains if I can."

"Have a good flight," Frank told him.

Lew finally released Ellen and, one arm still around her waist, turned to the pilot, saying, "Thanks."

"My pleasure. I needed the work."

"You ought to get out of there," Lew said.

The pilot ducked his head, like someone who is used to being beaten. Gesturing almost with hatred at the plane, he said, "That's all I've got. Things will get better. And I keep her gassed up and ready to go."

"Sure," Lew said.

Startled, the pilot looked skyward. "The rain!" he said, as Ellen felt a fat drop of water hit her arm. "Good-bye!" the pilot cried, scurrying back to his plane. "Good-bye!"

Frank, holding the manila envelope, said, "Glad you got back, Lew."

"Me, too. I didn't like it there."

"Come on," Frank said. "It's gonna rain like shit in a minute."

They walked back across the field, which now lay dry and expectant, strangely gleaming with pearl-gray light, awaiting its lover, the rain. Lew walked in the middle, the others unconsciously guarding him, protecting him. Frank said, "I'm sorry I sent you there. You know?"

"I don't blame you," Lew told him. His arm around Ellen's waist was nervously fidgeting. "I really don't. You didn't bring me all this way to lose me."

"That's right."

"The car's gone," Lew said. "So's the camera. Chase says forget them. I got my own stuff back, though."

"Balim'll cope," Frank said. "Are there any pictures in the camera?"

"No. I didn't get that far before they grabbed me."

Ellen said, "What happened? What went wrong?"

"A few years ago I worked for an army in the Sudan, backed by Libya. I quit, and they put my name on some enemies' list. Libya and Uganda are very tight these days, so on the Ugandan border they've got Libya's lists."

"Christ on a crutch," Frank said. "You go along and go along, and all of a sudden your past comes up and kicks you in the nuts."

*   *   *

The storm broke just before they reached the house. Before, there had been the occasional lone fat drop on the windshield, but all at once it seemed there was no windshield at all, just a massive waterfall, and they were behind it.

Or inside it. With the abruptness of a bucket's being upended, the world was suddenly nothing but falling water, splashing, ricocheting, thundering, drenching everything in sight. "Good *Lord*!" Ellen cried, her voice lost in the barrage. The long rains had arrived.

But Frank could be heard, storm or no storm. "Shit!" he yelled, flinging the wheel back and forth as though trying to shake the rain off the car. "Goddam son of a bitch!" he shouted, as the Land-Rover slued and slid forward into the unknown; not a thing could be seen through that streaming windshield. "You could have waited an hour, you filthy bastard!" he brayed at the sky, shaking his fist, and stuck his head out into the storm so he could see something of where they were going. And, "You're here!" he roared at them a few seconds later, as the Land-Rover sideswiped a parked Datsun and came to a stop in front of the house. Frank's head, out in the rain for half a minute, looked like something found four hundred years later in a sunken Spanish galleon.

"Come in for a minute!" Ellen shouted, not wanting him at all but thinking she should be polite.

He shook his head, spraying them with water. "I'm going home! And get drunk!"

Lew waved his hand at Frank and clambered out of the Land-Rover. Ellen followed, stepping directly into a lukewarm shower with the taps turned on too full. She ran through it, drenched to the skin before she'd taken a step, and tumbled with Lew into the house.

Standing in the living room, the roar of the rain all around them, they struggled with their sopping clothes, peeling the layers off their rubbery skin, just throwing the soaked stuff onto the floor. Ellen looked at Lew, and his tanned flesh was pitted and scarred all over, as though he'd been rolling in gravel. "Lew! What happened? What *is* that?"

He looked down at himself with apparent dislike. "Bites," he said. "I think I got rid of them all, but I'll keep washing."

"Got rid of what?"

"Lice. Ellen," he said with great weariness, "I really don't want to talk about it."

"Fine. Fine. What I think we ought to do is borrow Frank's suggestion and get drunk."

"Maybe so."

But the house was almost as wet as the outer world, and it took awhile to make a nest for themselves. Open windows had to be shut. Lew found a length of rope and rigged it up in the living room while Ellen dragged the pile of clothing into the bathroom and wrung everything out. Then, with the laundry hung and their bodies scrubbed dry—using every towel in the house—and wearing dry clothes, they shut themselves in the kitchen, and Ellen turned on the stove burners to bake away some of the humidity. Then at last, with the drumfire of rain held safely at bay, with the small blue rings of gas flame, even this minimal rusty kitchen became comfortable and homelike.

Then Lew talked. It wasn't true that he didn't want to talk about what had happened, it was that he didn't want to be questioned about it. He needed it to come out at its own pace, and with his editing. Ellen made scrambled eggs and toast, which they washed down with beer, and he told her some of what the State Research Bureau was like. She tried to maintain a blank alert expression, because she saw that every time she reacted, with horror or pity or revulsion, he backed away from telling her any more. But she was given enough to have a clear picture of the place.

As for his getting out, starting as an escape and ending as a kind of rescue, he seemed more reticent. It was clear that along the way he had injured, probably killed, one or more people, but he never made that part explicit, and when she asked him what the result of it would be, he dismissed it with quick contempt, saying, "Chase'll deal with that. He'll invent something. The truth doesn't mean anything there."

After a while they stopped talking and merely sat together at the kitchen table, Lew brooding, Ellen watching him. She had never in her life been so acutely aware of another person. She knew how much comfort he needed, and how unready he was to accept it, so she merely watched him and waited.

After a while, he said, "I'll tell you one thing."

"Yes?"

His expression was grim; his eyes gazed away at something she couldn't see. "There's more to it than coffee," he said. "There has to be."

PART TWO

16

Lew had experienced African rainy seasons before; but to have gone through them was not the same as getting used to them. You didn't ever get used to them.

He was supposed to fly with Balim to Nairobi to meet some Kenyan coffeegrowers on some sort of business. The weather had not changed—water and mildew were spreading like a curse from God— but when Ellen phoned the airport control tower that morning, they told her takeoffs and landings were possible at both Kisumu and Nairobi, and that the cloud cover was so low they should be able to fly above it the whole way. So Lew phoned Balim with that information, and he said they would go ahead.

They drove from the house directly to the airport, where Balim had been delivered by his son. In the damp empty waiting room Balim looked eager but just a bit apprehensive. He was dressed for the weather in a hugely voluminous black raincoat, which made him look like a beach ball in mourning. "Well," he said, "it isn't pleasant to fly in such weather, but oh, you know, the highway would be much much worse. Very dangerous."

"We'll be careful," Ellen promised.

"Bring back my father, Ellen," Young Mr. Balim said. "He's the only one who knows what we're all doing."

They got very wet crossing the field to the plane, which a sopping employee of Balim's was untying from its mooring ropes. Because Balim was a bit too chubby to be comfortable in the rear seats, Lew went back there while Balim sat beside Ellen. The interior of the plane became steamy at once, smelling unpleasantly of wet clothing.

To Lew, the little windshield wiper swiping back and forth against the glass in front of Ellen's face was thoroughly inadequate for the job; it gave her a clear space the size and shape of a lady's fan to look through, which in any event kept covering over again with streams of water as they taxied to the end of the runway.

Balim was the sort who chattered to distract himself from his nervousness. While they waited out at the end of the runway, he told them about his first flight ever, which had been from Kampala to London, by way of Cairo and Rome, a trip lasting more than two days. It had been 1938, just before the outbreak of war, and he had been fourteen years of age and on his way back to school.

Ellen asked, "What school?"

"Eton."

"You went to Eton? I'm sorry, I didn't mean it that way."

But Balim was unfailingly gracious, even when struggling not to show that he was frightened. "I'm rather surprised at it myself," he said. "I had hoped to go on to Cambridge, but the war changed things."

Lew, intrigued, said, "What was your subject?"

"History. Asian history, primarily. Unfortunately, mostly from the English point of view."

Ellen said, "You and Frank have something in common, then."

"Oh, we have rare old arguments. History, after all, is nothing but interpretation."

"I have clearance," Ellen said, meaning the other conversation she was listening to, in her earphones.

While Balim several times patted his seat belt to be sure it was still in place, and started some rambling panicky sentence about having visited Cambridge once before the war and having been impressed by the trees, Ellen accelerated and the little twin-engine plane first rolled then scampered down the rain-slick runway, propellers chopping up the raindrops and throwing out behind them a wake of fine silver mist.

Then the plane lifted, as though it had taken a sudden quick ingulp of breath, and in the next second they were a flying thing, inches from the ground, then feet, then yards, then bearing no relationship to the earth at all.

The rain and their weight made the little plane fight hard for altitude, struggling up through the downpour, poking into the dirty clouds, then being engulfed in gray dimness, water streaming everywhere, the plane bucking in the weird air currents inside the clouds. Then all at once they burst through into sunlight so bright and clean and astonishing that all three of them cried out in wonder. "Ah!" said Ellen, and "Jesus!" said Lew, and "Oh, my Lord!" said Balim. The sun.

Seen from above, the clouds were clean, a great soft white comforter spread over the king-size bed of the world. The sky had the utter mile-after-mile clarity of a September blue. And the sun was a great golden round smiling king of creation, happy to see them.

"I'd forgotten," Lew said, "what the son of a bitch looks like."

The plane flitted on, between sky and cloud, a cheerful toy left to play on its own while the titans were elsewhere; at lunch, or taking their naps. Their clothing dried, and the air in the cabin became sweet. Balim stopped patting his seat belt. Ellen relaxed her grip on the stick and looked at her reflection in the mirror she'd mounted on the post between windshield and door. Lew sat back and grinned, stretching luxuriously. The sun shone, and all was right with the world.

* * *

The descent into Nairobi was like a self-inflicted wound. With obvious reluctance Ellen pointed the plane's nose downward, picked fastidiously at the wispy top threads of the clouds, then all at once dropped down from sun through sunny translucence through eerie white through increasingly dirty gray, with water droplets running rearward along the side windows. Then they dropped out of the cloud layer, like a bedbug out of some grungy flophouse mattress, and there below lay Nairobi, sopping wet and feeling very sorry for itself.

Wilson Airport was just beyond the unfinished new airport. Ellen had to circle while a KLM flight landed and a small private plane took off; then she came down through the bead curtains of rain toward the runway, which looked as slippery and treacherous as glass. Balim started six or seven sentences on as many topics, finished none, patted his seat belt a lot, and they were on the ground, taxiing forward, losing speed, not fishtailing or somersaulting or nose-diving or doing any of the other things they'd all been more than half expecting.

It seemed strange to leave Ellen here, but of course the pilot stayed with the plane. She would deal with airport formalities and buy gas and then wait for Lew and Balim to return.

The rental car was waiting: a four-door maroon Peugeot 504. Balim sat in back, visibly delighted to be no longer in the plane, and Lew drove through Nairobi, following Balim's directions.

Wilson Airport was south of the city, while the coffee plantation they wanted was to the north; unfortunately, there was no way to go around the town. Still, despite the rain and despite the congestion, traffic scooted along at a pretty good clip. Lumbering trucks, little rusty taxicabs, wetly gleaming Mercedes-Benzes, saturated bicyclists, and completely oblivious pedestrians all contested together, weaving a manic tapestry on the wet streets.

In all the cultures in the world, the rich live on the hills above the city. Leaving behind the crowded, raw-looking, hurriedly constructed streets of the main part of Nairobi, Lew steered upward through decreasing traffic and increasingly expensive-looking houses. After a while the streets became wider and sported gentle curves, sure signs of wealth. They passed the German Embassy, two other official residences. They passed a boarding school where the visible children were all white.

"This is why Kenya has remained a stable country," Balim said from the backseat, "while so many other independent African nations have fallen away into bankruptcy and corruption. Kenyatta is of the Kikuyu tribe. When independence came, the Kikuyu thought they would be moving into these houses, but they did not. The whites are still here; the Indians are still here; the successful blacks are still here. That's why international commerce can continue in Nairobi, and Kenya remains solvent. It would have been very popular politics to give these houses to the Kikuyu down from their mountain villages, but it would have killed the country. And where would we be today, eh, Lew? You and I?"

"I don't know where you'd be, Mr. Balim," Lew said, grinning at him in the rearview mirror. "I'd be in Alaska."

"We owe much to Jomo Kenyatta," Balim said.

The city itself was left behind, and then the suburbs, and still the Peugeot climbed upward into the foothills of the Narandarua Range, north of Nairobi. A group of black schoolgirls in bright purple jumpers, carrying many-colored umbrellas, waved and laughed at them as they drove by, and a few minutes later Balim said, "That is coffee."

This time Lew frowned into the rearview mirror. "What is?"

"The shrub growing on both sides of the road. We are in the plantation."

Lew then realized they were driving through cultivated fields. The shrubs were about three feet high, very bushy, and with intensely green leaves. In the rainswept distance he could see their parallel rows curving across the hillside, like a drawing in a children's story, grainily reproduced.

"Beyond the next curve," Balim said, "there is a white house on the left. That is our destination."

"Fine."

The land sloped down on that side, and the house would have been very easy to miss, being set low and back from the road and surrounded by trees. A rain-gullied gravel driveway lay just beyond the curve; taking that, Lew circled down and around amid the trees and came to a stop at the side of the house, facing a three-car white wooden garage.

Before they could open their doors, a broadly beaming skinny black man with a huge black umbrella appeared beside them. He gestured for Lew to wait in the car and opened the rear door for Balim. Having safely escorted Balim from car to house under the umbrella, he returned for Lew. "Good rain," he said, smiling and nodding as they hurried toward the side door. "Excellent rain."

"Very good rain," Lew agreed.

Lew's first impression inside the house was of darkness, as a setting for a tiny woman dressed all in white. This broad brushstroke was followed almost immediately by far too many details. The woman was very old. She was clearly an Indian, and in fact with her round spectacles she looked absurdly like Mahatma Gandhi. The white swath of cloth covering her from neck to toe was a sari. The rings on her tiny gnarled fingers were all of a style: intricate dark-gold vinelike bands clutching small glistening stones of red or green.

The black man with the umbrella disappeared down a narrow dark corridor crowded with furniture. There were dark-green walls, mahogany sideboard, rococo gold-framed mirror, small Persian rugs spaced on the gleamingly waxed dark floor, a wooden staircase leading upward with black steps and white risers and banister.

Balim's normal politeness was redoubled in here, intensified into an almost palpable concern, as though this old lady were both extremely fragile and terrifically important personally to Balim. "Mama Jhosi," he said, "may I introduce a young friend of mine from America, Mr. Lewis Brady. Lew Brady, may I take pleasure in introducing Mama Lalia Jhosi, who is the mistress of this magnificent house."

Lew could rise to formality when required. Taking Mama Jhosi's hand—a collection of pencil stubs in a tiny leather sack—into his own, and half bowing over it, he said, "I am very pleased, madame."

"You are tall," she said. Her voice was as gnarled as her hand, rough and very faint. "A man should be tall."

"And a woman should be beautiful," Lew said, smiling broadly to show he meant to compliment her, and released her hand.

The giggle and head bob she gave were astoundingly girlish—heartbreakingly girlish—in acknowledgment of the gallantry. Then, stepping slightly to the side, she said, "And may I present my grandson, Pandit Jhosi. Mr. Lewis Brady."

The grandson was eleven or twelve, a slender solemn boy with soft Indian skintone and features, and huge dark eyes. He wore sneakers and blue jeans, but his white-and-blue vertically striped dress shirt was buttoned at neck and wrists, making him look like a miniature of a formal Indian shopkeeper. Lew saw in his eyes that he was intelligent and shy; a bright boy who knew it was appropriate now to shake Lew's hand but was too shy to initiate the move. Lew helped him out of the impasse by extending his own hand, smiling, saying, "Pleased to meet you."

"And you." The boy's handshake was correct; two pumps, and release.

His grandmother touched his shoulder. "Tell Ketty we would like tea."

"Yes, Mama."

Balim said gently, "Pandit, Lew Brady knows very little about coffee plantations. Why don't you take him with you to the kitchen and tell him about them?"

Ah. The pilot stays with the plane; the chauffeur waits in the kitchen. Whatever Balim's business in this house, it didn't include Lew, who grinned at the seriousness with which Pandit accepted the task, saying to Balim, "Yes, sir, I'd be happy to," then looking up at Lew to say, "We have a very modern kitchen."

"I'd be interested to see it."

As Pandit led Lew down the long corridor, Mama Jhosi ushered Balim into a room to the side. Now they could talk Hindustani together without rudeness. Lew was still grinning at the courtliness with which people around here got their own way, when Pandit opened a door at the far end of the corridor and ushered him into a gleaming large kitchen, which was, as he'd been promised, very modern. Copper pans hung over a large pale-wood central table. The appliances along the walls were all brushed chrome or white porcelain, and included a large separate freezer. The uniformed black woman reading a newspaper spread on the table was middle-aged and just a bit hefty. Pandit said to her, "Ketty," and then flowed away at her in Swahili. Ketty nodded, folded her paper, got to her feet and, turning away, presented a huge behind, tightly swathed in the black uniform skirt and framed by the string and side hems of her white apron.

Pandit said, "Would you like some tea?"

"Thank you, yes."

Lew sat at the table, across from where Ketty had been, and drew her folded newspaper close. But then he saw it was in Swahili, and pushed it away again.

Pandit brought to the table: two teacups with saucers and spoons; two small plates with butter knives; a teapot on a tray, the pot covered by a quilted tea cosy; a small silver tray holding a silver cream pitcher and a silver bowl containing lump sugar; two linen napkins; a butter dish; a saucer of lemon circles; a graceful china ashtray; a plate containing an assortment of cakes and pastries. Meantime, Ketty was assembling a similar though larger grouping on a silver tray; as she carried it out of the room, moving in a stately manner only partially undercut by her absurd rear end, Pandit sat down across the table from Lew and said, "Are you very much interested in coffee plantations?"

Something told Lew this was a kid with whom honesty was the best policy. "Not really," he said.

"I am, of course," Pandit said. "But it is my job to be."

"Because you'll inherit."

"I already have some managerial responsibilities," the boy said.

Lew grinned at him, hoping he'd understand the grin was one of comradeship and not mockery. The boy was so solemn and intelligent, and yet still a kid. "I saw the coffee bushes on the hillsides," he said, "when we were driving in. I can see there's a lot of responsibility there."

"Oh, that isn't all ours."

"No?"

"No. It used to be, but when my parents died and we came here, my grandmother had to sell most of our land."

Already knowing the answer, Lew said, "Came here? From where?"

"Uganda."

"Ah."

"Have you been to Uganda?"

"Yes," Lew said.

"I was seven when we left," Pandit said, "so I don't really remember it."

"It's not a pleasant place," Lew said. "This is much nicer."

"Still," Pandit said, "I would like to see it someday. When things are different, of course."

"Of course."

Getting to his feet, Pandit said, "The tea should be ready." He removed the cosy, picked up the elaborately black-and-gold pot, held the top with his fingertips, and gently swirled the tea for a moment. Then he poured out Lew's cup, and the room filled with a delicious aroma. "Sugar?"

"One lump, thank you."

Pandit gave him sugar, using small silver tongs. "Milk or lemon?"

"Milk. That's fine." This was the pervasiveness of British civilization: in the middle of a coffee plantation, they sat down to a formal tea.

At last Pandit, having poured his own tea, covered the teapot with the cosy, sat down again, and they both chose pastries.

Lew said, "What are you interested in besides coffee?"

"Football," Pandit said.

"Oh, really?"

"I am a very big fan of the Italian team," Pandit said, his eyes shining.

"The Italian—" Then he caught on. "I'm sorry," he said, "I was confused. I thought you meant American football."

"No, soccer. I don't like American football." Then, catching himself in a possible discourtesy, he quickly asked, "That doesn't offend you?"

"Not at all," Lew said, smiling at him. "What don't you like about American football?"

"It keeps stopping," the boy said. "Every time it starts, you just begin to get interested and it stops. Football—excuse me, I meant to say soccer—soccer isn't like that. I find it much more exciting."

"I suppose it all depends what you're used to," Lew said. "Baseball, now, in that game nothing *ever* happens, and yet it's still the most popular sport in America."

"That's the way it is with cricket," Pandit said, and shrugged. "Cricket's all right," he said dismissively.

There was a door in the far wall; this now opened and a girl came in, carrying two string bags, both filled with various small packages. She was dressed in tan slacks and a tan raincoat and round soft rainhat. "Ah," she said, smiling at Lew and then at Pandit, "you brought a friend home from school."

Pandit, flustered but still the gentleman, jumped to his feet, saying, "Amarda, this is Mr. Lewis Brady. Mr. Brady, may I present my sister, Amarda Jhosi."

Lew rose, hit his head on a hanging copper pot, winced, grinned, said, "Ouch. Hello."

"Oh, those pots," she said with a commiserating smile. "We aren't used to men around here. Tall men, I mean," she said, bowing a bit at her brother. She looked to be about twenty, with Pandit's large liquid dark eyes but her own softly oval face. The Indian Princess, Lew thought.

"I'll get you a cup," Pandit offered.

"Thank you. It's beastly outside."

Lew watched, not yet fully realizing that he was smitten, as she removed her hat and shook out her thick black hair. The hat and raincoat went on a chair; she wore a white-on-white blouse, and around her throat a thin gold chain. She unloaded the string bags quickly, putting things away in the refrigerator or on shelves, while Pandit set a third place at the end of the table, between the males. He poured the tea, added a lemon circle, selected a brownish square piece of cake for her dish, and was just sitting down again when she joined them, saying, "Perfect." Seating herself, she said, "But why are we hiding out here in the kitchen?"

"Mama is in the parlor with Mr. Balim."

Her manner at once changed; understanding came into her face, and something else. Giving Lew a quick look of unconcealed distaste, she said, "I see."

The smitten one cannot stand rejection. Lew said, "Is it that distasteful to break bread with the chauffeur?"

The look she gave him now was honestly bewildered. "I beg your pardon?"

"I could wait in the car, if you prefer."

Pandit, shocked at this breach of etiquette but determined to maintain his own civility, said, "Surely not!"

"Chauffeur?" echoed Amarda Jhosi; then she said, "Oh, I see what you mean. No, to be honest, I hadn't even thought that word."

Himself bewildered now, Lew said, "What word did you think?"

"It doesn't matter. Have some cake."

Ignoring the pastry plate she held up for him, he said, "Miss Jhosi, what word did you think?"

She hesitated, frowning at him, wanting it to be forgotten. But when she saw he intended to stick on this point, she gave an annoyed little headshake, put the cake plate down, gave her brother a little apologetic look, frowned at the lemon circle drifting in her tea, and said, "If you insist, the word I thought was *thief*."

Lew was so angry he could barely control himself. The source of her mad against Balim was her own business, but he wouldn't let her tar him with the same brush. Holding his voice lower than usual, to keep from shouting, he said, "What have I ever stolen from you, Miss Jhosi?"

Her annoyance showed itself again in a quick glare, and she said, "You know what I'm talking about."

"No, I'm afraid I don't."

"Aren't you here right now to negotiate with my grandmother about the stolen goods?"

Stolen goods? Balim had said nothing about the reason for this trip, hadn't even suggested it was connected with their own coffee caper, but now the whole thing laid itself out in front of Lew's eyes, as clearly as if Balim himself had taken Lew into his confidence.

Here is a family, the Jhosis, who used to have coffee plantations in both Uganda and Kenya. They were among the Asians expelled from Uganda by Amin in 1972, when in some manner the parents of these two died—or were killed. That would have left the grandmother and the children with nothing but this Kenyan plantation, part of which they'd had to sell off because of their financial bind. On the other hand, here is Balim, who will soon be in possession in Kenya of tons and tons of smuggled coffee; somehow it will be necessary to reintroduce that coffee into legal channels of trade. Why not arrange for the coffee to be shipped from the Jhosi plantation, under the Jhosi brand name? In typical Balim fashion, he will be solving a problem of his own and helping needy co-nationals at the same time.

While Lew thought this out, Amarda Jhosi continued to study him, her expression gradually growing less certain until she said, "Didn't you know? Did you truly not know?"

"I suppose I should have guessed." Sighing, Lew took his napkin from his lap and dropped it on the table beside his cup and plate. "Thank you, Pandit," he said, getting to his feet. "I appreciated the tea, and the conversation."

Pandit stared at him, wide-eyed. "But where are you going?"

"I'll wait in the car. Nice to have met you, Miss Jhosi. That's all right, Pandit, I can find the door. And I promise I won't steal anything along the way."

* * *

He was reading the Peugeot owner's manual for the second time, without as yet having learned why the car was called a 504, when the front passenger door opened and Amarda Jhosi slid in, dressed again in her Burberry and rainhat. He looked at her, trying to appear stern to hide his leap of pleasure. "Can I help you?"

"You can accept my apology," she said. She removed the rainhat and again shook out her hair; a gesture he could grow very fond of.

"Apology accepted," he said in an offhand manner, as though her apology hadn't mattered one way or another; punishing her a little.

"I thought I understood things," she said. "You confused me."

"I'm sorry."

"Please, don't be mad at me anymore."

He had been more or less looking past her, at the rain-streaming side window; now he looked at her and saw that she was trying to be honest with him. She had the vulnerability of someone who has deliberately disarmed herself. As always, Lew's reaction to such risky vulnerability was to become extremely protective. "I'm not mad," he said. He touched his fingertips to her hand in her lap; it was wet with rain. "You didn't have to come out here in the rain to apologize to me."

She smiled, disarming them both. "I didn't," she said. "At least not *just* to apologize."

"I get it," he said, disappointed but not surprised. "You also want to pick my brains."

She frowned. "Sorry?"

"You want to ask me questions. You want to know what's going on."

"That's right." Then she shook her head and said, "No. Let me tell you what I *thought* I knew, and you tell me where I'm wrong."

"Sure."

"Some people are stealing a lot of coffee from Uganda, smuggling it into Kenya. They came to Mr. Balim to help them make the coffee seem legitimate again."

"I've been fighting the phrase 'launder the coffee,' " Lew said. But then, seeing she didn't understand that Americanism either, he said, "Never mind. Balim isn't an agent, he's one of the principals, but you've got the general idea. Go on."

"Mr. Balim came to my grandmother, knowing our financial troubles. I assumed you were one of the thieves."

"I am, I guess," Lew said. "But the word *thief* isn't quite the right one."

"Isn't it stealing?"

"From Idi Amin. Your family used to live in Uganda, didn't you?"

"Yes. Most of our holdings were there."

"How old were you when you left?"

"Fifteen."

"So you can remember the way it was, with Amin."

"Yes, I—" But then, all at once, her chin was trembling. She blinked and looked away, nodding. He saw her try to speak, but her control was slipping away and she couldn't do it.

"Hey," he said, startled and embarrassed. "Hey." He put an arm around her shoulders, touched her trembling jawline with his other hand, drew her close in, seeing the tears well up in her eyes as he pulled her close, tucking her head in against his shoulder and chest, holding her very tight, letting her sob it out.

She cried for a long time, while he kept trying to find the right thing to say, without success. Finally, sometime after the racking sobs had ended and her body had become merely soft and passive against him, her muffled voice said against his chest, "I'm all right now."

Reluctantly he eased the pressure of his arms, permitting her to move slightly away and lift her face to look at him. She was so beautiful, and so sorrowful, and so vulnerable, that he couldn't not kiss her. And her lips were as soft as the lawns of Heaven.

She responded. Her arm slid around his neck; the soft lips opened; the heat of their bodies commingled. He moved his arm, and his hand brushed her full breast, and her arm tightened around his neck. He held the breast, feeling the hardening of nipple through layers of cloth, feeling the warmth of her body, the sweetness of her tongue.

Which of them broke off first he had no idea; they seemed to do it together, at once, as though in response to some outside noise. But his mind had suddenly filled with thoughts of Ellen, of Amarda's youth, of the idea that he was taking advantage of her emotional condition, of their exposed situation here in the car in the daytime beside the house, and he pulled away from her just as she was pulling away from him.

They stared at one another, wide-eyed. Her softness and warmth were still with him, an invisible blanket warming but frightening him. He whispered, "I'm sorry."

"Oh, don't be," she said. She grabbed his wrist in her hand, squeezed painfully. "Don't be," she repeated, and turned away. Fumbling with the handle, she pushed open the door and hurried away into the rain.

17

The rain poured down, well into its second week; ten days and nights of drenching downpour. The pockmarked face of the lake was muddy, everything on the surface of the planet was saturated and soft, and everywhere you looked was water. The pregnant cloudbanks pressed so low to the ground they gave you a headache just thinking about them.

Frank Lanigan sat in the front of the boat, inside his slicker and rainhat and heavy boots, thinking about his headache. Behind him, Charlie scooped rainwater out of the boat with a coffee can, while at the rear the boat's owner sat by the outboard motor, steering them toward Uganda.

Uganda. There it was, visible in the downpour, dead ahead. The brow of a dark giant rising up out of the lake. A turd floating in a world of water. A brown-black otter, resting. The Mysterious Island of the ghost stories, where the shipwrecked sailors meet the crazed professor and the living dinosaurs and the things that suck your blood in the night.

Somewhere inside all his steamy cloying clothing Frank had a pint flask full of bourbon. The bourbon might help, but the job of getting to it would hurt far more, so he just sat there, cursing his fate, cursing Africa, cursing the rain, cursing Lew for not having completed this job the first time.

Slowly the broken coast of Uganda came nearer. Behind Frank, playing harmony to his thoughts, the boatman cursed his motor in a slow, almost loving litany, baritone voice and cough of engine blending into a lullaby of discontent within the endless barrage of the rain.

Bwagwe Point passed slowly on the left as they entered Macdonald Bay. Before the long rains this neighborhood had been alive with Ugandan soldiers on antismuggling detail, but in weather like this the smugglers and troops both stayed home. Everybody stays home, Frank thought in angry self-pity, except me.

The boat poked into the bay, putt-putting, almost drifting with some storm-induced tide, becoming a child's toy that bobbed in the great rain-drenched bathtub of the bay. They remained unchallenged, and Frank roused a little, thinking about the task at hand, wishing Lew could have been sent again (not even thinking about Ellen), and finally turning to yell, "Keep to the left, you asshole!" at the boatman, who was drifting them eastward into the middle of the bay, probably out of some subconscious desire to be back in—to the east of here—Kenya.

Shit. As usual, his most determined statements remained un-understood by their targets; fuming, Frank suffered through a translation of his command by Charlie, knowing that whatever Charlie was saying, it bore little or no relationship to the original.

Nevertheless, it worked. The boat angled left; it even seemed to increase just a trifle in speed. "It's along here," Frank said, then wondered whom he thought he was talking to. "I hate rain," he said, and slumped deeper inside his clothing.

Charlie's translation of Frank's shout at the boatman had somehow blossomed into a full-fledged conversation. Behind him Charlie rattled away, the boatman rumbled back; Charlie took his turn, the boatman his—a regular dialogue. Charlie pointed vaguely ahead and to the left, the boatman pointed vaguely a bit to the left of that, Charlie pointed somewhere else, the boatman pointed at his engine, Charlie pointed at Frank, and through it all they kept yakking away together, like long-lost brothers who had never cared for one another. "I think I'll kill them both," Frank muttered.

Through the curtains of rain, on the bank to the left, he could just make out their intended landfall: a muddy crescent where a faint two-track dirt road came down to the water's edge. "There it is, you goddam idiots!" he yelled, and cuffed Charlie across the head to distract him from his patter with the boatman. "Right *there!*"

"Yes, it is," Charlie said. Even in this downpour, still dressed in nothing but tattered shirt and trousers, he remained cheerful and unaffected. "We were just talking about it," he said, and calmly went back to his conversation.

"Lying bastard," Frank muttered.

The boatman steered them to the crescent, where they ran aground a good twenty feet from shore. Frank shook his head. "We got to do better than *that*," he said.

"Oh, sure," Charlie said. While the boatman unlocked his motor and tilted it forward, lifting the screw out of the water, Charlie hopped over the side, grabbed the thick frayed end of rope tied to the bow, and waded them ashore. Surprisingly strong for all his skinniness, Charlie pulled a good half of the boat up onto the mud with Frank and the boatman still in it. Of course, the mud itself was half water. When Frank stepped into it, his booted feet sank in halfway to the knee; pulling out, against the suction, he felt the mud doing its best to yank the boots right off him.

The boatman also clambered over the side, and now the three of them dragged the boat the rest of the way over the mud and up onto the solid cross-hatching of last year's dead grass. Like the Abominable Snowman, Frank lumbered around in the mud, plop-squirking at every step, while Charlie and the boatman were agile in their bare feet, slithering around like upright eels. That Charlie's squalid uncon- cern was somehow better attuned to the circumstances than Frank's careful preparations only made Frank's mood worse.

With the boat on relatively solid ground, they pulled the tarp off the two mopeds and carried them to the beginning of the road. Then Charlie stood grinning, the rain already washing the mud from his shanks, as Frank opened his slicker, opened the coat within, found the flask, and pulled it out. The first short swig of body-warming bourbon burned his throat and brought tears to his eyes, but they could count as tears of gratitude. Blinking them away, Frank knocked back another, longer swallow, then screwed the cap back on the flask and smiled as he felt the welcome warmth spread through his body the way molten steel runs to fill the mold.

But then, looking at the mopeds, he frowned again. It was a damned undignified mode of transportation for a grown man, this stubby motorized bicycle with the ridiculously thick wheels. But Maintenance Depot Number 4 was a good twenty miles up the road, and no other vehicle could have been brought here over the lake. "Might as well do it, then," Frank said, stowing away the flask and rebuttoning all his coats. Jabbing a dripping thumb over his shoulder at the boatman, he said to Charlie, "Tell him to wait."

"Oh, he knows," Charlie said.

"Tell him, if he doesn't wait we'll get him for it later."

Charlie looked dubious. "Later? If he leaves us here, we don't have any 'later.' He knows that, too."

So did Frank. "Will he stay?"

"He wants his money," Charlie said with a shrug. "If something scares him, he will go away."

"Shit." Shaking his head, Frank said, "Come on, then, let's get it over with."

They climbed onto the mopeds, both of which snarled into life at the first kick, and started up the faint double track into the low dense trees, Frank slightly in the lead on the right-hand rut, Charlie a bit behind him on the left. Looking back, Frank saw the boatman had climbed back into the boat, where he now sat, unmoving, his back against the upturned engine, forearms folded on his sunken stomach. He seemed asleep; or dead.

This road had been cleared by the railroad-building British seventy years earlier, and abandoned fifty years after that. The occasional passage of a farmer's wagon or truck in the twenty years since had been sufficient to keep the twin track visible against the ground, but not sufficient to keep saplings and brush from encroaching. "This'll be hell on the trucks," Frank said, shoving the moped through the tangle of shrubbery. He felt that he looked like the clown in the circus who rides the tiny tricycle, and he wasn't far wrong.

The forest was dense here, the old road completely covered by tree branches, which screened out most of the rain. Individual drops could be seen and heard—and felt—and the air seemed cooler and not quite so humid. The ground was just a bit less spongy. It was almost as though the rain had stopped barely a minute ago and these were the final droplets shaking out of the trees.

The effect of the mopeds' nasal roar was strange in this empty, wet forest. It seemed both very loud and utterly silent. It seemed to be posing some further corollary question to the old one about the tree falling in the forest. The only effect the engines seemed to have was that the quality of the empty silence behind them was more shimmering, more tense, than the empty silence in front.

The mopeds were theoretically capable of doing fifty miles an hour, but not in this terrain. They did manage short spurts of twenty, even twenty-five, but more usually traveled at fifteen and sometimes even slowed to ten or less. The land was a persistent gradual uphill slope, the forest unchanging all around them, here and there a small path— cut by humans or animals—leading away to the right, inland. The lake was never more than a few miles away to the left, but there was no hint of it.

Frank kept one eye on the odometer, and they had gone nineteen and four-tenths miles when some change in the mass of the sound filling his ears made him glance to his left, where he failed to see Charlie. Looking back, frowning, he saw that Charlie was stopped fifty yards back, standing beside his moped, cheerful and patient, gazing alertly this way.

"Now what?" Frank made a U-turn from the right track onto the left, not quite getting bucked off when the moped hit a root in the middle of the maneuver, and roared back to where Charlie stood, smiling in all innocence. "Whatchagot?"

"Path to the turntable." He pointed.

Frank looked, and damned if there didn't seem to be the faint remnant of a path there, leading away from the road. Squinting through rain and trees, shielding his eyes with his hand as though from sun, Frank thought maybe he could see some sort of building back in there. Hard to tell.

"You drove by it," Charlie said.

Frank understood then that Charlie was getting revenge for his having pointed out their landing spot. "You are a prick," he said. Getting off the moped, kicking its kickstand harder than necessary, he tromped away on the path toward the perhaps-building, knowing that if he looked back he would see Charlie as happy and guileless as ever. He didn't look back.

Charlie had been right; this was Maintenance Depot Number 4. The old engine shed was there, a long tall corrugated-iron structure open at the uphill end, big enough to hold a steam locomotive, sagging and rusty now but still intact. Beside it were piled half a dozen sixteen-foot rails, orange with rust. Trees and brush had so overgrown the area that one tree branch grew into the building through a glassless window.

Frank unlimbered two cameras and moved steadily around the area, taking pictures, wiping the lenses, crouching in positions where water could run down the back of his neck, while Charlie strolled through the open end of the engine shed and lolled at his ease in there, amid mounds of rusted metal.

The site was pretty much as described in that memo Chase had sent. Rusted track led down from farther up the hill, bifurcating, one line running straight down into the big empty maw of the engine shed, the other angling away to the right and leading to the old turntable. As to this track and turntable, all of which was frozen with rust, there was both good news and bad news. The good news was that the old switch was rusted in position to run a train toward the turntable rather than toward the engine shed, which was what they would want, but the bad news was that the turntable had been left positioned at an angle to the line of track. It was going to be a bitch to get that ancient rusty turntable unstuck and lined up with the track.

Oh, well; Frank took his pictures and kept going. Beyond the turntable, the track continued another twenty feet, almost to the dropoff; a sudden unexpected cliff, that was, with forest growth right to the edge and a nearly hundred-foot drop down into Thruston Bay, whose boulder-strewn shoreline looked in the rain like something from a gothic novel.

Frank next retraced his steps, past the turntable and the engine shed and the dozing Charlie and on along the line of track up the hill. Bushes and trees, some of them sizable, grew up between the rails all along the way. Then, abruptly, the rails stopped. The dismantled connecting plates lay on the ground to one side, and there was not even a hint anymore of where the old rails and sleepers had once lain. "Damn *rain*," Frank said, squinting, trying to see through the wall of foliage in front of himself, but there was nothing to see except greenery and water.

He got *really* wet shoving through that batch of growth between the old spur and the main rail line. He struggled through, kicking and punching, elbowing the tree branches, and all at once he popped out onto the single-track main line of Uganda Railways, the well-used rails wetly gleaming, reflecting the gray-white sky. Standing between the rails, Frank took more pictures, and observed with satisfaction that absolutely nothing of Maintenance Depot Number 4 could be seen from here.

The wet steel sleepers made slightly iffy footing as he tramped away eastward to where the level crossing still existed—though unrepaired—for the old access road. Up there to the left was where Lew had been grabbed by the State Research Bureau. Frank gave a dark glower in that direction; if it hadn't been for those bastards, Lew would have done the job then and there. Now they couldn't risk Lew's getting picked up a second time, so it was Frank who had to slog around in the rain, the faithful Charlie at his side (at Mr. Balim's order). And Lew was back in Kisumu, taking over more and more of Frank's regular job.

What the hell; he was here, and the job was done. Now all he had to do was go back to the engine shed, collect Charlie, and return to the boat. He started down the access road, stowing the cameras away in their canvas bag, and a sudden thought made him stop, lifting his head.

What if he *didn't* go back for Charlie? The son of a bitch would survive—this was his turf—but he'd be out of Frank's hair for a while, and maybe even permanently. And if he got back without the moped, that'd be a mark against him with Mr. Balim.

Frank could say he'd looked all over for Charlie, had shouted his name, but Charlie must have been somewhere asleep. Finally, afraid the boatman wouldn't wait any longer, he'd had to leave. (He would walk the moped the first mile, so the roar of its engine wouldn't alert Charlie to what was happening.)

Feeling like a kid playing hooky, excited and guilty and expecting to be caught at any second, Frank continued down the road. After he'd taken a few steps, exhilaration (and bourbon) rose up in him so strongly that he broke into a shambling downhill run.

It's a good thing he ran; there was only one moped there, at the start of the path.

The son of a *bitch*! The dirty unreliable bastard! Of course he was doing the same thing, and there wasn't a way on Earth to prove it. Frank could hear no engine sound, so Charlie was walking the moped the first mile, exactly as Frank had planned. If Frank tried to sneak up on him by walking his own moped, he'd never overtake the rat, but if he started his own engine, Charlie would hear it, would immediately start his, and would come tearing back with some innocent bullshit story about flower picking or something.

It wasn't fair. "Shit," Frank said, and started the moped, and bumpity-dumpityed away toward the lake.

18

The slide show of Frank's trip to Uganda took place in a smallish storeroom in Mr. Balim's second building. A number of sewing machines and shoe cartons and lounging employees having been removed, and a few folding chairs having been introduced, Isaac set up the projector and screen and took charge of the room lights, while Frank ran the show.

The audience was small and intent. Lew and Ellen and Balim and Young Mr. Balim and Isaac sat watching the screen as Frank flashed slide after slide, describing each picture in turn. Lew and Isaac held pads and pencils and made occasional notes.

"This is the bay, coming in. Tough to see with the damn rain, but there's no villages or houses right down by the water. All forest, thick growth.

"This is the landfall. It's mud up to your ass. Even if we go in two or three weeks after the rains stop, it's still gonna be like that. We'll have to bring enough planks to build a house or we'll never load the boats.

"You can see the road is clear. A lot of brush and shit, but we'll have big trucks.

"It's nineteen-point-four miles from lake to depot. I took pictures along the way to show how it was. Maybe too many pictures."

Balim: "No, no, Frank, this is very good. We'll want to see as much as we can, as though we'd been there ourselves."

Young Mr. Balim: "As Von Clausewitz said, the map is not the terrain."

Lew took his eyes off the screen, turned his head, and gazed at Young Mr. Balim. Von Clausewitz? Young Mr. Balim was smiling at Ellen's profile. He switched his smile to Lew, so Lew looked back at yet another blown-up slide of a forest trail in a drenching rain.

"This is about the steepest incline we hit. It never gets worse than maybe one in ten, one in nine. The trucks'll go down full and come back up empty, so there shouldn't be any trouble.

"Okay. Here's the path in to the depot. This could be a problem. It'll slow us down if we have to carry all that coffee out from the depot to the road, but you can see what it looks like. We won't get any trucks in there."

Balim: "Couldn't we clear the trees, make a road?"

"Clear the trees, sure. But there's no roadbed there, it's all erosion and gullies and roots and rocks and more shit than you can think about. You'd have to spend a day in there with a bulldozer."

Isaac: "That would leave a very visible scar from the air."

Lew: "How about a corduroy road? Chop down the trees that have to go, and use the logs for a road surface."

"You'd need too many logs. I paced it out, best as I could, and I make it ninety feet from the depot to the road."

Lew: "If the footing's that bad for the trucks, it'll be even worse for the coolies. Can they carry seventy-pound sacks through there?"

"Like I said, this is where we got a problem."

Young Mr. Balim: "Frank, there must already *be* a road in to the depot. That's what the access road was for."

"If there ever was, I couldn't find it. The way I figure, the access road runs up and down the slope, so rain doesn't hurt it. But the road in to the depot ran crosswise on the slope, so over the years the run-off just turned it back into gullies, and trees and brush grew up, and now that road is gone. A tree can grow a lot in twenty years."

Ellen (surprising them all): "How about a brush road?"

Lew (nervous for her): "A what?"

Ellen: "Taking your idea about the corduroy road, but you'd just use logs to fill the deepest ruts, then lay tree branches and bushes down over the whole thing. Drive a truck back and forth on it, keep laying brush and packing it down, and pretty soon the trucks themselves will tamp it into a road."

Balim: "Miss Ellen, have you seen this done?"

Ellen: "Twice, as a matter of fact. Once in Guatemala, when they were trying to get medical supplies in after an earthquake, and once in Oregon, where a man was building vacation houses on a lake he owned, and he was very short on capital. He built the first houses using the brush road, then put down macadam once they started to sell."

Balim: "What do you think, Frank?"

"I think it's a terrific idea. Stick around, Ellen."

Ellen: "I will."

Lew looked at her smiling face, feeling equal portions of love and possessiveness, and then grinned, very happy, when she winked at him.

Frank went on with the show. "Here's the depot. You see the rails there, we can use those when we connect to the main line. Building's intact, very good shape.

"Here's Charlie asleep. I couldn't resist it, just once."

Young Mr. Balim: "Charming. The drool, especially."

"Spur line. Tracks are rusty but usable. Switch here rusted into place, but it's the right place. A lucky break. But here's the turntable, our next problem."

Isaac: "It's angled wrong. Why on earth did they do that?"

"Beats me. We're gonna have to break it loose and line it up with the rest of the track so we can use the extra twenty foot beyond it. As it is, that train's gonna be so long you'll be able to kiss the caboose from the main line."

Balim: "Speed is everything."

"Don't I know it. Here's the track going up to the main line. We got a lot of trees to cut down."

Lew: "More matériel for Ellen's road."

"Check. Here's where the track stops. You notice you can't see shit, but the main line's just the other side of the hedge. And here it is, and now you can't see the depot."

Young Mr. Balim: "You'll have to cut an awfully big hole in that hedge to get the train through."

"We'll mask it when we're done. That isn't one of the problems."

Young Mr. Balim: "I *am* relieved."

"Here's where the access road crosses the track. Up there's where they nabbed you, Lew."

Lew: "We'll have to put up a plaque."

19

It was with exceedingly mixed emotions that Sir Denis Lambsmith, watching the passengers from the Entebbe-Tripoli-London flight emerge from the Terminal 3 passageway at Heathrow, saw that walking forward beside Baron Chase was Patricia Kamin, beautiful and stylish and utterly at her ease. Even at nine in the morning after an all-night flight, he thought, she was unruffled perfection.

He was delighted to see her, of course, delighted and astonished— but with Chase? What could be their relationship? Remembering his own three nights with her in Kampala—she had come to him every night, had left him thrilled and satiated, and had always been gone in the morning—he could only suppose her connection with Chase was sexual; but he didn't *want* to think that. He remembered that she had been seconded for a while to the Ugandan Embassy in London, so perhaps she was here on official business, and sharing the flight with Chase was mere coincidence. He clung to that shred of possibility as they approached him.

It was strange, but the white man looked more out of place in London than the black woman did. In Kampala, Chase was appropriate, of a type not unknown in that part of the world, but walking into London with his dark-blue canvas flight bag he looked like some prowling barbarian slipping unsuspected through the city gates. Patricia Kamin, who in Kampala was an exotic touch of sophistication in a pretty but small-time provincial capital, in London was a bird of magnificent plumage in its right setting; she might be this year's modeling find, or movie star, or diplomat's wife.

They both greeted Sir Denis with handshakes—Chase gripping him hard, as though to arrest him, Patricia's touch light and brief and stirring. Her eyes laughing at him, she said, "So this is how you look in London."

"And how *you* look in London," he answered. "More beautiful than ever."

"Gallantry," Chase commented without inflection, like a man identifying a kind of tree.

"You have luggage?"

"Of course," Patricia said. "Empty trunks, to carry home full."

As they walked toward the baggage area, Chase said, "We can drop Patricia at the hotel."

"Delighted."

"I'm here on business," Patricia said, answering his unasked question. With a mock grimace of distaste, she said, "Very boring. But at least there'll be time for shopping."

Perhaps we could go shopping together, Sir Denis wanted to say. The presence of Baron Chase inhibited him.

While Patricia and Chase waited with the few other milling passengers at the baggage carousel, Sir Denis went out to the car—a black Daimler parked in the Special Arrangements area behind the Annex—and collected the chauffeur to help with Patricia's putative empty trunks. There turned out to be only two of them, and not so large at that. "You can't intend much shopping after all," Sir Denis said.

"Ah, but I'll also buy luggage."

The gentlemen permitted Patricia to enter the car first, then Sir Denis as host—this being his nation—stood aside for Chase, which put Chase between the other two on the wide soft backseat. Too late, Sir Denis realized he would have preferred the possibility of leg contact with Patricia.

Up on the M4, heading for London, Patricia explained her mission: the Ugandan Air Force wished to purchase some computer equipment from an American firm, and she had to clear it with the American Embassy in London. "Any purchases of a military nature," she said, "even indirectly military, have to be approved by that man."

"Very powerful man." A ridiculous twinge of jealousy moved in Sir Denis's mind: the thought that Patricia was being sent on this mission because she could influence the man at the American Embassy with her sexual favors. To distract himself from that unwelcome—

and certainly unworthy—idea, he said, "I thought Uganda and the United States were at odds."

"Oh, this is a simple commercial deal," she said dismissively. "U.S. government permission is really a formality, just to guard against our buying things like atom bombs."

"You expect no difficulty, then," Sir Denis said, happy to have that ungracious suspicion put to rest.

Which Patricia did, emphatically. "If there were any difficulty in it," she said, "they wouldn't send *me*. I'm just a glorified courier."

Sir Denis smiled, extremely happy, then saw Baron Chase looking at him with a crooked grin. Flustered, imagining for just an instant that Chase could read his mind, Sir Denis sat back against the Daimler's upholstery and permitted the conversation to proceed without him.

*　*　*

Patricia had to be let off first, of course. Her hotel was small but elegant, on Basil Street in Knightsbridge. "*Very* convenient to Harrods," Sir Denis commented, risking another smile, willing himself not to know whether Chase was watching.

"That's why I chose it," Patricia said. Then she stood for a minute on the sidewalk while the chauffeur removed the luggage from the trunk and turned it over to a dark-blue-uniformed bellman who had trotted briskly out of the hotel. Chase was also staying here, but would be going on first to the meeting that had brought him to London.

While Chase was looking the other way, Patricia mouthed at Sir Denis, "Call me." He nodded, and his smile this time could have cracked his cheeks.

After they dropped Patricia off, the Daimler had to maneuver the endless stretch of traffic jam along Knightsbridge to Hyde Park Corner, then rolled through Green Park and past the Queen Victoria Memorial and St. James's Park along the Mall to the impressive multidomed sweep of Admiralty Arch. Trafalgar Square was also crowded with the usual black taxis, red double-decker buses, endless scooting little Morris Minis looking like dirty washing machines on wheels; the chauffeur steered them around past the National Gallery, took the left, shot up toward Leicester Square, made another left, and ducked into the underground parking garage beneath one of the new tall office buildings that the British appropriately call office "blocks" and that are making sections of London (or at least so Sir Denis thought) look more like some lesser city—Indianapolis, perhaps, or Montreal.

There was no conversation in the car after Patricia's departure, but in the elevator up from the parking subbasement to the twenty-third floor, Sir Denis said, "You realize, I'll only be introducing you. I won't be staying."

Baron Chase's cynical grin flickered again, like phosphorescent fire on a bog. "I know," he said. "Your skirts will remain clean."

"If you like."

And in fact it was close enough, Sir Denis had to admit. When he had left Uganda, three weeks earlier, he'd carried to Zurich with him the results of his strange conversations with Chase; the man's hesitancies, non sequiturs, moral probings, and the final message to Emil Grossbarger: "Tell our friend I can't discuss the details with neutrals. He must send me somebody of his own." Grossbarger had laughed when Sir Denis repeated this message and, like Sir Denis, had understood it at once, saying, "Zis is crooked business he hass for me." Sir Denis had agreed, and had been disappointed but not surprised when Grossbarger had gone on, "Vell, ve'll listen to him. It might be amusing."

In the next two weeks, Sir Denis had been home to São Paulo, and to Bogotá, and to Caracas; all on matters dealing with the concerns of the Bogotá Group but having little to do with the Brazil-Uganda deal. Coffee prices and coffee supplies this year were unusually volatile throughout the world; in addition to the untimely frost that had detroyed so much of Brazil's crop, an earthquake had reduced Guatemala's production to a fraction of normal, and continued civil war in Angola made the crop there uncertain. The Bogotá Group was concerned about stability in the coffee market. They liked the price high, but not too high; they liked their product's supply to be less than demand, but only slightly less.

Returning to London three days ago, principally to serve as a conduit of opinion between the Bogotá Group and the International Coffee Board, Sir Denis had found that Emil Grossbarger was also in town, and had a commission for him. "Zis Baron Chase is coming Sursday.

I shall meet viss him in my solicitor's offices. Vould you be so kind as to perform ze introductions? You should leave immediately afterward, of course," he'd finished, his mobile mouth moving, and had gone off into gales of laughter.

Sir Denis had agreed, realizing at once the two reasons for Grossbarger's request, neither of which had anything to do with formality or politeness. The first was that Grossbarger would want assurance that the man he was talking to was in fact Baron Chase and not some secondary figure sent by Chase in his stead for reasons of his own. And the second was accountability: Grossbarger might at some time in the future want to be able to prove that the meeting had actually taken place.

So it was that Sir Denis had traveled today out to Heathrow in the Daimler provided by Grossbarger, where he had been given the totally unexpected present of Patricia Kamin. His mind full of Patricia he now rode upward in the elevator with Chase, then led him down the corridor to Suite 2350: heavy mahogany double doors with the law firm's title affixed in brass letters—eight names, the last two separated by an ampersand, but nothing to indicate what business these eight men might have joined to undertake.

The receptionist, an American girl but with a narrow-nosed oval English face, recognized Sir Denis, announced him, and very shortly the secretary came out, an older woman, dowdily dressed in the seeming parody of a rural postmistress. Sir Denis and Chase followed her down the carpeted hallway past doors closed or ajar, from behind which came the murmurs of serious, intense conversations.

Grossbarger's London solicitor was named Lissenden (number five on the entrance door); rather than a working attorney, he looked most like the sort of tall graying distinguished actor who makes a living portraying lawyers and heads of intelligence agencies and sometimes— though not quite so effectively—doctors. He was emerging from his office as the others arrived; with a hurried wave, backing away as though embarrassed, he called too cheerily, "Well, I'll leave you to it!" and disappeared through another doorway. Sir Denis wondered if Chase understood that Lissenden was avoiding at all costs being introduced to Baron Chase; a quick glance at the man's profile proved nothing.

Emil Grossbarger was seated in a large armchair with its back to the sweep of plate-glass window; behind him, the low gnarled roofs of Soho could be seen far below.

Sir Denis performed a flat uninflected introduction: "Emil Grossbarger, may I present Baron Chase from Uganda. Baron Chase, Emil Grossbarger from Zurich."

"Forgive me if I don't stand," Grossbarger said, gesturing at the walker beside his chair. "I'm not ze man I was."

"I'm sure you are, Mr. Grossbarger," Chase said, stepping briskly forward to bow slightly as he took Grossbarger's hand. "The body may be less. I'd guess the mind is more."

"Vat a compliment!" Grossbarger said, actually squirming with delight, pumping Chase's hand. His mouth moved like a reflection in water, and to Sir Denis it seemed the old man really *was* taken with the flattery.

Releasing Grossbarger's hand, Chase said, "May I sit?"

"Do! Do! Of course!"

The room had been arranged as if it were a stage set with Grossbarger backlighted so that his face was a dimly seen silhouette against the glare. But Chase, acting not as though to counteract that design but merely as though his own passionate interest made him want to be closer to Grossbarger, at once pulled another chair across the pale-blue carpet, leaving darker lines of ruffled nap, and placed the chair diagonally to Grossbarger's right, so that now Chase would be facing him directly (without the window in his line of sight) while Grossbarger would have to turn his head somewhat.

But Chase didn't immediately sit. He stood behind the chair, both hands on its back, like an agnostic listening to predinner grace, while Grossbarger beamed at Sir Denis, saying, "Sank you for bringing zis chentleman to see me."

"My pleasure," Sir Denis said, but he could see that it was in truth Emil's pleasure, that Emil saw in Chase another player of The Game, saw at once the possibilities for both conflict and mutual understanding available only to those who share the same secret life and world view. Professional tennis players and military leaders and politicians all are closer to their opponents than to anyone in the outside world. The off-duty policeman would rather talk shop with a burglar than mortgages with the next-door neighbor. In the same way, Emil Grossbarger was already closer to Baron Chase than he would ever be to Sir Denis Lambsmith, and Sir Denis recognized this fact with an inevitable twinge of envy and a reluctance to depart.

However, Grossbarger's expression of thanks had been Sir Denis's cue to leave, and so he did, saying, "Well, as you know, I can't stay. But I was happy to be able to bring you together."

"Delightful," Grossbarger agreed, while Chase contented himself with a cold smile of dismissal.

As he was leaving the office, the door not yet completely closed, he heard Grossbarger say apologetically, "I am so sorry, Mr. Chase. My neck, ze strain. If you could move your chair just slightly. Sank you zo much."

He wanted me to hear him win that round, Sir Denis thought, and he walked back toward the elevator smiling.

*   *   *

There were fewer people in Harrods than during the holidays, but the customers were still primarily tourists from the Continent. Combining this fact with the high percentage of Pakistanis and Indians and other Commonwealth citizens among the store's sales employees, there tended to be any number of comic vignettes going on at all times. Appreciatively Sir Denis watched the performance as a Norwegian woman attempted to pay a Pakistani salesgirl for a Japanese calculator in kroner, but he felt rather sorry for the Danish man with scanty English attempting to buy an Italian suit in the right size from a self-important Indian salesman who had apparently no English at all.

For the most part, though, Sir Denis ignored the passing vaudeville of sales transactions between pairs of people who lacked a common language or currency or agreement on clothing sizes. Instead, he concentrated on Patricia's fashion show.

She was buying, as she had said she would, a great deal of clothing. She had been in her hotel room when Sir Denis had called her from the pay phone in the garage level of Grossbarger's solicitor's building, and she had clearly been delighted to hear from him. "Come with me to Harrods," she'd said, "and help me choose my wardrobe."

He had been happy to say yes. Grossbarger's Daimler had returned him to the hotel on Basil Street, where he'd wondered if Patricia might invite him up to the room; but she'd come down instead, and they'd walked the few blocks to Harrods, and now he was having the time of his life, seated on a small but comfortable chair while Patricia paraded before him in dress after dress, sweater after sweater, blouse after blouse.

Alicia, whom he had loved absolutely, had never given him this treat, had never even led him to suspect that such gratification existed. Her own clothes buying had been done almost exclusively in solitary twice-a-year campaigns; forays against the shops organized as by a general brilliant in tactics, from which Alicia invariably returned exhausted and triumphant. That the expedition could instead have a wonderful languorous hint of the harem about it, Sir Denis had never guessed; again his gratitude toward Patricia informed his more carnal feelings.

After an hour or so, during which Patricia selected a variety of garments and instructed they all be delivered to the hotel, she suddenly said, "I'm famished. Come upstairs, let me give you lunch on my expense account."

It was just lunchtime, and the broad, cream-colored, low-ceilinged room on the top public floor was half-filled, mostly with middle-aged women. Patricia selected their wine and guided Sir Denis in his choice of entrée with that easiness of manner that had only recently come to women; the motherly waitress seemed to admire it from afar, as though she found Patricia's manner as unattainable as her beauty.

Over glasses of Chablis, Sir Denis said, "When do you have to see your American Embassy man?"

"Oh, not till tomorrow. We're forbidden to do business the same day we arrive. Jet lag, you know."

"Chase seemed untroubled by jet lag." Sir Denis was chagrined to hear the jealousy in his voice: of Chase and Patricia? Chase and Grossbarger?

"Oh, Chase," Patricia said dismissively. "He isn't human, he's a cat. Do you know, he slept from the instant he boarded that plane until the announcement to fasten our seat belts for landing?"

"Did he really? I envy that." It was pleasant to find a safe outlet for the expression of his envy.

"He's so cold," she said, and shivered.

"He is that."

Suddenly much more serious, she leaned forward, reaching across to cover his hand with hers. "You ought to look out for Baron Chase," she said.

"Oh, I agree."

"No, I mean it." She hesitated, then plunged forward. "I can tell you things now that I couldn't say in Kampala."

Immediately there flooded into Sir Denis's mind the memory of his unguarded conversation with Patricia that first night she had come to his room. The next day he had been astounded at the openness with which he'd answered everything she'd asked, particularly given his memory of Chase's earlier warning that the rooms were undoubtedly wired. He was not a stupid man, and it had occurred to him to wonder if she had doped him with that wine, but ultimately he had decided she had not. He *wanted* to believe in her—that was the most important thing—but he had other evidence as well: the fact that he was a businessman dealing with businessmen and not a spy dealing with spies; the fact that his secrets were all so small and unimportant and mercantile; and the fact that she had come back to him the next two nights, when there had been no questions and no loose talk.

Now, in confirming to him again the warning that the rooms at the Presidential Lodge were bugged, she re-aroused that worry, and gave it an additional wrinkle of complexity. Was she guilty after all, and speaking to him now out of the subtlety of the spy? Or was her reference to the eavesdroppers the final proof of her innocence?

Exploring that ambiguity, as one pokes one's tongue experimentally against the aching tooth, Sir Denis said, "I seem to remember I told you far too many things in Kampala."

She closed her eyes as though embarrassed, her hand clenching on his. "Oh, I know," she said, and opened her eyes to stare at him. "We were too excited, my darling, and we got a little drunk. The next day I remembered— And how I led you on— Thank God you didn't say anything against Amin."

That possibility had never even crossed Sir Denis's mind; he'd been too concerned about his merchant's secrets. But if he'd said disparaging things about Idi Amin? If he'd made fun of the man? Less than two years ago, Amin had imprisoned a British writer named Dennis Hills for having said in a book that Amin was a "village tyrant." Hills had been sentenced to death, and had been released only when British Foreign Minister James Callaghan flew to Uganda to plead personally for Hills's life. (That time, Amin had been seated in a hut with a very low door, so Callaghan had to bow as he entered Amin's presence.)

Patricia smiled reassuringly, squeezed his hand once more, and said, "Well, it's over. We were lucky, my dear, and we didn't let it happen again."

"No, we didn't." With his free hand, Sir Denis lubricated his dry mouth with wine.

"The *point* is," Patricia said, returning to earnest seriousness, "Baron Chase is up to something."

"That wouldn't surprise me in the least."

"I suspect," she said, "he's planning to betray Amin in some way."

"If so," Sir Denis said, "he's either a braver or a more foolhardy man than I am."

"Please don't repeat this," she said, looking very tense and worried. "Not to anybody."

"You have my word."

"And don't let him involve you. Whatever it is he's doing, don't let him convince you to help him."

"Certainly not."

"Do you know why he's in London?" Then, obviously seeing the quandary in Sir Denis's face—should he mention Grossbarger or lie to her?—she laughed and patted his hand, saying, "I know about Emil Grossbarger."

"Good," he said, smiling back, relieved.

She released his hand to sip wine, then didn't take his hand again. "Officially," she said, "he's come here to talk with the Grossbarger Group—which of course means Grossbarger—"

"Of course."

"—about the planes for the coffee airlift to Djibouti."

Sir Denis lifted an eyebrow: so that was Chase's story. "I see."

She had been watching him keenly. Now she smiled again and said, "No, you don't believe it, either."

"I don't?"

"It's too small a mission," she said. "Anyone could have done it. I could do it. Chase could even have done it with a phone call."

"I agree."

"But Grossbarger requested the meeting personally," she said, "and asked for Chase."

"Direct action," Sir Denis commented admiringly.

"I'll tell you what I think," she said. "I think Chase is trying to make some sort of deal of his own with Grossbarger. Remember, in Uganda he wouldn't tell you what his message to Grossbarger was?"

That was one of the things he'd babbled away about that first night. Wincing at the memory, he said, "Yes, of course I remember."

"Well, somehow he did get his message through to Grossbarger, and Grossbarger is interested, and now they're trying to work out some sort of deal together."

"I daresay you're right," Sir Denis said; what he didn't say was that he knew for a fact she was right. Wondering if she knew *more* than he did, he said, "What sort of deal do you think it is?"

Unfortunately, she shook her head. "I have no idea. Could it have something to do with coffee? But Grossbarger has other interests, hasn't he?"

"Of course. Grossbarger is an investor, in whatever looks safe enough and profitable enough. The Grossbarger Group is venture capital at a very high level."

"But he'll talk with Baron Chase," she said, frowning with the intensity of her bewilderment. "What on Earth could Chase be offering him?"

"I've asked myself that same question a dozen times," Sir Denis said, "without finding a satisfactory answer."

"Is he selling Uganda?" That had been said facetiously, but then she frowned again, saying, "I wonder. *Is* he selling Uganda?"

"I don't understand."

"Revolution," she suggested. "Could Chase be talking to Grossbarger about financing a revolution? There'd certainly be profit in it if the revolution succeeded."

Sir Denis shook his head. "I know Emil Grossbarger fairly well," he said. "I imagine he's capable of very many things, but he wouldn't touch a revolution."

"Not under any circumstances?"

"Not under any circumstances. Revolution is emotion, and Emil Grossbarger won't put his money on another man's emotion."

Patricia laughed, in surprise as much as pleasure. "You read people very well," she said. "I wonder what you think of me."

"You know what I think of you," he said, and was gratified to see that special sensual smile touch her lips.

The motherly waitress was bringing their food at last. Patricia said, "I've done enough shopping for today. After lunch, I'd love to go back to the hotel and just rest awhile, but I don't want to run into Chase."

"Come to my hotel," he suggested, trying to be casual but already feeling the heat of arousal in his body.

"Delicious idea," she said, smiling again in that same way.

The waitress walked off frowning, glancing back over her shoulder at the stylish young black woman and the distinguished elderly white man.

*　*　*

Anne wasn't using the farm in Sussex that weekend, so on Saturday Sir Denis and Patricia drove down there in a rented Ford Escort. On the way, they talked together easily, comfortably, each dipping into that store of anecdote freshly available with the advent of a new partner. They touched on the question of Grossbarger and Chase only once, and glancingly, when Patricia said, "Why did you have to meet Chase at the airport?" He explained then his role in introducing the two men, and she said, "So you're the go-between."

"I suppose I am, in a way."

"I'm surprised they wouldn't tell you what it was all about."

"They think I'm too sort of honest," he said, with a self-deprecating smile.

She studied him sharply for a few seconds, then smiled, visibly relaxing, saying, "And of course they're right."

"Thank you," he said.

At Foxhall (pronounced *Foxell* or, when the natives were trying for wit, *Fossil*) Sir Denis turned left onto the small macadam road, barely two lanes wide, that led after several miles to the farm. "That's my land there," he said, nodding at the freshly turned earth under the cloud-filled sky.

"You farm it?" She sounded amazed and delighted.

Unfortunately he had to say, "No, I lease most of the land to local men. All I keep for myself is the house and the woods."

He had been hesitant at first about bringing her up here, but the closer they got to the place the more he knew he was doing the right thing. In the old days he'd had a great deal of pleasure and contentment here, but in the years since Alicia's death the farm had taken on a different meaning in his life; it had become a solitary place, where he could work and read, but not particularly a place of joy or serenity. Introducing Patricia to the farm would shake it up, renew his relationship with it. And perhaps with himself.

Leading from the road to the house was a quarter-mile gravel lane between fields; the one on the left recently plowed, the one on the right still with its spring stubble of dead stalks and fresh weeds. At first the house was invisible, its presence indicated only by the cluster of evergreens at the end of the lane, standing there like a Swiss Guard in uniforms of dark green. The house itself stood in their midst, a low two stories, half-timbered, with beams of so dark a brown they seemed black against the white plaster. Faintly visible behind and to the left were a springhouse and the nearest barn, both lumpy humble structures of native stone.

"It's beautiful," Patricia said, leaning forward to smile at the house through the windscreen. "It's a fairy tale."

Sir Denis smiled. A house of this design, nestled alone in the woods, always made people think of fairy tales. He normally responded to comments like that by saying, "If you owned it, you wouldn't think so. For me, it's plumbing problems, mildew, cracking plaster, field mice, and outrageous taxes." But with Patricia he forbore; he wasn't of a mind to spoil the mood.

The Kenwyns were a local farm couple who leased some of his land and who also took care of the house during those long periods when neither he nor his daughter was in residence. Sir Denis had phoned them from London this morning, so when he and Patricia entered the house, it had been aired out to some extent (though the mustiness of disuse remained faintly discernible) and most of the surfaces were dusted. The central heating (still considered a luxury in this corner of England) had been turned up, and a fire had been laid in the beam-ceilinged living room. Mrs. Kenwyn having asked if Sir Denis was bringing a guest, two of the bedrooms upstairs would have been readied; to avoid shocking local sensibilities, he would have to remember to muss up the guest-room bed before departure on Monday.

They carried the luggage upstairs, where Sir Denis pointed out the woods visible from the master-bedroom windows, stretching away for more than a mile into the countryside. "Later on," he said, "if you feel like it, we can go for a walk. I'm sure I have wellies you could wear."

"That's later," she said. "Right now, I very much want to be made love to."

"I am at your command," he said, and she took him at his word.

* * *

They never did get outdoors again that day. Between napping and lovemaking, Saturday was nearly at an end before they came back downstairs, he in his mildew-tinged old maroon silk robe, Patricia looking like a sexy, wayward little girl inside the massive quilted pink folds of an ancient robe of Alicia's. They made a supper out of tins, and Sir Denis lit the fire the Kenwyns had prepared in the living room. Seated on the long sofa facing the fire, they drank a Saint-Émilion from his cellar and talked about their lives from before they'd known each other, and the darkness beyond the windows was unbroken by any sort of light.

When she opened his robe and lowered her head to his lap he was no longer even astonished at the frequency with which she could arouse him. She stayed there, and drew the lightning out of him like drawing a wasp's sting out of one's flesh, and then they both fell asleep in that position, awakening much later, cold and stiff and giggling, the fire nearly out. Laughing and touching one another, they made their way upstairs to bed, and awoke to a wonderfully sunny Sunday. *"Now,"* she said, "I'll take that walk in the woods."

In the mud room by the rear door he had an assortment of wellingtons, knee-high lined rubber boots. She found a pair that fit well over her walking shoes, and they tramped through the spring-boggy woods hand in hand. She kissed him as a reward for finding a sweet-singing bird whose name he did not know.

They went for a drive in the afternoon, and stopped in a pub where the mackintoshed locals clearly couldn't tell whether they should be astounded by the black woman herself or by her choice of companion. That was funny, too, and on the drive back they made up the dialogue that must have taken place around that bar after their departure.

There was a restaurant in a town fifteen miles away—good plain food—where once again they were a sensation, but the proprietors and other customers were too well bred to make an obvious fuss. Returning to the house after dark, the black sky flung with high tiny stars and a gibbous moon, they found that the unseen Kenwyns had set a new fire in the living room that awaited only Sir Denis's match.

Patricia had completed her business at the American Embassy on Friday—the permission, about which there would be no problem, would be forthcoming to the computer supplier in the States—and would be taking an afternoon plane Monday to Rome, transferring there to an overnight flight for Tripoli and Entebbe. All her luggage and her new purchases (including a third suitcase, as threatened) were with her now, and Sir Denis would drive her straight to Heathrow tomorrow. In bed tonight he already felt her loss, felt nostalgic for the weekend even before it was over, and he slept with her head nestled on his shoulder, his arm curled around her back.

They were in the process of loading the car and closing the house on Monday morning when the phone rang for the first time all weekend. There was only one phone in the house, in the kitchen, and Sir Denis was a bit out of breath when he got to it.

It was Bentley, one of the men from the International Coffee Board's London office. "Forgive my calling you at your weekend retreat," he said, "but I wanted to get hold of you before you made any plans."

"Of course. Not to worry."

"The fact is," Bentley said, and Sir Denis could hear an uncharacteristic awkwardness in the man's voice, "you won't be involved with the Uganda transaction any longer."

His heart seemed to stop. In the other room, Patricia was humming some tune as she made a last stroll around the house. *I'll lose her*, he thought (not acknowledging to himself even then what the thought implied, what knowledge about her he was denying), but he kept his voice steady when he said, "I won't? Why on earth not?"

"Um," Bentley said. "I'm supposed to fob you off with some sort of answer, you know, but I can't help asking a question of my own. What's the relationship between you and Emil Grossbarger?"

"Emil—? I—I hardly know how to answer that. We get along; we work well together." *I'll lose her.* "What are you trying to say, man?"

"You didn't hear it from me," Bentley told him, "in fact you don't know this at all, but you're out at Grossbarger's request."

"That's impossible!" But even as he said it he could feel the floor of the world shift beneath his feet, could sense the stage sets of reality being reordered into a new perspective.

"I can tell from your voice," Bentley said, "that you don't know what this is all about."

"Am I that obvious? All right, then, I *don't* know what it's all about."

"Grossbarger went out of his way," Bentley said, "to assure us that he had no fault to find with you, either personally or professionally. He said he wanted to make the change for reasons of his own, and would always be happy to work with you again in the future."

"Then it makes no sense," Sir Denis said. *I'll lose her.* "Who's replacing me?"

"Walter Harrison."

Sir Denis knew him; an American, with a special interest in the Mexican coffee business. "Still someone from the Bogotá Group, then," he commented.

"I was rather hoping you could explain it."

In that instant the penny dropped, and Sir Denis could have explained it, but he did not. "I'm as baffled as you are," he said.

"As it now stands," Bentley told him, "you can go home at any time."

Meaning São Paulo, of course. "Thank you." Sir Denis said. "I'll talk to you before I go." *I'll lose her.*

Very hesitantly he returned to the living room, where the ashes in the fireplace were cold and dead. Patricia rose from an armchair, her expression concerned, saying, "What is it? It must have been bad news."

Staring at her more intently than he realized, willing the awfulness to be over as quickly and cleanly as possible, he said, "Emil Grossbarger has asked the Coffee Board to replace me on the Uganda sale."

"Oh, my dear." She stepped forward, reaching out to touch his arm.

"I can see what it is, of course," he said. "Grossbarger and Chase have come to an agreement, and they want me out of the way."

"So it *is* coffee." For just an instant her face was tense with calculation. Then she shook her head, and focused on him again, and smiled sadly at whatever she saw in his eyes. "Yes, of course," she said. "But this won't make any difference to us."

"It won't?" He was so convinced of their finish that he couldn't even try to hope.

"There are things I wish I could tell you," she said, her gentle hand pressing his arm. "But you'll see, my dear, it isn't over. Not between us."

He didn't believe her, but courtesy required him to pretend that he did. "Thank you, Patricia," he said. "If for nothing else, thank you for bringing me back to life."

"Stay alive," she said, with that well-remembered seductive smile. "For me."

"We should leave. You won't want to miss your plane."

20

Through April and into May, in the first five weeks of the long rains, Ellen flew only four round trips: three to Nairobi, and one all the way to Mombasa, seven hundred miles eastward on the Indian Ocean. Those few intervals above the clouds, in the beautiful gold of sunlight, made things not better but worse; each time, the return to Earth through those miserable clouds was an awful experience, leaving her bad-tempered for hours afterward.

The rain affected everybody. Even Frank seemed less boisterous and Mr. Balim not quite so smoothly self-assured. As for Lew, the rain and the forced inactivity were probably enough to explain his recent tension, his distracted, almost guilty manner, his impatience and suppressed anger. Still, Ellen thought there was more to it than that. She thought he was having an affair.

If so, it was the girl in Nairobi. The first flight there, Ellen's passengers had been Balim and Lew, and afterward Lew had described to her the Jhosi family, their current plight, and their relationship with the coffee-smuggling operation. The second time, a week later, Lew had been the only passenger, bringing papers for the grandmother to sign. He had been met at the airport by the granddaughter, Amarda, who was to drive him to the coffee plantation while Ellen refueled and dealt with the airport paperwork.

Lew had mentioned Amarda Jhosi in his account of the first meeting, but had referred to her only glancingly, as though she were unimportant, thereby leaving out far too much. He hadn't mentioned that she was beautiful, with large sad eyes. And he hadn't mentioned that she was in love with him.

Well, men had less sensitivity about such things; it was possible he didn't realize Amarda Jhosi was in love with him. Still, Ellen dated his increasing testiness and irritability from that second Nairobi trip, when he had been gone with the girl for five hours—to sign papers?—and had volunteered an unconvincing story afterward about traffic jams.

Ellen's third rainy-season flight had been the one to Mombasa, carrying Frank and two small canvas bags. Ivory or some other illegal commodity had been involved in that flight, she suspected, but she'd asked no questions and Frank had volunteered no answers. Because of the distance involved, that one had been an overnight trip, and Ellen had been fully prepared to fend off further unwanted advances from Frank that night in the Whitesands Hotel. It had been a pleasant relief when he had remained merely cheery and companionable, telling her over dinner comic or horrific incidents from Mombasa's history, and not once making even the most oblique suggestion that they might spend the night together. Since then, she had warmed more to Frank, and even thought of him now as a friend.

Finally, three days ago, there had been the third trip to Nairobi. This time, Mr. Balim was along as well as Lew, and from the conversation in the plane Ellen understood that Balim was bringing money to the Jhosi family to be used in connection with the smuggling. They would have to order and pay for thousands of sacks with their own plantation's imprint. They would have to arrange for transportation of the resacked coffee from the plantation, as well as for storage during the time the coffee was in their care.

The girl Amarda was at Wilson Airport again, to chauffeur them, and it seemed to Ellen the girl avoided her gaze. And this time, when the two men returned after four hours, Ellen thought there was a new amused twinkle in Balim's eye, the look of a man holding tight to a delicious and diverting secret.

During this period of rain-caused idleness, Ellen had taken to hanging out at Balim's place of business, where there was at least usually some sort of activity to watch, to distract herself. And she did enjoy talking with Isaac Otera, a decent and very sad man. Of course, Frank was always enjoyable to watch, crashing from wall to wall.

Today, arriving in midmorning, she found Frank dressed like some demon out of Kabuki, all swathed in shiny black raingear, stomping out of the office. Seeing her, he said, "You busy? Wanna go for a ride?"

"In the rain? Where to?"

"A town that never happened," he said. "Come on along."

"What the hell," she said, and went with him.

* * *

"Port Victoria," Frank said, squinting like a gargoyle through the wet windshield. "It was gonna be the champ, and it wound up a bum."

They were driving northwest out of Kisumu on the B1. The rain was in its medium stage—relentless but not a downpour—and Frank had covered the front passenger seat with a blanket to eliminate the traces of Charlie, so Ellen could ride beside him. She felt unreasonably happy and light, as though some stuffy, constricting woolen overcoat she'd been wearing for months had at last been flung off. Settling herself comfortably on the blanketed seat, smiling in anticipation at Frank's craggy profile, she said, "What happened to Port Victoria?"

"The British, to begin with," he said. "When they were building the railroad, they didn't know what the fuck they were doing. They had four surveys done, and no two of them agreed, but of course back then a successful survey was one where nothing or nobody ate the surveyor. About the only thing they all agreed on was the place where the railroad should meet the lake."

"Port Victoria," she suggested.

"Wait for it." He liked to tell his stories at his own pace, without being interrupted.

"Sorry."

"This place—okay, Port Victoria—it's up on the northeastern shoulder of the lake, with fairly high land right behind it. No swamps, see, but no mountains, either. It's at the outer southern point of Berkeley Bay, so the lake is right in front of it, with a natural deep-water harbor, and Berkeley Bay around to the side for protected mooring."

"Sounds good," Ellen said.

"It is good. It's terrific. That's why they named it Port Victoria, right? It was supposed to be the major port on Lake Victoria, both of them named after that queen."

"Something went wrong."

"Something always goes wrong," Frank said. "What happened this time, the British knew they were gonna end the railroad at Port Victoria, and they knew they were gonna start the railroad at Mombasa, but the seven hundred miles in between they were kind of fuzzy about."

Ellen laughed, saying, "Because of things eating the surveyors."

"Sure. It was so bad, they were still surveying out in front of the railroad while they were building it. And of course, the more detailed the survey, the closer they got to the reality on the ground, the more expensive it was. Like, a team would go through in the dry season and say, Fine, we got solid ground, just lay your track right down and zoom. Then the rains come, and it turns out there's absolute rivers there, the track washes away, and all of a sudden for every ten miles you've got to do six miles of bridges."

"Expensive," Ellen agreed.

"The British Parliament was paying for all this," Frank said, "and right from the beginning there was a strong minority that didn't want to build the railroad at all. They were the anti-Imperialists, called the Little England group, and they didn't want the interior of Africa opened up and colonized and made part of the British Empire. After ten years, when the cost of the railroad was just about doubled from the first estimate but they were actually getting close to the lake, the Little England bunch finally got their way. The money wasn't shut off entirely, but the faucet was turned way down."

"But they still reached the lake."

"Sure. At Kisumu. Fifty-five miles closer than Port Victoria, a swamp next to a stagnant gulf, and it's another forty miles across the gulf to the regular part of the lake. The British were just like anybody else: they spent like idiots when they didn't know what they were doing, and as soon as some ready cash would have helped they got stingy."

"So Port Victoria never happened."

Nodding, Frank said, "It would have been what Kisumu is, a rich trading town with tourist hotels and its own airport and all that shit. Instead, it's got a population of maybe a hundred, a little open-air village market, and that's all. Also, the last twenty-five miles in is dirt road."

"Dirt! In this weather?"

"It's not that bad," he said. "Most of it is rock. The way they build that kind of road, they just come in with bulldozers and scrape the topsoil away, and underneath you got rock. Anyway, back to the story. There's a kicker in it."

"A happy ending for Port Victoria after all?" Oddly enough, she had found herself sympathizing with the town, as though it were a person who'd been unjustly treated.

"In a way," Frank said. "All the regular commerce went to Kisumu, but that left Port Victoria with all its natural advantages and nobody to use them. The natural harbor, the firm uphill land, the protected bay. And besides that, you've got Uganda just ten miles across the water."

"You're going to say smuggling."

Frank laughed; history delighted him. "Sure, it's smuggling. The biggest smuggling port on the lake. The straight world got the swamp and the stagnant gulf and a town called Kisumu, sounds like a sneeze. The underworld got Port Victoria."

*   *   *

What Frank had called "mostly rock" turned out, in Ellen's opinion, to be mostly mud. When they turned left off the B1 at Luanda—the sign pointed toward Siaya and Busonga, without mentioning Port Victoria at all—they were almost immediately half-mired in a broad lake of orangy-red mud. The road was very wide, probably three lanes (if it could be said to have such things as lanes), with high mud walls on both sides to channel the rain and keep it from running off. Those walls were undoubtedly the topsoil that had, according to Frank, been scraped off when this "road" had been built.

They passed a group of schoolgirls in bright pink jumpers and white blouses, all carrying gaudily colored umbrellas. A few glowered at the truck in sullen suspicion, but most showed cheery smiles under their umbrellas, and many waved.

Everywhere she went, Ellen saw these groups of schoolchildren, the girls in bright-colored jumpers, the boys frequently in short pants and white shirts and blue blazers. The strangest thing was to see a group of neatly dressed teenagers walking at the end of the day across the stubby fields toward their homes; a cluster of low mud huts, lacking electricity or running water. How do they get up in the morning in such hovels, she wondered, and manage to turn themselves into clean, pressed, shining-faced students? How far they were traveling to reach the twentieth century, and how quickly and surely they were making the journey.

Their own journey, on the other hand, was rather slower and more uncertain. The Land-Rover slithered and slued along this endless rice paddy, the wheels throwing mud in all directions. (Frank had slowed down when they passed the schoolgirls so as not to splash them.) Here and there a solitary person walked, occasionally someone was to be seen hunkered under a large umbrella by the roadside waiting for God knows who or what, and once a dangerously skidding blue bus crammed with passengers came lurching the other way, the driver madly honking his horn in lieu of attempting to control the wheel. Frank eeled by him, and Ellen stared back at all the white-eyed black-faced passengers seen through the steamy windows frighteningly close.

There were no more history anecdotes on this part of the trip. Driving took all of Frank's attention and, as usual, most of his muscles. Keeping clear of the flailing elbows, Ellen sat close to the door and watched the muddy world go slowly by.

Frank had said Port Victoria was fifty-five miles from Kisumu, and at the rate they were going, it was beginning to seem it would take a week, when all at once the road made an abrupt right-angled turn at a village—not even a village; not anything at all that Ellen could see—called Busonga, and directly in front of them was a narrow, fast-running, muddy river and a small open ferry. "Good God!"

Frank was grinning at her as he wrestled the Land-Rover to a stop on the slippery macadam incline running down to the water. "Forgot to tell you about this," he said. "The ferry over the Nzoia. Little adventure to tell your grandchildren."

Suspiciously studying the ferry, which was inching this way from the farther shore, Ellen said, "You sure I'll *have* grandchildren?"

"I'm willing to do my part," he said.

She looked sharply at him, but saw that he was merely joking and not making a pass. "I'll think of something funny to say," she said, "when we reach the other side."

The ferry was merely a large square raft, with a filthy greasy big engine bolted to it on one side. A thick cable attached to metal stanchions on each bank dangled across the river and through the raft's engine so the ferry could slowly and agonizingly winch its way across the stream. In addition, another higher cable was slightly upstream; a third cable, one end of which was attached to the upstream side of the raft, was noosed around this higher one to keep the ferry from drifting too far downstream, thereby creating too much stress on cable number one as it was fed through the engine. Friction between the wire noose and the cable it was to slide along made the ferry move in slow uncertain fits and starts, like a very sleepy drunk.

The ferry had metal pipe railings on both sides, and twin narrow metal ramps for vehicles jutting out at front and back. At the moment there were about a dozen people standing clustered in the middle of the thing, dressed in red and white and yellow and pink, most holding umbrellas, forming a bright-colored temporary geodesic roof. More foot passengers waited on this side of the river; the monotony of their wait had been broken by the unexpected arrival of a Land-Rover containing two white people. Ellen stared back, but she grew bored before they did.

The man who ran the ferry was short, with a stout torso but spindly arms and legs like a spider's. Also spiderlike in his movements, he crawled and swarmed over his engine, making a great complicated to-do about the landing, with the metal ramps scraping up onto the macadam.

Despite the ferryman's angry shouts and warnings, most of the passengers had jumped off and gone on about their business before he'd finished docking to his own satisfaction. Then there was a semicomic moment when the waiting passengers all rushed on and the ferryman had to order them off again, with many yells and curses and flailings of his spindly arms, so the Land-Rover could be carefully maneuvered into position first. Ellen, feeling vaguely guilty that she was inside in the dry while all those people were out there in the wet, smiled apologetically at everybody whose eye she met, while Frank cursed under his breath at the contradictory instructions of the ferryman, who kept waving Frank to turn this way and that, when obviously the sensible thing to do was merely drive up the ramps and onto the ferry and stop.

Well, he did, at last, and the foot passengers followed, and the ferryman collected everybody's fare. The vehicle was charged four shillings—about fifty cents—while from watching the ferryman make change, it seemed to Ellen foot passengers paid far less.

"This is the most relaxing part of the trip," Frank said as the ferryman threw his engine into gear and the metal ramps scraped back again off the macadam. Suiting his actions to his words, he leaned back in the seat, folded his arms over his chest, closed his eyes, and smiled in lazy comfort.

And the strange thing was, he was right. The motion of the ferry, the combination of hesitant forward motion with the constant sideways thrust of the river, was oddly soothing, the physical equivalent of a lullaby. Their progress was slow, easy, soporific, and out of their hands. The river was so narrow that even with its rapidity and muddiness it didn't look really dangerous, and the other passengers under their roof of joined umbrellas seemed pleased by their presence, as being an entertaining break from routine. The far shore, which was much steeper, approached slowly through the rain, and Ellen found herself relaxing more than she had done in a month. The tensions went away; the frustrations faded; the uncertainties grew less important. "I want to stay here forever," she murmured, and beside her, Frank comfortably chuckled.

The routine between frantic ferryman and disinterested passengers was repeated on the opposite bank, and so was that between ferryman-as-incompetent-direction-giver and Frank-as-long-suffering-driver. But at last they were off, and spurting up the muddy slope, people ducking out of the way of the great gobs of maroon gunk thrown back by the tires straining for purchase. They reached level ground and a much narrower road, arched over by rows of trees. "That was fun," Ellen said. "Thanks."

"You don't get any of those in— Where are you from, anyway?"

"Everywhere. I was an Army brat. Air Force, really. My father was a pilot."

"You learned from him?"

"Starting when I was fourteen. He's flying for PSA now."

They talked awhile about cities and countries where Ellen had grown up, finding that while they'd both lived in several of the same places, it had never been at the same time. But Ellen loved meaningless coincidences as much as anybody, and was pleased whenever it turned out that Frank had been such-and-such a place three years after she'd been there, or two years before.

At a fork in the muddy road they turned left, and very soon overtook a monstrous sagging lumbering smoke-snorting truck, its load covered with tan canvas tarpaulins. The springs on its right side were completely shot, so that at all times it seemed in the process of falling over; even if the road had been wide enough to pass, that tottering hulk would have intimidated most drivers.

"Shit," Frank said. "They're supposed to be there already; they left two hours before us."

She had no idea what he was talking about. "Who?"

"Charlie," he said in disgust, pointing at the truck. "They can't take the ferry, so they came around the long way, through Sio."

"They have something to do with *us?*"

"That's our work crew," Frank said, and despite his annoyance he grinned. "We didn't come out here just to play might-have-been."

"Oh," Ellen said, suddenly realizing. "The smuggling capital." Of *course* this had to do with the coffee caper; for some absurd reason it spoiled things a bit that this expedition wasn't merely an outing for its own sake.

"That's right," Frank said. "The smuggling capital; that's good. Did you read in the *Standard* about the outboard motors?" The *Standard* was a Nairobi newspaper, also available in Kisumu.

"Outboard motors? No."

"You know Lake Naivasha? It's two hundred miles east of here, big lake. Already this year, every outboard motor on that lake was stolen; at least, every outboard motor that wasn't locked away in somebody's house."

"Is that true? Why?"

"To come here for the smuggling. Uganda's breaking down. This year, there'll be more import-export by smuggling than by regular trade."

Ellen suddenly had an image of them all—herself, Lew, Frank, Balim, even Isaac Otera—as carrion eaters, buzzards or hyenas, waiting on the sidelines for some stricken creature to die. It was a discomfiting vision. She said, "It seems tough on the people."

"Around Lake Naivasha? They'll recover."

"No, in Uganda."

"Uganda!" He seemed truly astonished. "We aren't screwing the *people*," he said, "they're the ones doing the smuggling. They're getting out from under their government, that's all, the best way they can, poor bastards."

"What's going to happen next?" she wondered. "In Uganda, I mean."

"What usually happens, I suppose," he said. "Things'll get worse."

* * *

Port Victoria looked like the cowtown in Western movies. Not the big town with the saloons full of fancy women, but the little nothing-town where the stagecoach changes horses. The dirt road—mud road, really—ended in a large scraggly weedy square with low stucco or cement buildings on three sides. Most of the buildings featured veran-dah roofs over mud or cement walks, above which were false fronts. Peeling old political posters glued to the walls looked like wanted posters from those same Western movies. A dozen or so adults and children lounged in the comparative dryness under the verandah roofs. Low hills surrounded the village on three sides, adding to the sense of frontier isolation. Only the presence of a small white British Leyland truck parked in front of what seemed to be a general store took the scene out of the American nineteenth century and put it in the African twentieth.

Was there a sense here of unfulfilled destiny? In this sleepy village did there still dream the egg of the merchant metropolis that had never been born? It was probably merely that she'd heard the history of the place from Frank, but it nevertheless seemed to Ellen that there was something vaguely sad about the town, sad in a way other than the sadness endemic in rural towns everywhere, more than that usual sense of personal loss, of stunted promise and missed opportunity. Here it was no mute inglorious Milton that was evoked, but the image of an entire city that had failed to be. The missing railroad yards, warehouses, docks, movie palaces, bars, mansions, slums, vitality, purpose; all seemed to hover minimally and unnoticeably in the air behind the reality of the town, the aura of a ghost too weak even to haunt the place.

And the second subtext here, of course, was the underworld: Port Victoria's secret life as a smuggler's haven. In addition to the bland reality of surface appearance, in addition to the ghostly echo of what might have been, there was also the hidden face of corruption. Everyone she saw might be a smuggler or a thief; every building might conceal booty. Smuggling always leads to further crimes, to bribery, theft, or murder; in losing its original destiny, Port Victoria had become something strange and fascinating and in a way pathetic, almost like a failed person. Looking around her, Ellen said, "It's a Graham Greene character as geography."

Frank glowered. "What?"

"Nothing. Never mind."

Frank had grown more and more angry at that groaning truck out in front of them, and once they reached the town's weedy square he took the immediate opportunity to yank the Land-Rover in a wide sweep around the other vehicle, honking furiously. "Stupid bastard!" he yelled, but since the windows were closed against the rain, nobody could have heard him but Ellen.

A bumpy muddy lane led downhill on the right side of the square, beginning like an afterthought between two of the verandahed buildings. Frank charged through there as though daring the Land-Rover to hit one of those walls, then skittered and skewed and side-slid down the long muddy slope between tiny flat-roofed houses that were more Caribbean than Wild West.

The lake was out ahead, at the bottom of the hill, with a strange

large round cane-and-reed hut off to one side. Ellen thought, Now
we're in the South Pacific. To the left, near the shore, was another
huge truck like the one now lumbering down the lane after them. As
Frank slued around and parked behind this second one, its doors
opened and two men climbed down, wearing shabby raincoats and
straw hats.

"Time to kick ass," Frank said, with clear satisfaction. Pulling on
his shiny black plastic rainhat, thus completing once again his Kabuki
demon costume, he kicked open the Land-Rover's door, splashed out
into the mud, and stood with arms akimbo in the very ideogram of
rage as the second truck wheezed and sagged around in a great semicir-
cle and came to a stop beside its brother.

Ellen also climbed out of the Land-Rover, wearing her red rainhat
and dark-blue raincoat and faded blue jeans and black knee-high boots,
and heard the two men in the straw hats jabber away at Frank in
Swahili. "Ah, shut up," he told them, and called across the Land-
Rover's hood at Ellen, "The stupid bastards won't learn English!"

"Very good English," one of the men said indignantly.

"Then *talk* English," Frank told him.

The man hesitated, frowning mightily, apparently having thoughts
about his dignity; then he rattled off some more words in Swahili.

"Shit," Frank answered, and turned to the two men who had
emerged from the other truck, one of whom was Charlie. "Where've
you been, you guttersnipe?"

"Oh, it's a very heavy load completely," Charlie said. He was the
only one present not dressed for the weather, and already his filthy
white shirt and baggy black trousers were soaked and clinging to him.
He seemed neither to notice nor care.

"Double shit," Frank commented. "You gonna go to work now?"

"Absolutely," Charlie said, and turned to speak Swahili to the three
other men, all of whom answered at the same time, each obviously
pleading his own special case. Charlie went on blandly talking through
their answers, and Frank turned away, shaking his head in disgust.
"Come on down to the lake," he called to Ellen, who was still standing
on the other side of the Land-Rover, "before I forget myself and stomp
these clowns into the turf."

They walked down the slope together in the rain, their hands in their raincoat pockets. Pulled up on the bank were several long narrow rowboats, brightly colored, most with a flat board at the back for mounting an outboard motor. Ellen said, "This is your natural harbor?"

"Sure." He waved an arm away toward the right. "Berkeley Bay in there." Jutting his chin forward, he said, "That's Uganda."

Straight ahead, a low hill rose out of the water, surprisingly close, looking like an island. Flying over Uganda with Frank, back when Lew was captured, Ellen had had no particular feelings about the land itself, but now that dark featureless hill in the rain, looming up out of the water, did bear an aura of menace. "It doesn't look pleasant," she said, and shivered inside the coat.

"The funny thing is," Frank said, "it *is* pleasant. The land, I mean. It's the lushest, richest part of the entire continent of Africa. Stanley said Uganda was the pearl of Africa."

"A pearl with a curse on it," Ellen said, and Frank laughed. Then he said, "You want another quote? This is from Sir John Gray, used to be Chief Justice in Uganda when the British had it. He said the history of Uganda is 'a crime to which there have been no eyewitnesses.' "

"But if the land is so rich—"

"Only man is vile."

Ellen turned away from that low hill across the water and looked back upslope, where Charlie and the other three men had pulled the tarpaulins off one of the trucks and had started to unload masses of concrete blocks by the simple method of standing up on top of the load and tossing them down into a messy muddy pile. When they landed on one another they chipped and broke, but the men didn't seem to mind. Ellen said, "What's that all about, anyway?"

"The hotel," Frank said, grinning with another secret joke.

"Hotel? Here?" She looked down at the shoreline, which was mud and weeds and grass; hardly a tourist's beach.

"Sure," Frank said. "Regional development. Build the joint up. Next thing you know, you got Elizabeth Taylor and Bianca Jagger dropping in. *Paparazzi* at Port Victoria."

Ellen laughed at the idea, then said, "Come on, Frank. What's up?"

"Balim had a little chat," Frank said, rubbing his thumb and the side of his first finger together in the universal sign language for a bribe's being passed, "with a fellow at the Ministry of Tourism and Wildlife."

"The Ministry of *what?*"

"Have I ever lied to you?"

"Probably," Ellen said. "Is there really a Ministry of Tourism and Wildlife?"

"Sure. Think about it; you'll see it makes sense. When the tourists come to Kenya, it's to see the wildlife."

"Not much wildlife around here," Ellen said, glancing around again, "apart from Charlie."

"*Look* at those idiots," Frank said. Crack, crack, the concrete blocks were bouncing off one another.

"Frank, why a hotel?"

"Okay." Looking away toward Uganda, he said, "When this fucking rain stops, we're gonna go over there and get ourselves several *tons* of coffee. We're gonna need boats to ship it over here. We're gonna need trucks to get it to the plantation."

"The Jhosi plantation," Ellen said, with a sudden surprising spasm of misery.

"Right," Frank said, not noticing. "We're gonna need work crews here to load and unload. We're probably gonna need storage facilities, because the coffee'll come in quicker than we can truck it out. Now, you see what this town looks like. How much traffic you think they get on that road, the average day?"

"Not much." Coming in, they'd met that one blue bus, and had seen three men riding bicycles laden down with huge burlap sacks; Frank had said those were smugglers.

"That's right. Sometimes a truck or two, even a legitimate delivery to the market. But not heavy traffic. A lot of smuggling goes through here, but it's all small-time."

"Of course."

"Now," Frank said, "not everybody on this old planet is as easy-going as you and me. Here and there you've got busybodies. Here and there you've got people who might even rat to the cops when they see something they don't understand."

"I'm beginning to get the picture," Ellen said.

"For the next couple months," Frank told her, "there'll be trucks going in and out of here every day. There'll be work crews. There'll be construction materials, including all the wood we'll need to make the rafts to bring the coffee over. There'll be storage facilities."

"But at the end," Ellen pointed out, "there will be a completely useless hotel."

"Paid for by international development funds."

"Oh. I see."

"Cute, huh?"

Ellen nodded. "Balim is very very clever, isn't he?"

"Balim is a fucking genius," Frank said.

*　　*　　*

The only fly in the ointment, Frank explained, was that he was going to have to spend a lot of time here, making sure the work was done right, the supplies weren't stolen, and the truth about their plans didn't come out prematurely. "Originally I'd figured Lew for this job," he explained, shaking his head in disgust, "but I got to admit I'm the one to do it. I know how to deal with these Bantus."

Yes, Ellen thought, the white man's method. Kick ass. Yell, scream, get red in the face. And on his side, the native smiles and nods and works as slowly as possible and pretends to be stupid, and all the time he's robbing you blind. And both sides are satisfied with the arrangement.

"The worst of it is," Frank was saying, "I can't be too visible here, because I'm white. Some son of a bitch'll tell the police at Kakamega there's a white man hanging around Port Victoria, and we're screwed. So I'm gonna have to camp out."

"Camp out? In a tent?"

"Yup. That's why I came out today, to pick the site. Up in the hills there. If I leave it to Charlie, he'll pitch the fucking tent on a scorpion's nest. And if I live through it, he'll act stupid, like it was a mistake."

"I was just thinking the same thing," Ellen said.

"Come on for a hike."

They walked back up from the lakeshore through the unending rain, and Frank spent a useless moment by the trucks yelling at Charlie about breakage. Then they walked on, diagonally away from the village, up a steep rocky slope covered with gnarled low shrubs and stubbly green new growth. Bony trees were farther up toward the ridge.

Looking back, Ellen saw two small boats approaching the shore near where they'd been standing, each carrying two men and several lumpy sacks. The sound of their outboard motors was obliterated by the rain. Smugglers, probably; no, certainly.

The steep hill made for hard climbing, particularly since both the mud and the rocks were slippery under their boots. Concentrating on the climb, they spoke no more until they reached the ridge and had started down the much gentler slope on the other side. Perhaps because of the earlier mention of the Jhosi plantation, during the silent walk uphill Ellen brooded on her problems for almost the first time since leaving Kisumu, and after they'd reached the top she astonished herself, as they walked along on the nearly level land, by suddenly saying, "Frank, do you know that Lew's having an affair?"

He frowned at her, uncomprehending. "With you," he said.

"No, with somebody else."

"Greedy bastard."

The phrase made her believe Frank really did know nothing about it, so she said nothing more. They walked along, Frank glowering out ahead of them, apparently thinking about nothing but the right place to pitch his tent, until he looked at her again and said, "Who's the lucky girl?"

"It doesn't matter."

He stopped entirely. "Listen," he said. "Are you one hundred percent sure?"

"Of course not. Nobody is until the other person suddenly tells you. And the other person always does suddenly tell you."

"People are shits," Frank said.

"True. I was hoping you could confirm or deny."

"Lew doesn't confide in me," Frank said. "Not that kind of thing, anyway. He'd be afraid I'd go sniffing after you myself."

"He'd be right," she said, smiling despite herself.

He held a hand up, dangling it from the wrist as though broken. "I got burned once."

"Oh, it wasn't that bad." Not liking the way the conversation was tending, she looked around and said, "How about over there? For your tent."

He stared in the direction she was pointing. "Where?"

"There, where the land rises a little."

They walked over to the spot, a low knob or mound, overgrown with weeds and shrubs but treeless. The bony trees were all around, like layers of barbed wire protecting this hillock. Neither the town nor the lake could be seen. "Possible," Frank said. "Very very possible."

"It'll be drier than the land around it, but still protected."

"Sure." Frank turned in a great circle, looking at the view without delight. "Home sweet home," he said. "Jesus. In some previous life I must have been one hell of a villain."

21

Lew was at the wheel of the Morris Minor, in the rain, with Ellen in the passenger seat beside him, on their way to Balim's office. And it was at the corner, barely half a block from their house, that he saw the gray Citroën parked on the verge and knew at once it was Amarda Jhosi's car.

Amarda herself was behind the wheel; he saw her smile through the rain-streaming window as he drove by. Had Ellen seen? Glancing at her, he saw she was looking for something in her shoulder bag.

Driving on, he experienced a sudden surge of erotic memory. The second trip to Nairobi in particular came back to him with the force of hypnotic suggestion. That was the time Balim had not come along, and Amarda had met him in that same Citroën. "I just have something to pick up at a friend's house," she'd said as they'd driven away from the airport (and Ellen). "It isn't out of the way." The friend, of course, had not been at home, and when Amarda had said, "You might as well come in," the radiance of her smile had answered all his questions. She was the round-breasted Indian Princess, slowly smiling, soft and young and very willing to learn.

The third time, with Balim along, the connection with Amarda had been more hurried, more guilty, less ecstatic; but still he had followed her eagerly into the storage shed behind her house, rolling with her on the rough burlap sacks, surrounded by the clatter of the rain.

There had been no more trips to Nairobi, which was just as well. Amarda was wonderfully enjoyable, but she was also dangerous, and while she had asked for nothing, he couldn't help the guilty feeling that he had taken her gift somehow under false pretenses. It was better to let the affair die from inanition.

But now Amarda was *here*, in Kisumu, smiling at him half a block from the home he shared with Ellen. Do we really have to pay for our falls from grace, every single one? *I don't want to lose Ellen*, he thought, and glanced at her profile beside him in the car. It was probably just his imagination, but she looked awfully stony.

* * *

Lew had to struggle to keep his mind on what Balim and Isaac Otera were saying. The railroad that came to Kisumu, they told him, was not the main line it had once been. The true main line now angled northward at Nakuru, then ran west into Uganda, leaving the much-struggled-for track to Kisumu nothing but a branch. This branch had been more recently extended northwestward, paralleling the lakeshore but running farther inland, and terminating at Butere, thirty miles away.

It now appeared that at some time in the last two weeks a shipment of sewing machines—fifty-seven machines, crated separately, from Japan—that should have been delivered to Balim here in Kisumu had unaccountably not been offloaded from the freight train and had wound up in the terminus at Butere. "Now," Isaac said, showing his annoyance by shuffling the various documents and manifests and flimsies in his lap, "some railway officials in Butere are making trouble."

With his sad smile, the smile suggesting that yet again the human race had justified his worst suspicions, Balim said, "It's a bribe they want, of course. *Chai.* The questions are: first, How much? and second, To whom? It is one of those moments, my dear Lew, that call for a firm hand and a white face."

Lew grinned, trying to appreciate Balim's humor and stop thinking about Amarda *here in Kisumu.* Did she mean to talk to Ellen? What was going to happen? He said, "I've got the idea." To Isaac he said, "Do we have a name?"

"Two names." Isaac extended a small sheet of paper marked in blue ink with his small neat handwriting. "One is Kamau Nyaga, who calls himself assistant terminal manager. I phoned a railway friend in Nakuru, and at the moment the manager's position at Butere is unfilled, so this fellow is making hay while the sun shines."

Balim chuckled. "An odd metaphor, under the circumstances," he said, with a nod toward the windows, against which the rain was streaming.

"Lew knows what I mean," Isaac said, at his prissiest.

"Yes, I do." But, he thought, what does *Amarda* mean?

"The other," Isaac went on, "is called Godfrey Juma. He is freightmaster and has been there for a very long time."

"We have bribed him before," Balim said drily. "That is, Frank has. You can give him Frank's best."

"I will."

"Unfortunately," Isaac said, "we cannot tell from here which of these two has authority, or even the physical control of the shipment."

"We don't," Balim pointed out, "wish to bribe the wrong person."

"I see that," Lew said.

"It's as bad as having two women," Isaac said with a sigh.

Lew peered sharply at him; had he meant something by that? But Isaac's face was as open and innocent and humorless as ever. Feeling grim, Lew got to his feet, saying, "I'll see what I can do."

"Merely do your best," Balim suggested. "Romance them both, but only plight your troth with one."

Oh, for God's sake. "That's what I'll do, then," Lew said, and got out of there before they could drive him any more crazy.

* * *

The gray Citroën was in his rearview mirror, beyond the rain-running back window. Being on a mission where face was of importance, Lew had been given one of Balim's better cars, an almost undented black Peugeot. He had barely steered it out of town, heading northwest through the rain on the B1, when the gray Citroën appeared behind him.

He didn't notice it at first, because he'd been thinking about Ellen.

Was it possible for a woman to clench her lips? Leaving Balim's building, going out to the rain and the Peugeot and the uncertainties of both Butere and Amarda, Lew had kissed Ellen good-bye, and it had seemed to him that her lips were harder than usual; corrugated, almost. Or was that merely paranoia? Or guilt? "Shit," he said out loud, driving along, and that was when he glanced in the rearview mirror and saw the Citroën.

His first impulse was to hit the accelerator, but of course he couldn't do that. Nor could he hit the brake and stop, not here on the main road out of Kisumu. So he kept driving until he reached Kisiani, where he took the small unpaved turnoff to the left. Not far out of town he found a place where farm vehicles had beaten a path in to the right past a cluster of trees. He made the turn, jounced around behind the trees, and stopped.

The Citroën was huge in his mirror, like a brooding shark. Lew stepped quickly out into the rain, wanting the meeting to take place in her car, not his.

"Surprised?" she said, smiling at him in uncomplicated happiness as he slid into the Citroën.

"More than I can say." Slamming the car door, he took her in his arms and kissed her; not because he wanted to, but because he knew very well it was what he was supposed to do.

But then he did want to.

*   *   *

It was in the role of hero that he had first met her. He was the hero and she the damsel in distress. He was the handsome stranger and she the beautiful virgin in the bosom of her family. He was Lochinvar and she— Except that, in the poem, Lochinvar's damsel was named Ellen.

His own Ellen had seemed an irrelevancy then, not mentioned in sagas. But she did exist, the outer world did exist, and the wall he'd built between reality and fantasy had crumbled this morning when he'd first seen Amarda's car half a block from his house. The damsel in distress doesn't drive two hundred miles to get laid.

In the Citroën now, sex finished, the beast slaughtered yet again, the two of them sprawling on bedlike reclining seats, it was possible at last for Lew to move in the direction of rational thought. So far from being a helpless orphan, Amarda at twenty was a grown woman capable of getting what she wanted out of this world. How much did she want Lew, and for how long? How much trouble did she want to make? What did she intend to do about Ellen?

The Citroën was like some cave on an asteroid somewhere. The interior was very warm now, the windows completely steamed over, and the rain—filtered through tree branches—thudded erratically on the roof. In this setting, the girl naked and luscious beside him, Lew set out to end the relationship. "Um," he said.

"Don't say anything." Her murmuring voice was languorous with the satisfaction. Her small warm hand traveled slowly down across his chest and belly.

"Um!" He sat up, turning away from her hand, trying desperately to think of something to say. "What time is it?"

"The clock works." Her rejected hand, not seeming to mind, gestured idly toward the dashboard.

He barely looked at the thing. The point wasn't the time but his reaction to time. "I've got so much to do today," he said.

"Mmmmmmmmm."

Dear Lord. He risked a look at her; how could he give that up? Almost without his collaboration, his hand stole forward to touch that breast. "You are something," he said.

But then all at once *she* was brisk, sitting up, stretching—he held the bowl of her belly and dreamed he'd live in the cave forever— saying, "It *is* late. I have to get back; I have to see Mr. Balim."

Cold reality. Drawing back his hand, hunching himself protectively over his lifted knees, he said, "Balim? What for?"

"That's why I'm here." She leaned forward to pull a box of tissues from the shelf under the dashboard, then looked back with her sunniest smile. "Aren't I clever?"

"I'm sure you are."

Cleaning herself like a cat, she said, "My grandmother had more questions. Also bills to be paid, extra expenses. I convinced her I should drive here today, much better than asking poor Mr. Balim to fly to us every time."

"Of course."

"You make me so messy," she said comfortably, balling up tissues.

Her grin when she looked sidelong at him was filled with the innocence and freshness that made him her fool. "I wanted to see you on your home ground."

"Am I different?"

"Sadder, I think. I don't know why."

"Ellen," he said, forcing the name out before he could stop himself. He *had* to bring this to an end, no matter what his body wanted.

She looked first startled, then hurt, as though he had betrayed some pact between them. "Oh, dear," she said.

"I don't want to lose Ellen," he said. "But I don't want to hurt you."

"And you think it has to be one or the other."

"Sometimes I think it'll be both."

Turning away, she rubbed a small circle in the steam of the side window so she could peer out at rain-soaked farm fields. "Ellen is very beautiful."

"That isn't—"

"And very sophisticated." Amarda turned back to him, an intelligent, wistful child. "She is very exciting," she said, "and *you* are very exciting."

"Amarda, don't—"

She put her hand over his mouth, to silence him. It was the hand she'd used to clear the steam from the window, and it was cold and damp. She said, "Lew, please. Wait. Do you have any idea what my life is like?"

That stopped him. Had he ever wondered about that? When Amarda was not imprisoned in the tower in his mind, what *was* her life like? She took her hand back from his mouth, but he didn't speak.

She said, "We're poor people, who were rich. I was born in Africa, but I'm a foreigner. Even if there were Bantus in whom I was interested—and there are not—I would not be permitted to become friends with them. And they could only want me to humiliate and cheat."

"Class," he said, floundering. "Other people, other—" His hands made vague gestures.

"—Indians," she finished for him. Her eyes burned with an intensity he hadn't known she possessed. She said, "Three generations of Africa have emasculated our men. You see them on the streets in

Nairobi and Mombasa, narrow boys in fancy silk shirts, buying and selling cheap cars and cameras. I shall inherit land; the family will survive; we won't always be poor. Those boys would love to court me, give me rides on their motorcycles, marry me, take my land, give me babies, and forget me." She shrugged, a very bitter gesture. "One day, that's what will happen."

Thinking of Young Mr. Balim, knowing she had told him the truth, he still tried to deny it, saying, "That doesn't have to—"

"But it does." Now she looked at him as though *he* were the child. "What do you think? Shall I go to London, walk along Sloane Street, be discovered for the fashion magazines? Shall I return to India, a land even my *father* wasn't born in, and find hundreds of lovely friends, thousands of eligible suitors?"

"Oh, Amarda." He couldn't even argue anymore.

More softly, resting her hand gently on his, she said, "Lew, don't you know how exciting you are to me? There in my kitchen, with your breezy manner of adventure and derring-do, and even a thrilling suggestion of crime in the background. Not some awful crime like murder, but a thrilling crime: smuggling, piracy. Lew, you were the only hero I'd ever met."

They'd *shared* the fantasy! "Oh, Jesus," he said, wanting merely to undo everything. After all, she really was the waif, and she did need his protection. And he had no solution for her. He wasn't a hero, he was a fraud.

She said, "Lew, I know you're not *my* hero. We can just pretend for a little while, and then you'll go back to your airwoman."

He shook his head, eyes downcast. "I'm sorry."

"I'm not." Her more impish smile showed now, the way she'd smiled while taking him into the empty borrowed house. "It's wonderful with you," she said.

"And with you."

She leaned forward to kiss him, very chastely, closed lips to closed lips. "Next time in Nairobi," she whispered.

Next time. Why was he so weak? Why couldn't he stand up and say *no* like the hero she claimed he was? "All right," he said.

* * *

Her fragrance filled the Peugeot because it was on his body. He drove north, switching to the B8 at Luanda (where Frank and Ellen had taken the road the other way, to Port Victoria), and arrived at Butere shortly before two o'clock. The railroad station, a small brick colonial reminder, was a very sleepy place, with a dozen skinny ragged men snoozing or smoking in the dank waiting room, away from the rain.

He found Kamau Nyaga, the assistant terminal manager, in his office. Nyaga was a short and stocky man with a thick moustache and large black-rimmed glasses. He had the pouty expression of the petty tyrant, and at first he apparently thought he would play the game of making Lew wait.

No, he would not. Lew didn't have Frank's hearty bonhomie with these minor-league pests, that palsy shoulder pat of friendship which nevertheless implied the punch of punishment. What Lew had instead was an undisguised contempt, suggesting a barely restrained rage at the shabbiness and venality around him. If the minor officials went along with Frank because they wanted him to remain friendly, they went along with Lew because they didn't want him to go crazy.

Nyaga pretended to read documents while Lew stood across the desk from him. Lew counted privately to three—not very slowly—then leaned forward, resting his palm and splayed fingers on the paper Nyaga was perusing, and said, "I'm here for Mazar Balim's sewing machines."

"Sewing machines?" Not yet intimidated, merely indignant, Nyaga reared back in his squeaking chair and glared. "Who do you happen to be?"

"The representative of the owner. You were told I was coming." Picking up the handful of documents from the desk, Lew flipped through them, saying, "These aren't about our sewing machines."

Nyaga was on his feet; he was squawking like a rooster. "Privileged documents! You can't—! Unauthorized—!"

The terminal manager's was a very small office; still, Lew gave it the most dramatic gesture the space would permit, flinging his right arm out, hurling the handful of papers with disdain at the side wall. As they fluttered to the ground, he said, "I'm here for sewing machines."

Nyaga was looking everywhere at once: at Lew, at his denuded desk, at the open door (to cry for help from the layabouts outside?), at the crumpled papers on the floor. "This office," he managed to say, his voice trembling with emotion, "is for railway business. It is not for rowdies and—and—and—crazy persons."

"I understand there will be," Lew said, his manner still contemptuous but now less threatening, "certain storage charges." Looking around, he found the room's second chair in the corner behind the door, and dragged it over with his foot hooked in a rung.

"Charges," Nyaga said, as though coming to consciousness after having been stunned with a brick. "Yes, of course. Property cannot be stored for free." When Lew sat down, Nyaga returned to his squeaking swivel chair behind the desk.

Lew said, "Mr. Balim has obtained a legal opinion that the railway should pay us interest on the money lost because of the delays in this shipment."

That statement was banal and stupid enough to reassure Nyaga, who actually smiled in response, saying, "To resolve that question in court obviously would involve even more delay."

"Mr. Balim would prefer not to cause trouble." Lew shrugged and curled his lip to make clear his own quite different preference. "He is prepared to pay reasonable storage charges."

"He is a businessman," Nyaga said in a relieved tone. Opening and shutting desk drawers, he muttered, "Storage charges, storage charges . . ."

"Are the sewing machines still in the same freight car?"

Nyaga stopped. He blinked, and licked his lips. "Goods wagon?" he asked. "Well, no. But reloading is not a problem." He busied himself again with his desk drawers.

"Where are they?"

"Not a problem at all."

"Where are they stored?"

"Well, here. Of course here. Here at the railway station. Ah, this is the proper form." He brought up a pad of receipt flimsies and began to insert several well-used sheets of carbon paper. "Let's see, storage nine days—"

Lew said, "I'll want to check the machines, of course, be sure they haven't been damaged."

"Yes, yes. First we deal with the storage charges, and then—"

"You don't know where they are," Lew said.

Nyaga gaped at him. "I beg your pardon?"

"You don't know where the sewing machines are!"

Lew jumped to his feet, the wooden chair tipping over behind him,

Nyaga blinking up at him through his black-rimmed glasses. "You goddam fraud," Lew told him, "you were gonna collect your *storage charge* and then send me out to Juma!"

"Juma? Juma?" Nyaga couldn't seem to figure out any response other than faked indignation. "Who is this Juma?"

"Your *freightmaster*, you fucking asshole!" Lew pointed a rigid finger at the astonished Nyaga's nose. "If you come out of this office, I'll wring your neck like a chicken."

Leaving, he slammed the door so hard everybody in the waiting room woke up.

* * *

Godfrey Juma was a different kettle of fish, an older, grizzled, no-nonsense sort of man, who took *chai* when it came his way because bribery was part of the world order, but who nevertheless found pride and dignity in knowing his job and doing it well.

Unfortunately, he didn't know where the sewing machines were, either. "Believe me, sir, I would be happy to take your money," he told Lew, the two of them standing under the corrugated roof out of the rain at the end of the platform, with various pieces of rolling stock on the several tracks beyond. "But as it happens, the crates were stolen."

Truly irritated, Lew said, "Stolen! How? When? Why didn't somebody report it?"

Juma pointed. "Sir, do you see that goods wagon?"

The freight car in question was new, silver-sided, with the slanted red KR of Kenya Railways. "I see it," Lew said. He was about to become dangerous.

"Your shipment arrived in that wagon. I at once saw it had not been consigned to this station, and so I had it shunted onto that track to await further instructions."

"Yes?"

"During my period of being off-duty," Juma said, "our terminal manager—"

"Nyaga." Were he to look over his shoulder, Lew knew, he would see the round-eyed, round-mouthed, round-spectacled face of assistant terminal manager Kamau Nyaga peering through his rain-bleared window, like a squirrel waiting for the dogs to pass.

"That is the man." Juma nodded, his expression carefully neutral.

"For greater safekeeping," he said, "or so he claimed, Mr. Nyaga had the crates removed, you know, to that shed." He pointed to a small corrugated-metal building surrounded by weeds, off to one side of the yard.

"Yes?"

"I feared they would *not* be so safe in that location, so I did instruct my crew to return them to the goods wagon. Somewhere in the process, then or later, very distressingly, they disappeared. I believe they were Mr. Nyaga's responsibility at the time of disappearance."

Lew nodded. "And he blames you."

"Sir, I'm afraid that is so."

Except that the goddam sewing machines were gone, it was a comic situation. The two bosses, knowing there was money to be made out of that shipment, stealing it back and forth from each other until some third party—or possibly either Juma or Nyaga himself—retired the booty from the game. Being tough, but not physically threatening, Lew said, "The railway committee of inquiry will certainly figure out who's responsible."

"Committee of inquiry?" Juma took on the worried look of an aging man thinking about his pension. "Why would there be a committee of inquiry? There are railroad-yard thefts every day."

"Mr. Balim is insured," Lew lied. "The insurance company will insist on an inquiry."

"Oh, the insurance company." Juma looked more and more worried. An insurance company was a much more serious threat than some minor Asian merchant.

Lew said, "Frankly, I suspect the committee of inquiry will find reasons to be displeased with *both* you and Mr. Nyaga."

"Unjust interpretations, you know, sir," Juma said, scraping his work-roughened hand over his grizzled cheeks, "could of course be made against my actions. Believe me, sir, if I could hand over those sewing machines, I would, and charge you nothing for them."

"I don't like to see an older man driven out of his job," Lew said. "Do you suppose Nyaga knows more than he's telling?"

"I wish he did, sir." Juma shrugged fatalistically. "But I'm afraid he is the victim in this case as much as I."

Lew had pressed as hard as he could, and nothing had come of it.

Juma couldn't help him; Lew had no doubt the man would if he could. Was it worthwhile to roust Nyaga again, go back into that office and rough him up a little? No; Juma's reluctant exoneration of Nyaga had been an expert's opinion.

While Lew had been thinking things over, Juma had been staring out mournfully over his small messy rusty freight yard, as though seeing it for the last time. Now, suddenly enlivened, magically taller, more sure of himself, with the fresh gleam of hope in his eyes, he spun back to Lew and said, "Sir! Perhaps after all there is a way out."

"Yes?"

"Come with me, sir."

Juma led the way down the concrete steps at the end of the platform and out across the freight yard in the rain. They had to step high over the rails, skirt the larger and dirtier puddles, place their feet carefully on the rain-slick metal ties, hunch their necks down into their collars to keep the droplets from slithering in.

At the extreme far corner of the yard, near the tall barbed-wire-topped fence, stood one of the older freight cars; peeling maroon paint and the old multicolored seal of the East African Railways Corporation. Undoing two large padlocks, Juma pushed open the side door and said, "There."

The wooden floor of the car was at chest height. Looking in, Lew could see stacked large crates—somewhat shorter than coffins—covered with stencils and pasted-on travel documents. "What is it?"

"Outboard motors. Sir, see for yourself."

They climbed up the metal rungs into the cool but dry car, and Juma used a large screwdriver from his hip pocket to pry the lid off one of the crates. Inside, nested in Styrofoam and wrapped in grayish clear plastic, lay a 120-horsepower Evinrude outboard motor, gleaming in orange and white and black enamel, its small fanlike propeller painted a dull green.

"There are forty of them." Juma said. "Worth more than fifty-seven sewing machines."

Considerably more. Lew said, "You're suggesting a trade?"

"A goods train is being made up this afternoon, to return to Nakuru," Juma said. "I can put this car on it, assigned to Kisumu. Mr. Nyaga knows nothing of this shipment, sir."

"Ah-hah."

"I shall telephone to my friend Mr. Molu in the Kisumu freight office, and he will understand that you shall be picking up the shipment on behalf of its consignee."

"Who is this consignee? Who do these motors belong to?"

"Oh, no one, sir," Juma said. "An Asian, sir, you know, that sort of bad man. He was going to use these engines in his smuggling, you know, on Lake Victoria."

"Oh, yes? What's this Asian's name?"

"Hassanali."

Lew remembered having heard Balim speak disparagingly once or twice about a man named Hassanali, an out-and-out crook, a man who made a practice of sailing too close to the wind. "What happened to him?"

"Oh, he killed a boatman, sir, who had cheated him. You know there is no honor completely among those thieves, sir. The police have got him now."

"So he has other things to worry about than his outboard motors."

"Oh, yes, sir." Patting the sleek flank of the exposed motor, Juma said, "You can rescue these beautiful machines from a life of crime, sir."

"Save them from being used in smuggling," Lew said, and laughed, feeling better than he had in days. There was nothing like absurdity to put things back in proportion. Even Amarda would pass. "Come along, Mr. Juma," Lew said. "We'll have tea and talk this over."

22

There are spirits in the air, and in the ground, and inside trees, who make it their business to call human beings to their deaths. This is why, when a male child is born in many African tribes, he is not initially given his true name, but is lent a temporary false appellation to confuse the spirits of death. Should the child survive his first few years—and most do not, despite this subterfuge—he is given his permanent name.

But even this is not his *real* name. That he selects for himself at puberty, and will probably never tell anyone. Thus the African travels under an alias at all times, secure in the knowledge that *nobody knows who he really is*.

However, the process of naming has two further ramifications. The African may privately rename those persons who are important in his life; this secret name, which he will not tell the person thus dubbed, gives him an important power over that person. And of course when traveling among people other than one's own tribe, one permits these strangers to cloak one with some nonsense syllable or other, to be shrugged off once the foreign travel is complete.

So Charlie's name was not Charlie. That was merely the bark he responded to when among the animals; that is, persons who were not Kikuyu. His death-fooling temporary name was long in the past, his permanent name was spoken exclusively by members of his branch of the Kikuyu in the villages along the western scarp of the Narandarua Range, and his real name was known only to himself.

Among the animals, the only one so far honored with a name by Charlie was Frank. Charlie had named him Mguu, and it gave him secret pleasure every time he saw the man to know that he alone knew this was Mguu. The name was from the Swahili—Mguu was not worth a name from Charlie's native Kikuyu dialect—and means "foot." It seemed to Charlie that *foot* expressed Mguu very well; his stamping around like an elephant, his roaring, his rushing into situations without thought or preparation. Also, Charlie had seen in the cinema cartoons about a blind white man named Mr. Magoo, and this seemed to add a proper dimension: Mguu, the blind foot.

*   *   *

Late afternoon. During a pause in the rain, Mguu left his tent and crossed the clearing to where Charlie squatted, skinning a not-quite-dead gazelle. "Charlie," Mguu said.

Charlie stood, smiling his cheeriest smile, the red knife in his red hand. Mguu pointed at it. "Put that down."

"Oh, sure, Frank." Negligently Charlie stuck the knife into the gazelle, which in gratitude expired. "What may I do?"

"It was only a joke," Mguu said, his expression mean. "I know that, Charlie."

Charlie looked alert, inquisitive, ready to help. He wiped his bloody hand on his shirtfront.

"But," Mguu went on, "the joke's over. So now one of two things is gonna happen. Either you'll give me back my malaria pills, or I'll twist your scrawny neck, leave your body here and your head over there, and drive back to Kisumu for a fresh supply of pills."

Behind Charlie's bland smile and gleaming eyes, the speedy brain buzzed, till all at once the smile blossomed into a tooth-baring, hearty, friendly laugh, and Charlie said, "A joke! That's right, that's right, Frank, I can never put anything over on you!"

"That's right," Mguu said.

The westward sky, over the lake and under the clouds, was gossamer-white and pale blue, descending to lavender at the watery horizon, with an undercoating of gold. Charlie and Mguu walked out across the scrubland, some distance from camp, before Charlie shinnied up a flat-topped tree, causing a white-winged bateleur eagle to rise skyward in heavy flapping irritation. Riffling through the dry ordure of the eagle's nest, Charlie grasped what he was looking for and descended with the bottle intact, which he plunked with the pride of the successful hunter into Mguu's palm.

In the lengthening shadows Mguu looked back toward camp, then up at the nest in the tree. "Some hiding place for a joke," he said.

Flying insects were beginning to swarm, including no doubt some of the thirty-eight varieties of mosquito which carry malaria in this part of the world. "If a thing is worth doing," Charlie said, "it's worth doing well."

* * *

Early next morning, Charlie and Mguu came down the hill in a fresh downpour, paused at the hotel construction site so Mguu could shout and puff and wave his arms at the men digging the hole for the footing, and then they gathered the drunken boatman and putt-putted across the mouth of Berkeley Bay and past Sigulu Island, and so out across Lake Victoria, now well within the territory of Uganda. The gentle rain slackened and after a while stopped; looking back, Charlie could see it still falling upon Kenya.

The last time they had come to the landfall at Macdonald Bay, Charlie and Mguu and the boatman had built a blind to conceal the two mopeds. It had not been disturbed, and the mopeds were still there, though wet and rusty. It was not raining at this moment, but it had done so recently, and everything in the woods was wet. Mguu refueled the mopeds from the can in the boat, and when they started the engines the racket seemed to shiver the raindrops off the leaves.

Yesterday afternoon, a truck carrying Michelin tires had crossed from Kenya into Uganda at Moroto, far to the north of here. The border guards who had been bribed there by the driver to permit him to bring in this illegal shipment without filling in the required forms or paying the usual taxes and fees had been led to believe this was merely a normal smuggling operation, tires bound for Masindi, a prosperous upland town to the west of Lake Kyoga. They had been unaware that in the hollow center of the stacks of tires there were seated four men, hired by Mazar Balim with the assistance of Lew Brady. The four men had track gang experience with Kenya Railways, and they were traveling with a variety of tools: shovels and prybars and wrenches and sledgehammers. They also shared their hiding place with bedrolls and several cartons of tinned or packaged food.

Last night the truck, having followed back roads southward past Lake Opeta and Mount Elgon, had eventually reached the spot on the Tororo-Kampala road where Lew had been arrested by the State Research Bureau men. There, under cover of darkness, the truck had been driven as far as possible down the old service road and the laborers had emerged from their cocoon of tires to carry their tools and provisions down to Maintenance Depot Number 4. And now this morning Charlie and Mguu were coming to the depot to give the men their instructions.

The four were lolling at their ease inside the engine shed. What work they had done so far was in the realm of housekeeping; they'd cleared some of the rusted garbage into far corners of the shed, blocked two broken windows with old sheets of corrugated metal, and created a fireplace of rocks beneath another window, which would serve as a rough-and-ready flue. They had surely heard the roar of the arriving mopeds, but they were still lying around their small fire, telling lies and laughing, when Charlie and Mguu walked in.

Mguu began by carrying on about the fire. Charlie was supposed to translate—into Swahili, as only two of the men were Kikuyu, the others being animals—but instead he said to Mguu, "These men know about smoke completely, Frank. There are farms all around here; the farmers light fires in their fields; no one will think about a little smoke."

That calmed Mguu, though he did stay grumpy. He ordered the laborers to rise and follow him outside, where, with much arm waving and kicking at the rusted rails stacked beside the shed, he explained what they were supposed to do. Charlie translated, interpolating asides that made the laborers bite their cheeks to keep from laughing.

Yes, they understood. Yes, they saw that the turntable must be moved to align with the track. Yes, they agreed that the buffer at the end of the track must be removed and the track extended with these rusty rails to the lip of the gorge. Yes, they followed the reasoning behind the idea that they must cut a hole in the thick shrubbery and hedge between the spur track and the main line, but that they then must create a removable blind of branches on some sort of framework to conceal the hole they had made. Yes, they heartily concurred that they must not be caught by the Ugandan police or Army. (If they were caught, however, it wouldn't be a total disaster, since these four hadn't been told the ultimate purpose for their work.) And, at long last, yes, they accepted the deadline of one week. All would be accomplished. And now let us have some beer.

"I don't know about those birds," Mguu said, later that afternoon, as they tromped back to the access road and their mopeds.

"Oh, they'll do very fine," Charlie said. "I vouch for them."

Mguu gave him a hard look. "*You* vouch for them? Jesus."

He prays a lot, Charlie thought.

* * *

The man tried to run away, but Mguu shouted him down. It was a wonderful thing to see, as effective as another man throwing a rock; Charlie much admired it.

They had come out of the woods, and there was the man, poking around their mopeds. Charlie had seen at once that he didn't have the manner of a thief but instead the manner of curiosity. It was only that he tried to run away that made him seem like a thief. And then Mguu roared, and the man dropped, and now he crouched there beside the road, waiting, sitting on his heels, trembling slightly, his head bowed down between his knees.

Charlie and Mguu strode forward and stood over him. Charlie could see he was not Kikuyu, but possibly Luo or some other lake tribe. "Stand up!" Mguu yelled. Charlie repeated that in Swahili, not yelling, and the man slowly uncoiled and stood.

He was a very raggedy man, the kind you would see on construction projects in Nairobi pushing a wheelbarrow full of concrete blocks. His torn clothing was gray; his knobby knees were gray; his bare feet were beige and cut-covered; his hands were swollen from work or disease; the leathery brown skin of his fingers ballooned up around the orange nails.

"Ask him," Mguu said, "what he's doing here."

Charlie asked. The man, sullen but submissive, answered, *"mfupa,"* which means "bone."

"Ah," Charlie said. He had already decided this raggedy man meant nothing. He explained to Mguu, "He says he's a peddler. He buys and sells bones."

Mguu looked startled. "Bones!"

"There's a living for a poor man in bones," Charlie said gently. "And cloth, and other rubbish."

"Oh," Mguu said, in sudden understanding. "A rag-and-bone man. We used to have those in the States."

"Used to have?" Here was another unexpected window into that other world so far away. Charlie was always interested to learn more about that place of fantasy. "*Used* to have, Frank?"

"Nobody does that anymore." Mguu dismissed the idea with his typical curt hand wave, while continuing to glower at the boneman.

"Nobody?" In Charlie's mind loomed an image of the homes of America—they looked like cinema motel rooms—with all the corners piled with unclaimed rubbish. Could that be true? He'd never seen such a thing in the films, but it was well known the cinema lied about real life. If it were really so, what an opportunity for some enterprising boneman!

But Mguu's attention was fixed on this current boneman, who looked not enterprising at all. "There's no bones *here*," he said, angry and dangerous. "What's he doing *here*?"

Charlie put the question. The boneman mumbled something imcomprehensibie, which Charlie translated as "He doesn't know."

"Doesn't know? He damn well better know!"

Charlie rephrased the question. The boneman mumbled more nonsense. Charlie shrugged. "He just doesn't know, Frank."

"He's *going* to know," Mguu said, and before Charlie could blink, Mguu had punched the boneman in the face.

The boneman sat on the vine-covered ground. For an instant, as though all of creation had been startled by Mguu's violence, nothing happened. Charlie, the boneman, Mguu, all three remained unmoving. Then Mguu, opening his punching hand as though it were stiff, said, "Ask him again, Charlie."

Stooping in front of the boneman, Charlie could see that his eyes were turned inward, his jaw muscles were slack, his hands were at ease in his lap. Straightening, Charlie said, "He thinks now about dying."

"A good thing to think about," Mguu said, misunderstanding. "Tell him, he gives me a straight answer or he *is* dead."

"No, Frank," Charlie said. But how to explain what was happening? He had noticed over the years that the whites didn't seem to have this capacity for death that was so natural in the tribal African. In a situation of hopelessness or misery the African, armed with his fatalism, could merely sink into a lassitude and then slip quietly out of existence. It was very well known, but not to the whites.

Or not to most whites; one white doctor to whom Mr. Balim had sent Charlie three years ago had said it was because the tribal Africans were all sick anyway. They all lived with malaria (which infected everybody but only killed one percent of blacks) and several other diseases, against which a certain level of immunity or accommodation had been developed over the millennia. But still their bodies were weakened, and it was easier for them to let loose their grip on the reins of life.

It was an explanation Charlie himself didn't believe—he knew it was merely sensible at some point to die, and the African is sensible— but perhaps it was an explanation that would please Mguu.

No; it was too complicated. Charlie couldn't go through all that. He merely said, "Frank, this is just a poor boneman, looking in the woods for what he can find. He knows no answers at all, and he thinks you'll go on hurting him, so he is thinking about dying to be away from all this."

"What?" Mguu hunkered down to look at that closed-in face, with the eyes like those of an animal caught for too long in a leg trap, no longer struggling, prepared now for death. "Bah," Mguu said, and stood up, brushing his hands on his trousers, looking almost embarrassed. "What a country," he said, and turned away and tramped back toward the mopeds.

But Charlie had kept watching the boneman—had those eyes minutely glistened when Mguu turned away? Charlie frowned, studying that ragged head.

Up the road, Mguu called, "Come on, Charlie!"

Charlie squatted, looking, and the empty eyes looked back. Did or did not something move inside there?

"Charlie!"

It occurred to Charlie he should kill this boneman right away, this instant. But he couldn't kill coldly, like a white man; he had to build a rage first, an emotion for killing.

"God*damm*it, come on!"

Toward Mguu, of course, such an emotion would be easy and very quick to build. Charlie stood, his own mind filling with the fatalism he imputed to the boneman. Either he *was* a boneman, and would matter to them no more, or he was something else, and would return to their lives.

Charlie rejoined Mguu, and they climbed on the mopeds and started for the lake. When Charlie looked back, just before the first curve, the boneman had not moved.

23

Walking down Greek Street at two in the morning, past the all-night sex shops with their white-painted shopwindows and glaring red-lettered signs, Baron Chase was stopped by two weaving, smiling, slender Jamaicans who seemed to be high on dope and not liquor. "Mon," one of them said, "mon, give me a bob."

"Get out of my way," Chase said.

The evening rain had stopped, but the sparkling wet streets remained deserted. The two blocks farther on to Shaftesbury Avenue with its lights and traffic and pedestrians might as well have been two miles; they might as well not be in London at all. The smiling Jamaicans crowded closer, smelling absurdly of coconut, the spokesman saying, "And a bob for my friend, mon, we want an egg."

"If I had you in my country," Chase said, his voice low and compelling, "I would have your ears removed and roasted in the oven and fed you for your dinner."

"What country is that, mon?" the Jamaican asked, giggling as though it were all a joke, as he reached out for Chase's sleeve.

Chase's hand came up, too fast to be seen. The heel thudded upward into the Jamaican's nose, shattering the bone, shoving the splinters up into the man's brain. Dying, his wide eyes already filming, the Jamaican collapsed slowly backward onto the uneven wet slate sidewalk.

The other one ran. He didn't wait to see what happened to his friend nor to find out what Chase meant to do next. He simply spun shakily on his heel, regained his balance, and dashed tottering around the corner of Manette Street and out of sight.

Chase walked on, ignoring the twisted man on the sidewalk, who looked as though he'd been flung there from a truck. *What country is that, mon?* echoed in Chase's ears, and he walked down to Shaftesbury Avenue and turned right toward Piccadilly Circus.

Uganda. Violent Uganda. Depraved Uganda. Horrific Uganda. *My country.* He could feel it repainting him in its own colors; he had to get out.

London seemed so tame. There had been a period in his life when his greatest pleasure was London after dark; so much more accessible than Paris. To walk the streets of Soho and the West End after midnight with his pockets full of pounds, among the prostitutes and the sharp-nosed petty crooks and the innocent schoolboys out on a fling, to choose one's amusements, playing different parts every night; that had been the Technicolor of his existence, and now it had all faded. A few years of *open sesame* at the State Research Bureau—his private nonfaked Madame Tussaud's—had turned the rest of the world pale.

In Piccadilly Circus, the restless motion of the night crawlers still continued, though it was less crowded than it had been at midnight, when he'd last walked through. The puffy-bodied sullen-faced girls in their miniskirts and shoulder-padded jackets and eyes heavily under-lined in black, the skinny awkward long-necked boys in their tight black tubular pants and their sweat shirts reading UNIVERSITY OF MIAMI (bought here in London on Oxford Street), the nervous sagging-bellied older homosexuals stumbling toward the humiliation they half craved and half dreaded, the brassy semipro hookers always in pairs and wearing blond wigs like wood shavings; they all still promenaded, restless and purposeless, their eyes and mouths dissatisfied and guarded against further hurt. The coughing black taxis curved ceaselessly past the statue of Eros in the middle of Piccadilly, heading elsewhere, scooting away, very few with their amber FOR HIRE signs lit; not here.

There was no actual sense of order, but the trend of pedestrian flow was clockwise, echoing the movement of the traffic. Joining the minority that trekked in the opposite direction, Chase studied the faces and the bodies as they came toward him. And this place might as well as be the exercise yard of a concentration camp whose comman-dant, with a more than usually macabre sense of humor, has dressed his charges out of captured theatrical trunks.

What shall I have tonight? What here will best ease for a little while the boredom? The hour was late; the pubs were closed; the air was cold and dank from the earlier rain; the desperation all around was rising closer to the surface; whatever Chase wanted from this chorus line was his for the beckoning.

The fourth time he passed the same pair of boys, painfully thin, dressed almost identically in bulky black cable-knit sweaters and tight blue jeans and cracked cheap "western" boots, their hands and necks gray—not with the dirt of toil but with the grime of sluttishness— he shrugged to himself and nodded to them, then took the next turning at Glasshouse Street, the dark narrow block behind the brightly lighted curve of Regent Street. Glancing back when he reached the far corner, he saw them trailing almost reluctantly after him; smiling, he turned right on Regent Street past the gleaming huge shopwindows filled with clothing to be worn in a world those boys would never know.

He could have anything, anyone, from that sink. His trend increasingly had been to choose boys, but he told himself that meant nothing. Boys were simpler somehow, that's all. And since he never permitted anything to be put into his own body, but only inserted himself into them, he was clearly not homosexual.

Once free of Piccadilly Circus, the empty cabs switched on their FOR HIRE signs; Chase hailed one before he'd walked as far as Beak Street. "One moment," he said to the driver, "for my friends."

The driver, a narrow-faced Jewish Cockney, twisted to look back at the approaching boys. "It's your life, gunnor," he said. "Innit."

"It is." Holding the door open, Chase ushered the now shyly smiling boys into the cab. "Enter my golden coach," he said.

*   *   *

At ten in the morning the hotel-room phone rang. Chase, blurrily waking, fumbled for the receiver, muttered something into it, and heard Emil Grossbarger say, "Zey have brought him back."

Chase's mind was filled with the wisps of dreams, red and black silhouettes fast receding, no longer forming their story, leaving only a faint nervous residue of terror. He had no idea what Grossbarger was talking about. "What? Who?"

"Sir Denis Lambsmitt. Chase, vat do you know of ziss?"

"Lambsmith?" Orienting himself, remembering who and what he was, Chase sat up straighter in the bed. "What do you mean, he's back?"

"I had him removed from ze Uganda negotiation," Grossbarger said. On the phone, one became more aware of the husky power of that voice, still potent with the strength that had been stolen from his body. "Vunce ve made our own arrangement, you und I, my dear Baron, I vished zat man's keen eye removed from ze arena of our activities."

"Yes, yes." Impatient with himself, rubbing his sleep-blurred face with his free hand—smelling faintly of soap from last night's shower, after the boys had been sent away—Chase said, "Who brought him back?"

"Your government. Vy did zey do zat?"

"I have no idea," Chase said, astonished to realize it was the truth. He had not the vaguest idea who in Uganda would have done this, or what they could have had in mind. It was frightening to have such sudden unexpected ignorance about the arena in which he struggled for survival.

"I vant him out of it," Grossbarger said. "Ziss is very important to me."

"I can, um—" Chase shook the sleep webs out of his brain. "We can contain him. I assure you he won't know what's going on."

"I vant him *avay*! Und not killed, zat tips our hand. Out of ze operation *complete*."

In Grossbarger's intensity, Chase found the sudden shocking realization of just why the man was so upset. Yes, and why he had wanted Lambsmith removed in the first place. With hatred at this knowledge welling up inside him, hatred and rage, Chase became calmer, more assured, more hidden. "I'll cut short my vacation, Emil," he said, using the older man's given name for the first time, doing it deliberately, to twist the knife in them both. "I'll go back to Kampala today." He should in any event; clearly, he had been away too long. "I'll find out what's happened."

"Und you *vill* remove Sir Denis Lambsmitt from ziss operation!"

"You have my guarantee."

"Our partnership depends upon it."

Chase cradled the phone and sat a moment longer in bed, brooding at the mirrored bathroom door, in which he could see reflected the room's main window. It wasn't Sir Denis's keenness, the likelihood of his discovering their plot, that was agitating Emil Grossbarger so much; no, not at all. Chase saw through that. The fact was, Emil Grossbarger *liked* Sir Denis Lambsmith, he considered himself Sir Denis Lambsmith's *friend*, he was trying to protect his *friend*, ease his *friend* out of the area of danger.

Who would do that for me?

In Chase's world the evidences of friendship were so few that he almost never had to remember the existence of such a thing. To have it flaunted in his face here and now, under these circumstances, involving two such creatures as Grossbarger and Lambsmith, was galling, insupportable. Who would concern himself for Baron Chase in that way?

They use me, that's all. Even Amin doesn't really like me.

Chase picked up the phone to change his airline reservation.

*   *   *

In one of those coincidences that aren't so farfetched as they at first appear, Sir Denis was on the same plane. He had been in London, he explained, at meetings with the Coffee Board, when the request had come in from the Ugandan government that he be reinstated as the Coffee Board's mediator. He had learned this news not much sooner than Chase, and both men had promptly made arrangements to return to Kampala, Chase to see what he could do to regain control of the situation, Sir Denis at the request of the Ugandan government. The most sensible route for them both was the all-night London-Tripoli-Entebbe, Air Uganda flight.

They met in the VIP lounge at Heathrow, where Chase was savagely delighted to see the man who had just become his enemy, and where Sir Denis obviously had to use all his diplomatic skills to suggest pleasure on his side at the encounter. After normal greetings and expressions of surprise and joy, they got themselves drinks at the bar, and then Chase insisted on changing his seat assignment so they could travel together. "You needn't do that, if it's too much trouble," Sir Denis said, and Chase smiled, showing his teeth. "No trouble at all," he said.

The lounge receptionist made the change, and Chase carried his new boarding pass over to where Sir Denis sat by the windows, leafing through an old issue of *Punch*. Moving dots of red and white light in the blackness beyond the windows defined the wanderings of taxiing planes. "Not a bit of trouble," Chase announced, and settled with angry happiness into the overstuffed chair to Sir Denis's right.

Sighing, Sir Denis closed the magazine and showed its cover to Chase, saying, "I fear I'm no longer English. I'm away from the country too much these days; half the cartoons in here make no sense to me."

"England is a club," Chase said, as though agreeing with Sir Denis's point. One of Chase's grievances was that he himself was Canadian, which was one small step from being nothing at all.

"England is a club? Perhaps so." Sir Denis smiled ruefully, dropping the magazine onto the table beside his chair. "I may have permitted my membership to lapse."

"At least we got you back onto the Brazil-Uganda team," Chase said with his most welcoming smile.

Sir Denis looked at him keenly. "Did you have something to do with that?"

With a modest shrug, Chase said, "You seemed the right man for the job. I merely said as much to Amin."

"I see. Thank you very much."

Sir Denis's disappointment was evident, and Chase laughed to himself because he knew why. Sir Denis had assumed it was Patricia who had worked his renomination; and in fact it might well have been. Chase smiled at the thought of what hoops Patricia would run this old fool through. "It was my pleasure," he said.

* * *

Amin himself met them at Entebbe. He was in another of his personae, that of the distinguished statesman. His medium-gray single-breasted suit was beautifully tailored to maximize his shoulders and chest while minimizing his gut. His tie was a dark blue, modestly figured with silver lions rampant, and his shirt was snowy white, still faintly marked with the creases from its folding by the manufacturer. His feet, which were of normal size, looked tiny in their shiny black shoes under his imposing top-heavy figure. Only the bulging side pockets of the suit jacket—containing, as Chase well knew, wads of cash in shillings or pounds or dollars, to be spent or given away as whim might dictate—spoiled the tailored perfection of his figure.

Amin came out of the terminal building alone, striding across the tarmac toward the plane as they disembarked. His happiest and most welcoming smile beamed out at them, and he strode forward with his hand already outstretched. As the other passengers—Ugandan or European businessmen—glanced nervously and curiously out of the corners of their eyes, Amin approached Sir Denis and pumped his hand, saying, "My friend-ah, my friend-ah. How could I continue without you completely? That-ah mee-nister that-ah *fired* you is *gone* from that post. *Gone* from my-ah government-ah completely. When I-ah *hear* what he do, I act-ah at *once*."

He's taking the credit for it himself, the wily bastard. Chase stood to one side and smiled, willing Sir Denis to see his stance as that of the modest civil servant permitting his superior to claim the rewards for his own unsung work.

As for Sir Denis, he seemed, at least on the surface, honestly de-lighted to be in the presence once more of President for Life Idi Amin Dada. In fact, he said so. "I'm delighted, Your Excellency. I hope I may go on being of use to you."

"Oh, yes. Oh, yes, we-ah work together like-ah—" Briefly, Amin was seen to flounder for a simile; then he found it: "—like-ah Cain and Abel. *Brothers*."

"Brothers," agreed Sir Denis, utterly unflappable. "Delighted," he repeated; so even he was at a loss for words.

Amin didn't bother to shake hands with Chase, but he acknowl-edged his presence with a big grin, saying, "Welcome-ah home, Baron. You been-ah now gone too long."

So he had. "It's good to be back," Chase said, returning Amin's smile.

"My right-ah hand," Amin said, and grinned again at Sir Denis, saying, "What-ah you think-ah my Baron? Maybe I make him now a duke."

It was a joke Amin had essayed before; Chase responded as he always did: "Oh, no, sir, I'm content to be a lowly Baron."

"Modest completely. Come along-ah."

Here in Uganda the rainy season was less relentless than it was to the east, through the Rift Valley, and today was one of the periods of respite. Though the tumbling clouds still roiled across the sky, there was a faint glow in the air and a soft warmth that was not quite too humid for comfort. From the dankness of London to the austere aridity of Tripoli to the tropical breeze of Entebbe was a journey from Purgatory through Hell to Heaven. Meteorologically speaking.

Today's car was the black Mercedes convertible, the one the Israelis had imitated last summer in their raid for the hostages. That false Mercedes, emerging first out of the bowels of the landed lead aircraft with the flags of Uganda and of Amin's presidency fluttering above its headlights, had distracted and confused the airport garrison just long enough. For weeks afterward Amin had refused to travel in his own Mercedes, as though blaming the car for his humiliation, but he hadn't been able to keep away from it permanently; the meanings and symbols of the Mercedes-Benz were too powerful.

The chauffeur stood at natty attention beside the car, all four doors of which were open. Air Uganda ground crew in their white jumpers were stowing the luggage in the trunk. Amin told the chauffeur in Swahili, "I'll drive. Go back in one of the other cars." (Chase understood Swahili very well—better than any of them, including Amin, guessed—but he would never speak it. His unsuspected fluency was yet another small weapon in the arsenal of his self-defense.)

The chauffeur saluted and marched away like a windup toy. Amin bent his smiling black head toward the aged white head of Sir Denis, as if he were a solicitous keeper in an old-age home, saying, "I'm-ah drive you. I'm-ah show you the beauties of my country. You sit-ah now in front with me."

"An unexpected pleasure," Sir Denis said. (How he's squirming, Chase thought in elation, watching Sir Denis's unruffled surface.)

Chase had the wide backseat to himself. The top was down, and when Amin jolted the car forward—he drove too fast, too carelessly, too inexpertly, and had already gone through several crashes—the wind of their passage yanked at Chase's thinning hair as though to scalp him. Brushing the wisps of hair off his forehead, he looked back and saw the two cars of bodyguards following at a discreet— but not too discreet—distance.

There had been attempts made on Idi Amin's life. No matter

how spontaneous his actions appeared, he was always well guarded; too many men in Uganda needed him, not merely for their livelihoods but for their lives. If Amin *were* to be assassinated, it would change nothing for the country, since the structure of oppression would remain in place. But the struggle among the lesser Nubians to take Amin's place would be more horrific than even Chase could imagine.

Up front, Amin was talking at Sir Denis, giving him a travelogue filled no doubt with inaccurate statements about Uganda's history, its flora and fauna, and Amin's own development plans for the nation. Chase didn't even try to catch the words as the wind whipped them past him. He already knew more true facts about Uganda than Amin did, and as for Amin's development plans, those began and ended with the so-called "whisky runs," flying coffee to Stansted in England and Melbourne in Florida in the United States, returning with the liquor and luxury goods that kept the Nubians in line. That was the development plan, and it worked considerably better at achieving its goal than most plans in the Third World.

Chase spent the drive brooding on his own development plans. What he was trying was much riskier and more subtle than the whisky runs, but if it worked it would give him just as much security as the whisky runs gave Amin. Money. A lot of money. Money to retire on, perhaps in some lesser island in the Caribbean, from which he could still make his occasional trips to London. And to New York, as well. And all his life he had wanted to test the rumors about New Orleans.

Amin was the first to see the trouble ahead. That was like him, part of the secret of his success; he had a cat's sensitivity to potential danger.

They had reached the city and were driving along Kampala Road, lined with shops that had once belonged to the now-expelled Asians. Half were now closed, for lack of capital, lack of expertise, lack of initiative. Among the few battered vehicles on the street, the gleaming expensive Mercedes seemed like a visitor from another planet. Much more typical was the lumbering, plank-sided, blue-cabbed truck that came crawling out of a side alley ahead of them, filling the road, seeming to take forever to get out of the way.

Chase didn't see the other truck until after Amin was already in action. The second truck had been parked on the other side of broad Kampala Road, and it was with unusual speed that it abruptly started up and swung across the lanes of traffic to meet the first truck head-on, effectively barricading the road.

But Amin was fast, and when necessary he was incredibly decisive. With a sudden loud growl, like a lion disturbed at its meat, he slammed his foot on the accelerator, twisted the wheel, and ducked down as low as possible behind the steering wheel.

Acceleration yanked Chase out of his reverie. He too could act fast in a crisis, and afterward he realized it was the threat to his relationship with Grossbarger should Sir Denis be killed that made him, even before protecting himself, pull forward against the acceleration, slap Sir Denis on top of his white head, and yell, "Down!"

The Mercedes had leaped up onto the sidewalk. A woman was walking there hand in hand with her young son. Men with machine guns were coming out of an abandoned storefront just ahead of the car. The driver of the plank-sided truck was desperately trying to shift the ancient gear into reverse. The woman flung her son at the street just before the Mercedes smashed into her and threw her away like an empty cigarette pack.

Then Chase was on the floor in back and could see no more, and bullets were shredding the windshield; another windshield to be replaced. He could feel the car scrape through between the concrete storefront and the rear bumper of the truck. The Mercedes rocked on its springs, seemed about to fly, bounced instead off the sidewalk and back into the roadway, and at last slackened its pace.

Rising hesitantly upward, Chase looked back at the pitched battle around the trucks. Amin's bodyguards were exchanging shots with the attempted assassins, who were now doing their vain best to flee. If they were lucky, they would be killed cleanly this minute, by gunfire.

April; it was only April. This was the third assassination attempt this year, and like the others it would be reported in no newspapers, on no television broadcasts, through no wire services.

I'm right to get out, Chase thought. It's breaking down.

Up front Amin was laughing, was slapping the shaken Sir Denis

on the knee, was already turning the near-miss into a triumph, a
joke, an anecdote. He had told Chase, and he apparently meant it,
that he knew no assassin could kill him because he had already seen
his own death in a dream. It would not happen, he'd assured Chase,
for a long long time.

24

Naked, standing in front of the mirrored dresser in Frank's bedroom,
Ellen reflected again that sex never seemed so wonderful after the event
as it always did while it was going on. By moving her head a bit she
could see Frank, sprawled on his back on the bed, on the new coral-
colored blanket he'd thrown over it after ousting the stupid dog,
George. Both pillows were bunched now beneath Frank's head as he
idly scratched his hairy stomach and smiled in sleepy contentment.
He had a good time, the bastard, she thought.

The only sound was the continuing chatter of the rain, a rustle like
a million chipmunks gnawing rotted wood. If it hadn't been for the
rain—

It had started at the end of March, the rain, and today was the
nineteenth of May. Seven weeks of rain. Cracks appeared in walls;
leaks developed in ceilings, warps in doorjambs. Dresser drawers stuck;
flour and beans and bread rotted on their shelves; the green-black stain
of mildew spread over everything in the world like some sort of
surrealistic total eclipse.

If it hadn't been for the rain—

Probably, Lew wouldn't have taken up with that Asian girl in
the first place. It was surely his own forced inactivity, brought on
by the endless rain, that had led him to distract himself with that
creature. In normal circumstances it would not have happened. Not
with Lew the man he was. And not with Ellen the woman she knew
she was.

If it hadn't been for the rain—

She herself would have been more occupied, more content. She would have been flying three or four times a week rather than three or four times a month. She would have spent time and thought and care on that awful little house they'd been lent, and by now she would have made it into something like a home. And she wouldn't have had all this empty time in which to brood and grow touchy and miserable, in which to plot shabby revenges.

If it hadn't been for the rain—

Frank too wouldn't have grown bored and tired. His camping-out adventure on Lake Victoria, just perfect for his twelve-year-old-boy's mind, would have contented and amused him. He would not have come back to Kisumu dull and restless and angry. He would have permitted their relationship to remain at that level of nonsexual friend-ship which had been with such difficulty attained, and which was the only possible long-lasting relationship they *could* have. He would not, on his return from Port Victoria, have thrown just one more pass, out of general irritation and ennui.

And she would not have accepted.

Stupid, stupid, stupid. They had gone to bed together, they had enjoyed it, and from now on, the whole situation was going to be that much worse. And all because of the rain.

"Penny for your thoughts," Frank said, and then, as though as a result of his having spoken, he hugely yawned.

"I was thinking how much I hate this rain."

He chuckled, very comfortable, and said, "You've got a beautiful ass."

"Thank you."

"I'll tell you what *I* was thinking, and this isn't bullshit. You know I don't do this kind of bullshit."

"Mm?"

"You're the best I've ever had," he said. "It's God's truth, may He strike me dead, I thought I was gonna fall out of my skin a couple times there. I thought I was dead and fucking an angel."

She laughed, rising partway out of her funk, saying, "What a hand you are with a compliment."

"Lew doesn't deserve you."

Oh, no, none of that. Suddenly decisive, Ellen turned away from the mirror, crossed the bedroom in two strides, knelt on the bed and straddled him, her pubic hair brushing his belly. Her fingers, not gentle, counted their way up the ribs on his left side. He winced away but wouldn't move his hands from behind his head to defend himself. He watched her, surprised, amused, interested, not alarmed.

She pressed her fingernail into his flesh between the third and fourth ribs, just under the nipple. "If Lew ever hears about this," she said, bearing down, meaning every word of it, "if Lew so much as ever *suspects*, I'll put the knife in right there. I will, Frank."

Frank chuckled, trying to pretend the fingernail didn't hurt. "Lew would do it first, honey," he said. "Don't you worry, old Frank has no death wish."

She relaxed the pressure but didn't yet move her hand. "Just so you understand."

"I read you, loud and clear."

She started then to climb off him, but he put his hands on her waist, pulling her down to sit on his stomach. She could feel him rising again against her buttocks. He said, "Don't go, I like you there."

So did she, goddammit. She was angry, she was bad-tempered, she was rain-obsessed, she was driven mad by inactivity, but at the same time she did like those hammy hands on her waist, she liked the nudge of that hard cock against her cheek.

He was something different from Lew, he was blunter and more stupid and less sensitive, but there were moments when crudity had its own charm. Almost against her will, she could feel herself softening to complement his hardness, she could feel the juices begin to flow. Knowing what he wanted, she lifted herself slightly on her knees, inching backward toward him—

And stopped. Frowning, she lifted her head like a herbivore in the forest who's heard a distant sound. His hands on her waist pressed her farther back toward his waiting member, but she didn't move. "What's that?" she said.

"What's what? Goddammit—"

Pushing his hands away, she climbed off the bed and went over to the nearest window. She pulled the curtain aside and looked out, listening to the splashes of individual water drops falling from branches and eaves.

It was true. And something in the quality of the light, the altitude of the clouds, told her this was no mere respite, this was the real thing. She looked back at Frank, bewildered on the bed. Her eyes were shining. She didn't need him at all. "The rain has stopped," she said.

PART THREE

25

Lew walked into the room carrying a two-by-four and a battered black attaché case. He put the case down, hefted the two-by-four, and faced his student body.

They reminded him somewhat of his truckers' class back in Valdez, except that he doubted he'd have as much trouble getting this mob to fight back. There were forty-eight of them here, in this large littered storage room in Balim's second building. They were Balim's employees, or the friends or relatives or fellow tribesmen of Balim's employees, and it was his job over the next few days to turn them into something approaching an invading army. At the moment, what they most looked like was the Saturday-night overflow from a tough-neighborhood bar.

Charlie had been assigned to Lew as an interpreter, and stood beside him now, chewing a piece of sugarcane and looking extremely relaxed. Lew gazed over his troops, most of whom looked no more than mildly curious at what was about to happen, and said to Charlie, "Tell them to sit down."

Charlie spoke. Since the crew was a mixed tribal bag, mostly Luo and Kikuyu, he spoke in Swahili, a language of which Lew had only a smattering—certainly not enough to cope with the slurring elision-filled singsong rapid delivery of Charlie. But surely it was taking too long to translate "Sit down," and Lew noticed that many of the men exchanged amused glances as they settled themselves on the dusty floor.

"Charlie," Lew said. When the man turned his small alert face, Lew said, "Charlie, all you have to do is translate what I say."

"Oh, sure," Charlie said.

Lew hefted the two-by-four. "Tell them," he said, "I am now going to show them what to do if a man comes at them with a stick."

Charlie nodded, and spoke in Swahili. Again there was a ripple of amusement among the seated men. Charlie turned back to Lew, ready for the next translation.

"Right." Lew held out the two-by-four. "Take this."

"Sir?"

"Go ahead, take it."

Confused but obedient, Charlie took the piece of wood, transferring his sugarcane to his left hand.

Lew stepped back about three paces. "Come at me with the stick, Charlie," he said.

Charlie looked blank for a second, then frowned down at the two-by-four and back up at Lew. "I *pretend*? Pretend to attack you?"

"If you want," Lew said indifferently. "Whatever you want to do."

With a little smile, Charlie turned to the audience and spoke again in Swahili. An appreciative murmur spread through the men; several hid big grins behind their hands.

Lew said, "I didn't give you anything to translate, Charlie."

"I just told them what will happen," Charlie explained. "So they will not be startled."

"Fine. Come on, now."

"Okay."

Charlie came forward, pretending to pretend. Lew had expected that—a deceptively mild approach rather than a lunging screaming performance—and he saw the instant when Charlie's eyes changed, just before the quick leap forward and the slashing swing of the two-by-four, aimed squarely for Lew's head.

Lew stepped forward inside the swing, his left arm going up at an angle to deflect the blow upward, at the same time that his right foot was coming up very hard into Charlie's crotch. Charlie screamed, a very satisfying sound in any language, and shriveled to the ground like an ant on a burning log. The two-by-four hit the floor and bounced away.

The men loved it. They laughed; they clapped their hands; they said admiring things to one another. Lew bent down to place a solicitous hand on Charlie's shoulder, saying, "You all right, Charlie?"

Charlie couldn't quite raise his head far enough to look up but he did manage to nod.

"Will you still be able to translate? Should I get somebody else to translate?"

"I can do it." Charlie's voice sounded as though it were being strained through canvas.

"I need good translations, Charlie. Accurate translations. You're sure you're up to it?"

Now Charlie did lift his head. He and Lew studied one another, their faces just a few inches apart, and Lew watched Charlie work out the equation in his own mind. Bad translation equals extreme pain. Good translation equals an end to pain.

Slowly, Charlie nodded. "I can do it," he said.

"Fine. Let me help you up."

Charlie stood, his posture and expression those of a very old man. Lew made a little show of dusting him off, while the watching men giggled and slapped their knees. Then Lew said, "Ready?"

Charlie swallowed noisily. Standing a bit straighter, he said, "Yes. Ready." His voice wasn't normal yet, but it was better.

"Good. Tell them the purpose of that demonstration was to prove that a weapon does not make a man invincible."

From Charlie's tone, and the men's interested reaction, he was translating verbatim now. Satisfied, Lew went on: "But we are not going into Uganda to *look* for a fight. There's a shipment there, to be loaded and unloaded. That's what we're going for. Most of us will not be armed."

There was a stir of dissatisfaction when Charlie translated that last sentence. Lew said, "If Ugandan Army or police attack us, we will leave Uganda at once. My job is to teach you how to get back to the rafts in case of attack. In other words, how to retreat, while those with guns protect your rear."

One of the seated men made an indignant statement. Charlie said, "He says, give them all guns, they'll protect themselves." He was clearly pleased that Lew was being given some trouble.

Lew nodded. "Look at the man next to you," he told them, and waited while they listened to the translation and then did actually look back and forth, confused and self-conscious, laughing at one another.

Lew went on slowly, giving Charlie plenty of time to put it all in Swahili: "That man beside you has very little experience with guns, and no experience at all with war. Imagine you are walking in the woods, with an entire army somewhere around. Imagine that man now sitting beside you is also in the woods, somewhere nearby. There's a commotion up ahead. People are shooting; people are yelling. With all the trees and bushes, you can't see what's going on, you can't tell who's who. Do you really want that man now sitting beside you to have a gun, out there in those woods, near *you?*"

There was general discontent at that. Several of the men had things to say. Like most people, they wanted to believe they were capable of decisive heroic action. Probably the most difficult part of Lew's job—in the armies he'd worked for, as well as here—was to get people to understand their limitations. Once they'd accepted how ignorant and unready they were, they'd be prepared to start listening to instruction.

Charlie, having a wonderful time, turned back to Lew. "They say—"

"I know what they say."

Hunkering down in front of the attaché case that he'd brought in here like any schoolteacher entering any classroom, opening it so the lid obscured the contents from his students, Lew took out two pistols, both Italian-made Star .38 caliber. Shutting the lid, he stood and faced the group, the pistols held loosely in his hands. "Tell them this, Charlie. If any man here thinks he knows guns well enough to be trusted with one in Uganda, he can prove it by dueling with me now." At continuing stunned silence from his left, he said, "*Tell* them, Charlie."

Charlie did, and the men became wide-eyed and silent. Lew went on: "We'll stand on opposite sides of this room, each of us holding his pistol at his side. Charlie will count to three, and then we will both begin firing, and continue until somebody has been hit. I won't shoot to kill; I'll aim for the knee."

They discussed it among themselves. Lew continued in a negligent manner to show them the pistols.

At last Charlie, his manner betraying a surprised and reluctant admiration, said, "They don't want to do it."

"Tell them this. *I'll* say what they know and what they don't know. And if anyone disagrees with me, he can always call my bluff."

Charlie translated that with as much relish as when he'd thought it was Lew who was in trouble. The seated men looked mulish and resentful as they listened, but not actually rebellious.

Lew put the pistols away, snapped the case shut, and went on with his lecture.

"I don't want any of you to die in Uganda. I don't want you to shoot each other, and I don't want you to be shot by the police. Mr. Balim knows I have worked as an instructor in different armies, and he has asked me to teach you what you have to know to be safe on our trip together. We only have a few days, so if you don't want to learn, or you don't like the way I teach, you can leave. No one will argue with you."

Lew looked around the room, expecting that this bluff also would not be called. The men were being offered a very healthy bonus for this work, and had been told only the bare minimum they needed to know: that they would travel over the lake to Uganda, that they would work as loaders there of a "shipment" (they hadn't been told of what), and that they would travel back to Kenya the next day. Lew expected a combination of greed and curiosity to keep them all actively involved.

He was right. They settled down at last, and he talked to them about the terrain they would be covering. He explained how, in heavy woods, even a group their size could avoid being seen from the air. He told them how to react under fire: never run in a straight line, and—most important—never assume immediately that they're shooting at *you*. "You're hiding behind a tree. They're shooting at some other guy. You panic and run. *Now* they'll shoot at you, and probably hit you, too."

He told them what to do in case they were captured: "Tell them everything they ask. Tell them the truth, cooperate, give them anything they want. Let them see how scared you are. And keep a very sharp eye out for a chance to get away. Listen to me, this is important. If you come on like a tough guy, they'll beat you down and eventually they'll kill you. If you behave like a nervous wreck, and answer all their questions, they won't worry about you very much, they might even get careless with you. In a battle, there's lots of distractions. If you see a chance to run, take it."

Out of the attaché case he brought an example of the one weapon he wouldn't mind their carrying: a woolen sock, filled with sand.

"Just tie it loosely. If you think you're about to get caught, untie it, dump the sand out, throw the sock away. Then you've never had a weapon at all."

They enjoyed the sock full of sand; from the way they pointed at Charlie and laughed and said several things, they wanted Lew to demonstrate the weapon on Charlie. "What are they saying?" Lew asked, straight-faced.

"Nothing," Charlie said. "Just nonsense."

Lew moved on. He was starting to get into the question of hiding in the woods during a police sweep when Isaac came in with an interruption. "Mr. Balim says he's sorry, but you can't work with these people tomorrow."

"Why not? We don't have much time. And this was his idea."

"Mr. Balim says, you can have them every day after tomorrow. But, he says, you must fly to Nairobi tomorrow morning."

Nairobi. Amarda.

Lew hadn't thought of her since— Since the rain had stopped? Since she had driven away from Kisumu two weeks ago? Since last night's muddled and mostly forgotten dreams? If he never saw her again, the affair was over. "Isaac," he said, "I've got these people to train. Can't you make the trip this time?"

"A black man, a black Ugandan, deal with an Asian family?" Isaac shook his head with a rueful smile. "Besides," he said, "I'm supposed to go on a trip with Frank tomorrow."

"A trip? Trip?" Irritable, Lew looked around at the observing, interested men. "It isn't fair to them," he said.

Isaac said, "Lew? What's wrong?"

Meaning that he wasn't behaving sensibly. Isaac would begin to wonder why he was making such a fuss over the training of these laborers—earlier, in Isaac's presence in Balim's office, Lew had given no such indication of concern for these men—and he might even begin to suspect the truth. "All right," Lew said. "Sorry, Isaac, I don't mean to be bad-tempered. I'm just having a little trouble with this crowd, that's all."

"Then you won't mind a day off," Isaac said.

Ellen will fly me; *Jesus*. "Not a bit," Lew said, forcing a cheerful grin. "Nairobi, here I come."

26

"The border," Isaac said. His mouth was dry; his eyes kept blinking; his hands trembled on the steering wheel.

"You wanted an adventure," Frank said from the backseat. "Here it is."

Looking in the rearview mirror, Isaac saw Frank lounging at his ease back there, his tie somewhat askew, his suit jacket open, his white shirt rumpled at his waist. Frank seemed happy, unconcerned, merely amused by Isaac's fear. I must be like that, Isaac told himself. I must watch Frank, and if he is not afraid I must also be not afraid.

And if the moment comes when Frank *is* afraid?

Turning his mind sternly away from that question, Isaac slowed the gray Mercedes to a stop just before the red-and-white-striped pole that blocked the entry to Uganda. On the left stood the small shed containing customs officials and border guards. Two sloppily uniformed men with repeating rifles strapped to their backs leaned negligently by the shed door, watching the Mercedes without expression.

Frank leaned forward, extending his document wallet over Isaac's shoulder, saying, "Here you go, old son. Knock 'em dead."

"Or vice versa," Isaac said. His voice was trembling, spoiling the unaccustomed effort at a joke. He hated that.

Frank laughed. "Just don't tell 'em your right name."

"No fear of that."

Very reluctantly, Isaac opened the Mercedes door, stepped out into the warm sunlight, adjusted his chauffeur's cap and dark-blue chauffeur's jacket, and walked on watery legs toward the shed.

After Lew Brady's experience, back before the rains, it had been decided that no one connected with this operation dared enter Uganda again using his own name and ID. Therefore, through various contacts of Balim's in Nairobi, false documentation had been arranged, so that now, when it was necessary to go to Uganda in a more open manner than the lake route Frank had twice used, they were (they hoped) prepared.

Isaac, grown increasingly discontented with his clerk's role, had purchased false identification for himself as well, explaining to Balim that Frank would need from time to time a translator who looked more civilized than Charlie. Also, Frank would surely welcome the presence of someone who already knew the ground. And, finally, there were things to be done in Uganda that only a black man could do, and whom could Balim trust for those things more than Isaac? Balim had responded by reminding Isaac that the first law of survival was never to volunteer; then he had accepted the voluntary offer. So here Isaac was, willy-nilly, a man wanted by the Ugandan police, a man high on Idi Amin's personal death list, walking—however shakily—directly into the lion's den.

Inside the overheated metal-roofed shed were half a dozen soldiers and customs officials, all looking bored and mean and half-drunk, as though they might murder him, or at the very least pull off his arms and legs, merely for a moment's amusement. Without a word, looking neither left nor right, Isaac put Frank's documents and his own on the chest-high counter dividing the room, then stood there like an exhausted horse, waiting.

After a moment, the oldest and least-dangerous-looking of the men came forward and began slowly to study those papers: Frank's green American passport, Isaac's red Kenyan passport, Frank's letters and other identification, Isaac's driver's license, the Mercedes registration.

These papers claimed that Frank was an American named Hubert Barton, an employee of International Business Machines, on his way to Jinja to discuss a computer installation there with an attorney named Edward Byagwa. (Photostat copies of correspondence between Byagwa and IBM were included.) The papers also identified Isaac as a Kenyan national named Bukya Mwabiru, employed as a chauffeur by East Africa Car Hire, Ltd., main office in Nairobi. The Mercedes registration showed it to be owned by the same company (of which Mazar Balim owned thirty percent).

The border guard frowned his way through these documents one by one, mumbling to himself from time to time, his lips moving. Finally he glowered at Isaac and said, "Barton."

"In the auto." Not trusting his voice—it might break, crack, fail entirely, somehow give him away—Isaac spoke as few words as possible.

The guard moved slightly to his left, so he could look through the open doorway and see Frank sprawled on the backseat of the Mercedes. "Why doesn't he come in here?"

"Air conditioning," Isaac said, and even essayed a shrug. "He's an American."

The guard grunted. Saying nothing else, he brought up stamp and pad from under the counter and stamped both passports, then wrote illegibly over the stamps. However, instead of giving the papers back to Isaac, he lifted a leaf in the counter, stepped through, lowered the leaf, and marched out of the shed, carrying the papers.

Isaac followed, half-afraid the other guards would yell at him to stay. He trailed the guard over to the Mercedes, where the man gestured with the papers for Frank to open the window. Frank did, and the guard said, severely, *"Jambo."*

"That means 'hello,' doesn't it? *Jambo* yourself, pal," Frank said. "Jesus, it's hot out here. Anything wrong, driver?"

"No, sir," Isaac said.

"Well, *jambo* some more," Frank told the guard, and pushed the button to reclose the window.

How can he *do* that? Isaac asked himself. Frank's nonchalance, rather than reassuring him, was just increasing his terror. And this is the easy part, he reminded himself gloomily.

The guard, rebuffed, frowned a moment longer at the car, as though considering whether or not to search it (not that there was anything to be found in it). Then, abruptly turning away, the man handed the documents wordlessly to Isaac and gestured at one of the lounging soldiers to raise the barricade. Isaac, his hand trembling so hard he had trouble opening the car door, slid in behind the wheel, dropped the papers on the other leather bucket seat, watched the red-and-white pole lift out of the way, put the engine in gear, and for the first time in three years moved onto the soil of Uganda.

The memories flooded back. Not just his family (*that* memory was never far away), but everything else he'd had and no longer possessed. His house, his friends, his work, the relationships with people at the

Ministry for Development, even the four peach trees in his backyard. His future, too, the future that hadn't happened and now never would—that also shone in on him with the sunshine through the windshield, closing his throat with the pain. He drove, eyes forward, hurting so much that he didn't want to move any part of his body.

The land was familiar, the sunlight familiar, the ribbon of road familiar. The few vehicles they passed bore yellow license plates as in Kenya, but beginning with *U*, not *K*. The people in the occasional village were more brightly dressed than in the countryside around Kisumu.

God help him, God help him, he was home.

27

For Idi Amin, the least enjoyable aspect of his office was his office. He very much liked to be out on maneuvers with his Army, or observing a flyby of his Air Force, or making a whirlwind tour of "inspection" in a jeep at the head of a convoy of troop-filled trucks, racing through the small towns, laughing at the dogs and the babies and the chickens as they scurried out of his way.

Official dinners, they were also nice. And official lunches, official teas, official cocktail parties. Also official tours of locations such as Owen Falls Dam (making sure those thrown-away bodies which had not yet been eaten by the crocodiles had discreetly been removed the day before) or the Field Marshal Idi Amin Air Force Base at Nakasongola, seventy miles north of Kampala. (The air base was a particular favorite, though also something of an embarrassment. Amin, early in his presidency, had ordered it built, with its modern camouflaged underground hangars, because he wanted to protect his Air Force from the fate that had hit the Egyptians in the 1967 Six-Day War, when the Israelis had destroyed virtually the entire Egyptian Air Force on the ground on the very first day. However, Amin had only about twenty modern warplanes in his Air Force, which he couldn't bear to keep so far away from himself, so the Field Marshal Idi Amin Air Force Base normally stood empty while his total Air Force remained at Entebbe, where the Israelis had wiped it out last summer. He had new planes now, though, and always ordered a few of them to Nakasongola before an inspection.)

Unfortunately, for the leader of a modern nation there's more to the presidency than Army maneuvers and VIP inspections. From time to time he must seat himself in his office, listen to a lot of boring details from various ministers, make decisions, give orders, and even occasionally sign something. (He *really* disliked that part. He had learned late in life how to sign his name, and he remained convinced there was something funny about the look of it, that it didn't have in some strange manner the appearance of a real signature. He thought other people could see the difference and were deliberately hiding their knowledge from him.)

As with many men who have reached the top in the world of power politics, Idi Amin's talent was not for governing but for climbing. Now that there was nowhere left to climb, he was frequently bored or resentful or ill at ease, as though it were the world's fault he had nothing left to do with his skills. Again as with so many such men, he had turned his energies to the obsessive struggle to *retain* the power he'd achieved, even if his enemies and competitors were frequently no more than ghosts.

But you can't chase ghosts all the time, no matter how many you've made. Today, all his appointments finished, nowhere else to go, Amin prowled the large plush room he'd inherited from Milton Obote, drinking beer and thinking about next month's Commonwealth Prime Ministers' Conference to be held in London. The British had been making a fuss lately about his attending; they said bad things about him and didn't want him to go. They claimed it was because of the way he treated his enemies, but he knew that was false. Didn't all strong leaders treat their enemies harshly? Of course; how else could you intimidate them, keep them in check? It was simple hypocrisy.

There had even been discussion in the British papers about his meeting with Queen Elizabeth. If he were to attend the conference, naturally he would with all the other heads of state be on the reception line to meet the Queen (whom in any event he had already met six years ago), and these newspapers had raised the question as to whether or not this Queen should shake Idi Amin's hand. Yes, and he knew why, he knew why *that* was such as issue. "Amin's red hand," they called it, but they meant Amin's *black* hand. Yes, they did.

Back in the 1950s, when he was in the Army, then called the King's African Rifles, he was the only black enlisted man on the Nile Rugby Team with all those white officers. Every time they played a game in Kenya there would be a reception afterward, and while the rest of the team enjoyed the festivities Idi Amin would sit alone in the bus, waiting to be driven back to the barracks. Yes, he knew what color hand they didn't want their Queen to touch.

"Sir?"

Amin had been deep in the past, staring sightlessly out his window, clutching his beer bottle by the neck. He was six feet four; he had a big gut he hadn't owned back in 1951 and 1952, when he was heavyweight boxing champion of Uganda; he filled this room with a brooding intensity. He looked over at his secretary, a uniformed soldier, a Kakwa like himself. He liked to have people around him who spoke his tribal dialect; in it he said, hoping for something interesting, "Well? I am very deep in thought here."

"Your Excellency, Mr. Chase wonders if you could spare five minutes to see him."

Chase. It was possible that Chase would be amusing, particularly if he was here to talk against Sir Denis Lambsmith again. "Yes, I'll see him," Amin said, then added, "No, wait. Tell him I'll see him soon, he should wait."

"Yes, Your Excellency."

Amin, smiling, watched the secretary-soldier close the door; then he turned back to the window and to his thoughts.

On the whole, he would prefer to attend that conference. Such official occasions were among the best parts of being a head of state, and it was always enjoyable to twit the British and strain the fabric of their surface politeness.

Also, there was London, which he liked very much. Amin had been to several places outside Africa—to Rome to see the Pope, to New York to address the United Nations—but his favorite trip had been back in 1971, the summer after he had taken power, when he had gone up to London to see the Queen. They'd had lunch together, and he'd explained at length his economic and educational plans for Uganda. Of course, that had been before he'd understood the depth of British faithlessness.

Chase. He was Canadian, of course, not British, but how much of a distinction was that? An African from this tribe and an African from that tribe were as different as winter from summer, but all white men—at least, all English-speaking white men—were the same. When it came to white people, he could only agree with the attitude of Roy Innis, who back in March of 1973 had made him a life member of CORE, the Congress of Racial Equality.

In preparation for an enjoyable conversation with Chase, Amin went back to his desk, unlocked a side drawer, and took out the Xerox copy of the letter, which he spread in front of himself on the desk. He still wasn't a very good reader, but he'd had this one read to him by a trustworthy educated Nubian, and by now he had it memorized. It was typewritten, with neither date nor business-address heading, and it looked like this:

Dear Emil Grossbarger,

When we last talked, I assured you I would be able to have Sir Denis Lambsmith removed from the Brazil deal. Unfortunately, I was wrong. Amin has decided for reasons of his own that he wants Lambsmith around, and has even gone so far as to insist that Lambsmith be at Entebbe to oversee the physical departure of the coffee.

It would be difficult, probably impossible, for us to communicate directly before the deed is done. I know what you said when we were last together in London, and I know you were quite serious. On the other hand, when we reach a spot where simply nothing can be done to alter the situation, the sensible man accepts reality as it is and goes on from there. On the assumption that we're both sensible men, I am continuing to work as though our deal were intact. You have my assurance that no harm will come to Sir Denis.

It was signed *Baron Chase*. Amin studied that signature as though there were something to be learned from it. The capital *B* and capital *C* were large and round, like village huts. The other letters, except for the *h* in *Chase*, didn't properly exist at all, but were represented by wandering trails, like animal paths leading from a water hole. On the other hand, the *h* was a guidon, a straight knife-edged flagpole with a tiny pennant at the top. *Baron Chase.* Very interesting.

Chase had written the letter just before the end of the long rains, a few days after his return from London. He had already, as he stated in the letter, done his best to poison Amin's mind against Sir Denis Lambsmith, but from what Patricia Kamin had told him, it was Sir Denis whom Amin wanted near him, and nobody else. Sir Denis was a skin-deep man, a technocrat without imagination. He didn't have the imagination to be dishonest or clever, and he had no secret plans or intentions in connection with this coffee sale.

Which was true of no one else involved. The Brazilians and the Bogotá Group were shifty, clever, very knowledgeable, out for their own advantage at every instant. Emil Grossbarger, of course, was completely untrustworthy, and Chase was a schemer by some sort of inner compulsion. No, it was bland unthreatening Lambsmith with whom Amin wanted to deal, particularly when his judgment of the man was supported by Patricia's spying.

And when his other spies could protect him from the other actors in the play, including Chase.

This letter had reached Amin by a means almost as circuitous as the route it had taken to Grossbarger. Chase had brought it, already sealed, to an English pilot named Wilson, one of the regulars on the Stansted whisky run. Swearing Wilson to secrecy, Chase had given him some money and asked him to carry the letter to England and from there mail it to Grossbarger in Zurich. Wilson had agreed, had carried the letter to Stansted, had there steamed it open and made a Xerox copy, had resealed the letter and mailed it to Grossbarger, had brought the copy back to Uganda, had requested a personal meeting with the President, and had given him the copy and his story. Wilson's reward was already in his personal Swiss bank account.

The question now was: What were Chase and Grossbarger up to? If it was merely that Chase was taking an extra little bribe on the side, that he was pressuring Grossbarger with some nonexistent problem solvable by money, then more power to him. Amin saw no reason to interfere with other people's little scams, so long as *their* scams didn't interfere with *his*.

But there was something about this letter, something that just didn't sound right. ". . . before the deed is done." ". . . as though our deal were intact." What deed? What deal? The "deed" *could* merely refer to the sale and shipment of the coffee. The "deal" *could* mean nothing more than a side-issue bribe. Still, there was something wrong, and the main problem was why Chase and Grossbarger wanted Sir Denis out in the first place. And why did Chase find it necessary to assure Grossbarger that "no harm will come to Sir Denis"? Were they afraid he knew, or would learn, something of what they were up to?

If so, that was even more reason to keep Sir Denis around. If he *were* to learn anything about Chase and Grossbarger, Patricia would soon get it from him, and then Amin himself would know.

So. Inasmuch as possible, the problem of Chase was under control. Slipping the letter back into the drawer, dropping the beer bottle into the basket under his desk, Amin buzzed his secretary.

"Send in Mr. Chase."

* * *

"Good morning, Mr. President," Chase said.

Amin smiled. Chase had always maintained a proper formality in his presence, and even though Amin knew the formality was duplicitous and only a surface sham he enjoyed it. It was a confirmation of who he had become. "Good-ah morning, Baron," he said, his voice rumbling like a sleepy purr. "My only Baron," he added.

Chase would go on standing, though at his ease, until and unless Amin invited him to sit down. "You're looking well, sir," he said. "I understand you were jogging this morning."

"Basket-ah-ball game this afternoon," Amin said. "With-ah my flyers." He meant the pilots of his Air Force, bright hard young men who treated him with a delicate combination of barracks-yard camaraderie and careful respect. Some had been trained by the British, some by the Israelis, a few by the Russians, or the Americans, and the most recent by the Libyans.

"Good luck," Chase said. The closest he came to informality was occasionally to drop the "sir."

"Thank you." Amin grinned. "My-ah T-shirts now come," he said, and gestured to a stack of cardboard cartons in the corner. "Take one."

"With the picture?" Smiling his amusement and anticipation, Chase went over and opened the top carton. "Shall I try one on?"

"Of course," Amin said. "How-ah you gonna know if it-ah fit?"

Unselfconsciously, Chase slipped off his tan sports jacket, his light-green figured tie, and his white shirt. His chest and back were very white and pasty, padded with unhealthy-looking fat in globules under the skin. Old wounds puckered and scarred his torso and upper arms, as though once, years before, he had rolled in barbed wire.

He's been in many battles, Amin thought, studying the man, and all at once he remembered his own testimony before the Commission of Inquiry back in 1966, looking into an ivory- and gold-smuggling operation out of the Congo as a consequence of which Amin had wound up with forty thousand pounds in his Kampala bank account and a lot of gold bars in his house. Amin had told the Commission of Inquiry—which had ultimately found nothing against him—that he'd served in Burma and India during World War II; in fact, he hadn't even joined the Army until 1946, and the only "war" he'd ever been involved in was a punitive expedition with the Fourth King's African Rifles in 1962, organized to put down some cattle rustlers in the Lake Turkana section of Kenya. The accusations that time against his platoon, of torture and murder, had faded away into an inconsequential muddle, as they always did.

Chase pulled on one of the T-shirts and turned to face Amin, arms spread out. "How does it look?"

"Fine," Amin said, laughing, looking at the blown-up black-and-white photograph spread across Chase's chest.

Two years ago, during the Organization of African Unity summit meeting here in Kampala, Amin had arranged to be carried to the meeting seated in a litter borne by four British businessmen who lived in Uganda, and followed by another white man, a Swede, carrying a tiny parasol on a long stick to shade Amin's head. A news photograph had showed Amin, in the litter, waving happily to a cheering crowd, and it was this photograph Amin had now had reproduced on several thousand white T-shirts.

Looking down, Chase said, "It came out very well. The white man's burden, eh?"

"That's-ah right! That's-ah right!"

Neither of them mentioned that the right-rear bearer of the litter, an Englishman named Robert Scanlon, had recently been killed with a sledgehammer over at the State Research Bureau because of a business dispute with some people there.

Coming back over to the desk, patting the photo on his chest, Chase said, "This is what I wear today."

"Oh, no," Amin protested, "not all-ah day. You look-ah so nice in you clodes."

"Underneath, then," Chase said. "It'll be my secret."

"One-ah you secrets," Amin said with an amiable smile. "Sit-ah down, my little Baron."

"Thank you, sir." Chase settled himself into his accustomed chair and said, "What I'm mostly here to talk about is coffee."

And Sir Denis Lambsmith? Amin's eyes brightened. "Yes?"

"The train can roll this week. Friday. Will the planes be there?"

It was Amin's style to divide tasks among several people, so that only he ever knew the full dimensions or the complete story of what was going on. While Chase was dealing with Sir Denis, and to a lesser extent with the Brazilians (and on his own hook with Emil Grossbarger), it was Amin's Deputy Minister of Development who'd been given the job of seeing to it that the Grossbarger Group provided the eight transport planes that had been agreed on. The planes were to be at Entebbe when the initial trainload of coffee arrived, and they would shuttle this first consignment of coffee to Djibouti, where it would be loaded onto ships in the Indian Ocean.

But there was a problem, and Chase unfortunately had now pointed to it. "We gonna get the planes," Amin said, exuding confidence. "There's-ah still one-ah two details-ah to be work-ed out."

"Positioning costs," Chase said. "I heard about it."

"You hear about a lot-ah tings," Amin said, displeased.

"I was wondering if there was anything I could do to help."

"It-ah will work itself out," Amin told him, shutting the door on that conversation. "And-ah dah train can still go on-ah Friday, even if we got to-ah store dah coffee a day or two day at-ah Entebbe."

As was so often the case when things became irritating for Amin, the problem was money. The planes were being chartered from a firm based in Switzerland, which was insisting on what it called "positioning costs" before it would divert eight aircraft from their current work in Europe. It was the firm's contention that to "position" each large cargo plane, fueled and with crew, at Entebbe would cost thirty-five thousand dollars U.S., money it was demanding in advance.

Since the Brazilians and the Grossbarger Group had already paid Uganda the advance money—and it had already been spent—they could not be called upon to pay these unexpected costs. However, Uganda's foreign-exchange position—as usual precarious—would not permit a payment of two hundred eighty thousand U.S. dollars prior to shipping the coffee and being paid the other two thirds of the price.

At the moment, Amin's people in Kampala and in Zurich were attempting either to convince the charter company to trust Uganda—a sovereign nation among nations, after all—for payment later, or to find some other air cargo company that would. So far, things weren't going too well, though it was possible they could still make a deal with an American company, Coast Global Airlines, which had already in the last few years made lesser coffee shipments from Uganda to the United States. Coast Global's primary problem seemed to be finding sufficient spare planes and crew for the job.

Chase rose, saying, "Well, if everything's in hand, I'll be off."

"Yes," Amin said. It was disappointing that Chase hadn't once mentioned Sir Denis Lambsmith. Amin watched him cross the room back over to his clothing, and then added, "To Jinja."

Chase looked surprised, but not worried. "That's right," he said. He put his white shirt on over the Idi Amin T-shirt, and buttoned it up.

"To see a lawyer," Amin said, his friendly smile unchanged. "Name of Edward-ah Byagwa. Wha-ta you need-ah lawyer for, little Baron?"

"I'm buying some land near Iganga," Chase said. "Used to be church land." Smoothly he knotted his green tie.

"*Buy*-ing?"

Chase grinned, making them conspirators together. "You know me," he said, shrugging into his tan sports jacket. "I like things to be nice and legal."

"I know you, little Baron," Amin agreed. "Have a good-ah time, in Jinja."

Chase paused at the door, looking back, grinning again with the open smile that Amin knew to be his most thoroughly false expression.

"So you knew I was going to Jinja," he said. "I can't get anything past you, can I?"

"I hope-ah not," Amin told him. "I hope-ah not completely."

28

Sex last night, and sex again this morning. He's feeling guilty, Ellen thought, because he's on his way to see his girl friend. She watched Lew's profile as they drove to Balim's offices, and in his expressionless face she read deceit, guilt, and self-indulgence.

She hadn't told him about her conversation yesterday with Balim, nor did she see any reason why she should. He'd want to know why she was quitting Balim to work elsewhere, and that would lead inevitably to the name of Amarda Jhosi, and Ellen simply didn't want that whole scene. She didn't care to learn whether Lew would deny everything, or promise to reform, or even attempt to defend himself. When a thing is over, it's over, that's all; and this phase of Ellen Gillespie's life was *over*.

In Balim's office she sat quietly to the side, in the brown armchair into which Frank normally flung himself, while Balim explained today's problem to Lew. "The grandmother," he said, with an embarrassed little smile, as though she were his own grandmother and he were solely responsible for her. "The grandmother won't stay in place."

"I don't think she likes us," Lew said.

"Poor lady." Balim sighed. "What she doesn't like is the position in which she finds herself. The moral niceties in stealing from Amin, who stole from her, are too subtle for Lalia Jhosi. What is wanted here is reassurance, someone to convince her she hasn't fallen in with thieves."

"Then you should talk to her yourself," Lew said. "Or send Isaac. That's what I told him yesterday."

Ellen looked sharply at him. *Had* he tried to get out of this trip? But that was just guilt again, and cowardice. The main difference between men and women, Ellen thought, is that men have so much simpler emotions; they can't deal with complexity. If Lew were really trying to avoid Amarda Jhosi, it could only be because she was making him confused.

"Ah, no," Balim was saying, "you are the man for the job. I am a merchant, and undoubtedly a shady character. At first I was a very good friend to bring my compatriots, my fellow refugees, this opportunity. But as time has gone on, Lalia Jhosi has come to realize that I am merely a sharp practitioner, the sort of Asian who gives Asians a bad name. As for Isaac, he would surely alarm the old lady by talking politics. She wants involvement with politics even less than with crime; after all, she's already seen what politics can do."

Lew glanced with a kind of frustrated anger at Ellen, then said to Balim, "But what am *I* supposed to do?"

"Be a clean-cut American boy. A fighter for justice and a defender of the oppressed."

"Oh, come on."

"No, I'm quite serious," Balim said, and Ellen believed he was. "Lalia Jhosi is impressed by you. You remind her of the hero in American films. So you go to her and you reassure her that what we are all engaged in is an adventure, *but* an adventure with a moral purpose."

"Oh, boy," Lew said, shaking his head.

"You don't talk about profit, as I would have to do. You don't talk about politics, as Isaac would have to do. You don't talk about the mechanics of the thing, as Frank would have to do. You talk about good and evil, and you show her that *we* are the good guys."

"The good guys."

"That's right. You'll have no trouble with it, Lew, I promise. Just go to Nairobi and be a hero."

*   *   *

As Ellen landed in bright sunlight and taxied the plane to an available pad at Wilson Airport in Nairobi, Lew broke an extended silence between them by saying, "Why not come along?"

She had been listening to the tower and thinking about other things. She stared at him for a blank second, then said, "To the coffee plantation?"

"Sure. It's a very interesting place."

He wants me to protect him from that girl, she thought. But she wouldn't do it, she wouldn't let him force her to make his decisions for him.

Besides, it was already finished. As they left the office in Kisumu, Balim had said to her, quietly so Lew couldn't hear, "No change?" and she had shaken her head, to which he had given his sad fatalistic shrug. And in any event she had the appointment here, all set up. "Oh, I don't think so, Lew," she said, turning down the invitation. "There's really too much to be done at the airport."

He was surprised, and showed it. "Too much to do? Come on, Ellen, you spend most of your time just hanging around, reading magazines. You've told me so yourself."

"Well, today there's too much to do," she said, turning the plane in a tight U and stopping on the pad. "And I really don't want to go."

"Why not, for God's sake?"

She shut down both engines, then looked at him frankly and clearly. "I'm not interested in the Jhosi family, Lew," she said. "Nor in their coffee plantation. Nor in a nice drive through Nairobi."

He had understood her subtext; she saw his face close in defensive anger. "Have it your own way," he said.

"Thank you."

She climbed down from the plane, and he followed. He started to help her tie it down, but she said, "Go on, Lew, the grandmother's waiting." They could both see, some distance away beyond the chain link fence, Amarda Jhosi standing beside her car on tiptoe, happily waving, like the girls in war movies welcoming their men back from battle.

Lew hesitated, obviously torn, looking between Ellen and the waving girl. "You sure you won't come?"

"Positive."

He nodded, as though coming to a decision. "See you later," he said, and walked off.

She kept her back turned, busy with the ropes to tie the plane down, until she was certain they had gone.

* * *

Among the tiny cubbyhole offices for the various small cargo and charter air services, Ellen found the one marked CHARTAIR, LTD. in sky-blue letters that leaned speedily to the right. Inside, a worried-looking black man sat crowded in between large dark filing cabinets, as though the cabinets were guards sent to keep him here until time for the execution. His desk was messy, his wastebasket overflowing, and the small blackboard on the side wall listing future charters was so cluttered with half-erased or crossed-out numbers and names that it made no sense at all. "I'm looking for Mr. Gulamhusein," Ellen said.

The condemned man lifted his worried head. He held a ball-point pen in his hand, and two red pencils were stuck in his woolly hair above his right ear. In a surprisingly firm and self-assured voice, belying everything else about him, he said, "You would be Miss Gillespie?"

"That's right."

"Mr. Gulamhusein phoned from Nairobi," the man said. "He has been unfortunately delayed, but he will be here within the hour."

"That's all right," Ellen said, though she was disappointed that she couldn't get the details over right away. "I have other things to take care of. I'll be around the terminal." She left the man there and walked toward the airport manager's office with her documents, trying not to hear herself thinking that she should have gone with Lew to the plantation.

* * *

Mr. Gulamhusein was another Asian, an overgrown fig of a man with a smoothly smiling exterior which seemed to be imperfectly shielding panic. But he was efficient; he had brought the employment contracts and the Ugandan immigration form and the other papers.

The condemned man had relinquished his seat between the filing cabinets to Mr. Gulamhusein and had gone away for a cup of tea. Mr. Gulamhusein unceremoniously cleared the messy desk by piling all the papers in a kind of compost heap to one side, then neatly laid out the documents he'd brought in his shiny black plastic attaché case, saying, "You will want to read everything most carefully before you sign."

"I couldn't agree more," Ellen said, and settled down to read.

Because of the eight-hour time difference between Kenya and New York, she had had to get up at two in the morning, night before last, once she was sure Lew was asleep, and drive to Balim's office (having earlier gotten his permission) to make the phone call to the pilots' agency at Kennedy Airport. She had used them before, and in fact they'd gotten her the job in Alaska. All she'd said this time was that she wanted a job anywhere in the world, but when she'd mentioned that she was calling from Kenya, the man at the other end of the line had become very interested, saying, "We may have something right there, very near you. Short-term job, but it ends in the States."

"Perfect," she'd said.

It would take a second phone call, and the man had agreed there would be someone in the office at eleven that night, which for Ellen would be seven the next morning. And when she made that second call, the deal was arranged.

So here she was with the East African representative of Coast Global Airlines, a large American cargo company, reading the contract for her employment. Sometime tomorrow, Wednesday, a plane lacking a copilot would be arriving at Entebbe from Baltimore. Ellen, at Coast Global's expense, would be flown by charter from Kisumu to Entebbe to become that plane's copilot. Her documents from Ugandan immigration would permit her to stay in the transient aircrews' accommodations at Entebbe, but not to leave the airport. On Friday, she would crew as the plane, fully loaded, went to Djibouti on the Gulf of Aden and returned empty. There would be three, and possibly four, round trips, but in any event she would be paid for four. On Saturday or Sunday she would crew back to Baltimore, where she would be paid. And by then, according to the man at the agency, they would surely have another more long-term job lined up for her. It couldn't be better.

The strange thing was, she was so involved in her own plans and her own unhappiness and her own determination to get out of this situation that had become intolerable to her that it never even entered her mind there might be any connection between the cargo she would be flying to Djibouti on Friday and the trainload of coffee Lew and the others expected to be stealing any day now.

"Everything's fine," she said, putting the papers down on the cleared part of the desk. "May I borrow a pen?"

"Certainly." It was an expensive silver fountain pen, which he uncapped before handing her. Watching her begin to sign and initial the various papers, he said sympathetically, "You were not content in your previous work?"

"That sums it up," she said, and smiled through her doubts, and handed him back his pen.

29

So he knows I'm going to Jinja.

That same sentence kept recurring in Chase's mind as he drove east on A109, amid the groaning trucks that gave an impression—utterly false—of a soundly functioning economy. So he knows I'm going to Jinja.

And he *tells* me he knows.

Meaning there are further things he doesn't know. For instance, he doesn't know *why* I'm going to Jinja, because if he had the slightest suspicion about the truth, I'd already be dead. Or wishing I were.

But it also means he's suspicious of me, more than in the normal way of being mistrustful. He thinks I'm up to something, but he doesn't know what it is, so he's poking at me a little to see what happens.

Poke all you want, Idi. All you do is strengthen me in my resolve.

Until very recently, he had thought he would continue on here for a while, possibly even a year or two, after making his double killing on the coffee deal. But this operation was making him nervous, and now Amin's attitude was making him even more nervous. Once the coffee was gone, why wouldn't Amin begin to believe that Chase had had something to do with its disappearance?

So the thing was to get out, right away. Not *with* the coffee, no; he had no desire to be present when Balim and Company received their little extra surprise. But at the same time as the coffee went, he would go. His papers were such that he could leave at will, so why not slip out of the country as soon as the word came that the coffee had actually been stolen? There was no reason why not, and plenty of reasons why he should.

Jinja, the source of the Nile, that romantic ideal of the Victorian imagination, has today become a plain and ordinary town, part small manufacturing center and part bedroom community for the civil servants at Kampala, fifty miles away. The whole is brooded over by the Army's Jinja Barracks, site of the first massacre of Idi Amin's rule, when several hundred officers and men from suspect tribes—Langi and Acholi, mostly—were herded into a small building and machine-gunned.

Not far from the Barracks was the business center of town. The lawyer Edward Byagwa's office stood upstairs from a now-defunct shoe store, once owned by Asians, then given to an Army officer from the Barracks, who, not knowing how to reorder, abandoned it when the stock ran out. Byagwa shared the second floor with a dentist, who hadn't been seen for about two months. His family remained hopeful.

Byagwa's secretary in his reception room was his wife; a fairly good guarantee of loyalty, assuming there were no domestic difficulties. She was a stocky unattractive woman who was reading an old copy of *Queen*, and who looked up with a mixture of apprehension and annoyance when Chase walked in. Seeing he was a white man, and therefore unlikely to be dangerous to her, she dropped the apprehension but kept the annoyance. "Yes?"

"Baron Chase. I'm expected."

"You're *late*. The others are already here." Not rising from her desk, she gestured at the inner door.

"I am *Captain* Baron Chase," he said, smiling at her, "an adviser to our President."

She stared at him, the threat sinking home. In Uganda, no one was permitted to call himself "President" of anything, not of a club or a company or a trade union. No one but Idi Amin. For another person to give himself the title "President," no matter of what, was a capital offense. So this man was telling her that he was close to Amin and that he was, after all, potentially dangerous to her, and that she should irritate him only at her risk.

Yes; she understood. Her mouth opening into a wide O, she started hurriedly and awkwardly to her feet. But then Chase smiled, arresting her with his hand, saying, "No, don't get up. I can find my way."

The inner office had a wall of windows overlooking the street, covered by a layer of thin curtains. The furniture was scanty and functional, placed for efficiency rather than beauty on a worn gray carpet; an Army uniform was folded on one chair. The walls were pale green and contained no decoration other than the attorney's framed documents.

Entering, Chase first saw Frank Lanigan, sprawled on a wooden-armed chair like a defeated gladiator. The man was dressed in suit and tie, but looked as ridiculously crumpled as ever. "Hello, Frank," Chase said, smiling. "Long time no see."

"Not long enough." But Frank did get to his feet and consent to shake hands. They both squeezed hard, but stopped before it became a contest. "This is Isaac Otera," Frank said, gesturing to a black man in chauffeur's uniform.

Isaac Otera, Chase knew, was Balim's office manager and the one who was supposed to get the trucks. He certainly didn't look the part. And why is the man staring at me like that?

Neither Chase nor Otera offered to shake hands, and it was with some relief that Chase turned to the third man in the room, the attorney, Edward Byagwa. "Our host, I believe," he said.

Byagwa did want to shake hands, and Chase obliged, finding the lawyer's paw soft and pulpy, like the rest of him. Byagwa had a round head and a round face of polished bronze, with a very wide mouth and bulging eyes. He's stuck midway between frog and prince, Chase thought, amusing himself, as he released the man's hand.

Edward Byagwa was many things, too many things, and some inevitable day he would overstep himself. His wife outside was right to be apprehensive. An active churchgoer, Byagwa appeared in court frequently to defend priests and ministers against accusations ranging from treason (the storing of weapons in church basements was a popular charge) to the holding of services allied to one of the banned Christian sects. At the same time, he served as a go-between in smuggling operations involving Army officers and government figures, and had allegedly been very helpful back in 1973 in getting automobiles across the border into Kenya. (The ousted Asians had left behind many fine cars, but the Ugandan shilling was then already worth only a fraction of the Kenyan shilling, and true profit could be turned on those cars only if they could be gotten out of the country. That was the first time in Amin's reign that the border with Kenya was closed; Amin closed it himself, to try to keep those cars in Uganda. Byagwa had helped many important people to realize their profit after all.)

Because he was so useful to the people in power, Byagwa dared more than most lawyers could these days in helping his church friends. And because he had been so useful, and knew (quite literally) where so many bodies were buried, he was not bothered, as he might otherwise have been. This office, for instance, was not bugged, nor was his telephone tapped, making this one of the very few places in Uganda where the present meeting could have occurred.

"Well," Byagwa said, coming around from behind his desk, "you'll want to talk together." And he smiled and bowed and departed, carefully closing the door behind himself.

"We might as well get down to it," Frank said. "Get changed, Isaac."

But Chase shook his head and put his finger to his lips. Frank frowned, and they all listened, and heard the hall door close. Frank strode to the inner door, opened it, and demonstrated to Chase that the reception room was empty. "Okay?"

"Not yet."

Chase looked around the office and decided the most logical place to start was the desk. The drawers were all innocuous, except that the bottom left was locked. Lying on the floor under the desk while Frank and Otera watched in bafflement, Chase found the tiny wire emerging from the bottom of the desk under that locked drawer. Carefully tacked into place along a seam between two pieces of wood, the wire ran to a tiny button microphone at the outer corner of the desk.

"Good," Chase muttered. He used the screwdriver from his pocket-knife to pry the microphone loose from the wood, then yanked it to break the wire and crawled out from under the desk. "Byagwa would also like to know what's going on," he said, dropping the microphone onto the middle of the attorney's green blotter. "And what's in it for him."

"The dirty bastard," Frank said, glaring at the button on the green.

"Ah, well," Chase said. "Who among us is above such little tricks? Now, Frank, we can get down to it."

So they did. Chase settled himself in the chair behind the desk, and Frank took a white envelope from his pocket and dropped it disdainfully next to the microphone. Meantime, Otera started to change from his chauffeur's uniform to the uniform on the chair, transmogrifying himself into a captain in the Ugandan Army.

Inside the envelope, Chase found the confirmation from the Zurich bank. Thirty thousand dollars had been deposited by Balim into his new account there. "Earnest money," he had described it to Balim, when insisting on some cash payment in advance. To protect Balim, the deposit had been made in such a way that he could order it withdrawn and redeposited into his own account at any time within thirty days. Balim had accepted this concept of "protection" because he had assumed he would be alive in thirty days.

"Good," Chase said, stowing the confirmation away. Then he brought from his inner jacket pocket a large manila envelope. Pushing the microphone to one side, he emptied papers from this envelope onto the desk, saying, "Let's see what we have here. Identification for Mr. Otera. You're Captain Isaac Gelaya now," Chase told the man, who was across the room putting on his military trousers. "I gave you your own first name, in case anyone calls to you."

"Thank you."

Otera seemed very muted for some reason. Was it funk? Chase frowned from Otera to Frank, wanting to point out that a misstep now by Otera could destroy the whole operation.

Frank read the unspoken concern and shook his head. "Don't worry about Isaac. He's very deceptive. He looks like a mild-mannered fella, but inside he's a killer."

Otera smiled a mild-mannered grateful smile, and zipped his fly.

Not completely convinced, Chase returned to the papers on the desk. "Here's the authorization for today's truck. And this is for the ones on Friday."

Frank said, "It's definitely Friday?" Behind him Otera, knotting his brown uniform necktie, became very still.

"Definitely Friday," Chase said.

Otera came forward, tie knotted a bit unevenly, legs awkwardly rigid. "Let's get it over with."

"Straighten your tie," Frank told him, as Chase handed him the documents.

Otera stood silently, nodding and fussing with his tie, as Chase explained what each piece of paper was for. But when Chase started to tell him how to get to Jinja Barracks, the man interrupted, saying, "I know Jinja."

Chase looked at him, the rigid face, the office-worker appearance, the wound-up-spring determination. A Ugandan, he suddenly realized. Refugee. A fled civil servant. Much became clear, including why Chase had been feeling such hostility from the man. "Then you know the Barracks are within walking distance," he said.

"Of course. Frank, here are the keys to the car."

Taking them, Frank said to Otera, "We'll see you from the window when you drive by."

"Yes."

"And you know where we'll meet."

"Of course."

Frank and Otera shook hands. Chase, seated at the desk, watched with a small smile as Otera left, then watched Frank go over to the windows, pull the curtain back a bit, and gaze out at the street. Talking to his back, Chase said, "Your life is in that man's hands, you know, Frank."

Frank didn't look around. "Better than in yours," he said.

30

By the time they reached the plantation, Lew and Amarda weren't speaking. She had wanted to stop at that availably empty house, but he had refused, and when she'd asked why, he'd had to tell her it was finished between them. And because it was so difficult to say such a thing, he'd had to build up a head of steam and then practically yell it at her. "There's no future in it, that's all! It's pointless and it's making trouble and it has to stop!"

"What sort of trouble? What are you talking about?"

"Just trouble." He could feel himself being sullen, and he blamed Amarda for making him be that way. "I don't want to lose Ellen, that's all."

"Over me?"

"Over anything."

"I'm not worth such a risk."

"If you say so," he'd said, knowing he was ungracious, but unable to carry the burden any longer.

And that had been the end of the conversation. For the rest of the drive, Lew had felt rude but virtuous—not an unpleasant feeling.

At the house, a stony-faced Amarda led him into a small, overly furnished, stuffily hot room where her grandmother, today in a light-green silk sari, sat reading from a book with a blue-velvet cover and gilded pages. The old woman lifted her head, the reading lamp with its dark glass shade reflecting from her round spectacle lenses, and gestured for Lew to sit in an elaborately carved armchair facing her. "I'll get tea," Amarda said.

The old woman closed her book but kept her finger in it to mark her place, and remained silent until Amarda had gone out and shut the door. Then her first words weren't encouraging. "I have no idea, Mr. Brady, why your friend Mr. Balim has seen fit to send you to me."

Neither did Lew, if it came to that. "Well, Mama Jhosi," he said, speaking softly and leaning forward as though to protect her from storms and abrasions, "Mr. Balim seemed to think there was some sort of problem."

"It is not a problem," she said. "I have changed my mind, that is the only thing. As for the money, Mr. Balim knows I shall return it from our next harvests."

There was a faint flowerlike scent of perfume in the stuffy warm air. Lew said, "I'm not here to talk about money, Mama Jhosi."

"Of course not." She made a small perhaps unconscious movement with the book in her lap, suggesting her desire to return to it.

Lew's hands felt too large, too cumbersome. Not knowing what else to do with them, he gripped his knees as he leaned toward her. "Please," he said, "would you tell me why you've changed your mind?"

"My grandson," she said.

"Pandit." Lew smiled in remembered pleasure. He'd seen the boy twice and had enjoyed their conversations both times. "A very nice boy."

"At school now. But the home is also a school."

"Of course."

"I do not expect," she said, her eyes small and unreadable behind the reflecting lenses, "that Pandit will have a very easy life."

"It's starting well, at least."

"You mean material comfort."

"That, too," Lew acknowledged. "But what I mostly meant was the home he has here, and the people around him. You, and Amarda."

As though on cue, Amarda entered with a tray bearing tea things, and for the next few minutes the ritual of an English tea interrupted the conversation. Amarda was silent, unsmiling, rigid. Was the old lady aware of the tension emanating from her granddaughter, and would she have any idea of its cause?

When they were all furnished with tea and little cakes, the grandmother said, "Amarda, I was explaining to Mr. Brady why I have changed my mind about Mr. Balim's so thoughtful proposition."

Amarda sipped tea, expressionless, not looking at Lew. "Does Mr. Brady understand, do you think, Mama?"

"I had not completely made my point." To Lew she said, "I was talking of Pandit, and I was saying that the home is also a school, and I was about to suggest that the sense of self and the sense of morals Pandit learns in his home will be very important to him in later life."

"Absolutely," Lew said. The tea and cakes had given him something to do with his hands, but the hot tea had combined with the airless warmth of the room to create a stuffy, clogged, distracted feeling.

"Pandit has seen Mr. Balim here," the old lady went on. "He has seen you here. If we continue as originally envisaged, the day will come when he will see many truckloads of coffee here which he will know we have not grown on our few acres. He will ask questions."

Amarda said, "He has already asked questions, Mama, about Mr. Balim and Mr. Brady. Mostly about Mr. Brady."

Glancing at the girl, Lew could read the hostility behind the neutral facade. It had, of course, been bad tactics to break with her before this meeting; a quick roll in that house in Nairobi and Amarda would be on his side now. But he couldn't have made himself treat her that cynically, so now she would do her subtle best to sabotage his mission.

If only Ellen had come along! Not only so he could prove there was nothing between himself and Amarda, but also to help with the old lady. Mama Jhosi would have been impressed by Ellen, and would have realized any plot with Ellen in it couldn't be all bad.

But Ellen had been difficult, and Amarda had set herself to be impossible, so Lew was left to struggle here on his own in this hot mummified room. Struggle and fail, no doubt; so he might as well get it over with. "I believe, Mama Jhosi," he said, "I understand your point. If Pandit sees a criminal act performed in his own home, with the connivance of the two people he most looks to for moral guidance, what will happen to his own moral and ethical self?"

The old lady smiled, and made a small gesture with both hands. (She still held her book, marking her place.) "You do see," she said.

What Lew saw, all at once and startlingly, was that he was exactly following Balim's instructions: he was talking morality, good and evil. But he hadn't intended it—he'd had no clear idea *what* he might say—and it seemed to him Mama Jhosi, rather than he, had led the conversation in this direction. But was Balim right, yet again? Baffled but emboldened, Lew returned to the attack.

"I see and I sympathize. And you may well be right. At Pandit's age—what is he, twelve?—a simplistic morality may be the best approach. There'll be time later, I suppose, for him to learn how to think through the knottier moral questions."

Amarda gave him a quick look of annoyance, but her grandmother frowned, shaking her head slightly, saying, "Knottier moral questions? I see no moral question at all. The subject is stolen coffee. Thievery."

"Of course." The heat was his friend now; it bound them all together as in a secret hiding place. He said, "Mama Jhosi, may I tell you a story from my personal experience?"

"If you wish."

"I am not a criminal by profession. I am a soldier."

"A mercenary," Amarda said.

"That's right. My usual job is instructing recruits. Several years ago, you may recall, one of the factions in the Congo civil war took to rounding up groups of white missionaries, white medical people, and so on, and massacring them."

"And nuns," the old lady said. "I remember how sad that was; they killed many nuns."

"I was just going to mention nuns. There was an orphanage—" Then Lew stopped and grinned and waved his hand in a negative gesture, saying, "The children were already gone; this isn't a tear jerker story."

"I beg your pardon?"

Amarda said in her neutral voice, "He means he will not try to sway you with sentimentality."

"Oh, I see." She was no longer marking the place in her book with her finger. She seemed almost to be smiling. "So there shall be no orphans in this story."

"Only the nuns," Lew promised. "Eleven of them, French-speaking. We had no transportation and we couldn't take them on into the thick of things with us, but we didn't like leaving them there. Now, there was a Land-Rover we'd seen, that had some journalists in it, that had been left with its driver while the journalists walked ahead. We went back to the Land-Rover, and the driver said he had to stay there and wait for the journalists. So we pulled him out of there, and we stole his Land-Rover and brought it to the nuns. One of them could drive, and away they went. The journalists were very angry."

"Yes," the old lady said. Now she was definitely smiling, while Amarda was cold and tight-lipped.

"Now, that's not a particularly *knotty* moral question," Lew said, "but it's beyond the level of subtlety you want to permit for Pandit. We did steal that Land-Rover."

"Oh, now, Mr. Brady," she said dismissively, as though disappointed in him, "that was in a war. Things are different in a war, everybody knows that."

"*You're* in a war, Mama Jhosi," he told her. "Forgive me, but you must know you're in a war, whether you want to be or not. Idi Amin is waging war against you and a lot of other people. He has already harmed you in this war, as you well know. And he's harmed Pandit, too."

"A war is battles. It isn't coffee."

"Money from coffee is the main thing keeping Idi Amin in power. And his victims are just as dead as if they'd been on a traditional battlefield. But all right," he said, sitting back, raising his hands as though to acknowledge defeat. "The point you're making is your own relationship with your grandson. I can't argue against that. The operation will go on in any event, as you realize."

Amarda said, "Of course it will. My grandmother doesn't suppose she is stopping the theft from happening."

Theft. Thanks a lot, Amarda. Lew said, "Even at this late date, I'm sure Mr. Balim will have no trouble finding another coffeegrower happy to take your place. Someone for whom the issue is money alone, without the satisfaction you might have in avenging yourself just a little against Idi Amin. That other person's *motives* will be less moral than yours would have been." Leaning forward once more, Lew said, "Mama Jhosi, it was out of his fondness for you, and his awareness of your treatment at Amin's hands, that Mr. Balim came to you in the first place."

"I am sure that is true." The old lady was agitated now; her fingertips silently tapped the blue-velvet cover of the book in her lap. "I have not discussed this with Pandit," she said. "Amarda, have you?"

"Yes," Amarda said. She hesitated, reluctant to go on, then looked hard at Lew, saying, "He sees it the way you do, Mr. Brady. A heroic adventure against the forces of evil." Turning back to her grandmother, she said, "Pandit thinks Mr. Brady is a hero. Like a footballer."

"A footballer?" The old lady studied Lew with mock severity. "Without a poster, I hope."

"No poster," Lew said, smiling.

She shook her head, thinking things over. Amarda sat rigidly, eyes lowered, looking at nothing but the tea service. Lew had won, and he knew it, and the astonishing thing was that Amarda had made it possible. The faint perfume hung in the close air, and he thought of Amarda's bedroom, somewhere deep inside this house, which he had never seen.

Mama Jhosi sighed. "There seems to be no completely satisfactory answer," she said, and looked speculatively at Lew. "But I suppose it won't hurt Pandit to have his heroes, if he shows some care in his choices. You may tell Mr. Balim that I will keep to our original agreement."

* * *

Amarda walked Lew down the hall toward the front door. "Thank you," he said.

The look she gave him was cold and unfriendly. "For what? I told the truth, that's all."

"You didn't have to."

"But I did have to." Stopping in the hall, facing him, she said, "I behaved properly. To Pandit you are still a hero, but to me not anymore. And when I think of you from now on, I will say to myself, '*I* behaved properly.' "

"I still thank—"

"Wanube is waiting for you in the car. He works for us. He will drive you back to the airport."

Lew would have tried to speak again, to thank her or say good-bye, but she turned on her heel and walked away.

* * *

At the airport, smiling, happy, he found Ellen reading a magazine in the waiting room and said, "Everything's fixed." And he meant— and he wanted her to understand—that *everything* was fixed. Not just the job Balim had sent him to do, but also the entanglement with

Amarda. That too was fixed—forever—and with very little damage on either side.

"That's fine," Ellen said, rising, stowing the magazine in her shoulder bag; but for some reason she didn't seem particularly interested or involved.

Lew had been assuming her bad temper was the result of some suspicion she had about him and Amarda; couldn't she see there was no longer anything to be suspicious about? He was sorry she hadn't been out front to see him arrive without the girl. Nailing home that message, he said, "Some employee of the family drove me back. An old man, a Kikuyu, named Wanube. Maybe the slowest, vaguest, worst driver I've ever seen. I finally took the wheel while he sat in back. Come to think of it, maybe that's what he had in mind."

"Probably so," Ellen said, still distracted. "You ready to go?"

"Sure. Ellen? What's the problem?"

Now she did finally look at him, and he saw her eyes come into focus. "Sorry, Lew," she said. "I was thinking about something else. You talked the grandmother around, did you?"

"That's just what I did. I think she half wanted to be talked around, anyway."

"So Mr. Balim was right to send you. Come on, let's get back and give him the news."

They walked out the terminal's side door and headed for the plane. Lew said, "Ellen? What's wrong?"

"Nothing," she said, and suddenly became much livelier. "Just half-asleep from sitting around, I suppose." Looping her arm through his as they walked along, she said, "There's no reason we can't be friends."

Now, what did she mean by *that*?

31

At the very first bureaucratic foot-drag, Isaac forgot to be scared. He almost forgot who he really was, and what this charade was all about, because what came flooding into the forefront of his mind was his normal technique for dealing with minor-league officiousness, clerical obstructionism, and the arrogance of petty authority. When the motor-pool sergeant, a sloppy man in a sloppy uniform, said indignantly, "We can't break into our schedule to service a truck for you now, you should have phoned yesterday," Isaac's immediate answer was to point to the phone on the sergeant's desk and say, "Put me through to the commanding officer."

Now, if he'd stopped to think about it, that was just about the most dangerous thing he could have done. These documents from Chase should carry the day with the Jinja Barracks motor pool—and in fact they'd gotten him through the gate and this far already—but in order to divert suspicion from Chase later on, the documents could eventually be shown to be forgeries. If the sergeant were to call Isaac's bluff and put him through to the Barracks commander—which is exactly the way some truly self-important bureaucrats would have handled the situation—Isaac could well be in deep trouble very fast. He could see the sequence now: the commander sides with his sergeant, and in order to complain about the lack of advance warning, he puts a call through to the individual in Kampala whose signature was on this requisition. "What order for a truck? *I* never—" Isaac's heart began to pound.

But. "No need to be that way, Captain," the sergeant said, at once losing his fine indignation and becoming mulish and sullen, like a man who's already been chewed out by his superiors more than once for unnecessary interference. "I'm just saying we don't have a truck for you at this exact instant."

Isaac had the man on the run now. Suddenly cool—really and truly cool, he was astonished to realize—just as though he weren't standing in this office in this low concrete-block building next to the motor pool, deep within Jinja Barracks in Uganda, with thousands of Amin's troops all around him like piranha fish around a drowning kitten, still thoroughly cool, Isaac made a show of looking at his watch. "At what instant do you suppose you *will* have a truck for me?"

"That's hard to say." The sergeant made an effort to reconstruct his former indignation. "You come in here; you disturb the schedule; I don't know what's going to happen next."

"Well, I know, my friend," Isaac said. "You see who signed this order?"

The sergeant looked again—reluctantly, it seemed—at that very important signature. "Yes, I know, I know."

"This isn't for *me*. I'm a captain. Do you think, if that truck were for me, I'd drive it myself?"

"Oh, I understand," the sergeant said, unbending a little, as though in acknowledgment that he and the captain shared the same fate: constant harassment from above.

"If I am late with that truck," Isaac said, "I'm sorry, but I won't take all the blame myself. I didn't get to be a captain *that* way. Do you understand me, sergeant?"

The sergeant did. He also understood why Isaac had made a point of emphasizing their comparative ranks. "Yes, of course," he said, looking worried.

"So I'm sure we'll both do our best," Isaac suggested.

"Certainly. Why not? Hmmm, let's see, I'll have to, um . . ." He took down one of several clipboards in a row on the wall over his desk and leafed through the papers on it. "I'll just check outside," he said. "You understand, I'll have to give you a truck already in process of being serviced for someone else. This alters the schedule a great deal. Well, I'll see what I can do. I'll be back."

The sergeant bustled out, carrying the clipboard with him. Isaac went over to the window to watch the man walk out across the motor pool, where a few dozen vehicles, ranging from large tractor-trailer rigs to buses to jeeps, were parked higgledy-piggledy on the tan dirt, in no discernible design. The sergeant's implication of neat, orderly, bustling, highly organized activity orchestrated to a tight schedule was belied by the sloppiness visible everywhere and the inertia common to those few troops he could see.

Strangely, Isaac felt less sure of himself, less concealed and more in danger, now that he was alone. He seemed to need someone to pretend in front of before he could feel secure in his impersonation.

The sergeant was out of sight, somewhere in there among the trucks and buses. What if he'd seen through Isaac's disguise? What if he'd already guessed that the documents were bogus, and even now he was on the phone somewhere out there, calling for a squad to come arrest the impostor?

Four men came into view from behind a building to the right, carrying rifles as though they were fishing poles after a long day without a nibble. Isaac stiffened, all the old fear coming back. Once again he was hidden in that shrubbery in the warm night behind his house, looking at all the lit windows and listening to the machine-gun fire within.

The four soldiers drifted laggardly by, not quite dragging their rifles in the dirt. The sergeant, moving with self-satisfied fussiness, reappeared among the motor-pool vehicles and came marching back to the office, where he said, "Well, I succeeded for you. It wasn't easy."

"I'll have a truck soon?"

"Ten minutes, no more." He returned his clipboard to its nail on the wall with a solid slap of self-satisfaction at a job well done. "It's being gassed up now," he said, "windshield cleaned, everything fine."

"That's good." Isaac touched the other requisition on the sergeant's desk. "Now, about this for Friday."

"Twenty trucks." The sergeant, very dubious, shook his head.

"Three days from now, plenty of warning," Isaac pointed out, and they spent the next fifteen minutes haggling over that, the sergeant at last promising that he would do *his* best—he couldn't answer, of course, for incompetent staff or careless previous drivers or the importunings of even more important individuals than the one whose signature was on this request—but at least *he* would do his best, and quite possibly, at noon on Friday, twenty trucks would be ready and forthcoming. "It helps," the sergeant explained, "that you won't need drivers."

A knock on the door was followed by the appearance of a grease-covered skinny man in uniform trousers and dirty undershirt, who said the truck was ready. "Exactly on time!" the sergeant exclaimed inaccurately. "Come along, Captain."

The truck was just outside, a five-ton Leyland Terrier, several years old, with a black canvas cover on an aluminum frame over the bed. The engine was running; that is, it was loudly coughing and missing. "Not warmed up yet," the sergeant said. Extending another clipboard and a ball-point pen, he said, "No dents or scratches. Sign here."

Isaac wrote on the form under *Comments:* "Many general dents and scratches." Then he signed, with something of a flourish, "Captain I. Gelaya." Pleased that he'd signed the name without hesitation, relieved and happy that he was getting away with this so easily, he handed the clipboard back.

"Isaac!"

Responding automatically to his name, and also to the sound of a familiar voice, Isaac turned, and his heart leaped into his throat.

He was face-to-face with a man named Obed Naya, who was also in the uniform of an Army captain, but who wore his uniform legitimately. An old friend, Obed Naya, a onetime classmate at Makerere University. A man who'd had dinner at Isaac's house, who had danced with Isaac's wife. He had entered the Army after university, in the latter days of the Obote presidency, and he and Isaac had seen less and less of one another after Amin had taken over. He was now something in engineering for the Army, and he knew who Isaac really was, and Isaac no longer had any idea who Obed Naya might in the last few years have become.

Brazen it out. What would Frank do? "Obed," Isaac said, forcing a broad smile onto his face, stepping forward with hand outstretched. "It's been a long time."

Delight was being replaced by confusion in Obed's eyes as they shook hands. He blinked at Isaac's face, then at his uniform, his captain's bars. Utterly bewildered, he said, "I had no idea you, uhh . . ." And Isaac could see him beginning to remember the truth, what had really happened to his old friend Isaac Otera.

"They had me up north for a while," Isaac said, babbling to keep

Obed from speaking. He squeezed Obed's hand hard, begging him to go along for the sake of their old friendship. "But now I've been transferred again. Amazing how things change, isn't it?"

"Yes . . . yes."

"Well, I mustn't keep my General waiting. It's been wonderful to see you again, Obed." Isaac stopped and peered intently at Obed's stunned face. "I mean that," he said. "Wonderful to see you again, see that you're healthy, you're all right. We'll have to get together soon."

"Yes," Obed said in a faraway voice.

Isaac felt his old friend's eyes on him as he climbed up into the truck's dirty cab and forced the floor shift into first gear. What was Obed thinking? What conclusions would he draw? Would he permit Isaac to get away, out of friendship or bewilderment, or would he suddenly raise the alarm? "This impostor—!" But he remained silent, beside the truck, his face a mask of shock.

The truck jolted forward. Isaac fed the gas slowly. He didn't want the engine to stall; he didn't want to seem to run away. In the rearview mirror on the truck door beside him, he could see Obed staring.

* * *

Up ahead, the Mercedes turned off the road at the spot where Lew had been captured by the men from the State Research Bureau. Isaac, following in the clumsy truck, looked in his mirror and saw only empty road behind him. He made the turn off the highway.

It was an hour since he'd driven away from Jinja Barracks, shaking at the wheel of the truck with pent-up fright and the nearness of his close call with Obed. Willing his hands to behave themselves on the steering wheel, he'd driven the truck through town and past the building holding the lawyer's office. He'd leaned out the cab window on the way by, pretending to stare at something up ahead, so Frank could get a good look at him. Then he'd circled the block twice, and the second time Frank had pulled out in front in the Mercedes, leading the way east out of Jinja toward the Kenyan border.

And now, with no trouble at all, here they were on the old access road, overgrown with shrubbery, rutted and pitted underneath. Ahead, the Mercedes moved at barely five miles an hour, rocking and dipping on the uneven ground as though it were a small boat in a choppy sea. The truck followed in a more elephantine manner, its big tires crushing down the rocks and roots that made the Mercedes dance.

After a quarter of a mile, the Mercedes stopped and Isaac braked the truck behind it. Frank came back and said, up through Isaac's open window, "No problems?"

"No problems. I ran into an old friend, but he didn't give me away."

Frank looked startled, but then he grinned. "Didn't give you away, huh? Isaac, you're wasted in an office; you were born for this life."

"I'll be glad, just the same, to be back in that office."

"Sure you will. Park this thing off to the right here, out of the way. We're far enough now; we can't be seen from the highway, and we can't be seen from the railroad."

"Fine."

Isaac put the truck where Frank had suggested, then joined him in the Mercedes. He got into the backseat where his chauffeur's uniform awaited him, and changed clothing while Frank bumped and groaned them on down the road. When the Mercedes stopped, Isaac looked forward and saw the gleaming steel stripes just ahead.

"Come on," Frank said. "Come look at our model railroad."

They got out of the car and walked down to the railway line. Looking back up the hill at the Mercedes, parked incongruously in the middle of the semitropical forest, surrounded by trees and vines and brush, Isaac was confused for a second because the car *didn't* look as out of place as it should; then he realized that luxury-car advertising for years has featured lavish color photos of gleaming expensive automobiles in the woods or on deserted beaches or perched on mountaintops. Now I know why they were there, Isaac thought. Their drivers were stealing coffee.

Frank said, "What are *you* grinning about?"

"A stray thought. Not important."

"It's somewhere down this way," Frank said, and led the way along the rail line to the right.

Isaac couldn't help looking back over his shoulder along the track from time to time, even though he knew no train would be coming. As part of his clerical role in this operation, he had learned the current status of Uganda Railways, and it was scanty indeed. There was no

longer passenger service on the main line between Kampala and the
eastern border with Kenya at Tororo. Generally speaking, two daily
trains now passed this spot, one in each direction, both freights, both
traveling at night to avoid the heat of the sun.

Frank stopped, in the middle of the tracks. Hands on hips, white
shirt sweat-damp beneath his rib cage, he stood glaring this way and
that, saying, "It's around here someplace."

"What is?"

Isaac slowly turned in a circle. Fore and aft, the rail line was flanked
by near-jungle growth, hedges and shrubs and limber small trees
crowding in on both sides, green walls ranging from eight to twelve
feet in height. There was a special small mower locomotive made for
this sort of climate, manufactured in Cleveland in the United States,
with whirring cutter blades mounted on both sides; three or four times
a year, that engine had to be run up and down the line to cut back
the encroaching plant life. With the sudden new spurt of growth
following the long rains, the mower engine would be due soon for
another run.

"*Hey!*" Frank yelled, as though to somebody. "*Goddammit, where
are we?*"

Nowhere, as Isaac could plainly see. Way to the east, the track
curved gently out of sight around to the left, still enclosed by greenery
except for the one break at the access road. The same was true to the
west, except that the curve to the right was closer and there were no
breaks for roads.

"Goddammit," Frank said, "do we have to walk all the goddam
way around the other way?"

"I don't know what you're looking for," Isaac said, and then he
shrieked and jumped back, nearly tripping over the rail, as a huge
section of greenery to his left all at once *opened up!*

"*There* you are," Frank said.

"Wa—wa—wa—" Isaac stared at a tangled green mess of leaves
and branches, eight feet square, that had simply separated itself from
the real world and turned itself into a door, into something from a
fairy tale.

From behind this now slightly ajar impossible door, a voice suddenly
cried in Swahili, "It's falling!"

"It's falling?" In his bewilderment and panic, Isaac still remembered his duty as translator; Frank had no Swahili. "It's falling," Isaac told him in English.

"*Shit!*" Frank cried, and leaped forward, arms outstretched.

And it *was* falling. This segment of the green wall had now become a green wave, a tidal wave toppling slowly over onto them. "I can't hold it!" cried the Swahili voice.

Frank had flung himself against the shrubs and saplings, was contesting his own weight against theirs. Isaac, reacting more slowly, now jumped to help him, at the same time crying out in Swahili, "We're pushing!"

But it didn't matter. The thing, whatever it was, leaned now off-balance, and the demands of gravity were inexorable. Slow, painfully slow, but nevertheless inevitable, the section of wall bore down on them. The voice from beyond it despairingly called out the name of a tribal snake god for the Lake Turkana region, and Frank and Isaac both collapsed backward onto the track, under a massive blanket of green.

Isaac, quite naturally, began to thrash about, but Frank yelled, "Don't break it!" and Isaac stopped, baffled. Don't break it?

The wall or wave or blanket or fantasy or whatever it was teetered now on the southern track of the rail line, leaving just enough leeway so that a man could crawl out from underneath, scratching his hands and making his chauffeur's uniform filthy in the process. Clambering to his feet, hatless, covered with leaves and stones and dirt, Isaac found himself facing a barefoot man dressed in blue work pants, naked to the waist, who was grinning sheepishly and saying, "It takes more than one man to hold it."

"What's the son of a bitch say?"

Frank had crawled out from under the thing on the other side, looking just as messy as Isaac and twice as angry. Isaac translated what the man had said, and, "No shit," Frank commented. "All right, just so it isn't busted."

Now Isaac looked down at the thing. On this side, there was a complicated trellislike arrangement of sticks and bamboo poles, lashed together, and with many tree branches and shrubs in turn lashed to the poles. The whole thing was two to three feet thick, and had to be very very heavy.

"We'd better get it back into place," Frank said. "Tell him to call the others."

"He says," Isaac translated, "to call the others."

"Very good." Turning away, the man trotted off downhill.

And now for the first time Isaac looked through the magic doorway. A path as broad as a railway line extended away down the slope, and after a few yards there actually was a railway line on it, old and rusted. The old tracks ran directly downhill, becoming quickly obscured because of all the undergrowth choking them. Nearer, tree stumps and disturbed earth showed where the rail line had been cleared and the pathway to it created.

Isaac became aware of a sound that had been obscured when the wall was in place. It was the whine of a chain saw. Now, over it, came the sound of the blue-trousered man calling. The saw stopped; another voice answered. The voices rang clear and echoing in the upper branches of the trees, disturbing birds, which fluttered briefly, calling to one another, then settled back again.

"If he knew one man couldn't do it," Frank grumbled, "then why the fuck did one man *try* to do it?"

"Because you have such a loud intimidating voice," Isaac told him.

Frank thought about that. Isaac could see him trying to remain stern and angry. "If I'm so fucking intimidating," Frank said, "how come you talk to me like that?"

"Because I see through you," Isaac said.

Up through the woods, along the rail line, the blue-trousered man returned with three other men, all dressed in a similar style, though two did wear frayed and torn shirts. The three newcomers were highly amused at the sight of their blind lying on the tracks, and they made several remarks at the blue-trousered man's expense. He laughed along with the others, so it was all right.

The four men, with Frank and Isaac helping, lifted the blind and jockeyed it back into position, where it was wedged in so tightly by the branches on both sides that it didn't even need to be tied in place.

All six men were now inside. Frank said, "Let's see how they're coming along," and they all walked back down the hill, following the old rail line. They had to struggle through trees and thick undergrowth until they came to another cleared section, where the broad path began again. Once more, tree stumps and fresh shallow holes between the rails showed just how much plant growth had had to be removed. And looking down the line, Isaac could now see the engine shed and the spur track angling away to the right.

One of the men, who wore a pale-green dress shirt from which the sleeves had been raggedly cut off, gestured to the uncleared portion of track from which they'd just emerged and said to Isaac, "Tell him we'll do that last."

Isaac passed the message on. Nodding, Frank said, "Smart. Another layer of protection." Isaac translated that, and the man in the green shirt smiled.

Walking on, they followed the spur down to the turntable. One of the potential problems, Isaac remembered, had been that the turntable was rusted into place at an unusable angle. But now it was aligned, fitting almost perfectly with the rails.

All four men wanted Isaac to explain to Frank just how difficult that job had been, how many tools they'd broken, how long it had taken. Isaac translated about half of it, and in the translation back, he made Frank's casual acceptance of their work sound much more enthusiastic than it was.

They had done a lot in five days, beginning in rain but latterly in drying sun. Beyond the turntable, the old bumper had been removed and was lying unceremoniously in the shrubbery to one side of the track. The track itself had been extended with rails from beside the engine shed. Lacking ties or sleepers, they had half buried thick logs at intervals from the end of the original track to the gorge and then attached the rail plates and rails to those. It was a makeshift, tottery affair and couldn't last long, but it only needed to last one day.

What the men were working on now was the path from the engine shed out to the access road, creating a surface that would permit trucks to pass. Trees and undergrowth were being cut away and the resulting logs and branches used to fill in the ruts and gullies that crossed the route. Less than a quarter of the distance had been covered, but they could already see that it would work.

"Okay," Frank said, stamping up and down the completed portion. "This fucker's gonna do the job." Then he grinned at Isaac and said, "This was Ellen's idea, remember?"

"Of course—"

"Let's—" Frank stood looking around, hands on hips in his usual expression of impatience.

"What is it?"

"A plank, board—something." Frank held his hands about a yard apart.

Isaac translated the request, and one of the workmen immediately laughed, nodded, and trotted away to the engine shed, to return a minute later with an old one-by-six, originally part of a window frame, both ends rotted away by dampness. "Perfect," Frank said, and pulled out his boot knife.

They all stood around watching as he laid the board on the ground, knelt over it, and carved the thick letters into the time-grayed wood, revealing slightly darker wood underneath. When it was finished, the board said: ELLEN'S ROAD. "There," Frank said.

Isaac, during the carving, had explained to the workmen that Ellen, Mr. Balim's white woman pilot, was the one who had thought up this road. They had all seen the woman around Balim's office, had thought of her as eminently fuckable, and were well pleased to have the road named after her. (Although in its earliest days Swahili had developed a written language and literature using Arabic orthography, that false start had been swept away and replaced by the European alphabet when the Portuguese overran the Arab merchant towns along the Indian Ocean early in the sixteenth century. Today the literate speaker of Swahili uses the same alphabet as the literate speaker of English; "road" in Swahili is *njia*, but "Ellen" is *Ellen*.)

After much discussion about the perfect location for the sign, a roadside tree near the engine shed was chosen, one of the workmen shinnied up, and the board was nailed into place. As the nailer slid back down, the others raised a cheer, which rang through the woods.

Well, well, Isaac thought, the world of the active man can be rather fun.

But now they got back to business. "Three days," Frank told the workmen, through Isaac, and they all grinned and nodded and said there would be no problem. "Okay," Frank said. "We'll go out this way. I don't wanna mess with that blind again."

The last several uncleared yards of Ellen's Road were rough going, particularly since Isaac was wearing ordinary shoes, as would befit the chauffeur of a Mercedes.

At the access road, Frank stopped and looked downhill. "Twenty miles to the lake," he said. "Easy as falling off a house."

Behind them, the chain-saw buzz started up once more. That nasal noise somehow only re-emphasized the quiet and the peacefulness of this forest, the tall graceful yellow-barked thorn trees, smaller trees of a dozen kinds, several varieties of purple acanthus, hibiscus in many colors, ground orchids, and here and there the creeper vine called *setyot*, which flowers only once in every seven or eight years; there are tribes who wait for its flowering before initiating their youngsters into manhood. Songbirds moved through the higher branches, keeping their distance from the chain saw and the movements of men.

"It's beautiful here," Isaac said, gazing around, watching a robin-chat—a small bird with yellow face and breast, gray wings, snowy white head—soar from branch to branch, pausing at each to announce one or another of its many brief songs. "Beautiful, peaceful." Sadly, nostalgically, thinking of Obed Naya, he said, "What a wonderful country this could be."

"Nice place for a battle, though," Frank said critically, studying the forest around them. "Particularly if you were attacking from uphill. Well, come on, let's get you back to that office you like so much."

32

Late Tuesday afternoon, and Sir Denis was exhausted. He could hardly keep his eyes open, and the softness of the Daimler's upholstery, the smoothness of the drive, the calm skill of the chauffeur up front beyond the glass partition; all struggled passively against his desire to stay awake. "My Lord, but I'll be glad when this is over," he said.

Beside him, a fur wrap over his useless legs, Emil Grossbarger snorted, saying, "Also I. Ziss Amin is not a businessman."

"I don't know why he insisted I be there when the coffee is shipped.

As though I were some sort of dispatcher. But he made it a condition of the sale. Yet another condition of the sale." Sir Denis yawned. "The last, I hope. Excuse me."

"After ziss, you can go home to São Paulo, you can rest."

"I'm not as young as I used to be."

There was a little silence in the car while they both pondered that statement; neither of them was as young as anybody used to be. Outside, the modern glass-and-concrete banking towers of Zurich went by, pink with embarrassment in a mountain sunset. A Volvo with red United Nations license plates rode for a while ahead of them before turning off toward the lake. How odd it was that so many offices of the United Nations were here, in Switzerland, a country that didn't even belong to the UN. Perhaps, Sir Denis thought, the rest of the world is trying to learn the secret that's kept the Swiss out of every war fought since 1521.

"I had you removed, vunce, from ze Uganda transaction."

This was the first either of them had mentioned that. On Sir Denis's arrival this morning from London, to meet with Grossbarger for the first time since his removal and reinstatement, he had wondered how the man would act toward him, and how he himself would behave in return. And the answer had been, they would both ignore the incident.

They had had a good lunch in Grossbarger's private dining room, in his apartment atop the tower containing his offices, during which no word of hostility or explanation was either requested or offered. Much of the conversation, in fact, had been about the wild mountain scenery, dark green below and gray-white-black above, forming the unexpected cyclorama background to this hard, modern, commercial city. "Ze mountains mock our little buildings," Grossbarger had said, smiling conspiratorially at them out his forty-seventh-floor window.

But now, at almost the last minute, as Grossbarger accompanied Sir Denis to the airport, the subject was all at once brought up. "I had you removed, vunce, from ze Uganda transaction."

"I know that," Sir Denis said, treading carefully. No inflection in his voice, he said, "I've wondered why you did it."

"You must know," Grossbarger answered, "zat not all ze coffee sold in ze vorld is of an unquestionable pedigree."

"Smuggling, you mean. The ICB does what it can."

"Vich is nossing," Grossbarger said, patting his fur lap rug in evident satisfaction. "Vat can your Coffee Board do ven legitimate roasters collude in ziss smuggling?"

Roasters was the coffee industry term for the companies that bought the coffee from the growers, prepared it, and packaged it for retail sale. "We know the problem," Sir Denis said, "but a roaster has no obligation—moral or legal—to question the bona fides of every shipment of coffee he buys."

"Of course not! And in any event, legitimate growers also collude, helping to bring smuggled coffee back into legitimate channels. Even governments, my friend, have been known to turn a blind eye and a ready palm ven ziss smuggling goes on."

"Are you suggesting the coffee Uganda is selling the Brazilians is smuggled from somewhere else?"

"Oh, no, no!" Grossbarger's mobile mouth expressed eleven kinds of amusement. "Uganda does not smuggle coffee *in*. Uganda smuggles coffee *out*. Particularly very recently as ze social structure zere breaks down. Do you know ze nation called Malavi?"

"Malawi? Yes, of course, in Africa."

"East of Zambia, souse of Tanganyika."

"Tanzania," Sir Denis corrected.

Smiling slyly, Grossbarger said, "Nostalgia. In any event, Malavi is really outside ze African coffee-growing belt, alzough it has in recent years exported some small amount. But zis year! My friend, zis year Malavi is a *major* coffee producer!"

In principle, Sir Denis disapproved of such occurrences in the world of coffee, no matter how common they were or how they were winked at by all concerned. But Grossbarger's delight was so infectious that he couldn't keep from returning the smile, saying, "How fortunate for Malawi's growers."

"Growers zey are, perhaps. Harvesters zey are, certainly. You know, my friend, ve Sviss"—that said without the faintest hint of irony or discomfort—"have known for centuries ze value of having a *lake* as a border viss anozzer country. So hard to patrol a lake, you know. And it iss almost as zough ze colonial powers vere consciously turning ze continent of Africa into a gigantic board game called 'Smuggling' ven zey laid out ze national boundaries. Lake Victoria borders sree nations, Lake Nyasa sree, Lake Tanganyika— Is ze *lake* still called Tanganyika?"

Acknowledging the teasing with a head bob and a grin, Sir Denis said, "Yes, it is. Your former German colony is still referred to in the name of the lake."

"Good. Lake Tanganyika borders *four* countries! How can zere be legitimate business at all?"

"I sometimes wonder," Sir Denis said. "But I don't understand the connection with, um—"

"Viss my kindness toward you?" Looking pleased with himself, ruffing up the fur throw, he said, "Oh, yes, kindness, I am not being ironic. You see, my friend, I vas given information zat somesing vould happen to zat coffee shipment."

"You mean theft?"

"Eggzactly. Seft und smuggling go togezzer. Just ze ozzer day I vas reading in ze paper, a truckload of coffee vas hijacked in Nairobi by two men viss guns. Eighty-five sousand English pounds' vorth of coffee in vun truck. Vell vorth ze attention of any gunman."

"What is supposed to happen to the Ugandan shipment?"

"I don't know." Grossbarger shrugged, looking away now at tiny patches of farmland, neatly planted, small and artificial-seeming against the backdrop of the mountains. The airport wasn't far. "Perhaps nossing," Grossbarger said. "But to be honest, Denis, if somesing does happen, I vished you not to be harmed."

"Harmed?"

"Oh, yes, I am serious. Zese people, you know, zey are not chentlemen like you und me. Und in ziss case, zeir opponent, ziss Idi Amin, he is also not a chentleman. I felt zere vas danger to anyone involved."

"Emil," Sir Denis said, earnestly and awkwardly, "I am touched, and I thank you. But I could wish you'd spoken to me directly, to learn if I wanted such protection."

"You vould say no! In your position, *I* vould say no! So I tried surreptitiously to have you removed from ze scene of danger, und I failed. Und so now I tell you ze truth, so you may defend yourself. Somesing may happen to zat shipment. Keep out of ze vay, if it does."

Smiling, Sir Denis said, "I don't fancy arguing with gunmen."

"Good. Anozzer sing. Ze vorst sing you could do vould be speak to ze Ugandan officials. Ve have no proof; ve have no facts; ve have no suspects. But if somesing does happen, und you have varned zem in zis vague vay, zey will detain you for questioning for ze rest of your life."

"Yes, I see that." Sir Denis rubbed a hand over his face. "And I thought my only problem was exhaustion."

The Daimler was turning in at the airport entrance. "Keep vell, my friend," Grossbarger said.

*   *   *

The stewardess woke him in Rome, where he must change planes.

The stewardess woke him in Tripoli, where he must change planes.

The pilot woke him at Entebbe. "We're here, sir."

Here? Sir Denis opened stinging eyes and looked at morning, somewhere on the planet. "Wum—" his mouth tasted terrible, full of woolly caterpillars. "Where?" he asked.

The pilot, a young Libyan Muslim, easygoing and self-confident with his modern skills, had seen these overly tired businessmen before, pushing themselves till they dropped. "Entebbe, sir," he said. "Wednesday morning, May twenty-fifth, nineteen seventy-seven. End of the line."

"End of the line," Sir Denis said, moving his stiff, cramped body. *I am sixty-one years of age.* "Yes, thank you."

33

Lew stared at her. "You're doing what?"

"I'm leaving," Ellen said. "I've got a job."

"A job?" They were seated at right angles at the kitchen table, in front of breakfasts of coffee, melon slices, and thick pieces of toast. Warm sunlight angled in through the open windows, gleaming on the surfaces they had together cleaned and polished, shimmering on the curtains Ellen had hung, highlighting the white-painted shelves Lew had put up. He frowned down at the food on his plate. "You've *got* a job. Balim," he said as though accusing her of disloyalty to the firm.

"He knows about it." She seemed awfully goddam calm, but on

the other hand, this wasn't a surprise to *her.* "He's getting a new pilot."

"A new—" There were so many spiky points on this ball she'd thrown him that he didn't know which one to grab for first. "What kind of job? Where are you going?"

"Back to the States."

The States. Was there a glimmer of understandable sense in that? Almost hopefully, because then at least he'd have some idea what was going on, he said, "Are you homesick? Is that it?"

But she laughed, as though relieved at the opportunity to break the tension—break *her* tension, not his—and said, "No, Lew, I've never been homesick in my life. I'm an Army brat, remember? I wouldn't know where home is."

"Then— Then, *what?*" The name *Amarda* trembled on his tongue, but it was just possible that Amarda was not the problem, and it would be stupid to open up that subject if he didn't have to. "Ellen, what is it?"

"You and me," she said. "Lew, do you remember who you were before you knew me?"

"Who I was? What do you mean?"

"You got along in life. You had friends, you had lovers, different people important to you at different times."

"Oh, now, wait a minute."

But she was inexorable. "Then we met," she said, "and we got to be very important to each other for a long while."

"We still are."

He tried to take her hand, but she moved it away. "No, we aren't. It used to be— Well, you went to Alaska to be with me. I came here to be with you. Now I'm going to the States. Will you come with me?"

"Come with—? How can I? The job—the coffee job—it's just about to happen!"

"Lew," she said, "the worst thing in the world is to try to hang on after something is over."

He was finally getting used to this. He sat back in the chair, pushing his plate away, and looked at her. "For you it's over, is that it?"

"For you, too," she told him. "You just haven't thought about it yet. Would you like to drive me to the airport?"

A new astonishment. "When?"

"I should leave in about fifteen minutes. I'm already half packed."

He could feel the bitter twist in his lips when he smiled. "No long good-byes, huh?"

"That's right. If you don't want to drive me, that's okay, I understand. I'll call Bathar."

"Young Mr. Balim? I'll drive you."

"Thanks, Lew."

He watched her get to her feet, a beautiful woman, in some weird way at the center of his life. "If everything's so goddam over," he said, "how come I'm still jealous of that twerp Bathar?"

"Habit," she said, smiling. She started away, to finish packing or whatever, then paused to say, "I told you where I'm going. If we were still now what we once were, I wouldn't want to go, and you wouldn't want to stay here without me."

"Not that way, Ellen," he told her. "I went to Alaska with you because I wanted to be with you, not because you were challenging me to prove myself. What you're doing now is something else; heads you win, tails I lose."

"Nobody wins, Lew," she said.

* * *

By the time they reached the airport he was more or less acclimated to the idea. He would still much prefer her to stay—he had no thought, for instance, of haring off after Amarda again now that the coast was clear—but if it wasn't right for Ellen, then he knew there was no way he could keep her. It was hard, but he knew he shouldn't even make the attempt. The day of the caged bird is over.

Still, it was tough to have this new weight on his chest, and even tougher that the only person he could go to for comfort and solace was the cause of it. And would no longer be available. He couldn't argue her out of her decision—at some level that he wasn't yet ready to deal with, he even thought she might be right—but he couldn't be as casual as she was, either. (He knew her calm was possible because she was the one making the move, and because she'd already had a while to get used to the idea.) Still, an emotional scene could only spoil their memories of one another; she wanted to go out on an easy level, and he could give her at least that much. What was roiling inside could stay there.

They'd been almost completely silent on the drive out to the airport, absorbed in their separate thoughts, Lew working his way through this new idea of what life was now going to be like, but as they walked from the car to the terminal it occurred to him to wonder about the details of her transition. "What plane are you taking? What's the route?"

"They're sending a charter for me from Entebbe."

"Entebbe!"

"Yes, I've got a one-shot job with an American carrier called Coast Global. A little cargo ferrying to Djibouti, and then I go back to the States with the plane and look for another job after that."

Lew had seen the truth right away. "Jesus, Ellen," he said, "when do you do this little cargo ferrying?"

"Friday."

"Hah!"

She stopped and stared at him, and he could see she was just about to get angry. They'd been doing very nicely, dealing with the emotional quagmire of their breaking up, and here Lew was suddenly filled with mysterious laughter, bubbling over with chipper secrets.

He explained: "It's *our coffee*, honey!"

Then she got it. "For God's sake! It has to be."

"So we're still in the coffee business together," he said grinning, taking her arm, walking her into the terminal. "In fact, here's something to think about."

"What?"

"If the coffee actually shows up where you are, you'll know old Lew isn't doing too good."

*   *   *

It was the same plane and pilot that had brought him back from Uganda in April. Uganda Skytours. The plane looked the same, but the middle-aged American pilot—owner, with his wife, of Uganda Skytours—looked just a little seedier, a little more desperate.

Nevertheless, Lew was glad to see him. They shook hands, and Lew said, "Ellen, this is Mike. He brought me back, remember?"

"Yes, I do."

"And now he's taking you away."

She shook the pilot's hand, saying, "How are you?"

"Can't complain," he said, which was patently untrue.

"Mike'll take good care of you." Lew was feeling extremely awkward, unable to work out how to say good-bye.

"Be ready when you are," the pilot said, and tactfully walked back over to his plane.

"Have a good flight," Lew said.

"Have a good robbery."

So he took her in his arms and kissed her, and she felt just as good as ever. And she responded just as well. "Jesus," he whispered into her hair, "can't we—"

Her body went rigid, pulling away from him. "Don't."

He released her, but he had become filled now with this urge to make things become somehow different. "Listen," he said, and in desperation he finally did bring out the dread name: "Amarda—"

"No," Ellen said, and touched his lips with her fingertip to make him stop. "I knew about that," she said, "and that was part of it, but it wasn't really the main thing."

"What was?"

She paused, as though she hadn't really thought about it before, and with some suggestion of surprise in her voice, she said, "You know, I think it was the rain."

There was no answer to that; he knew all at once exactly what she meant. But even though it was a perfect exit line—and they both knew that, too—he had one more thing to say. He took her arm and they walked toward the plane, and he said, "Listen, don't get married or anything."

"I wasn't planning to, but why?"

"I'm likely to show up in your life again someday."

She smiled, apparently pleased at the idea. "I wouldn't be at all surprised," she said.

PART FOUR

34

The train was made up at Tororo, on the Kenya-Uganda border, on Wednesday morning. It consisted of thirty-three enclosed freight cars with a combined carrying capacity of over nine hundred tons. (Coffee this month was selling on the commodity markets for seven thousand dollars U.S. a ton; when full, the train would carry six million dollars' worth of coffee.)

At the head of the train was a steam locomotive of the 29 Class, originally put in service in January of 1953. On the black metal side of its tender still showed the white letters EAR, for East African Railways. On its round front face, beneath its headlight, was a brass plate with the number 2934, and on both sides of the cab, under the windows, were brass plates bearing the name *Arusha*. All 29 Class locomotives were named for East African tribes.

In the four years since Idi Amin had broken up East African Railways, there had been virtually no replacement of Uganda's rolling stock. (By contrast, Kenya had in this time almost completed its transition from steam locomotives to diesel.) Uganda's locomotives were old and tired; the freight cars were rusted and worn, many of them with broken boards and loose trucks and wheels with flat spots that needed regrinding. Maintenance was at emergency level only, new parts were hard to come by, and there was generally a disinterest in keeping the line at full efficiency. The present management, placed there by the present government, treated the railway as a found object, to be used for as long as it lasted and eventually to be thrown away and forgotten.

Two little Class 13 shunting engines plied back and forth through the yard, finding the most serviceable of the remaining cars and lining them up on one track, where the yardmen hooked up the couplers and the hydraulic hoses for the brakes. (The electrical systems had broken down in so many of the cars that it wasn't worthwhile even to attach those cables.) On the side of each chosen car a yardman scrawled with white chalk KAHAWA—*coffee* in large scraggly letters.

Finally the coal-burning locomotive, the *Arusha*, was backed into place at the head of the line of cars, and the last couplers and hoses were attached. The engineer and fireman took their positions in the locomotive cab, and just before noon the engineer pressed down the long lever and the *Arusha* moved slowly forward, the complicated network of bars that connected the big wheels lifting and falling, the shiny-rimmed wheels turning almost delicately along the track. (Far above, the Uganda Skytours plane flew over, its nasal roar buried in the chuff-chuff of the straining *Arusha*.)

A series of crashing jolts ran back through the thirty-three empty cars, as the couplers down the line lost their slack and one after the other the cars reluctantly but obediently joined the march. As the yardmen walked away, thinking about their lunches, the coffee train moved slowly out of the yard and onto the main line.

Gathering speed, black smoke and white steam angling back against the blue sky, *Arusha* and her children ran north toward Mbale, twenty-five miles away. From there, she would angle on a great curve north-westward through the waist of the country, traveling from the Kenyan border on the east up through Soroti and Lira and Gulu and then curving around southwestward to Pakwach on the Zaire border in the west, where the Victoria Nile from Lake Victoria meets with the Albert Nile from what used to be Lake Albert but is now Lake Mobutu Sese Seko. (There was also now a Lake Idi Amin, farther south toward the Tanzanian border region of West Lake, whence the forces would eventually come to overthrow Amin.)

The distance to be covered by the train was just over three hundred miles. The rail line itself continued on from Pakwach, turning north-ward again and running a further fifty miles up to Arua, from where Idi Amin had originally come. But there was little coffee up that way, closer to the Sahel, that sub-Saharan area of dryness and frequent drought, where the desert is on the move southward.

The train being empty and the land for the most part relatively flat, they made very good time when in motion, running at sixty miles an hour through the lush Ugandan landscape, the empty cars rattling and chattering along the way. But from Mbale on, they had to make frequent stops, dropping off cars at every freight station they came to. By Friday, on their return, these cars would be full to capacity with sacks of coffee.

Wednesday night they lay over in Gulu, two thirds of the way to Pakwach. In the morning they would finish the western journey, and tomorrow afternoon they would start the return.

35

The night Patricia confessed she was a spy was also the night Sir Denis proposed marriage. The proposal came first, with them together in his bed at the Nile Mansions Hotel, and her immediate thought was: How they'll laugh when they listen to the tape! "Don't, my dear!" she said, trying to cover his mouth with her hand, but the damage was done. The words were on the tape, forever.

Also the words before that. She didn't need to give him the doped wine anymore; he was willing, and more than willing, to tell her whatever she asked. Was it because he was naive, or because he understood she was spying on him and he was willing to pay this price to keep her? She knew he was in love with her, and for the first time in her life a man's love had made her feel guilt.

When they were apart, it was easy to be dismissive and scornful about his love, to disbelieve in it and remain unaffected. After all, he was thirty years older than she, he was white, he was an English aristocrat. His "love" for her could be nothing but lust, mixed with that famous English craving for degradation.

But when they were together, she knew the love was real. She had another human being's life and happiness in her hands, and she didn't want them. She wanted power, but not this way. She wanted control, but not if it was only to destroy.

Patricia was also an aristocrat, though she would never tell that to

Sir Denis, fearing he would fail to understand and would be conde-
scending to her. For what did the English understand of royal lines
outside Europe; except, perhaps, for India? But Uganda too had noble
families, a history of kings and courts.

In the old days, the largest and most powerful tribe in the area
now Uganda was the Baganda, which controlled the land on the north
side of the lake. The Baganda lived in cities, wore fine clothing, had
established a sophisticated legal system, possessed excellent houses
rather than the mud huts of the tribes down in the Rift Valley. The
king of the Baganda was called the Kabaka; it was Kabaka Mutesa II
who, in accepting the gift of a rifle from the English explorer Speke,
sent a page from his court outside with it to shoot a bystander to see
how well the weapon worked. And it was from the line of Mutesa II
that Patricia Kamin was collaterally descended.

When the British took over Uganda, it was the Baganda tribe from
the southern half of the country who provided the civil servants, later
the university professors, the doctors and lawyers, and the local political power. And when eventually the British departed, leaving the
Nubians from northern Uganda in control of the Army, it was to a
very great extent the Baganda who controlled the government. The
later accession of Idi Amin was originally seen by many Ugandans
approvingly as the revolt of the poorer-educated northern underclass
against the oppressive aristocracy of the southern Baganda.

Patricia's father had been a literature professor at Makerere University—English literature, naturally, not African. She had grown up in
an atmosphere of combined luxury and tension. She was among the
select few on the inside, while the unshod many were always visible
wherever one turned. Some people were struck to pity by this circumstance; some became embarrassed and fled to London or Paris or New
York. Patricia became hardened.

She had spent three years in London finishing her education, but
the clammy climate and the color of her skin kept her from settling
there. At home she was the right color, but more than that, at home
she was an aristocrat, *and everybody knew it.*

Independence had made it more difficult to be ostentatiously an
aristocrat. Whatever might be said against the colonizers—and a lot
could be said against them—they had more or less effectively kept
the lid on tribal conflicts and bloodlusts during the three generations

of colonial rule. The removal of that overseeing power had quickly shown that three generations weren't enough; the old hatreds, the old feuds, were as alive and virulent as ever.

Patricia's father had died, of natural causes, and quite coolly she had looked for another protector, finding him in an Army colonel, a Langi named Walter Unbule. He had looked up to her as the blue-blood she was, and throughout the Obote years his own star had seemed to be in the ascendant. But then Amin came in, and Colonel Unbule had been among those massacred at Jinja Barracks in 1971.

Seeing very early that the rules had changed, and that the new rules would be much tougher than the old, Patricia had gone directly into Amin's camp for her next protector, finding him in the State Research Bureau, another colonel, this one a Lugbara (Amin's mother's tribe) named Musa Embur. He was married, which made it better; a man is always more solicitous of his mistress. Once or twice he had offered to marry her as well—multiple marriage was legal and common in Uganda, and at the moment Amin himself had four wives—but Patricia preferred the freedom of action implicit in her present situation. And besides, Embur had introduced her to Amin.

Amin frightened her, and excited her. Without his power he would have been nothing but a clumsy bear, not even amusing, but the natural way he wielded his power—as though of *course* he would be powerful, answerable to no one but himself—gave him a fascination to which very few women were immune.

For the past two years Patricia had been a spy for Amin, mostly responding to rumors that this or that individual high in government was disloyal, was possibly even thinking of a coup. Amin told her whom to go after, and what he wanted to learn. She had exposed some plotters and had proved some others blameless (a few times too late to make any difference to the suspect), but until Sir Denis Lamb-smith she had never grown to care for any of the men she came in contact with.

What was she to do? It was only as a spy that she would be allowed to continue her relationship with this man, but she no longer wanted to play that part with him. And what secrets did he know, in any event? He was an honest businessman, nothing more. Even when it seemed there might be something, there was not.

Tonight, for instance, before the proposal of marriage, he had told her that Emil Grossbarger believed the coffee shipment was in danger of hijack. But had he any proof, any names, any hints, the slightest suggestion of what the plot might be or who was Grossbarger's informant? Nothing. Sir Denis knew nothing, and it was cruel to play him this way, and she'd already known she wanted to stop even before he'd said that dreadful thing about marriage. "Don't, my dear!" she said, in panic, thrusting her hand against his mouth.

He misunderstood, of course. "It's the age difference, you mean. Patricia, my darling, if I—"

"No no no, please," she said, terrified he would make even more of a fool of himself for the microphones. "Come along," she told him, climbing out of the bed, pulling him by his long white arm. "Come on, now, we'll take a shower, we'll talk later."

"A shower? At a moment like—"

"*Please.*"

Responding at last to the urgency in her face and voice, he permitted himself to be dragged from the bed and herded into the bathroom, where she turned on full-blast both the hot and cold faucets in the shower, then turned, smiling, to say, "Now we can talk. The microphones can't hear us."

"Oh, my Lord," he said, blushing like a boy, his face and neck suffusing, becoming thoroughly red. "I completely forgot about those blasted things. Chase warned me, of course. My, we *have* given them an earful, haven't we?"

"On purpose," she said.

He leaned closer, apparently believing he hadn't heard. "What was that?"

"It was my job to get you to talk," she said, looking him directly in the eye. Her own eyes felt skinned; they burned with every tear she'd left unshed her whole life long.

He studied her as though he were no more than a kindly counselor, to whom she had brought a small but nagging problem. "So you *are* a— It sounds ridiculous to say it, the word itself is ridiculous."

"I am a spy." She pronounced the word carefully and distinctly, to rob it of ridiculousness.

"I'd wondered, of course," he told her, sadly shaking his head. "I will admit it crossed my mind. But to spy on *me*?"

"I did. I was ordered to." She held tight to his forearms. "I gave you drugs to make you talk. I have been performing for the microphones."

"Hardly that," he said, smiling wanly at her. "I can see where I must appear a doddering old fool, but—"

"No!"

"—but I can't believe it has been entirely performance. Were it, you wouldn't tell me now."

"Of course not."

"I haven't known many secrets, have I?"

She managed to return his smile, saying, "Absolutely none. Has there ever lived such an innocent?"

"Keep me innocent, Patricia. Marry me."

"Please—"

"Stay with me for whatever years I have left. Live with me where you will. São Paulo, London, somewhere else. Wherever you prefer. But not in this country."

"Not in Africa!" she said, startled by her own vehemence.

"I agree."

"But we *can't*; this is just fantasy. You and I—"

"The age?"

"*And* the race."

"Nonsense," he said, dismissing that. "Day after tomorrow, this annoying transaction will be at last completed. I shall leave Uganda, and you shall come with me."

"We can't just—"

"Hush," he said, and hushed her by kissing her. "Shall I let you go, now I've found you? Let us have that shower while there's still hot water left, and go to sleep, and dream whatever we dream, and talk again tomorrow."

"All right," she said, too drained to go on arguing.

"Somewhere without microphones," he said. "If there is such a place in Kampala."

36

Wednesday night, Lew couldn't stand the silent house, so he went for a drive westward along the gulf shore, not realizing until he was passing the place that he had repeated his route that time with Amarda. The memory of her, slippery and agile in the humid car, with the steam on the windows and the rain chuckling on the roof, came back to him alone in this other car now in the night like a physical presence, angering him and making him feel stupid. What Ellen had said about the rain was true—the rain and the long wait when nothing really was happening—but without Amarda they would have survived. Even to remember Amarda now, much less to remember her erotically, showed how little he could trust himself. "I am a fool," he muttered, glowering out the windshield, "and I do have to go on living with me."

The African roads at night were populated, people strolling along singly or in groups, walking at the edge of the road itself because the verge was too uneven or too overgrown. They walked in darkness, lit only by stars, and suddenly appeared like apparitions in his headlights. He had to keep steering around them. None hitchhiked or even acknowledged his presence, except that if they were walking toward him they lowered their eyes against his lights. Mostly they were raggedly dressed and walked slowly, ambling along as though to no particular destination. Their society is so mysterious to me, Lew thought, that I don't even know why they go for walks at night.

Not wanting to return past the Amarda spot, he continued on until he found a rutted stony dirt road leading away to the right. This too was dotted with strollers, and eventually it led back to the main road, the B1, which in turn brought him to Kisumu and home, where he found Frank and Young Mr. Balim getting drunk in his kitchen. "We brought you beer," Young Mr. Balim said, smiling like a used-car salesman.

"And drank it," Frank said. "We figured you needed to get cheered up."

"But you weren't here," Young Mr. Balim said. "So we started without you."

"I'll catch up," Lew promised, understanding at once that this was *exactly* what he needed.

There was lots more beer in the refrigerator. It was already well after midnight, but for the next three hours they drank together in the kitchen, telling one another stories, many of them about women. (Ellen wasn't mentioned; Lew didn't feel like talking about her, and the others respected his silence.)

Young Mr. Balim described the tragedy of his life. "Women love me," he explained. Like his father, he had the ability to smile in various sad and unhappy ways. "They find me irresistible," he said, and sighed.

"That must be tough," Frank said, looking surly.

"Yes, it is," agreed Young Mr. Balim. "For what they love is my exoticism. Not eroticism, exoticism. To most women—except to Indian women, of course; I'll have nothing to do with *them*—I am something different, an exotic specimen. They must have me. They want to know what I'm like."

"How come Indian women?" Lew asked. I am not thinking of Amarda, he told himself. "How come you got nothing to do with them?"

"First I tell you about these other women."

"The ones who love you," Frank said, looking increasingly surly. "All these cunts finding you irresistible."

"Those precisely. 'What is this Bathar Balim really like?' they ask themselves. 'He is very pretty,' they say."

"Mp," said Frank, and took a long swig of beer.

"So they pursue me," Young Mr. Balim said. "And how can I refuse them?"

"Get to the point," Lew said, because he wanted to go back to the question of what was wrong with Indian women.

"Well, they seduce me, don't they?" Young Mr. Balim asked, but went on without waiting for an answer. "And they find I am merely a man, don't they? Not exotic at all. Erotic, certainly, but not mysterious, not dashing, not romantic. Not a hero. I cannot *help* but disappoint them. And so they reject me for being ordinary after all." He sighed, and smiled in utter dejection and drank beer.

"You ain't ordinary," Frank told him. Lew could tell that Frank was thinking about getting into a bad mood. "You're a *prince.*"

"No fights in my kitchen," Lew said.

Frank gave him an indignant glare. "Who's fighting? I just said he was a goddam prince; am I right, Bathar?"

"We are all friends," Young Mr. Balim said. He blinked a lot, as though trying to get himself under control.

Lew said, "Tell me about these Indian women."

"What about them?"

"You said you wouldn't have anything to do with them."

"Oh, that's right. Absolutely." Nodding in agreement with himself, gazing at his brown glass beer bottle, Young Mr. Balim fell silent.

Amazed at his own patience, Lew said, "How come?" And then, because he feared a certain discontinuity in Young Mr. Balim's thought processes, he laid the whole question out again. "How come you won't have anything to do with Indian women?"

"Oh," he answered scornfully, "it's because with them it's nothing but fuck-fuck-fuck."

Frank, who had been nodding, sat up straight. "What's that?"

"Yes, that's all they care about," Young Mr. Balim said, dismissing all Indian women with a disdainful shrug. "Just fuck-fuck-fuck and that's all."

"Bathar, pal," Frank said, "I don't get your objection."

"Well, what *are* we to them? Nothing, just a penis."

"A what?"

"Cock," Lew translated for Frank.

"They don't care about men at all," Young Mr. Balim explained, becoming more earnest, more doleful, less cynical, as he warmed to his subject. "It's a society of women, is all, with men on the outside looking in."

Frank glowered, apparently dubious. "You mean they're dykes?"

"No, no. It's all fuck-fuck-fuck with men, but the rest of their lives is women. In India it's the same, and here, and everywhere you find our Indian culture. The young man marries, he brings his young wife home; right away the *important* relationship is between the mother-in-law and the daughter-in-law. They talk together; they live together; they have secrets together; *they* are the true loving pair. And then the young wife sees her husband, and she says, 'Oh, yes, fuck-fuck-fuck, make babies, now go away,' and she wipes herself off and goes back to the mother-in-law and they talk secrets together and giggle behind their hands." He drank beer, and became so extremely sad that the smile was hardly visible at all. "It is terrible to see your culture from the outside," he said. "Very disheartening."

It seemed to Lew that Young Mr. Balim's complaint was somehow an inversion of the social structure American women recently had been criticizing, with the sexes reversed, but the idea was too tenuous for him to try to put it into words. Besides, he was more interested in trying to make Young Mr. Balim's opinions about Indian women cast some light on his own relationship with Amarda. (He'd forgotten he wasn't thinking about her.) The fuck-fuck-fuck part was all right, but what about the rest of it? Did it alter his view of what had been going on in that small hot stuffy room in her house the last time he'd seen her? Amarda and her grandmother; he tried to visualize those two giggling together behind their hands, talking sexual secrets about men. Strangely enough, it was easier to see the grandmother that way, and what did *that* mean?

Soon Frank fell asleep, his head bouncing on the table. "I gotta go to bed," Lew announced, struggling to his feet, agitating the table so half the empties fell over and Frank snorted and opened one red eye.

"I shall take Frank home," Young Mr. Balim said. He seemed as neat as ever, but a bit less ironic and more human. Drink apparently was good for him.

"Do what you want," Lew suggested. "I'm going to sleep. I got a war to go to in the morning."

* * *

At eight-thirty, worn out and hung over, Lew arrived at Balim's buildings to find Balim's old canvas-covered trucks in the yard in back, with his forty-eight troops messily loading the food and bedrolls and clothesline and cable and tarpaulins and empty oil drums and cartons of tools and all the other miscellaneous supplies. The forty Evinrude outboard motors Lew had got in trade for the fifty-seven missing sewing machines were already loaded.

Frank appeared unaffected by last night's debauch, except that he seemed to be having a bit of trouble with his balance, as though something had gone agley in his middle ear. He would sway every now and again, while standing perfectly still on an unmoving flat surface. Otherwise, he was the usual Frank, bellowing and belligerent, slowing the loading process by repeatedly confusing the troops.

As for Young Mr. Balim, he was nowhere to be seen, but a hint to his condition might be garnered from the reproachful look Mazar Balim gave Lew when he came out at one point to check their progress. Lew gave him back a sickly smile, and tried to act as though he for one had had little to drink and a full night's sleep.

Finally they were ready to go. All the men except for the drivers and two assistants were seated in lumpy crowds in the beds of two of the trucks, and all the supplies had been jammed into the other two. Frank and Isaac and Balim had a little private conversation while Lew sat on the running board of one of the trucks and drank the coffee Isaac had kindly brought out to him. Then Balim and Isaac both came over to smile at him and shake his hand and wish him luck. And then they really did leave.

Frank rode as passenger in the first truck, Lew in the second. The theory was that they would look like work crews and supplies for the hotel being built at Port Victoria. Frank was generally assumed by those locals who had seen him to be an engineer or architect or some such thing, and Lew should be able to slip through under the same mantle.

The first part of the trip was relatively smooth, and Lew fell asleep before they were even out of town. He had a wonderfully healing and restful snooze for an hour and woke up when he was almost thrown through the windshield. "Yike!" he cried, and the bucking cab bounced up again, slamming him back into the seat. He clutched at the door and dashboard for handholds, while staring at the driver, who gave him a huge slant-toothed grin and said, "Sorry."

Lew got his body under control, and the driver got the truck under control. They were now on dirt road, or rather rock road, a kind of washboard surface made by scraping away the thin topsoil. The thrown-up dust from Frank's truck just ahead was already clogging Lew's throat. The usual streams of pedestrians watched them drive by, and presumably then died horribly in the great cloud of orange dust the four trucks must leave in their wake.

Lew studied the driver, a youngish man with long muscular arms and protruding crooked teeth and large cheerful eyes. "You speak English?"

The driver smiled at him again and shook his head. "Some words," he said. Then he faced front, watching men in the truck ahead hilariously try to play a game of *kalah*—the stones kept flying out of the cups at every bounce—while he proceeded to recite for Lew's benefit the English words he did know: "Money. Whore. Policeman. Boss. Fuck. Beer. Dead. Pissed-off."

It went on like that. He knew about a hundred words in all. Well, it was a kind of conversation.

* * *

Port Victoria reminded Lew of Ellen, because she'd been the one who'd described it to him, after her jaunt here that time with Frank. Without knowing its strange history—or nonhistory—it seemed to him nobody would think the place remarkable. It was just a little market village, that's all, like hundreds of others, with some fishermen's small houses along the steep road down to the shore. He didn't see any aura of strangeness or loss, but maybe that was because he was once again feeling the loss of Ellen. He dismounted from the truck when they arrived at the work site, eager to have something to do to distract himself.

Frank was now very cheerful. His problem with balance seemed to be gone, so maybe he too had had some sleep in the truck. He said, "What do you think of the place?"

The hotel was truly abuilding. The concrete-block exterior walls were virtually finished to their completed height of two stories, with rectangular openings showing where doors and windows would someday be placed. To the side, some sheds made of cardboard and rusty metal housed supplies and workmen. Just beyond, Charlie was pissing on a bed of lilies.

"I can't believe that hotel," Lew said. "We're actually building a goddam hotel."

"After this is over," Frank said, hooking his thumbs in his belt, "a couple years, maybe I'll come back, stay in this joint, sit on the terrace up there with my vodka-and-tonic and just look out over the lake at where we did it."

"You drink beer," Lew reminded him meanly.

"After this caper I'll drink vodka," Frank assured him. "And fuck college women."

Charlie came over, shaking the last droplets off his cock, which he then stuffed inside his disreputable pants. "All ready to go," he said.

"Don't tell *me*," Frank snapped. "Tell those other assholes. Start unloading. Shit, man, we got our fortunes to make."

Lew looked for the first time out over the water. He'd seen the maps, so that low green range of hills over there was Uganda. I am here, he told himself, to steal a train.

He found himself grinning.

37

For lunch, the engineer and the fireman ate sandwiches and drank beer on a pleasant sunny knoll overlooking the swift-moving Albert Nile. During the meal they were both bitten by various disease-bearing insects, but apart from the occasional itch they suffered no ill effects. They had been bitten by these creatures ever since infancy, as had their parents and their parents before them. Various low-level fevers and agues had struck them in their early childhood, and they had been among the minority in their age group to survive. They were immunized now, by nature's method, which is wasteful of life but effective, and which leaves the body permanently weakened, like an automobile that has been in a frame-wrenching accident.

When the engineer and fireman strolled back to the Pakwach East yards, the four freight cars—which they would call "goods wagons," in the British style—were just about filled with the sacks of coffee. They signed papers, and then phoned ahead to Lolim, their next stop, to say they were leaving Pakwach and to give an estimated time for arrival at Lolim. They had to do this by public telephone because Uganda Railways had no communication system of its own—certainly no radios in the locomotive cabs—except for hand-cranked field telephone sets at the signal boxes, whose wires were generally strung from tree to tree along the rail line, when they weren't stolen.

By the time they had steam up, the cars were ready and sealed. It was only fifteen miles to Lolim; the fireman delayed them for a moment, but merely to go buy two more bottles of beer. Ugandan beer, brewed from bananas, is very gassy, very tasty, and very strong. The train with its four cars pulled out of the Pakwach East yards, rejoined the main track, and rolled up the slight incline northeastward toward Lolim.

Neither the engineer nor the fireman was political; nor was either particularly religious, though both had come from Christian families. The engineer was a member of the Basoga tribe, which in the old days had ruled the land just east of the Baganda and were very nearly as advanced. The fireman was a Karamojong, from one of the few families to have come south and abandoned that tribe's traditional nomadic cattle-herding drought-plagued hand-to-mouth existence in Uganda's far northeast. Neither of them thought of himself first in terms of tribe or religion or politics. They had been railroad men all their adult lives, and they would go on being railroad men.

Amin's decision four years before to dismantle East African Railways had troubled them both, but only for practical and personal reasons. In practical terms, it meant their trains no longer could be serviced at the fine modern workshops in Nairobi. And in personal terms, it meant they could no longer go on jaunts to Nairobi and Mombasa, rough colorful cities they found more exciting than Kampala. But the decisions were not theirs to make; they shrugged and went on about their jobs.

Ahead, Lolim. They tossed the empty beer bottles from their moving cab into the newly green fields and sounded the whistle high and clear for the level crossing at the edge of town.

38

Idi Amin was drunk. He had become drunk at lunch, and now he was getting more drunk. Seated on a wooden chair, holding in his left fist a third-full quart bottle of Johnnie Walker Red Label scotch whisky, he stared blearily at the face of the colonel who—he well knew, he well knew—had schemed to bring together the entire Langi tribe in a plot against him. "You were very bad, Colonel," Amin said, and waggled a reproving finger in the colonel's face.

The colonel's eyes and mouth were closed. Small clumps of dried blood under his nose had made it seem he had an imperfect moustache. The colonel had been dead for four months and his body had long ago been thrown to the crocodiles in the Nile at Owen Falls Dam, but his head was still here, in the freezer in the Botanical Room at the Old Command Post, one of Amin's lesser dwellings in Kampala. Three other heads of former enemies were in here at the moment, plus two human hearts, but it was to the colonel that Amin directed his reproaches.

He had started drinking today before noon, and at lunch had had to put up with lectures on economics from a Saudi Arabian who was here to discuss financial assistance for Uganda but who in fact spent all his time criticizing Amin's handling of the nation's economy. The Saudi Arabian seemed totally unaware that his arrogant "expertise" was simply the oil-wealth cushion he was reclining on, and that he knew no more than Amin about actually managing financial affairs. Amin had drunk heavily throughout lunch to help him put up with this popinjay, and then had retired here to the Old Command Post and its Botanical Room to go on drinking and to take out his bad temper on his defeated enemies.

A knock sounded at the locked door, across the room behind him. Amin reared up, heavy head turning, staring this way and that for enemies. He glowered at the four sleeping heads in the freezer, and it occurred to him to wonder why they couldn't be delivered with their eyes open. As they were, they didn't appear to be paying attention. He would have to talk to Minawa about that.

The knock repeated, more insistently. Amin muttered something and heaved himself up out of the chair, pressing his palm to the freezer for support. "One minute!" he called, first in Kakwa and then in Swahili. "One minute," he muttered in English, "one minute, *sir*," and looked around for somewhere to put down the whisky bottle.

There were a refrigerator and a freezer here in the Botanical Room, side by side. The refrigerator contained beer and other drinks, because Amin liked to entertain close friends in this room. The two were kept locked with a single chain and padlock. Now, closing the deep-freezer of his enemies, Amin fumbled with the chain and padlock, fastened them, and moved toward the door. By the time he reached it, his manner was much less drunk; only his breath and the increased redness of his eyes gave him away.

The person at the door to the outer room was a servant named Moses, a Bagisu from the slopes of Mount Elgon, a placid man, eager to please, with a very ready laugh, who famously loved Amin's jokes and sense of humor. Amin didn't realize it, but whenever it was necessary to give him a message while he was drunk or in a bad mood, the other servants always sent Moses, because he was least likely to be killed or beaten.

"Ah, Your Excellency," Moses said. "Colonel Juba calls. He has a tape for you to listen to. He says he thinks it's very important."

"He thinks so, does he? Colonel Juba thinks Colonel Juba is important." The colonel was in charge of the network of spy microphones, and many of the colonel's tapes had in truth turned out to be very interesting indeed. Nevertheless, the lunch and the whisky had put Amin in a bad mood, which he was reluctant to give up. "Maybe someday I'll take one of those tapes," he said, "and shove it up Colonel Juba's ass, and spin him in a circle, and listen at his mouth."

Moses was delighted at the image. "That *would* be something," he agreed, laughing and nodding.

Amin's mood was improving by the second. "Order my car, Moses," he said. "I'll listen to this tape."

"Yes, Your Excellency," Moses said, and went laughing away across the main room while Amin strode off to piss and wash his face and change his lunch-stained safari suit.

* * *

The tape was of Patricia Kamin and Sir Denis Lambsmith, and when it reached the point where Sir Denis proposed marriage Amin, who had been smiling in anticipation of something special, roared with laughter and slapped his knee, looking around to be sure the other men in the room also got the joke. Then he said to Colonel Juba, "That's it, is it? She really got him, that girl. She's a holy terror, that girl."

Colonel Juba was a thin man, painfully thin inside his Army uniform, with a long bony face and a permanent look of disapproval. "No," he said. "It was the part before that, about the coffee."

Amin was still feeling the effects of all that drink, although he had gratefully accepted a cup of coffee on arrival here at the State Research Bureau building. The tape was still running on. "Run it back, play it for me again," he said, then frowned, because the tape now was nothing but a rushing sound, like a great wind through tree branches. "What's that?"

"They're taking a shower together," Colonel Juba said. "They take many showers together."

"A very clean girl," Amin said with a big grin. "And a very clean white man."

The technician rewound the tape, and Amin listened for the second time to the part that Colonel Juba thought important. With Juba and two technicians and two other officers in the room, Amin thought it important not to appear stupid, so this time he listened much more carefully.

SIR DENIS: You know, Emil Grossbarger told me why he wanted me out of this sale.

PATRICIA: So it *was* him?

SIR DENIS: Oh, I knew that all along. I could never understand why.

PATRICIA: Maybe he's up to some hanky-panky.

SIR DENIS: He says he heard somebody's going to try to steal the shipment.

PATRICIA: *What?*

SIR DENIS: It's nothing. Some rumor he heard, Lord knows where.

PATRICIA: The shipment, it's— It's too *big*. Hundreds and hundreds of tons.

SIR DENIS: I know that. He just thinks conditions here are too unstable. If something went wrong, he thinks I might get hurt. It was an act of friendship, believe it or not.

PATRICIA: Yes, of course it was. You should be flattered to inspire such friendship.

SIR DENIS: You inspire greater feelings than that, Patr—

At Colonel Juba's gesture, the technician switched off the tape. The colonel said to Amin, "Well? What do you think?"

Amin brooded for half a minute, much more sober now. He was not an intellectual man, but he was a cunning and clever one. His mind was like an anthill, the busy self-involved thoughts scurrying along the narrow channels. "Send them away, Juba," he said, and sat nodding while Juba told the other men to leave.

When they were alone, Amin said, "Baron Chase has been talking to that Swiss man."

"I was thinking that," Juba agreed. It had never been a secret that Juba was among those who disliked and mistrusted Baron Chase.

"We haven't known what he's been saying to the Swiss man."

"He won't sleep with Patricia."

Amin chuckled. "I think he likes to fuck boys."

"We could send him a boy."

"No. He wouldn't give himself away that easy. He's very clever, very cunning." Amin recognized his own qualities in other men, and was an excellent judge of whether or not they could be used against him. "He has been restless here for some time," he said, brooding, remembering his recent encounters with Chase. "Very restless. And he was gone a long time in London."

Juba waited patiently. He had already come to his conclusion as to what move to make, but of course he'd heard the tape almost an hour before Amin. And he never had cared much for Chase.

"All right," Amin said at last. "Take two men you trust, you know what I mean. Pick up Chase, but secretly. There are people in government who shouldn't know about this, not till it's over. So just you and me, and your two men."

Juba nodded. "Good," he said.

"Find out what Chase and this Swiss man are up to."

"Carefully?"

Amin thought again, but this time very briefly. "No," he said. "Baron Chase is spoiled for us now. We won't need him anymore. Squeeze him dry."

"And then?"

There was a catchphrase Amin used with his closest confidants, which meant that the person should first be tortured—not for information, but as punishment or for exercise—and then murdered. He used the phrase now: "Give him the VIP treatment."

"Good," Juba said.

Amin added, "But save the head."

39

Charlie didn't understand Lew Brady. The man wouldn't play the game. Since Monday, the beginning of the training sessions, Charlie had been assigned to Lew Brady as translator and it hadn't been any fun at all. Brady apparently didn't realize that one of the fringe benefits in this job, one of the little extras that made the work appealing, was Charlie's right to make fun of his employers. If he didn't have that, then what was the point?

And he didn't have it. Charlie was a fast study, and on Monday he had learned that when he translated Lew Brady's statements he'd better do so word for word. The flights of fancy, the scatological asides, the absolute poetry of his translations of Mguu's bellowed orders had made the entire work staff happy for years. Now here was this fellow taking himself seriously and bending Charlie's bones whenever Charlie wanted to have a little fun. The result was, in addition to the boredom of doing the job right, he was losing face with the other men, who knew what Brady had done to him and why he was being so cowed.

Maybe it would be necessary to kill Lew Brady.

Not so easy, though. Charlie considered going to a witch doctor—the best killing witch doctors came from the Luo tribe, right around this area—but what if word got back to Brady? Or even to Mr. Balim, whom Charlie revered in an almost theological way.

Charlie saw Mr. Balim as a being apart from other men, not to be compared either with his own Kikuyu tribesmen nor with the animals that populated the rest of the world, but as completely something else. In Charlie's mind Mr. Balim was a great benign sun that beamed upon him, that could read his mind without condemning him, and that understood Charlie's intelligence and humor and wisdom in a way no other mind had ever done. Mr. Balim gave him authority, Mr. Balim gave him responsibility, and then Mr. Balim completed his joy by giving him absolute understanding combined with absolute acceptance. He knows my heart, Charlie told himself; if ever he would tell his secret name to another human soul, it would be to Mr. Balim.

For some time, Charlie had been trying to think of a private name for Mr. Balim, but so far without success. No word, no name he could think of, was grand enough.

As for Lew Brady, he would soon find a name for him. He was close to deciding on Gijjig, an adaptation of a Kikuyu word for "venereal disease," though he had to admit the name contained more in it of spite than relevance. Perhaps a name would come; if not, Gijjig would do.

"Charlie, goddammit!"

It was Mguu, interrupting Charlie where he squatted thinking about Lew Brady. Charlie looked up in amiable fashion. "Yes, Frank?"

"Goddammit, Charlie," Mguu said, "don't shit on the flowers."

Charlie looked down between his knees. In truth there were lilies there, but so what? He'd chosen this spot because he intended to wipe himself with a few. "What's wrong?" he asked.

"The locals don't like it," Mguu told him. "They been bitching and complaining; every time somebody wants flowers for their house, they're all over shit from you. Besides, you're right out in plain sight. Do it up the hill there."

Charlie hadn't actually started to relieve himself, having been concentrating so thoroughly on Lew Brady, so now he merely shrugged and straightened up and pulled up his pants. "Whatever you say,

Frank," he said. "I just wanted, me, to be close by in case you needed something translated."

"Oh, fuck off, Charlie," Mguu said.

"Okay, then, Frank."

Charlie drifted on up the hill behind the hotel site, toward where they'd been camping out. He would have done his shitting in some declivity in front of Mguu's tent, but he doubted Mguu would be using the place again.

At the top of the hill he turned to look back, and the scene below reminded him of pictures in the book *Treasure Island*, which he had read in school when he was a boy and learning English because his mother—now dead—wanted access to the riches of the city. She had understood clearly that English was the language of the city, and would twist Charlie's arms or ears if he did badly in his lessons. In her dream, Charlie would grow up speaking English, would travel to the city in the little *matatu* bus—really just an enclosed pickup truck with two benches in the back—and there he would in some magical manner become plugged into the society of the rich. The money and the clothing and the food and the leisure would somehow flow out of the city and through Charlie and spread like a warm glow all over his mother.

What happened in reality was, Charlie grew up to be Charlie, and his mother died of various illnesses and a lack of medical attention at the age of thirty-seven. Which doesn't mean she was wrong.

And which does mean that when Charlie stood on the hilltop now and looked down at Port Victoria's shore, with Berkeley Bay to the right and the open immensity of Lake Victoria to the left and the green hump of Uganda straight ahead, what he thought of was the pictures accompanying *Treasure Island*.

Most of the men were hard at work down there, swarming over the rafts, while Mguu strode back and forth like a Long John Silver who'd regrown his leg, and Lew Brady played Tom Swift (more of Charlie's schooldays grab bag of books in English) by overseeing the uncrating and assembling of the outboard motors.

Ten large rafts were being built along the shore, each twenty feet square, made of twenty-foot-long planks nailed to twenty-foot-long crosspieces, the entire arrangement then lashed to empty oil drums.

Along one edge of each raft a rough-and-ready assemblage of planks was being fastened underneath the main wooden body, and then four of the Evinrude outboard motors were being attached to each of these assemblies. The reason for this awkward-looking mess was that the rafts would ride so high in the water that if the outboard motors were attached directly to the raft bodies their propellers would be completely up in the air. On the return trip, with each raft carrying tons and tons of coffee, that wouldn't be a problem.

Seen from the hilltop, the ten rafts were like some Lilliputian armada, about to launch themselves in a soup tureen, but they were more serious than they looked. The men's lives depended on these rafts, as Lew Brady had said (and as Charlie with perfect fidelity and increasing rage and boredom had translated), so they were taking their work with great seriousness. The ring of hammers beat out over the water and the land.

Charlie turned the other way, and something that might have been a gazelle ducked and leaped and flowed out of sight. Might have been a gazelle, but was not. Charlie pretended he hadn't seen it, and strolled along like any man looking for a place to shit. His search led him by many angles and ellipses closer and closer to the little bush-filled hollow in which—

"YAAAAA!"

Charlie leaped like a swimmer entering the pool for a two-lap race. The man—not at all a gazelle—surged up out of the brush like a startled quail, but wasn't fast enough; Charlie brought him down, arms entangling in the man's legs, the two of them crashing back down into the scratchy leaves and branches.

The man kicked and twisted and flailed about, utterly silent. It was the silence that told Charlie this was an enemy and not merely a sneak thief or a passing stranger. He held tight to whatever parts the man offered—a bony ankle, a bonier wrist—and slowly but inexorably he pulled the man out of the shrubbery and laid him on his back on the stony ground, where he gazed on his closed face and remembered that he had seen this fellow before.

It was the raggedy man, the boneman that Charlie and Mguu had surprised during their visit to the depot. Which was in Uganda. Which was a far far way from here.

I should have killed him last time, when I thought of it.

Charlie straddled him. "Oh, boneman," he said, his strong fingers toying with the man's Adam's apple as a kitten toys at first with a ball of string or a cat toys at first with a wounded bird, "oh, boneman, there is no false story you can tell."

The boneman apparently recognized that himself. He merely lay there on his back, arms under Charlie's knees, caramel-colored palms facing up.

"But you could tell me who sent you," Charlie said. His thumbnail drew a thin line of blood across that moving captive Adam's apple. "You *could* tell me that. Who spies? For what purpose?"

"I am an important man," the boneman said with an attempt at dignity, his voice hoarse as though from disuse. "If you kill me, you will be hunted down."

"By the Society of Bonemen?" In his combined comedy and rage— fueled by his recent thoughts about Lew Brady—Charlie overdid himself; he played too hard, the way the cat plays with the bird. Before he knew it he had crushed that Adam's apple, and the creature below him was gurgling and thrashing, eyes sticking out, tongue swelling.

"Oh, no good," Charlie said, sitting back on the animal's agitating stomach. "Very stupid. Mr. Balim would think I had become foolish. Oh, dear."

Leaving the boneman to gurgle himself to death, knowing his wisest move was not to mention this at all to Mguu, Charlie sighed and got to his feet and went away to find a socially acceptable place to relieve himself.

40

For many miles, the A104 parallels the northern railway line. At times the track is visible from the road, where they run next to one another on the straighter flatter stretches, while at other times the rail line is hidden by jungle or low hills. Baron Chase, driving north at the wheel of one of the black Toyotas belonging to the State Research Bureau, missed the coffee train in one of those latter areas, but when he reached Opit and saw that the loaded freight cars there were gone, he realized his error, reversed, and drove back south.

The train crew and yard crews had already done a lot, picking up the loaded cars from Pakwach East, then Lolim, Aparanga, Bwobo, Gulu, and Opit. And when Chase rearrived at Otwal, the train was just pulling out, now almost twenty cars long. Ahead were Lira, Aloi, Achuni, and Soroti, the largest town along the way, where they would undoubtedly spend the night. Tomorrow morning, they would have only Okungulo, Kumi, Kachumbala, and Mbale at which to pick up the filled cars. No later than lunchtime tomorrow the train should be full and traveling nonstop to Tororo to join the main line and turn westward for Kampala and Entebbe.

Chase traveled parallel to the train from Otwal to Lira, passing through field after field of coffee, the bushes all glossy green, already growing their next crop of cherries. A coffee tree left to itself will grow thirty feet tall, but the growers prune them to fifteen feet or less, for ease of harvesting. (In some places, like the Jhosi plantation, they are kept to bush height.) Toward the end of the rainy season these fields had crawled with harvesters, men and women and children, all circling back three or four times to pick each bright-red cherry when ripe. Once the rain was finished and the sun appeared, the cherries were spread on outdoor cement floors to dry, then were sent several times through fanning and hulling machines to remove dried hulls and interior yellow pulp, freeing the two beans that lie inside each cherry, their flat faces together. Two membranes still surrounded each bean, an inner delicate one called the silver skin and a more brittle outside one known as the parchment. These were removed in further cleaning machines, which led to sorting machines where the beans were separated by size, then to a hand-culling process to remove imperfect beans, and finally into a machine that weighed and bagged them ready for shipment.

Chase and the coffee train flowed and sailed through the coffee fields in their rolling green landscape under the high hot blue sky, here and there a field all white with clusters of jasminelike coffee flowers to counterbalance the smudgy line of black smoke drawn back from the locomotive over the full cars. The train whistle wailed at level crossings; the wheels of the loaded freight cars clattered and burbled along the rails; the cars all swayed at separate rhythms in the warm air. Driving along, Chase looked over at the coffee train and smiled. *KAHAWA*, said the white chalk letters, car after car, *KAHAWA KAHAWA KAHAWA*. *Mon*-ey-for-me, said the wheels on the rails, *mon*-ey-for-me, *mon*-ey-for-me, *mon*-ey-for-me. *WOOOO-oo-u*.

As the train slowed at Lira, Chase speeded up to dash over the level crossing just before the barriers were put down. His foot hard on the accelerator, he did the hundred sixty miles to Tororo in less than two hours, confident that his license plate—beginning with UVS, a declaration of the Toyota's official ownership—would keep any stray policeman from bothering him. At Tororo he turned west on the A104 and accelerated again.

It was not quite six o'clock when he turned off the empty highway onto the access road and bumped slowly down as far as the parked Army truck. He stopped the Toyota there, afraid it might get stuck farther on, and walked down past the railroad tracks to the path leading in to the maintenance depot.

The path had been rather astonishingly widened and smoothed; walking on it, Chase saw it would give the trucks no trouble at all. Even his Toyota would be able to traverse this new road. At the inner end, a board nailed to a tree gave the expanded path a name: ELLEN'S ROAD. Chase was reminded of World War II and the U.S. Marines on their South Pacific islands with their self-consciously humorous road signs: TOKYO—1,740 TIMES SQUARE—9,562.

The depot showed signs of activity, a great deal of cleaning up and rearrangement, but no human beings were in sight. Chase had been listening for the past five minutes or so to the repeated buzz of a chain saw; following the sound, he walked up the spur track almost to the hidden main line, where he found four men cutting away the last of the young trees and underbrush blocking the line.

Not knowing who Chase was, the four men were not at all pleased to see him. They looked actually threatening for a minute, until he mentioned the name Frank Lanigan. Then they smiled and relaxed and told each other in Swahili that he must be all right, just another of Balim's white men.

Chase gave no indication that he understood the Swahili. In English he asked, "Is Frank Lanigan here?"

None of them had English. He was forced to do charades, pointing at the ground while asking for Lanigan. It would have been easier, of course, merely to speak Swahili, but the habit of hiding that capability was so ingrained in Chase by now that it never even occurred to him to use it.

They finally did understand, and let him know through their own elaborate sign language that Frank was still in Kenya, but would be here tonight. Chase let them know he wanted to leave Frank a message, and they assured him with gestures that they would deliver it. "I hope so, you buggers," Chase said.

He carried a smallish notebook, on one page of which he now wrote: "Train maybe 3PM, maybe 6PM. No hue and cry at motor pool. C." Ripping the page out, he folded it in half and wrote on the outside "Frank Lanigan," then gave it with a stern warning in English to the spokesman for the group, a man in a filthy sleeveless green shirt, who smiled and nodded and repeated all his assurances.

Finally Chase retraced his steps, looking at all the work that had been done. They're working for me, he thought in secret pleasure. Only for me.

* * *

Chase's small neat house was in northwestern Kampala, off Bombo Road. He could see Makerere University from his front windows, and Mulago Hospital was up behind his yard. The house had belonged before 1972 to the son of a wealthy Asian merchant. Chase had kept most of the boy's toys—the pool table and stereo system and small private screening room—but had had to give up the silver-gray Porsche to a Public Safety Unit colonel who had obsessively craved it.

Generally, throughout the house, the Asian decorations had given way to Chase's simpler style. The rooms were more bare and Spartan now, and footsteps echoed as they would not have done in the past. A living-room wall on which had hung a tapestry carpet in vivid reds and greens now featured neatly framed black-and-white or color pictures of Chase himself with noteworthy figures of the day: people who had permitted themselves to be photographed with him during their stay in Kampala, or people he'd met while accompanying Amin on official visits overseas. Colonel Juba was studying these photographs with his disapproving air, hands clasped behind his back, when Chase walked in at a little after eight o'clock that evening. The two uniformed men with Juba, one showing a captain's rank, the other a major's, lolled at their ease on the overstuffed maroon mohair chairs left over from the previous occupant.

Seeing front-room lights on from the driveway, Chase had merely assumed his servant girl, Sarah, was doing some late cleaning up, but when he saw Juba and the other two—he recognized them, knew they were cronies of Juba's, but didn't know their names—he realized at once he was in trouble.

He didn't show it. "Colonel Juba! What a surprise. Is Sarah getting you something to drink?"

"No, thank you, Captain Chase. Is this really the Pope?"

Chase seldom used his Ugandan Army rank. To be called "captain" was another signal of trouble. Walking forward, his awareness strongly on the two seated men, both nodding and smiling and as yet taking no part in events, Chase said, "Yes, that's the Pope, all right. And that's me."

"Did you ask his blessing?"

Colonel Juba was a Muslim, like most of the men closest to Amin. Chase gave him an alert look, saying, "Do you think I'll need it?"

"Oh, we all need blessings," Juba said. "President Amin wants to see you."

"Personally?"

"Oh, yes. You can help him with that Swiss man who is buying the coffee."

Juba had gone too far with that. He was not as good at subtlety and double entendre as he thought. But Chase didn't show that he now knew not only *that* he was in trouble but also *why* he was in trouble. Instead, he smiled and said, "Anything I can do, as President Amin knows. Where is he today? The Old Command Post, isn't it?"

"No, he's at Bureau headquarters."

Serious trouble. Very very bad trouble. "We shouldn't keep him waiting, then," Chase said.

He knew, whatever might happen, he was leaving this house for the last time. But he didn't look back.

41

Just before sunset a car came sluing and sliding down the slope from the village of Port Victoria, skidding to a stop by the unfinished hotel. Lew had been sitting up on top of one of the completed rafts, looking westward out over the calm violet waters of the lake at the ochre ball of the setting sun. Thin lines of cloud bisected the sun to radiate colors in an extravagant display of blues and reds, magenta and maroon and indigo, rose and ruby and plum, gold and brass and aquamarine. The narrowing band of sky between sun and lake looked bruised, but the rest of the western sky was a topographical map of Heaven.

The colors affected the Earth as well, turning everything into Technicolor, brighter and ruddier and more golden than life. The men, their construction work finished, lay about on the ground with the unreal clarity of a Dali painting, and the arriving car semaphored golden and crimson greetings from its windshield. Lew turned to watch, and when the car stopped Young Mr. Balin came smiling and chipper out from behind the wheel while a somewhat less enthusiastic Isaac emerged on the passenger side.

Frank strode toward the car, his ink-black shadow sliding over the copper bodies of the reclining men. While he and Isaac talked together, Young Mr. Balim walked toward Lew, his smile at once arrogant and shy. "You're King of the Mountain?"

"Come up."

The top of the raft was a good yard from the ground. Lew grasped Young Mr. Balim's slender wrist and hauled him up, where the two could turn again and look at the sun, now shrunken slightly as though receding, and deepened to a rich cinnabar. Its bottom edge very nearly kissed the lake horizon. "Beautiful," Young Mr. Balim said. "I like your view."

"Thank you. I got the impression from your father this morning that you weren't feeling too well."

"Oh? What did he say?"

"Nothing. Just looked disapproving."

"Ha." Young Mr. Balim said, "He led *me* to believe you and Frank were utterly unscathed."

"Propaganda."

"I thought so."

The violet disk of the sun touched the water, then became minutely flattened on the bottom, like a locomotive wheel in need of regrinding. Lew said, "You here to see us off?"

"I'm coming with you."

Lew gave him a surprised look, and was startled to see the extent of Young Mr. Balim's vulnerability as he stood there in the red light, smiling painfully, braced to be made fun of. Quickly shifting gears, Lew said, "Then, welcome aboard."

"Thank you."

"You're welcome."

"I meant for not asking if my father knew I was here."

"Frank will."

"Oh, I know. Isaac did already. When do we leave?"

Lew nodded at the sun, continuing its lesson in conic section. "When that stops watching us," he said.

Frank and Isaac had come over, Frank belligerent and Isaac worried, and both now stood below them. The clarity of the light of just a few moments ago was gone, the redness becoming tinged with black, creating ambiguity. There was no ambiguity in Frank. "Bathar," he said, his hands on his hips, "your father is crazy."

"The sins of the sons," Young Mr. Balim said, with a graceful shrug.

"You're no fucking use over there, Bathar," Frank said. "You gonna carry sacks?"

"I shall play the lute."

"Oh, fuck off. Come on, Isaac, it's time we launch these mothers. You can translate; Christ knows where Charlie is. Lew, you keep an eye on Young Bathar."

Isaac gave them a nervous apologetic smile, then was drawn away in Frank's wake. Frank was already yelling at the prone men. Young Mr. Balim's eyes glinted in the red light as he looked at Lew, saying, "That puts us *both* in our place."

* * *

Twilight was short, and decreasingly spectacular, but as the colors drained out of the sky, swirling down after the sun into that slot on the western rim of the world, a hundred million stars gradually became apparent, very high crisp tiny points of white, with a quarter-moon at shoulder-height over the lake. In this uncertain and constantly shifting illumination, the rafts were one at a time wrestled over the muddy shoreline and out onto the warm water. Long planks were laid between each raft and the nearest reasonably dry ground, and everything was loaded. By the time the sky was almost completely black, except for a dark-reddish blur at one spot on the horizon, as though a city were in flames on the far side of the lake, they were ready to go.

The four outboard motors on each raft had been yoked together so they could be steered by a single L-shaped arrangement of boards. With the men distributed on each raft and the gangplanks pulled on board, they allowed themselves to drift a bit farther from shore before starting the engines. The first few made a kind of muted snarling sound, easily lost in the immensity of air over the lake, but as more and more engines turned over the quality of the noise changed, and by the time the full forty were running it sounded as though Berkeley Bay had been invaded by all the world's killer bees. In a straggling line, the ten rafts moved out onto the lake.

Lew and Young Mr. Balim traveled with three other men on the last raft, Lew manning the steering bar. The oil drums were lashed beneath the rafts, broadside to the direction of thrust, and their rounded metal sides slid through the water with a surprising lack of friction. There was no great speed to be had with these rafts, but the smoothness of the journey came as a surprise to them all.

Antismuggling patrols were likely, both ships and helicopters. To help evade them, the big gray tarpaulins were unrolled before the rafts crossed into Ugandan territorial waters at Sigulu Island, covering the passengers and supplies so that no reflection from metal, no distinctive shape, would give them away. Now the rafts had become twenty-foot-square gray islands, low and lumpy, almost invisible from the air. Lew and the other pilots remained outside the tarpaulins, watching the thin moonlight shatter on the water.

The men had used poles and mounds of supplies to prop up the tarpaulins enough to create tent spaces within, in which they sat and talked together, the soft burr of Swahili resonating out over the lake. Beneath that, and the sputtering roar of the outboard motors, the clicking sound of pebbles meant *kalah* was being played, in the dark. By touch alone, the players would know how many pebbles were in each of the twelve cups, and what the implications were after each move. Lew had played *kalah*, but never well, and would never play against these men for money; you had to be born and raised to that game. Like chess masters, the best players knew at all times where all seventy-two pebbles were and what every possible future sequence would create for the next five or six moves. In the old days, entire herds of cattle, hundreds of slaves, even entire kingdoms, were won or lost at *kalah*.

Young Mr. Balim sat just under the edge of the tarp, his back against two wooden cartons filled with fruit. After a long silence, while he looked back past Lew at the shoreline they were leaving, he said, "Do you know why my father agreed?"

"Did you need his agreement?"

"Ah, yes, I'm afraid so," Young Mr. Balim said, grinning. "He consented because he saw my restlessness was becoming again too strong, and it was time to give me a small concession. I may be twenty-eight, you know, but I am not my own man. By no means."

"Why not?"

"Money. I am like a wife, I am dependent on my father."

"Do you have to be? Can't you get money on your own?"

"Then I am a house pet," Young Mr. Balim said, easily shifting his justifications, "too spoiled by the easiness of my life."

"Then why come along tonight?"

"A conflict." Young Mr. Balim seemed to spend most of his time laughing at himself. "I want to be a grown-up, but I don't want to give up the easy life." Leaning forward, tapping Lew's boot for emphasis, he said, "Here's my harebrained scheme. I shall be a party to this escapade. My father will not be able to refuse me some small share of the profits. With that money I shall go back to London and set myself up in some sort of business."

"London?"

"Oh, yes, I love London. Nowhere else on earth for me. That's why my father gives me motorcycles instead of cash, you see; so I can't get away. He wants me to stay in Kisumu and take over his business someday. But what he refuses to think about is that the Kenyans will throw us out."

"You think so?"

"Why not? The Ugandans did, and there are constant rumors that the Kenyans will, the Tanzanians will. In Zaire it is already almost impossible for an Asian to live. They'll throw us out of all of Africa someday, you wait and see."

"You could be right," Lew agreed.

"And what price our Kisumu warehouses then? Oh, but London!" Young Mr. Balim beamed. "The worst they will do in London is insult me." Mimicking some nasal voice calling a dog, he said, "Here, Paki; there, Paki; go away now, Paki." He laughed and said, "So they call me Paki. I was born in Uganda of a man who was born in Uganda of a man who was born in India, but that's all right, I'm a Paki. And even a Paki can go to the West End, can shop in Harrods, can buy a little maisonette in Chelsea. A Paki can open a store, and the English will shop there. A Paki—I know a Paki who opened a little advertising agency for little Paki accounts—little travel agencies and tailors and so on—and he did well, and the English began to hire him. Because they saw he was good, you see, valuable to *them*. Give me a pragmatic people, and I won't care what they think of me."

Smiling, Lew said, "What sort of business will you open?"

"We wait upon opportunity," Young Mr. Balim said. "First this adventure, and then we settle down to Paki respectability."

* * *

The thirty miles to Macdonald Bay took just over three hours, of which the last part was the most difficult. The rafts weren't particularly agile and had to be jockeyed into position against a very narrow slice of muddy shoreline. Shutting down three of the four outboard motors on each raft, they eased in very slowly, the others drifting slightly while Frank went first, thudding his raft too hard into the shore, ripping loose one of the oil drums. His men saved the drum, unloaded the raft, and dragged it up onto the shore.

By the time Lew steered the tenth raft toward land, gently nudging the mud flat, the other nine had already been dragged as far as possible beneath the cover of the trees and, under the direction of Isaac and Charlie—a true odd couple, that—the men were further hiding the rafts with tree branches and brush. Once Lew's final motor was shut down, he could hear the receding whine of another motor going away inland; that would be Frank, traveling by moped up to get the truck.

The next three hours were all logistics, the slogging boring frustrating job of getting all your men and all your supplies to the place where they'll eventually be needed. Lew knew this phase from many battles in several wars and had long ago learned the only thing to do at such a time was to cease having opinions. It was a mistake to think that such-and-such an event *should* have happened by now, or that this person *should* have realized that fact, or even that somehow there *should* have been a better way.

There was no better way. No matter what you thought or planned, the truck would be overloaded the first time after Frank brought it down from the depot, and it would become mired three miles up from the lake, forcing everybody to trek those three miles, unload the damn truck, drag it out of its muddy ruts, and then reload it again, all by the shifting uncertain beams of several flashlights invariably being aimed at the wrong spot.

It was also inevitable that several fistfights would break out, that the soft ground of their landing site would be churned by all those feet into mud, and that when there weren't too few men for the loading at the lake there would be too few for the unloading at the depot. And it was probably even inevitable that the truck, on one of its return trips, would drive over a case of beer, smashing all the bottles and giving itself a flat tire, which also had to be changed by flashlight, the whole area stinking of beer.

What wasn't inevitable was that they would have called it Ellen's Road.

Lew hadn't known about that, and didn't see it until the end because he stayed at the lake during the whole transfer operation, traveling up with the last truckload, he and Frank in the cab, the final ten workmen and the last miscellaneous cases in the back.

Frank wrestled with the wheel, the truck grinding slowly up along the faint line of roadway, its headlights partially covered with tape but still showing the straight road steadily sloping upward, the dark trees and brush on both sides, here and there the startled red reflections of animal eyes. "I'll tell you something," Frank said.

"What's that?"

"This is exactly like the night before a war."

"I was thinking the same thing."

"Yeah, but do you know what makes this job better?"

"What?"

Frank released the wheel for just a second to jab a thumb over his shoulder, indicating the men out of sight and hearing beyond the cab partition. "Those assholes don't have guns," he said.

"I know what you mean. Unfortunately, the people on the other side do."

"We won't see no people on the other side."

"I hope you're right," Lew said, and awhile later Frank grappled the truck to a standstill, saying, "We'll walk in."

With the truck engine and headlights off, the world was at first absolutely black and absolutely silent. None of the starlight or faint moonlight reached down to here through the branches, and all of the surrounding animal life had been frightened into silence by the arrival of the truck.

But gradually new sounds filled the emptiness, the vague mutterings and jostlings of men in an encampment. And off to the left through the trees were glimmers of both flashlights and firelight.

"This way," Frank said.

They tramped in on a rustling roadway of crushed branches and leaves, soon seeing the depot up ahead, the dim forms of people moving against the lights. "So this is the place where I didn't get to take pictures," Lew said, and saw the sign on the tree, and said, "Oh, shit."

"What's up?" Then Frank followed Lew's gaze and said, "Oh. I forgot about that."

"Your idea?"

"Well," Frank said, immediately on the defensive, "she did design the fucking thing. And I put it up before she walked out on you."

"She didn't walk *out* on me," Lew said, obscurely angry. "Not the way that sounds."

Frank stopped and held Lew by the arm. "Listen, my friend. I've known an awful lot of women in my life, and sooner or later every damn one of them will leave you walking around, scratching your head, and saying, 'What the fuck was that all about?' "

"Frank, don't give me a whole locker-room—"

"Hear me out, goddammit."

"Let go my arm," Lew told him, "and then I'll listen."

Frank released his arm. "Ellen was a very good woman," he said. "One of the best. Too fucking good for the likes of you."

"*And* you."

"I know that. The point is, she packed up her little ditty bag and she *went*. And you can poke around for weeks if you want to, like you got a thorn in your paw. Or you can say, 'Screw it, there's more of them out there in the bushes.' What the hell, you did all right before you ever knew that particular woman."

With a crooked smile, Lew said, "Ellen made the same point."

"There, see? Be as smart as she is and you'll be a man, my son."

Lew said, "I'll tell you what the situation is, Frank, but I don't feel like talking about it a lot. Ellen leaving was like catching the flu. You get over the flu, but first it gets worse for a while. I saw that sign and I realized it was getting worse."

"Okay," Frank said. "I can follow that. Get well soon, pal."

"Thank you," Lew said, and walked on with Frank, not looking up again at the sign.

Some of the tarpaulins had been brought up from the lake and had now been made into lean-to tents. Cartons filled with large cans of stew were among the supplies; the tops had been levered off these, and the stew was heating in the cans over several small fires, filling the air with an aroma of dinner. The endless *kalah* games continued, beer had been distributed, men were laughing and visiting, settling down on blankets inside the tents, starting to relax at the end of a day of hard work.

Lew took a bottle of the warm beer and strolled around the encampment, not wanting conversation with anybody. Just uphill from the maintenance depot, away from the people, there was a clear spot in the roof of branches, where he could look up and see the stars. The moon had risen almost to its apogee. Ellen is ninety miles from here, he thought. Only ninety miles.

42

Ellen couldn't sleep, but she didn't want to admit the fact by turning on the light or getting out of bed. Her room here in the transient aircrews' quarters at Entebbe was small and clean but very cold and impersonal; more a prison cell than a hotel room. There was a slatted blind to cover the window, but she'd raised that some time ago so she could watch the quarter-moon climb diagonally up the sky, moving almost stealthily in its slowness and silence.

Is Lew in Uganda now? They'll be coming over tonight, to steal the train tomorrow, if nothing's gone wrong. Has something gone wrong? Is he in Uganda, or have they had to give it up for some reason?

Should I have stayed?

When she'd arrived here yesterday afternoon, it had seemed at first as though she were wasting her time, as though she should have stayed in Kenya merely because there was nothing for her at Entebbe. Certainly the planes weren't here, and the smiling false man from the government had lied to her for two hours before she'd finally browbeaten him into admitting the truth.

The truth was that everything was still tentative. It was still, even at this eleventh hour, possible that Coast Global would not be able to assemble sufficient planes, or sufficient personnel to crew them, in time for Friday's scheduled operation.

The contract Ellen had signed had of course given Coast Global an out, but it was the sort of boiler plate she'd come to accept in such contracts; it never meant anything. But this time it might. According to the contract, if for any reason the job she'd been hired for failed to materialize, she would be paid her expenses to and from her home (Kisumu!) plus one quarter of the agreed-on salary, which would probably be not much more than a thousand dollars.

And at the end of it back she'd be in Kisumu, instead of in Baltimore. Even with her airline discount, it would take most of her money to get to the States via commercial carrier. If she hadn't quit Balim, of course, he would have been obligated to pay her return fare, but now he was off the hook and Ellen was firmly on it.

Through all the irritation about money and contracts and lying government men, she had kept tucked away in the back of her mind one oddly comforting thought: if the job fell through, if she wound up back in Kisumu after all, it would be some sort of sign or something that she should stay with Lew.

Unless he'd already moved Amarda in.

Her thoughts had grown increasingly troubled, not eased by the five other crew members—casuals, hired like her for this one-time job—who'd showed up in the course of the evening and then this morning. And it wasn't till nearly noon today that they'd known for certain the job would take place.

The eight undercrewed planes had started arriving at three this afternoon, and the last hadn't showed until after nine tonight. With the end of uncertainty and the addition of all these other pilots and navigators, a certain conviviality developed, and during dinner in the otherwise empty airport coffee shop Ellen had smilingly turned down three separate propositions. So it was her own fault if she was alone tonight in this bed and unable to sleep.

The moon was nearing apogee, climbing just beyond the top of the windowframe. Is Lew in Uganda? Will the coffee show up here tomorrow? If it does, will that mean they didn't make the try, or that they tried and failed? The grayish pale moonlight inched out of her eyes and moved away down the blanket, and Ellen drifted into shallow unsatisfying sleep.

43

They took Chase to the State Research Bureau, pretending he'd meet Amin there to "help him" in some undefined way in connection with "the Swiss man who is buying the coffee." In other words, some corner of Chase's scheme had unraveled and Amin had sent Colonel Juba to pick at it and find out what it meant.

The first encouraging sign was that Juba didn't want anyone else to know Chase had been arrested. At the Bureau's front door, he went so far as to ask the guard, "Is the president here yet?" Chase presumably was not supposed to notice the guard's bewilderment, nor to hear the irritation in Juba's hurried "No matter. We'll wait in his office."

So. Amin was not certain he had Chase dead to rights. Juba and his two young assistants and Amin himself were probably the only ones who knew Chase was a prisoner. (Amin had to know; Chase was far too important for Juba to arrest on his own initiative.)

So they went to "Amin's office," a large square room with gray industrial carpeting and several Danish-style sofas along the wall, which was in fact one of the interrogation rooms, though Amin did use it sometimes in conferences with Bureau people. He also used it for occasional in-person interrogations of his chief enemies, and it was here he'd lost his temper and shot the archbishop. Chase was supposed to be thinking about these associations, of course.

What he was thinking instead was that Amin was too impatient a man not to be here already if he planned to take part in this interrogation. In leaving it to Juba, he was giving himself later deniability. More important, he was also confirming for Chase that he wasn't yet sure what was going on. They need to get it from my mouth, Chase thought, and they won't succeed.

Juba, having earlier proved himself inept at clever double entendre, now proved himself inept at the psychological ploy. The next three hours of waiting—ostensibly for Amin—were supposed to soften

Chase for the questions to follow, but the delay merely gave him time
to plan out his own strategy.

At first Juba tried to fill the time with light conversation, but made
the mistake of talking about foreign travel. Poor Juba had never been
out of Africa; Tripoli was his cosmopolitan city, where the Libyans
had taught him how to use his electronic equipment (some of which
probably had created this present trouble). Chase responded with amiable condescension, until even Juba saw he was being made fun of.
Then they sat in silence, unless Juba and his men spoke together,
which they did from time to time.

And here was an irony Chase could appreciate without approving.
After all his years of hiding his knowledge of Swahili, when these
three Africans spoke secretly together it was in Kakwa, their tribal
tongue, of which Chase knew only one word: *kalasi*, which means
"death." It might have been his imagination, but he thought he heard
them use the word several times.

Colonel Juba tried to maintain an atmosphere of menace with dignity, but the other two, the captain and the major, were in reality only
country boys from up north, basking in power and luxury, practically
hugging themselves with delight at their great good fortune. In a
well-ordered world—and they knew this better than anybody—they
would be at best laborers now, on a farm or a construction project,
and at worst they would be nothing at all, merely two more idle men
whose ugly bitter wives worked small parcels of land for their minimal
food supply. But here they were, because of Idi Amin, a "captain"
and a "major," with women and food and drink and clothing and
even cars available just for the asking.

The burlesque that Chase was not a prisoner extended so far as their
permitting him to go to the men's room by himself, though the
captain did stand in the office doorway watching the men's room
entrance until he returned. And after a while it extended to their
offering him beer, when the captain and the major both began to
drink. Chase accepted a bottle, but merely sipped at it, noticing that
Juba didn't drink at all.

Finally, after three hours of nonsense, Chase decided it was time
to force the issue. Rising—the captain and the major sat up, looking
as alert as possible after half a dozen bottles of beer—he crossed to

the desk, behind which Juba was seated filling out pointless forms, and reached for the telephone. "Perhaps the president has forgotten," he said. "He's at the Old Command Post, isn't he?"

"No need for that!" Suddenly angry, Juba slapped at the phone, glaring at Chase. "Just sit down."

"But if it's so important for the president to see me, we should—"

"He'll see you in his own good time!" Then Juba got himself back under control, and returned to the game of make-believe: "I'm sure the president doesn't wish to inconvenience you, Captain Chase."

"No inconvenience. Merely a desire to be of help."

"Then there's another matter you can help on, while we wait."

Chase was aware that the major was on his feet, prowling around behind him. They could at any time use physical torture, but they preferred the cat-and-mouse tactics until they grew bored. Chase had to sense Juba's state of mind very delicately, but didn't want to make his own move until he knew for sure the extent of the problem. He said, "What other matter is that, Colonel?"

"Sometime ago there was a white man imprisoned here. He caused some damage, and you had him released. Why?"

What was this? In his irritation—maybe the stalling tactic had gotten through to him after all—Chase snapped, "All of this was covered at the time. The man was named Lewis Brady, he's a gun-runner working for the Saudis, bringing weapons to Muslim revolutionary forces in Africa. He came here posing as a tourist to meet with me, unofficially, concerning arms shipments for friends of ours in the Sudan, to be shipped through Uganda. Libya unfortunately had his name on the wrong list, as a result of work he did for a pro-Libya faction in the Sudan several years ago. So he was arrested. When he didn't appear at our meeting, I naturally made inquiries, and I found him here. He was already making his escape when I intercepted him."

"There is no verification of this story."

"Verification? The man was here. Libya has acknowledged his work with their people in the Sudan. I have told you his mission. What more do you need?"

"The Saudis—"

"In the first place," Chase interrupted, really *tired* of all this, "we couldn't possibly make an open interrogation to the Saudis about one of their sub rosa projects. And if we did, they would quite properly deny all knowledge."

Colonel Juba sat blinking at his desk, annoyed and uncomfortable. He tried once or twice to find things to say, then finally blurted, "Do sit down! You make me lean my head back!"

"Sorry, Colonel.'

Chase started for the sofa, but Juba said, "No, here. Sit here," pointing at the witness's chair in front of the desk.

So the make-believe was coming to an end. To emphasize his dignity and authority, Juba went on pointing at the chair until Chase had settled himself in it. Then he said, "About this other matter of the Swiss man."

Chase smiled, leaning forward to put his elbow on the edge of the desk. "The Swiss man, yes. The one who is buying the coffee, as you put it."

"You told him the coffee would be stolen," Juba said, then immediately looked doubtful, as though wishing he'd been more roundabout.

"I told him the coffee would be stolen?" This was a distortion of the truth, but still it was more than Chase had thought these people might have. "Why would I say such a thing to a customer? And who says I did?"

"The Swiss man told it to the English Sir."

The fool! Grossbarger's enslavement to friendship had landed *Chase* in the soup. At his scornful best, Chase said, "And I suppose the English Sir told President Amin."

Juba looked smug; he was at last on sure ground. "He told Patricia Kamin."

So that was it. The Kamin bitch was the source of his trouble. He wasn't surprised; she'd been out to get him for a long time. His mind already dealing with thoughts of revenge, Chase said, "There seems to be something wrong here. Did I tell the Swiss man we must have good security because some Ugandan coffee has been stolen? That is possible. Did he repeat this to the English Sir? Why not? And did the English Sir— In bed, I suppose? With the Kamin woman, were they in bed when they talked?"

"That makes no difference," Juba said.

"So the English Sir, trying to seem brave and dramatic in bed with his whore, tells her a story about danger to the coffee shipment. And for this you bring me here at night, you waste my time, you tell me falsely that President Amin will be here, you—"

"You shut up now!" Juba banged his palm down flat on the desktop.

"I will not shut up! When President Amin learns what you have done—"

"These are his orders!"

Chase sat back, arms folded, gazing without expression at Juba. The situation was out in the open now, and he knew everything he needed to know. He had nothing further to say.

Juba too realized the situation had changed, and relaxed into the thug he really was. Speaking slowly, gazing unblinking at Chase, he said, "When you speak together with your friends, do you talk of 'the English Sir,' or do you say 'Sir Denis Lambsmith'? Do you think I am a great ignorant fool?"

"Not a *great* ignorant fool."

"Now you shall learn!" Juba gestured at his assistants. "Search him."

"Too late," Chase said. Withdrawing from its forearm holster in his left sleeve the chrome-plated Firearms International .25-caliber six-shot automatic, he fired once, the bullet hitting Juba just under the right eye with enough force to penetrate the brain and kill him but not enough to knock him out of his chair.

Chase was already moving, rolling leftward, kicking the witness's chair backward, rolling once toward the wall and coming up onto his feet with the automatic trained on the beer-slowed captain and major. Those two, nothing but big loutish boys with slow brains and too much good living, lurched in front of him, wanting to rush but afraid. "Move back to the wall," Chase told them.

They wouldn't. Uncertain but belligerent, they stood, weaving slightly, and the major said, "You shoot, they come here."

"Nobody knows there's a prisoner in here," Chase said. "Not even me. That's why you couldn't search me before. Move back to the wall."

"They *come*," insisted the major.

The captain said something in Kakwa. It was *infuriating* to have the wrong language! The major shook his head, then replied; by his eye movements, he was saying they should rush, one to the left, the other to the right.

No, no, can't permit that. The .25 automatic is really a very small gun; it won't slow people down, and it isn't accurate over much distance. Suddenly leaping forward, gun arm extended full in front of himself like a swordsman, Chase shot the major in the mouth, then jumped to the side, re-aiming at the captain.

Who stared with disbelief as his comrade slowly fell, hands to his face, then jerked once on the floor and was still. Terrified now, cold sober, a sudden white froth of sweat appearing in his wiry hair, the captain gaped at Chase and dropped to his knees. "Mercy!" he cried.

"Get up. I have use for you alive."

But the captain merely knelt there, clasping his hands, staring at Chase with full expectation of death. He had too little English, obviously, not much more than that ironic *mercy*; wherever could he have learned such a word?

In a hurry, Chase at last lifted his self-imposed ban and spoke in Swahili. "You will live if you do what I say. Get on your feet; go over there; stand facing that wall."

The captain, as astounded at hearing Swahili as if Chase had performed a Biblical miracle, scrambled to his feet, saying, "Yes, sir, yes, sir, I'll do what you say," in his own slurry rural version of the language. He retreated to the side wall and jittered there, the white foam of sweat sudsing in his hair and running in droplets down over his collar.

Chase found a total of four handguns on the two dead bodies. Returning the .25 to its forearm holster, he chose a Browning .38 revolver to carry. "All right, Captain," he said. "Now we go to work."

It was important that Juba and the others not be found yet, but fortunately in this building disposal of bodies was not a problem. Chase made the captain strip the dead men of their uniform coats, which bore their rank and symbols of office, and hang them with the other coats in the closet. Then he had him carry the major while Chase himself carried the thinner lighter Juba down through the empty midnight corridors—Chase knew where the sentries were and how to go around them—to the concrete-floored room at the back where bodies were placed prior to removal. There were only two corpses here at the moment; a slow night.

Juba and the major were dumped beside the first two. Then Chase said, "Give me your coat, Captain."

"Oh, sir," the captain said. "I did what you wished. Let me go home now. Far away from here, not even Uganda. Near Adi, sir," he said, naming a Zairian town just a few miles from both the Ugandan and Sudanese borders. "I go there, sir, I never come back."

"Give me your coat."

"All my family is there, sir. I go live with them, I never bother you again, sir."

In the end, Chase had to strip the coat off the body himself.

*　*　*

There were a few papers he could use from his own office in the Bureau building, a few weapons, nothing much. He sat at his desk a moment, looking around the barren room—he hadn't come here often, preferring his sunnier happier office in the Parliament Buildings—and reflected that this part of his life was over. Just in time, he had made his preparations for the future. On the other hand, the preparations themselves seemed to have hastened his departure.

Oh, well. In the world of the living, only Idi Amin and Patricia Kamin knew there was so much as a shadow over his head. His papers would still give him safe-conduct for some time to come, and his orders would still be obeyed. Leaving his office, he walked downstairs to the duty room, where he said to the duty officer, "Give me an arrest form."

"Yes, Captain Chase."

Chase filled out the form, naming Patricia Kamin as the person to be arrested, and giving both her home and Sir Denis Lambsmith's hotel room as possible locations where she might be found. In the appropriate block he wrote "Charge Not Specified." Under *Authority* he printed "IAD," which the duty officer would know stood for Idi Amin Dada. And under *Date of Implementation* he put not the usual "Immediate" but "Night, 27 May 1977." Meaning tomorrow night, Friday, after the coffee caper had been successfully pulled off. Finally, he wrote the word "Jinja," meaning she would not be brought here, where she might be able to contact friends in the Bureau to rescue her, but to Jinja Barracks, where she was unknown.

Returning the form, Chase said, "You see the authority."

"Oh, yes, Captain Chase."

"And the place."

"Jinja; yes, sir."

"And the date of implementation."

"Yes, sir. Tomorrow night."

"We must keep this quiet until then. We don't want to scare our bird away."

Laughing, the duty officer said, "No, Captain, we don't."

"There's one thing more," Chase said.

The duty officer waited, alert.

"This is not something to be written. This is from the President himself." Chase tapped the form with a fingertip. "Give her the VIP treatment."

PART FIVE

44

Eight a.m. The train—locomotive, tender, twenty-seven coffee-laden cars—pulled out of the yards at Soroti, headed south. A brief sprinkle before sunrise had left the world sparkling clean. The engineer and fireman, drinking their after-breakfast beer and feeling the deep vibration of the locomotive as it pulled eight hundred tons of coffee over the shining rails, sang happy songs together as they sailed along the track through the green countryside. They called to pretty school-girls crossing the fields toward the main road, carrying their books against their breasts. Some of the girls waved back.

* * *

Lew stood aside while the four men who'd built this blind carefully removed it, pulling it downhill and to the left, leaning it against a tangle of shrubbery. "Very pretty," he said, and stepped through the magic doorway in the jungle to look at the railroad track. "Very pretty indeed."

Young Mr. Balim, who claimed to speak Swahili sufficiently well for the task, had assigned himself to Lew as translator. Following through the gap, he said, "My goodness. To hear about it is one thing, but to see it is something else."

"Bathar, tell them this is a very very pretty structure. They did a Grade A job."

Young Mr. Balim's translation was at least close enough to wreathe the faces of the four men in proud smiles. They did a lot of nodding and pointing and talking, all of which Young Mr. Balim translated as "They say they had much difficulty, but they knew the job was very important."

"They did just fine. Thank them again."

While that was going on, Lew studied the rails. Unlike American track, which is laid with staggered joints so that each join is always at the midpoint of the opposite rail, the British habitually lay track with parallel joints. This practice makes for a marginally less solid line, but it does come in handy for hijackers intending to divert the track. "These joints here," Lew said to Young Mr. Balim, having walked down the line a bit to the west. "This is where we'll open the track. Ask them if they agree."

Young Mr. Balim posed the question, which Lew had asked since after all these men had been hired for their railway experience. And the answer was "Yes, they say that's the place they had in mind."

The up freight had gone by two hours ago, just after dawn, when the brief rain was stopping. The railway was theirs. "We might as well get the work crew up here," Lew said, "and get started."

* * *

Isaac, in his Ugandan Army captain's uniform, approached the truck, where Frank was suspiciously watching the twenty men chosen as drivers select clothing out of the boxes before climbing aboard. He looked as though he suspected them of lying about their ability to drive; which was in fact possible. Isaac said, "How does it look?"

"What? Oh, the uniform. Fine," Frank said. "You could strike terror in my heart at forty paces wearing that."

"That's reassuring," Isaac said.

"Good. Charlie!"

A part of Mazar Balim's business was a brisk trade in Army surplus and used clothing, which was where all the stuff in the boxes had come from. Charlie was helping the men find military-style clothing that fit, though what Charlie knew about right-fitting clothing was anybody's guess. He looked up at Frank's voice, said, "Yes, Frank?" and trotted over to receive instructions.

"Tell those clowns," Frank said, "we want those uniforms back."

"Okay, sure."

"Those duds are for sale in the shop in Kisumu, they're supposed to go back on the shelf when we're done, so they shouldn't get 'em all dirty and fucked up."

"Okay, fine."

Something about Charlie's translation struck the men funny; Isaac, listening, faintly smiled, until he saw Frank glowering at him, beetle-browed. "Did he tell 'em what I said?"

"Oh, sure," Isaac said, and in essence Charlie *had* delivered Frank's message. Isaac thought it better if Frank remained unaware of the details. He said, "Couldn't we speed up this loading process?"

Frank grinned at him. "In a hurry to get started?"

"No," Isaac said truthfully, "I'm in a hurry to get it over with."

* * *

The bank opened at nine-thirty, and Chase was its first customer, striding in with smiling confidence, greeting the assistant manager by name, handing him the forged request chit from Idi Amin for five thousand dollars U.S., in cash. (That, Chase knew, was the highest amount the assistant manager would give him without telephone verification.) "While you're getting it," Chase went on, "I'll just visit my box."

"Certainly. Of course. Miss Ngana? Would you take Mr. Chase to the safe-deposit boxes?"

Chase had always assumed that Amin knew what was in his safe-deposit box, so he'd never kept anything there but some jewels and personal identification. These he now removed, so that when he returned upstairs with the willowy Miss Ngana, he carried in his pockets about thirty thousand dollars' worth of ivory figurines and small pieces of jewelry in gold.

The small canvas packet was waiting on the assistant manager's desk. Approaching, Chase was overcome by a huge yawn. "Very sorry," he said, when he could. Not wanting to risk a return to his own house, he'd spent last night with a whore of his acquaintance, who had insisted on giving him his money's worth.

"Not at all," the assistant manager said, smiling. "Many mornings I feel the same myself."

"Coffee, that's what I need." Chase smiled his secret smile.

"And less love life," the assistant manager said, beaming broadly and nervously to show he had dared a joke.

"That, too. Well, good morning."

"Good morning, Mr. Chase."

Outside, Chase strode briskly to the Mercedes he'd commandeered last night from the Bureau building's parking lot. Stuffing the bag of money under the front seat, he started the engine and drove quickly away. He still had three more banks to visit, plus several shops.

Even success, though, had its bitter taste. Amin is taking millions out of this rotten country, Chase thought, and I'm taking thousands. Big fish, little fish. Ah, well; we all eat as much as we can.

*   *   *

Frank didn't realize it, but when he shinnied up a telephone pole wearing earphones connected to a dangling ball of wire he looked like some sort of bear act in the circus. That's why there was so much snickering going on below. He suspected the racket had something to do with him, however, and resolved to kick ass just as soon as he got to the ground.

The Ugandan telephone system had last been cared for by the British sixteen years ago. Since then, there had been very little maintenance and absolutely no upgrading. Half the glass insulators were broken or stolen, and the old wires themselves were frayed. The service box was dented and rusty, but when Frank opened it the old diagrams and layout in English inside the door were still readable. Still, he had to attach the alligator clips several times before he found the direct line from the railroad office at Jinja. "My, how they chatter," he said aloud.

Between the earphones and the alligator clips was a thirty-foot ball of wire, much more than enough to reach from here to the ground. Looking down, Frank saw Charlie directly below, gesticulating and grimacing for an appreciative audience. Taking careful aim, he dropped the earphones and was gratified to see them bounce off Charlie's head. "Watch out below!" he called amiably, then double-checked that the alligator clips were firmly in place, shut the service-box door, and shinnied back down the pole.

*   *   *

Ten-fifteen. If the train could be said to have a schedule, it was running ahead. There was something about the sunniness of the morning, the clarity of the air, that made even lazy people feel like working. The one car at Okungulo and the two cars at Kumi had been attached almost before the train was completely stopped, and now the same thing was happening at Kachumbala with its one car. The train was now thirty-one freight cars in length; only the two at Mbale were left to pick up. "We'll be in Kampala before dinner-time," the engineer said.

"If nothing goes wrong."

"On a day like this? What could go wrong?"

* * *

Lew had posted one sentry where the access road crossed the track, and the other fifty yards from the work site in the opposite direction, where the curve to the right sharpened. If either of them saw anything, he was to wave his arms energetically over his head. That signal would cause Young Mr. Balim to call out *"Chini!"* the Swahili word that means "down," which in turn would cause the work crew, carrying their tools, to scatter off the tracks and take cover in the underbrush on either side. Lew had made them practice this maneuver twice, and believed they understood it. As for Young Mr. Balim, he took his task with utter seriousness, striding back and forth beside the track, frowning first at one sentry and then at the other.

Even with nearly thirty men at work, under the instructions of the four former railway employees, it was a long and cumbersome job. Four spikes had to be levered out of every metal sleeper over a distance of some forty yards; that was nearly a hundred sleepers. The joint plates with their rusty nuts and bolts had to be removed at the point of the break. Then, inch by painful inch, the two lengths of rail, about seven tons of metal in all, had to be pried away from their nests in the sleepers and urged toward their new alignment. To do it, twenty men would stand in a row beside one rail, holding twenty prybars angled under it; at a signal, all twenty would heave upward and the rail would move; not very far, but it would move.

Meanwhile, the rest of the work force was digging shallow trenches for logs to be used as crosspieces on the new trajectory. Not only were one hundred sleepers at seventy pounds apiece too much to move in the time they had, but at the end of the exercise, in order to hide themselves, they would have to put this goddam track back together again.

While Lew oversaw the trackwork with the help of Young Mr. Balim, Frank roamed the entire area of the depot looking for trouble to yell at. Down the track a ways Charlie, now wearing the earphones,

hunkered against the telephone pole Frank had climbed, chewing
sugarcane stalks as he listened contentedly to the conversations from
Jinja railway station. If Frank in earphones on that pole had looked
like a performing bear, Charlie in earphones drooling under the pole
looked like a performing monkey in the same circus.

By ten-thirty the new spur was beginning to take shape. The south-
ernmost rail had been pried and levered and shoved and inched and
cursed into place, up on the logs, angling now leftward away from
its original bed, curving over the logs and down to meet the end of
the spur track, where it was over two feet too long.

"Shit," said Lew. "All right, we have to increase the angle up at
the other end."

With several spikes driven in near the spur end to keep that part
from moving, the workmen levered the other end back toward the
original bed, increasing the angle of the curve. The end of the rail
where it lay overlapping the rusty spur seemed to shrink, jerking
backward an inch or more at each heave.

"Chini! Chini!"

Young Mr. Balim was so excited at being useful, he was actually
hopping up and down, flapping his arms like the young traveler in
the Indian tales who sees the djinn. Most of the men wasted a few
seconds looking around for Lew, to see if this were another test, but
when they saw the sentry at the access road waving his arms over his
head they scattered in commendable fashion, leaving nothing behind
except a very oddly splayed section of line. The sentry stopped waving
and, apparently having already been seen by whoever was coming,
hunkered down on his heels beside the track like any unemployed
man waiting for a train; not to board it, to look at it.

From his concealment Lew could see the crossing, and what first
appeared on it was a cow, ambling along with slow purposefulness as
though returning from church. It was tan, tall, long-nosed, big-
shouldered, bony-legged, half-wild, looking more like an ox than a
cow, and nothing at all like the picture-book black-and-white cows
in American fields.

Beside Lew, Young Mr. Balim giggled. Lew shook his head, and
the giggling stopped.

Three more similar creatures now appeared, two of them stopping in stupid-cow fashion to graze on the crossing, where there was nothing green. The herder, a gray-brown boy of about seven wearing a crimson shirt and short brown pants and carrying a stick almost twice as long as himself, came up onto the crossing to lecture the dawdlers, his manner that of a patient but disappointed teacher in a class for slow pupils. He and the sentry nodded to one another, and two more cows stepped up onto the crossing, heads nodding as they wondered what the stopped ones had found to eat.

The boy had charge of nine cattle in all, and obviously knew them very well. And they knew him; he merely had to show the stick to get them moving. In three minutes the cattle had finished crossing the track, and a minute later the sentry waved the all clear.

As everybody came back up onto the track, Frank came stomping up the spur line and stopped to give a critical eye to their progress. "Coming along, huh?"

"Slow and unsteady," Lew said.

Frank nodded, looking at the track. The northern rail was still part of the main line, but the southern rail was curved down to the spur. "I never saw a railroad spread her legs before," he commented.

*　　*　　*

I'm getting too cocky, Isaac warned himself. It isn't this easy; something could go terribly wrong.

But at the moment things were going wonderfully right. The same motor-pool sergeant was in the office, and apparently Isaac had sufficiently cowed him last time, so that today all he wanted was to show how cooperative he could be. "Twenty trucks," he announced as Isaac walked in on the dot of eleven. "All gassed up and ready."

"That's fine," Isaac said. "I told the General we could count on you."

"You did? Thank you, that's very good of you. And accurate, accurate." Grabbing a clipboard off the wall, the sergeant said, "Come along and look at your trucks. Beauties, every one of them."

The sergeant had a strange eye for beauty. The twenty trucks lined up on the tan dirt of the yard looked as though they might have taken part in the retreat to Dunkirk: battered, filthy, canvas covers ripped, headlights broken, windshields starred, bumpers missing. Mostly British Leyland, but with a few Volvos and even some Mercedes-Benz and Fiat diesels, they looked more like vehicles coming in to the motor pool for general repair than going out for regular use. But so long as the tires were sound and the engines ran, Isaac wouldn't complain. "Many general dents and scratches," he wrote on the form on the sergeant's clipboard, and signed: "Captain I. Gelaya."

No old friend appeared today to stop his heart. It was clear that Obed Naya had not turned him in, had kept his own counsel. What had the man thought was going on? If only there were some safe way to get in touch, to thank him, but any contact at all would be dangerous to Obed. A letter or a phone call would attract the wrong attention. It would be a poor thank-you to get his old friend killed.

Once he'd signed for the trucks, he went back to the one he'd driven here and ordered the men out. In their ragbag of army clothing they looked about like the other soldiers at Jinja Barracks. Isaac enjoyed pretending to be a tough officer, barking at the men, ordering them into the trucks. Once he saw that in fact all the engines did work, he thanked the sergeant once more, promised to return the trucks by noon tomorrow, and led the convoy out of the Barracks and eastward out of town.

They were merely an Army convoy, one of the commonest of sights on Ugandan roads. No one gave them a second glance.

* * *

At a quarter to twelve, Chase came smiling out of the jewelry shop on Kampala Road. Ugandan shillings would be useless to him after today, so he had just converted most of his into a small but lovely diamond necklace. He should be able to sell it for at least twenty thousand dollars once he got to Europe.

This was his last stop. Eat lunch now, before departure? No; now that things were in motion he was increasingly gripped by a sense of urgency, a strong desire to keep moving. He could stop at a market, buy some food to eat on the way. Deciding that, he returned to the Mercedes, stowed the small flat box containing the necklace in the glove compartment, and drove away from there. Westward, away from Kampala, away from Jinja and the coffee train. Away from Uganda, away from the past. Away from danger.

* * *

Frank walked along the track to where Charlie half snoozed, smiling dreamily inside the earphones, listening to the busy talk of the workaday world. It was just noon. "Charlie," Frank said. "Where's the train?"

"Oh, hello, Frank. They just called."

"Who did?"

"Tororo station. Train gone through, making good time."

Frank stared at him. "Gone through *Tororo?*"

"Sure. Very fast train."

"Jesus H. Galloping Christ!"

Frank pounded back up the track to where Lew and the workmen were easing that second rail closer and closer to the spur. "Son of a bitch, Lew!" he yelled. "The fucking train's ahead of schedule!"

Lew looked down the track, as though expecting to see the thing coming. "Where is it?"

"Eighty miles from here. Gone through Tororo already. The bastards are highballing."

Lew looked around, then bawled, "Bathar!"

Young Mr. Balim appeared, as though from under a sleeper. "Here I am."

"Tell them," Lew said, "we've got to do this faster. The train's an hour from here."

"Oh, my gosh."

"Not an hour," Frank said. "They can't do eighty, not that full."

"Tell them an hour," Lew insisted.

While Young Mr. Balim translated—it griped Frank's ass that a punk like that could rattle off the fucking Swahili—Frank turned and saw an army truck just going over the level crossing. "Isaac's back! Get these people moving, Lew."

Frank trotted down the track to the access road, where truck after truck was now lumbering across. Who asked the goddam railroad to run *ahead* of schedule? Jumping up onto a passing running board, Frank rode down to where Isaac was directing everybody where to park. "Hey, Isaac!"

Isaac waved, grinning from ear to ear, the ultimate schoolboy playing hooky. "No trouble at all," he called. "I am reborn a highwayman."

Frank had no time for amenities. "Isaac, the train's running ahead of schedule. It's already past Tororo. Get your drivers up to help Lew move that fucking track."

"Tororo!" Turning away, Isaac started shouting panicky instructions at his drivers. *More* Swahili.

* * *

It was like a conga line, with Lew at the head, Young Mr. Balim behind him, Frank, Isaac, the four ex-railwaymen and the forty-eight laborers. Fifty-six men in a row, all stooping over to grasp the double lip of the rail in both hands, tensing, waiting.

"On three," Lew called. "You do it, Bathar."

Young Mr. Balim's voice sounded clear and musical over the tracks: *"Moja! Mbili! TATU!"*

The hundred twelve hands gripped; the fifty-six backs strained and lifted; the rail cleared the ground and moved leftward not quite a foot, and fell.

"Again!"

"Moja! Mbili! TATU!"

"Moja! Mbili! TATU!"

"Jesus," Frank grumbled, "isn't the fucker there?"

Lew looked down at the two lengths of rail, the main track gleaming, the spur orange-red with rust. We should have guessed, he thought. "It's there," he said. "Come take a look."

While the men all straightened and rubbed their backs, stretching and laughing at one another, Lew and Frank and Isaac and Young Mr. Balim and the ex-railwaymen all stood looking at the rails. Frank said it: "It's two fucking feet too fucking short."

Lew sighed. "We took two straight lines," he said, "and curved them. The outer curve has to be longer than the inner curve to come to the same place."

"Two feet. We'll derail the fucking train if we try to run it over that."

Lew turned to Young Mr. Balim. "These men have been working here for a week. Ask them if they've seen any short piece of rail we could fit in there."

Young Mr. Balim asked the question, but didn't have to translate the negative headshakes. Frank said, "Goddam son of a bitch dirty bastard."

Hardly noticing the fact, Lew had taken over. "Frank," he said, "we didn't come this far to get stopped by some little gap in the rail.

We'll work something out. You start them driving spikes. Have we got the measure?"

"Right here," Young Mr. Balim said, picking up the long notched stick they would use to be sure the rails were the right width apart.

"Give it to Frank. You and these guys come with me. There's got to be *something* in this depot we can use."

Frank stood holding the stick Young Mr. Balim had given him. He looked truculent and confused. "Now what?"

Lew said, "Frank, we've got the first rail spiked into place. You use the measure to put the second rail the right distance from it, and have the men spike it in. I'll be right back."

"Where's my translator?" Frank was demanding; as Lew led his party down toward the engine shed, Frank overrode Isaac's attempt to volunteer by bellowing, "Charlie, you asshole, get over here!"

The interior of the engine shed was an agglomeration of half-eaten food, ancient rotting leaves, animal and bird droppings, rusting tools and metal tables, rotted planks and foul woodsmoke. Lew and the other five searched through this mess without result; everything they came up with was either too long or too fragile for the weight it would have to support.

"Something," Lew said, hands on hips, glaring around. "Something."

"Not in here," Young Mr. Balim said.

"Outside, then."

Outside, beside the shed, there were still a few unused rails, but they were all sixteen-footers. No good. While the others scuffed through the trash beside the building Lew, not knowing what he was looking for, wandered alone down the spur line to the turntable, paused there to look around and see nothing of use, and walked on. The last of the added rails stopped less than five feet from the lip of the gorge. Far below, the water of Thruston Bay could be heard beating against the coastal rocks.

What could they use? Turning back, Lew was starting to retrace his steps when he saw the old buffer that had been removed from the end of the track now lying off to the right in the weeds. A trapezoid around a large thick rusty spring with a black rubber knob on the front, the frame of the buffer was made of *lengths of rail*!

"Jesus Christ," Lew said for his own benefit, then yelled, "Bathar! Bring 'em down here!"

*   *   *

There were gaps at both ends of the inserted piece, but neither was more than an inch long. Extra log supports were under the insert, which had been fixed in place with so many spikes it looked as though it had acne.

"All right," Frank said as he threw away the measure stick. "Now we've finally got the welcome mat, let's go steal the fucking train."

45

The train ran west from Tororo at fifty-five miles an hour. The heavy-laden cars roared and rumbled on their way, the wheels banging into the joints, the metal couplers gnashing together, the bodies swaying and jouncing left and right on their old springs. The locomotive strained forward as though representing steam engines everywhere, hurling defiance at the world of diesel. The big steel wheels ran so fast the connecting bars were a blur. Smoke and steam fled out the stacks, and the engineer wailed the whistle for the level crossings, where people stared as the huge snarling shrieking metal snake, a third of a mile long, went thundering by.

Back when they'd been picking their path through the Tororo yards, they'd had to slow to such a crawl that the fireman had hopped out, run to the station, bought two sandwiches and four beers, and was back aboard before the transfer was completed to the east-west line. But now, as they ate the sandwiches and drank the beer, there was nothing ahead but fine weather and clear track.

The little stations shot by: Nagongera, where the sleeping stationmaster leaped out of his chair on the shaded platform as though the devil himself were rushing by; Budumba, just before the clattering trestle bridge over the swampy southern toe of Lake Kyoga; Busembatia, where the train quivered and clanged over the switches that led to the northbound Mbulamuti branch loop; Iganga, where a school soccer game faltered to a stop as the white-shirted boys in dark-blue short pants turned to stare and the black-and-white soccer ball went bounding away on the green grass. The engineer laughed and sounded the banshee whistle one extra time for luck.

"Flag ahead!"

The engineer turned and frowned, and the fireman pointed dead ahead, where a very sloppy soldier beside the track waved a red flag vigorously over his head.

Automatically, the engineer released the throttle bar and applied the brakes, and they shot by the grinning flag-waving soldier. What did it mean? The next station was Magamaga, just before Jinja. Was there trouble there? Trouble on the track?

Down the line another soldier waved a red flag, and beyond him an Army truck straddled the rails, blocking the train.

"It's Army," the fireman said. He sounded frightened.

"We have to stop." The engineer sounded frightened, too. The Army. Who knew whose side the Army was on these days?

But stopping a train this big, this long, this heavy, was easier said than done. The brakes slammed on all the way down the line of cars, the impulse running back through the hydraulic hoses, the wheels under the cars shuddering to a halt, skidding and scraping along the rails, throwing sparks. The locomotive hurled up a great whoosh of steam, neighing like a fractious horse, not wanting to stop, fighting the brakes. The wide-eyed driver of the truck (an Asian, he looked like, what was an Asian doing in Uganda?) hurriedly drove off the track, but the train did finally grind down to a loud, steam-hissing, metal-banging, infinitely prolonged halt, forward motion ceasing just before it reached the spot where the truck had been.

The second soldier was an officer. The engineer, torn between worry and irritation, watched him trot this way along the gravel beside the track, still carrying his red flag. Far back, well beyond the last car, the other soldier had thrown his own flag away and could faintly be seen running in this direction.

The officer was out of shape; a desk man, probably. He was winded when he reached the locomotive, where the engineer yelled down to him over the continuing hiss of steam, "What's the matter?"

The officer gasped and blew for a minute, increasing the engineer's impatience, before he managed to say, "Trouble."

"Trouble? I *guessed* there was trouble. What sort of trouble?"

"You're being hijacked," the officer said.

The engineer didn't at all understand. "What's that?"

A voice behind him said, in English, "We're taking over the train."

The engineer and fireman were both fairly proficient in English, and they understood *that* sentence well enough. They spun around and stared in absolute amazement at two white men who had climbed up into the cab on the other side—while the Army officer had distracted them—and who were now standing there with guns in their hands.

"You—" The engineer couldn't figure out how to put his astonishment and disbelief into words in *any* language. "You— You can't— This is a *train*!"

The bigger older one said, "We know it's a fucking train, fella, and we're taking it over."

The Army officer had now climbed up into the cab, and the fireman said to him, "The Army? What does the Army want with our train?"

"They're not Army," the engineer told him. He'd at least worked out that much.

"Talk English," said the older white man.

The younger one stepped closer to the engineer. "You'll drive now," he said. "But slowly."

"It would have been a record!" wailed the fireman, the enormity of it coming home to him.

"Talk English, goddammit!"

The younger one gestured with his gun at the engineer. "Start now."

"Wait for Charlie," said the officer.

The older one said, "Fuck Charlie."

"No," said the younger one. "Where is he, Isaac?"

The officer leaned out the cab window. "He's climbing on the last car. Give him just a second . . . okay."

"Start."

The engineer started. Once again, smoke balls puffed upward; the wheels spun on the track; they caught; the locomotive surged forward.

Clang, clang, clang, the couplers crashed all the way down the line as the slack was taken up, and the entire giant snake lunged forward.

They passed the truck, stopped now on the dirt road beside the track. The driver—he *was* an Asian—waved and drove away as the train slowly gathered speed.

The younger one was carefully watching the engineer's moves. He means to run it himself, the engineer thought. Aloud, he said, "This is foolish, you know. What are you going to do with a train? When we don't arrive in Jinja, they'll come looking for us."

"Stop now," the younger one said. "We're here."

They'd traveled perhaps half a mile. "Here?"

The train was doing barely ten miles an hour, and was very easily stopped. But where was *here*? An empty stretch flanked by jungle growth, near a level crossing for an abandoned road.

"Last stop," the older one said. "Everybody off."

The engineer, the fireman, the Army officer, and the older white man all climbed down to the ground, where the older man yelled up, "Don't fuck up this train now! It's the only one we got!"

"I've always wanted my own train," the younger one said, grinning out of the cab at them.

The other soldier, the one they'd called Charlie, was running along the tops of the cars, leaping the spaces like a deranged impala. The engineer and the fireman looked around, wide-eyed, and here was *more* astonishment. Just up ahead, the track had been moved! While the rest of the line continued on as before, curving slowly away to the right, this one section had been curved sharply to the *left*, through a gap in the encroaching shrubbery and out of sight.

"Stand clear, now," the older white man said. "We got an amateur up there at the throttle."

46

Lew couldn't stop grinning. The train seemed to breathe under him, a huge panting powerful tame beast, waiting for his command. The throttle bar had to be held down to make the beast move; a safety measure, the dead-man's bar, so that if the engineer had a heart attack the train wouldn't continue on with nobody at the throttle.

It had been decided that Lew would drive this part, just in case they had to deal with an engineer of heroic cast, who might try to sabotage the train before it was well hidden. Now Lew touched the bar and felt the beast's vibration against his palm. He pressed, and the vibration multiplied a hundred times, and through a great rasping roar he heard somebody down there yell, "Easy! Easy! Not so fast!"

Not so fast? The train wasn't moving, so he must be spinning the wheels. He released the throttle, and the noise died away, and he settled down to learn this beast, which maybe wasn't as tame as he'd thought. He hadn't known he was going fast. He touched the bar again, and this time depressed it very very gently.

The roar started, but not so angrily. The vibration increased, but not so dramatically. The train moved! Startled, Lew released the throttle, and the train stopped.

"Will you quit fucking around up there?"

"Shut up, Frank," Lew yelled out the window, and put his hand again on the bar.

The roar. The increasing vibration. A jolt, and once again the train inched forward.

Lew kept his hand exactly where it was, and the train slowly gathered speed, and from behind him came the diminishing crashes of the couplers losing slack.

The train was doing at most five miles an hour, with the diverted track just ahead. As he looked down on it from way up in the cab, it seemed to Lew that what they had built was too flimsy, the logs too uncertain a replacement for metal sleepers, the bed too soft, the rails insufficiently spiked into place. It's a child's toy, he thought, and I'm bringing a life-size locomotive onto it.

If it fell over, should he stay with the engine or try to jump clear?

"Take it slow, Lew! Slow and easy!"

"Shut *up*, Frank!"

The locomotive sagged to the left as they moved down off the regular roadbed. The observers on that side scattered, and the locomotive hesitantly rolled down over a track that had suddenly become all hills and valleys.

"Don't stop! Keep moving!"

"Blow it out your ass, Frank," Lew muttered. Out ahead, as the locomotive slowly curved through the gap in the wall of shrubbery, he could see the ex-railwaymen and the workers, all expectant and excited, watching this huge black metal monster nose down into their world.

It was such a short distance from the solid main line to the solid spur line, but now it seemed a million miles long. The entire locomotive was on the temporary track, weaving from side to side as wood and metal groaned and cracked beneath the wheels. The tender followed like an obedient child, much more docile than its parent on the new line. The cars came along like sheep, one after the other, clanking, grinding, wheels screeching where the rails were too close together.

The locomotive dropped, on the right side, about an inch, lurching as though it had been shot. Lew lost control of the throttle, and when he grabbed to regain it he pressed down too hard. The wheels spun with that grating roaring sound, but then the right side lurched up again and the locomotive lunged forward onto the old spur track like a bear hurling itself away from thin ice.

That sound was a cheer! Lew looked out of the cab, and on both sides of the locomotive the men were yelling and grinning and clapping and jumping up and down. Even Frank was cheering instead of giving advice, and the former engineer and fireman were surreptitiously grinning at one another. Leaning far out of the cab and looking back and up, Lew could see Charlie about eight cars back, capering on the roof like a mannequin whose strings are pulled by a child.

Isaac, grinning like a Halloween pumpkin and carrying a walkie-talkie, climbed up into the cab. Pointing at Lew's own grin, he said, "You'll crack your face."

"So will you."

Now it was easy. While the men surged forward to grab for the ladders on the freight cars, climbing aboard for the ride, some going up top to the roofs, some hanging on the sides, Lew eased the locomotive on down the spur track. Smoothly and neatly, it rode the switch that diverted it from the engine shed toward the turntable. *Clack* went the wheels when they hit the minutely off turntable, and *clack* again on the other side.

Isaac said, "You know, that's a gorge just ahead."

"Oh, I know it."

At the end of the regular spur was more temporary track; again the locomotive sagged and hesitated. Lew took his hand off the throttle, and for an agonizing instant the train kept rolling toward the end of the track and the lip of the gorge. But then it faltered, and then it stopped.

Isaac's walkie-talkie cleared its throat with scratchy static sounds, then squawked in a parrot's version of Frank's voice saying, "Take it on down."

Isaac said, "It *is* on down."

"Repeat?"

"We're here, Frank, at the end of the track."

The walkie-talkie made indignant sounds: "I still got cars up here! I gotta get 'em off this track! Run the fucking engine into the gorge!"

Lew said, "Ask him if he wants to ride shotgun."

Another Americanism to confuse Isaac. "What?"

"Never mind. Tell them out there to unhook the cars from the tender. We don't want the whole train in the gorge."

"Right."

As Isaac started down out of the cab, Lew said, "And send somebody up with one of those little pieces of rail."

"Right."

That happened first; a grinning workman clambered aboard, toting a two-foot piece of rail from the dismantled buffer. He stood in the cab, grinning, looking around at everything, and Lew said, "Wanna ride over the cliff in it?" But the man had no English, and after a minute he left.

Down below, Lew could hear the walkie-talkie skreeking Frank's impatience, and Isaac calmly answering. Frank wanted the workmen, so Isaac called to them to hurry back up to the main line. Reluctantly they left, looking back, wishing they could watch the locomotive go over the cliff.

Meanwhile, two of the ex-railwaymen worked at unhooking the lead car from the tender. The other two had climbed to the top of the first two cars to turn the big flat wheels of the hand brakes.

"All set!"

Lew had already propped the piece of rail on the cab's windowsill, and now he lowered it gently onto the throttle bar. The engine roared, the wheels spun, and before he had the thing balanced they were already rolling toward the cliff. Quickly he lifted the rail, but the locomotive wasn't pulling any weight now, and saw no reason to stop.

Hell and damnation. Feeling the pull of that gorge, Lew dropped the rail onto the throttle, turned, and dove headfirst out of the moving cab.

He landed in a lot of sharp nasty branches, rolled over, sat up, and watched the front wheels of the locomotive run off the end of the track and dig a plowlike furrow into the ground.

The locomotive slowed; it strained; the rear thrusting wheels bit in hard against the rusty rails; the front wheels sliced slowly through that final five feet of earth toward the gorge.

Isaac had come running, squawky walkie-talkie in hand. "Are you all right?"

"Just look at that son of a gun."

Lew clambered to his feet, and he and Isaac stood and watched the locomotive doggedly commit suicide. It pushed, it strained, the tender patient and obedient behind it, until all at once chunks of earth gave way at the lip of the gorge, and the locomotive shot suddenly forward. "There it goes!" Isaac cried.

But not yet. Lew had had all the time in the world to climb in a dignified fashion down out of that cab. He and Isaac ran through the scrub to the edge of the cliff as the locomotive ground slowly forward, the front wheels now dangling free in space. The nose very gradually drooped downward, as though the locomotive were reluctant to see where it was going. Then it spurted forward, the front half stuck itself black and huge and defenseless out into the air, the wheels lost their traction on the rails, the rear lifted, the nose turned down, and with a sideways lurch as though acknowledging defeat, the great monster slid over the edge.

Thruston Bay was narrow and crooked and very deep, almost more a river than a bay, with steep clay cliffs on both sides, covered with tenacious shrubbery. The locomotive, immediately looking tiny and weightless when it was in the air, plummeted straight down, hit the cliff face a glancing blow midway, and then spun crazily the last fifty feet, shaking itself loose of its tender and hitting the water with a huge, satisfying, craterlike splash, into the bull's-eye of which the tender dropped like an unimportant afterthought.

There was an underwater explosion when the cold water hit the roaring-hot boiler, and the already roiled surface of the bay seemed to lift in a body, like bread rising. Then the surface ripped apart and the giant cough of the explosion was released, along with a great gout of steam. The steam fled away up into the air, dissipating, and the torn water fell back to form a surface again, which rapidly smoothed itself. The locomotive was gone.

Lew and Isaac stared at one another, their faces delighted and awed, like children on Christmas morning. "That," Isaac said, his faint and dazzled voice seeming to come from the tree branches above his head, "that, that was the most satisfying sight I ever did see in my entire life."

"What is so beautiful as a falling locomotive?" Slowly nodding, Lew said, "No matter what else happens to me in my life, that made it all worthwhile."

"Oh ho ho!" Isaac laughed, staggering backward. He might have gone over the edge himself if Lew hadn't grabbed his arm and pulled him back. "And Mazar Balim," Isaac cried through his laughter, "Mazar Balim said don't volunteer! Ho ho ho ho ho!"

A sudden thought left Lew stricken. "Oh, my God," he said.

Isaac's laughter cut off. "What's wrong?"

"We didn't take any pictures."

Isaac gave that serious consideration, then shook his head. "They wouldn't have come out. Something like that never does."

"You're right," Lew said, relieved. "In a photograph, it's just a toy train."

"We have the pictures here," Isaac said, tapping his head.

"Forever," Lew agreed.

Reluctantly, they turned away from the placid bay, to see the rest of the train rolling slowly toward them. Letting gravity do the work, the ex-railwaymen atop the front two cars turned the brake wheels, making tiny adjustments, permitting that great weight to inch slowly down the gradual slope but not to build up momentum.

"I hope they know what they're doing," Lew said. "After all this, I wouldn't want to see six million dollars of coffee go crashing into the bay."

"We wouldn't *want* a camera for that," Isaac said.

47

When the goddam cars at last began to roll forward, Frank knew they'd gotten rid of the locomotive. He'd yelled himself hoarse into that goddam walkie-talkie, and all he got for his efforts was a sore throat. But now at last the cars were moving, though awfully goddam slow.

Up toward the main line, the work crew was already busily pulling spikes from the temporary track. The engineer and the fireman, trussed with ropes, sat to one side, their backs against trees, and watched with unflagging astonishment. Charlie had been put back to work as Frank's translator, and was capering around in his usual style, while down the line Young Mr. Balim had been put in charge of the earphones, to spy on the railroad station at Jinja. Frank hated to have to admit that Young Mr. Balim could be useful, but there it was. At least Young Mr. Balim, unlike Charlie, could be counted on to report anything he might hear of interest.

The cars stopped. That was too soon; most of the last car was still on the rails that had to be moved. Frank yelled into the walkie-talkie,

"Move the damn thing!" He waited an eighth of a second and then bellowed, "Is anybody goddam *there?*"

It was Lew's voice that responded, not Isaac's. "You don't need the walkie-talkie, I can hear you without it."

"Then move the goddam train!"

"We did. The locomotive's gone. It was a very pretty sight, Frank."

Frank had no time for pretty sights. "I've still got wheels on the main line."

"The only thing we might do, Frank, is throw the first car over."

"Do it!"

"We won't have time to unload it."

"One fucking car? Don't be greedy, throw it over!"

"It's done," Lew promised.

Shaking his head, Frank stuck the walkie-talkie under his arm like a swagger stick and walked up to where the men were pulling spikes. Every spike was thrown away over the bushes and every log tie would be dragged off out of sight, and all the digging would be smoothed over. If there was time.

Two of the ex-railwaymen were up at this end of the work. One of them now came over to speak very earnestly at Frank in that goddam Swahili, all the while pointing at the end of the spur track. Probably wanting to know when they could separate that join. "We're working on it," Frank assured him. "I hope to Christ we're working on it."

The cars moved. They stopped. They moved again, inching along, the rear wheels of the last car creeping toward the joint and the start of the rusty spur track. They reached the joint, they flowed over it, they went on another two or three feet, and then they stopped.

"Now," Frank said, and the happy ex-railwayman went purposefully to the joint, carrying several tools.

Frank walked down the track to Young Mr. Balim. "Anything doing?"

Young Mr. Balim pushed one earphone back onto his head so he could listen simultaneously to Frank and Jinja. "Not a word," he said. "Most of the calls are about missing freight, not missing trains."

"It's early yet," Frank said. "They'll push the panic button, don't you worry."

"The missing train," said Young Mr. Balim, and smiled. "What a wonderment."

"It is kinda nice," Frank admitted, and looked back up the track to where fifty men were just starting to shuffle the northern rail back to its original position.

48

The city of Jinja, population fifty-two thousand, in addition to being the spot where the Nile emerges from Lake Victoria, so that it is therefore a port of some importance, is also a railway hub, an important freight stop on the main east-west line as well as being the western terminus of the northern loop branch line through Mbulamuti. The railroad station at Jinja, as a result, was kept manned all day even under the current reduced level of rail service.

The main office in the red-brick station building was a long narrow room in which an L-shaped, chest-high, dark-wood counter kept the public limited to one quarter of the available area, nearest the door. There was just enough space beyond the counter for two desks, two chairs, one tall filing cabinet, and a wooden pigeonhole arrangement on the wall, holding freight manifests and unsold passenger tickets. One of the two desks was assigned to the stationmaster (and ticket agent), while the other was for the yardmaster (and chief of security).

There was a great deal of pilferage going on in the railway these days, and no one seemed able to stop it. There was a general public suspicion, well founded, that railway employees were themselves responsible for a great percentage of the losses. The result was, most of the phone calls to Jinja station were from irate and suspicious freight customers whose shipments had disappeared.

The yardmaster, himself an honest man, could do nothing for such callers but sigh and agree and promise to look into it. His days were increasingly frustrating and unsatisfying, and if he could have thought of anything else to do with his life he would have quit this job long ago. As it was, he spent his time searching for honest men to stand guard over the yards, and apologizing to customers who no doubt thought *he* was a crook, too. A very sad situation.

At one-forty-five that afternoon, the yardmaster hung up the phone after one more such unhappy call, and looked up at the round railroad clock on the wall. "That freight didn't go through, did it?"

The stationmaster was working on the *fumbo* in today's paper. "I just can't get three down," he said. "A seven letter word meaning 'trade fair or international mart.' First and last letters both *O*."

"*Onyesho*."

"That fits!"

While the stationmaster laboriously printed in the letters, the yardmaster again frowned at the clock. "It must be nearly an hour since they went through Iganga."

"What's that?"

"The special train. The coffee freight."

"They'll be along."

"It shouldn't take an hour."

"Maybe they saw a pretty girl beside the line and stopped to bless her."

The yardmaster laughed. The phone rang, and he stopped laughing.

* * *

There was no direct rail service to Entebbe. After an early lunch, Patricia drove Sir Denis to Luzira, Kampala's port, where the major freight yards were located and where the train would terminate. This was an official trip, in order for the yardmaster at Luzira to show Sir Denis the trucks waiting to carry the coffee from the train to the aircraft at Entebbe.

As they drove, alone in the car, they talked about their plans. "I'm not making any promises," Patricia said.

"Of course not. We'll simply take each day as it comes." Sir Denis beamed on her. "I'm looking forward to showing you Brazil."

"Brazil." She shook her head, a bemused smile on her lips. "That's one future I never even suspected," she said.

* * *

Amin had anticipated a report from Colonel Juba about Chase sometime this morning. When the colonel hadn't appeared by eleven o'clock, Amin telephoned his office at the Bureau, only to be told the colonel wasn't there. Nor was he at home.

Amin came to the conclusion that Juba, to keep Chase's arrest secret, had taken him to some other safe place, such as a rural police station, until he'd extracted the man's story. "Inform me immediately," he ordered, and went off to lunch.

Today's lunch was more enjoyable than most. He was welcoming back his young Air Force men who'd just been ejected from the United States.

American companies such as Bell Helicopter had been training Amin's pilots for several years, but recently a few busybody American congressmen—mere publicity seekers—had applied pressure, claiming to be humanitarians, claiming the United States shouldn't do business with a country like Uganda—as though America's skirts were clean.

The bad publicity had frightened the American companies, though, and the whole problem had been compounded last October, when the only three Christian Ugandans enrolled with the eighteen Muslim Ugandans being trained by the Harris Corporation in Melbourne, Florida, had defected, asking the American government for political asylum and being granted it, and then of course telling all sorts of wild stories.

The upshot was, the several dozen Air Force men in the United States—some of whom had already received British training in Perth, Scotland—had all now left America and returned to Uganda, their courses incomplete. And it was to greet the last six of these, just back from Vero Beach, Florida, that was the purpose of today's lunch.

Amin loved contact with his brave young airmen. They reminded him of himself, or of the smoother and more sophisticated person he might have been if he'd had a firm proud good Idi Amin Dada to help *him* along the way in those early years. At the same time, it made him feel good to know he was still better than any of them. He could beat them at boxing, at basketball, at swimming races. And in the last analysis *he* was the father who made them possible.

There was much laughter and beer drinking at lunch, and many lies told about American women. Amin challenged all comers to arm wrestling, and won every match. His plan to buy long-range bombers and attack South Africa was discussed and given a respectful hearing. Amin emerged from lunch in a very happy frame of mind.

Which was at once spoiled, because neither Chase nor Juba had been found. Where were they? Amin gave orders, and soon learned they were positively nowhere in the Bureau building, though last night's duty officer did remember having seen Chase leave the place around midnight.

Leave? Chase? *Alone?*

A call to Chase's bank confirmed Amin's suspicions. The man had been in this morning, and his safety-deposit box proved to have been cleaned out. What was worse, he had apparently turned over a chit for five thousand U.S. dollars in cash, forged in Amin's name!

"He's running, my little Baron."

Calls to the airports at Entebbe, Jinja, Tororo, Soroti, and Kasese confirmed that Chase hadn't yet left the country, at least by air. No white man, in fact, had flown out of Uganda in the last twelve hours.

Which left the roads and the lake. The lake was very unlikely; Chase had no boat of his own and had never cultivated any acquaintanceship with boat owners. He had always made it plain that he didn't enjoy the occasional jaunt on Amin's yacht. He wouldn't like the sense of exposure, of limited options, associated with escape by water.

Which left the roads. "Call every border post," Amin ordered. "If Chase went through, we want to know where, and what name he used. If he tries to go through now, he should be stopped and sent back here. I don't care what condition he's in when he gets here, just so he can still talk."

*   *   *

The stationmaster put down his completed *fumbo* and yawned. Although the job had been much more strenuous back in the days of East African Railways, it had been more interesting, too. The stationmaster looked up at the clock, and was disheartened to see it was only five past two. Three more hours of boredom. "Say, old man," he said to the yardmaster, "where's that train of yours?"

The yardmaster was taking a correspondence course in accountancy from a British school in Manchester. After a long delay occasioned by his mail's having been held up, there being official displeasure between the governments of Great Britain and Uganda, three lessons had just arrived at once, and he was busily at work on them, between phone calls from dissatisfied customers. Glancing up from an extremely tricky problem in taxable versus tax-exempt interest income with or without compounding at various rates, he frowned at the stationmaster and then at the clock. "I just don't know what's happened," he said. "Could they be broken down?"

"They would phone us from a signal box."

"Let me call Iganga again," the yardmaster said, reaching for the phone, and when he got through to the Iganga stationmaster he said, "What time did that coffee train go through there?"

(Beside the track, seventeen miles away, Young Mr. Balim called, "Frank! The first question!")

"Twelve-fifty-five," the Iganga stationmaster said.

"It hasn't been through here yet. No word of trouble up there?"

"Not a thing. Did they break down, do you suppose?"

"They'd phone us."

"What's happened, then?"

"No idea. I'll call you back."

The yardmaster then tried to call the only other intervening station, just a few miles away at Magamaga, but there was no one on duty in the office there, and the phone rang uselessly in the locked room.

The yardmaster hung up. He thought for a few seconds, while staring sightlessly at his accountancy problem, and then sighed. "I should go look," he said.

"You think so?" The stationmaster, though he might regret the interesting days of hard work, did not believe in rushing unnecessarily in the direction of labor. "Why borrow trouble?" he asked.

"Oh, well, it's my duty, you know." Getting unhappily to his feet, closing his lesson book, and putting it away in his center desk drawer, the yardmaster put on his official dark-blue jacket and round hat and wheeled his bicycle out from beside the filing cabinet. (It was kept in here to protect it from thieves.) "I keep hoping I'll hear it coming," he said. "Ah, well. At least you can take my calls while I'm gone."

The yardmaster walked his bicycle out to the gleaming tracks in the sunlight, and looked both ways. No train. Shielding his eyes with his hand, he looked away eastward as far as he could see, and there was no train. In the opposite direction, the bridge over the Nile stretched out, empty and inviting. Behind him were the Jinja yards, dotted with aging goods wagons and just a few tottering old Class

13 shunting locomotives. All around, the town of Jinja slept quietly in after-lunch warmth.

The yardmaster climbed on his bicycle. Bending over the handlebars, he pedaled away slowly along the tracks toward Iganga.

*   *   *

The plane was a Boeing 707, old and sloppy, maintained just well enough to pass the required insurance and governmental codes. Ellen had familiarized herself with it this morning and didn't consider she would be putting herself at any particular risk in flying it, either to Djibouti or across the Atlantic, though it would likely be considerably less fun than Balim's little twin-engine six-seater. Now, dawdling over a late lunch in the coffee shop, she could look out the tall windows at the plane, and the other seven planes, all parked in a row on the tarmac. Three more 707s, one Lockheed C-130, and three Douglas DC-9s; a complete grab bag of not-quite-obsolete cargo planes.

At the table with Ellen were the other three members of the crew. The pilot and flight mechanic were both Americans; they had brought the plane in from the States yesterday. They were named Jerry (pilot) and Dave (flight mechanic), and they were both amiable laconic men who found the presence of a female copilot amusing, but not in a derogatory way. The navigator was a silent morose Italian named Augusto, who merely became more silent and more morose when Jerry and Dave decided his name was Gus.

Jerry, who wore a bushy moustache and a prominent thick wedding band, had made it clear last night, and again this morning, that he could take an interest in Ellen, given the slightest encouragement. Dave, who had the shock of unruly hair of the born sidekick, had made it clear that he felt Jerry had seen her first. Ellen had never been interested in such Rover Boy types, and her lack of response was only intensified by the fact that she was spending all her time worrying about Lew.

Which was unfair, damned unfair. When you break up with a man, he isn't supposed to force you to go on thinking about him by immediately flinging himself into danger. No matter what Ellen might want to do or think about, she was limited to this: she would sit here in Entebbe Airport and wonder if the coffee would show up. If it did, she would then have to wonder what that meant. And if it didn't, she would have to wonder if the hijack had gone smoothly.

If I had his address, she thought crossly, trying to follow an anecdote of Jerry's about flying Air America in Laos back when opium was the most important cargo, I'd send him a letter bomb.

Someone was approaching across the nearly empty coffee shop. How will they phrase it? Ellen wondered, and invented a monologue: *We're sorry, but you can go home now. Somebody took our coffee. They got away clean. Thank you and good-bye.*

It was the waitress. She said, "Would you like more coffee?"

* * *

At twenty past two, Chase and the Mercedes-Benz were nearly to the Rwanda border east of Kabale, near the Rwandan town of Kagitumba. Once safely across the border, he would drive the less than eighty miles to Rwanda's capital, Kigali, where he would be able to charter a plane for anywhere. Probably he would choose to continue westward to Kinshasa, capital of Zaire, from where he could take a commercial flight to Europe.

From Kampala, Chase had driven southwest and then south around Lake Victoria. At Masaka, eighty-five miles from Kampala, he had stopped at the village market to buy fruit and beer and a few pieces of greasy cooked chicken. At Rakai, thirty miles farther on, he had turned off onto a dirt lane leading in to tiny Lake Kijanebalola, where he had found an isolated place in which to remove the two back door panels, stuff his money and jewelry and secondary papers into the window wells, and replace the panels.

After Rakai, Chase had taken minor roads westward, in the general direction of Lake Idi Amin. At Gayaza he'd turned south again, avoided the Tanzanian border running along the Kagera River, and now at last he found himself on the threshold of Rwanda.

The border station was a small shed of concrete block and various mud huts with thatched roofs. Several children playing in the dirt remained hunkered on the ground but watched with silent intensity as Chase left the air-conditioned splendor of the Mercedes for the humid heat of the real world.

There was nothing here, nothing but the shed and the huts, the tentative, worn blacktop of the road, the red-and-white border pole barrier, the children, the tan dusty soil, the single telephone line strung high on narrow wooden poles, a faint smell of some sort of flesh burning. As Chase strode toward the shed, perspiration already starting on his forehead and in the small of his back, a plump dark man bustled out of one of the huts, rubbing sleep from his eyes and pulling on his uniform coat. He was hatless and barefoot. *"Jambo, jambo!"* he cried.

"How do you do," Chase said, smiling. "I'm sorry, I have no Swahili."

"Oh, yes. English fine. You, sir," the plump guard said, gesturing for Chase to precede him into the shed. Behind him, a skinny weirdly boned woman wrapped in a cheap bright-patterned red cloth emerged from the hut, carrying an old desk drawer full of forms and stamps and pencils.

Chase had to duck his head to get through the doorway. The interior of the shed contained a wooden tabletop supported on old beer cases. Two backless chairs faced one another across this table.

The plump guard, entering, gestured to the chair Chase was to take, then settled himself with comic grandeur on the other. The woman came in, put the desk drawer handy to the guard's right elbow, and stood to one side behind him, hands clasped in front of her crotch.

Chase handed over his Ugandan passport, saying, "As you see, I am a member of the government."

"Ah! Fine!" said the guard, using his English. *"Very* fine." He took the passport and opened it.

Chase saw him change; that was the first thing. The guard was not a subtle man, nor a very bright one. His smiling face became stiff with shock; his shoulders hunched; he began very rapidly to blink.

So I didn't have this much time after all, Chase thought. He folded his arms, the fingers of his right hand snaking in under his left sleeve toward the automatic.

The guard stared too long and too unseeingly at the passport, attempting to compose himself. Then he looked up, still furiously blinking, and gave Chase a huge smile in which panic was the chief component. "More papers," he said. *"Me* papers." Then he turned to the woman, as though instructing her in what papers she was to get; but what he said in Swahili was, "Get Ulu and Walter. This is the man the President wants. When he goes out, they must shoot his legs."

"All right," the woman said. Now she too was ineffectively hiding fear and excitement and panic.

"But they must not kill him," the plump guard said. "The President wishes to speak to him."

I bet he does. Smoothly rising, drawing the automatic from his sleeve, Chase said in Swahili, "Don't move." He didn't shoot them right away because the sounds would attract Ulu and Walter.

The damn woman. The gun frightened her, all right, but it frightened her the wrong way. Instead of freezing, she screamed and jumped and then *ran at Chase*! She dashed at him the way the dazzled rabbit hurls itself into the automobile's headlights, and to the same effect: Chase killed her.

But it was no good. He'd had to shoot, and yet she kept coming. He shot again, and she threw her arms around him in an embrace of death. The miserable little .25 had no stopping power.

The dying woman encumbered him, pressing his gun hand between their bodies. By the time he freed it the plump guard was ready, the desk drawer held high over his head, papers and rubber stamps flying every which way as he brought the drawer crashing down onto Chase's wrist.

Then two men came running into the shed and knocked him down.

They were both the dead woman's lovers. It was all the plump guard could do to keep them from kicking Chase to death.

49

Lew and Young Mr. Balim stood on the track and watched the last two dozen spikes being driven into the sleepers. The rails had been put back where they belonged. Two of the ex-railwaymen were attaching the joint plates, spitting on them, smearing them with dirt to hide the new scratches. Most of the work crew had already left, going down with Frank to start the unloading.

Young Mr. Balim finished rolling the long wire around the earphones, then tucked the ball of phones and wire under his arm; there was no longer any need to eavesdrop on Jinja. "Wouldn't you like to be here?" he asked. "I mean, when they realize the whole bloody train is gone."

"But there isn't any *here* here," Lew told him, and gestured at the ongoing line of the track. "Just twenty-five miles between Iganga and Jinja, and no train."

"The look on their faces," Young Mr. Balim said, chortling, and the look on *his* face changed when he glanced back up the track leading toward Jinja. "Now what?" he said.

Lew turned, and here came the sentry he'd posted down there, pelting along the track, risking his balance by waving his arms over his head as he ran. Lew said, "Find out what it is."

Young Mr. Balim trotted forward, calling in Swahili. The man stopped to answer, pointing behind himself. Young Mr. Balim turned back to Lew. "He says, a man on a bicycle."

"Christ." Lew looked back at the men hammering in the spikes; only a few remained undriven. "Tell them to forget all that. Just get down and out of sight. With their tools."

"Right."

While Young Mr. Balim did that, Lew waved vigorously at the other sentry down by the access road. Go away, he waved. Get out of sight. Go down the road. The sentry seemed confused for a moment, but then he saw the workmen hurrying to hide and he responded with a comprehending wave and then trotted away.

The first sentry had already without pausing run through the opening in the hedge, and now the workmen streamed after. Lew went last, pausing for one quick look around, then jumping over the rail and trotting down through the gap.

Half a dozen workmen were poised to slide the blind back into place. They were jockeying it into position when the cyclist first appeared around the curve to the west, riding in the narrow dirt strip beside the railway's gravel bed. Weary, perspiring in his dark-blue official Uganda Railways jacket and dark-blue round hat, all unknowing he pedaled doggedly past the scene of the hijacking, his right sleeve brushing the blind, his movements watched through twenty tiny chinks in the shrubbery. On he went, pursuing the lost train as doggedly as he pursued his course in accountancy. He didn't know it yet, but he would bicycle all the way to Iganga.

50

"Your Excellency," the uniformed male secretary said, "very good news. Captain Chase has been found."

His ebullient mood having been spoiled by the defection of Chase, Idi Amin had taken to his porch at the Old Command Post, where he now sat with a bottle of beer and four of the returned airmen. They'd been striving very hard to recapture the amiability and self-satisfaction they'd enjoyed at lunch, but without much success; the jokes and laughter and reminiscences, even Amin's, were too obviously forced. It was harder and harder for Amin to ignore the fact that he wasn't happy, and the airmen were right to become increasingly nervous, though not smart to show it.

But now, in a flash, everything changed. The sun shone. Amin's merry smile spread across his face, his eyes lit up, he even clapped his big hands together, the long fingers splayed wide and only the palms hitting, as when children try to applaud. "Ah, *now* we have something!" he cried. "Where is this scoundrel?"

"Major Okwal is on the phone, Excellency."

"You boys wait here," Amin said, heaving himself to his feet. "I'll tell you about *this* scoundrel."

The secretary led the way to Amin's office, where the phone waited off the hook, then bowed and departed, shutting the door. Amin sat at his desk, picked up the receiver, smiled like a lion who sees a zebra, and said, "So, Major Okwal? You have him?" It was Amin's practice not to identify himself on the phone, assuming that everyone would know who he was.

"Yes, Excellency." Major Okwal was a Lugbara, Amin's mother's tribe. A colorless man, he had attained a middle rank in the State Research Bureau, where he was an effective if not imaginative interrogator. Amin treated him as he would a dull inoffensive cousin.

"Where is he?"

"Near Kabale."

"Ah! Trying to escape into Rwanda, was he? Who caught him?"

"The border guard there. Sergeant Auzo. A very good type of man, sir."

"I was a sergeant," Amin said reflectively. A vision of the sink from which he'd emerged shone briefly like black steel in his eyes. "I like to encourage the better men in the ranks," he said. "Send me his name."

"Yes, sir, at once."

"And when shall I have my hands on Captain Chase?"

"Ah," said Major Okwal. "Unfortunately, Sergeant Auzo is short-handed; he doesn't feel he has a proper or a secure escort to return Captain Chase."

"Oh, yes. Oh, yes." Amin nodded, eyes brooding at the opposite wall. "We shall want this fellow back *posthaste*," he said, using the English word, which had for him a tone of officially demanded speed that no Swahili word could convey.

"Of course, Excellency."

"Send me— Hmmm. What of Colonel Juba?"

"No sign, Excellency."

"He wasn't with Chase, then?" It had seemed to Amin that Chase had either murdered Juba or corrupted him, and that both were equally possible. He would have thought that of any man.

"Oh, no, sir," Major Okwal said. "The colonel and his two aides are both completely missing."

"*And* his two aides?" Amin couldn't help but smile; he couldn't help but admire a villain as vicious as Chase. It would be a pleasure to break him. "Send me General Kekka," he said.

"Yes, Excellency. At once, sir."

Amin hung up and sat brooding a long moment, the leftover smile still visible on his face. His hands moved together as though cracking nuts.

*   *   *

General Ali Kekka was a very tall and very thin man of fifty-three, a southern Sudanese very much of the breed called Nubian. His skin was quite dark and lusterless; his cheeks were sunken; his eyes looked at the world without expression. Amin knew that two years ago General Kekka had gone to Mulago Hospital complaining of headaches, that a brain tumor had been diagnosed and an immediate operation urged, and that General Kekka had refused, out of a primitive fear of the knife. The tumor would kill Kekka within the next few years, but in the meantime he was a coiled spring, a man of such sudden, brutal violence that even the men who worked with him at the Bureau were made afraid. Even Amin, who found his affliction useful, felt a sense of wariness in the presence of Ali Kekka.

They sat together on the porch of the Old Command Post, from which the young airmen had been banished now that Amin had more serious things to think about. "Ali," Amin said, "our friend Baron Chase has turned against us."

"Of course he has," Kekka said. "Every white man will turn against you. And most blacks."

"He has stolen from me," Amin said, his manner patient and slow-moving, like a man training a hunting dog. "He has some plot against me which I don't know yet."

"We'll ask him."

"Yes, we will. Ali, he tried to run away, he was caught down on the Rwanda border. I want you to go down there, take a platoon of men, and bring him back."

"Yes, Field Marshal."

"He must be alive when he comes to me; he must be able to talk."

"Yes, I agree."

"Take him to my office at the Bureau building. Draw as little attention as possible."

"Then is it the VIP treatment?"

"Not yet," Amin said. "When you bring him back, Ali, call me at once. I shall deal with my little Baron personally."

* * *

Amin stood on the porch looking down at Kekka's black Mercedes as it wound away down the drive toward the road. He smiled in anticipation. It was not quite three o'clock.

"Your Excellency?"

Amin turned to see who was in the doorway, and found Moses, the cheerful servant whose job it was to tell him bad news. "Yes, Moses?"

"Ah, Your Excellency," Moses said, his normal ebullience stripped away, leaving him sad and troubled. "Bewildering bad news, Your Excellency."

Amin took a step forward. Had they bungled, had they accidentally killed Chase? Or had he gotten away again? "What is it, Moses?"

"The train," Moses said, and shrugged as though to absolve himself of blame. "The coffee train."

Relieved that it wasn't about Chase after all, it was nothing of importance, Amin said, "What about the train?"

Moses wrung his hands. "It's gone!"

Amin failed to understand. "What's that you say?"

"Oh, Excellency!" Moses cried, instinctively backing away. "Somewhere between Iganga and Jinja, the great huge train was magicked! It's gone entirely! Disappeared!"

51

Thirty-two freight cars made a stylized curving scrawl down from the beginning of the spur line past the maintenance depot, over the turntable, down to the end of the permanent track, and on out the temporary rails almost to the lip of the gorge. From the air they were virtually invisible, except that if you knew where the train was, you would understand the occasional glint of reflected sunlight up through the trees.

Each car contained approximately four hundred sacks of coffee of one hundred thirty pounds weight, for a total of twenty-six tons. In all, the train carried just about seven hundred fifty tons of coffee. Each truck could carry no more than twenty tons at a time, so two round trips from them all would be necessary. But that also involved twice shifting seven hundred fifty tons of coffee by hand: from the train to the trucks, and again from the trucks to the rafts. It was going to take several hours, and during most of that time they could expect to be the object of a very determined search.

Lew had posted Isaac as sentry with a walkie-talkie up where the access road crossed the railway line. Young Mr. Balim, with the other walkie-talkie, sat like a slender young Humpty Dumpty atop one of the freight cars, where he could command a view of the entire scene and attract everybody's attention if necessary. One of the ex-railwaymen stood on the roof of the first car, his hand on the big flat wheel of the brake. Four trucks had been driven in to the depot and backed up to the first four cars, and now they were being hastily loaded by over fifty men, including Frank and Charlie and Lew.

The first loading job went quickly. They were exhilarated from their success in capturing the train, and they were still fresh, the earlier track work forgotten. It was not quite three in the afternoon when they started, and in twenty minutes the trucks were full. Immediately three men piled into the cab of each, with Frank and Charlie in the lead truck, and the vehicles groaned away over Ellen's Road, their wheels digging deep into the logs and brush, mashing everything down to a mulchlike muddy smoothness.

As soon as the first trucks were out of the way, another four were driven in, turned around, and backed up to the same freight cars, which were now less than half full.

With twelve fewer in the work crew, this second group of trucks took longer to load. But there was a reward ahead for those who still labored here, because, when the trucks were just over one-quarter full, these four freight cars were empty. Jamming the big sliding doors open on both sides of the cars, everybody jumped out onto the ground, chattering and laughing together because they knew what was going to happen next.

Young Mr. Balim climbed down to the ground, where Lew said, "You could have stayed up there and just walked back a few cars."

"If an error occurs," Young Mr. Balim said, "I prefer to watch it from here."

Up on the train roofs, two of the ex-railwaymen were tightening down the brakes on the fifth and sixth cars, while down below a third unhooked the coupler between cars four and five. The other ex-railwayman, having loosened the brake on the first car, stood poised to do the same atop the second. The word was yelled to him, and with a flourish he spun the wheel.

At first, despite the slope, the cars didn't want to move. Then Lew,

with Young Mr. Balim acting as translator, got the watching men to
come in and push. Slowly and silently, all at once losing their reluctance, the four cars rolled forward, gathering speed. The ex-
railwayman stayed on the roof of the second car, laughing and waving
to everybody.

Lew said, "That nut's going with it!"

But he wasn't. As the cars hit the temporary track, the ex-
railwayman leaped the twelve feet to the ground, rolled, and sprang
to his feet. The workmen gave him a huge cheer and laugh, and the
four freight cars rolled out into space to tumble end-over-end down
through the air, crashing into the water with a crazy series of splashes
and bangs, the second car bobbing on the surface long enough to be
rammed broadside by the third, then all four wriggling and collapsing
downward into the water, after their leader and out of sight.

After that experience, it was obvious that everyone had to have a
beer before going back to work. While the ex-railwaymen eased the
rest of the train down so the next four cars were lined up with the
half-full trucks, two cases of beer were brought out from the engine
shed, where they were being kept relatively cool. The engineer and
fireman, having sworn oaths to be on their good behavior, were untied
from all those ropes and allowed to join the festivities. Beer bottles
were distributed, and success was generally toasted.

Meanwhile, Frank and Charlie and the others in the first four trucks
ground slowly but steadily along the access road toward Macdonald
Bay, twenty miles off. The road sloped downward over the whole
distance, so that gravity assisted them to some extent, but with the
road so chancy and the trucks so overloaded they couldn't average
much better than fifteen miles an hour. They hadn't yet reached the
bay before the celebration back at the depot was finished, the second
four trucks were fully loaded, and they too were on their way, reducing
the work force back there by another four.

At last the bay appeared, sparkling and empty, the mud flat surrounded by the ungainly huge rafts covered with brush, as though a
beachfront community had been flattened by a hurricane. Everybody
climbed down from the trucks, and Frank bellowed the first raft into
the water, with Charlie's left-handed assistance. Then, while Frank
and Charlie went to work unmounting the outboard motors and re-

mounting them higher on the raft body, the other ten men started moving sacks.

On the twenty-foot-square surface of the raft they could lie one hundred twenty sacks, in six rows of twenty. The contents of the four trucks would fill this raft, making an unwieldy-looking monster ten layers high, crisscrossed for stability and standing nearly twelve feet tall. In theory, it wouldn't tip over and it would float.

The first full sack was carried up the plank and onto the raft at five minutes past four.

52

The station clock read five minutes past four when Idi Amin marched into the tiny railway station at Iganga, followed by half a dozen Army officers and uniformed members of the State Research Bureau. Glaring around, Amin said, "Now you'll tell me what this is."

Two men were present in the uniform of Uganda Railways, both looking scared out of their skins. The fat one pointed at the thin one and said, "This is Jinja yardmaster, Mr. President. He brought me the information."

"*What* information?" Glowering upon the Jinja yardmaster, Amin said, "Explain yourself."

"Yes, Mr. President." Though terrified, the man was trying for a dignified professionalism. "Iganga station having informed me," he began, passing the buck right back to his compatriot, "of the coffee train having gone through here at twelve-fifty-five, when it had not appeared at Jinja by two o'clock I became alarmed. Having checked again with Iganga station, Mr. President, that the train had indeed passed through here at that time—"

"Yes, yes," Amin said, slapping the air in his impatience. "The question is, where is the train?"

"Gone, Mr. President. I'm sorry, sir, but it's disappeared. Sir."

"Trains do not disappear," Amin told him reasonably. "You are a trainman, you should know such a thing. Just the size of a train, the very *size* of the thing, will tell you that. Then again, there are the tracks. The train cannot leave the tracks. Not and get very far," he added, joking, looking around with a big smile to see if his entourage were laughing. They were.

The yardmaster was not. "Excuse me, Mr. President," he said. "I rode here on my bicycle from Jinja, along the permanent way. There was no train, sir."

Amin gazed upon this man. Would anyone have the effrontery to make Idi Amin the butt of a practical joke? Would either of these rabbits dare to lie to their president? Speaking slowly and heavily, gesturing pedagogically with one finger in the air, Amin said, "Be very careful now, you. Be very careful, the two of you."

The Iganga stationmaster, having falsely believed himself to have been safely forgotten, gave a little jump of fear. The Jinja yardmaster stood tall against his fright and said, "Yes, Mr. President."

"Now, you," Amin said, pointing at the Iganga stationmaster, the weaker of the two rabbits. "You say this train passed through here at twelve-fifty-five."

"Yes, Mr. President."

"A long train full of coffee. A huge long— How many cars?" he demanded of his entourage.

"More than thirty, Your Excellency," someone said.

"Good." Returning to the Iganga stationmaster, Amin said, "Now, this long train of more than thirty cars passed through this station at twelve-fifty-five. And did it return?"

The Iganga stationmaster was too frightened to keep up with sudden leaps like that. "Sir? Mr. President?"

Amin was becoming irritated. "The train! Did it *come back through* the station?"

"No, no, of course not, Mr. President! It went through, westbound, at twelve-fifty-five, traveling very very fast—oh, more than ninety kilometers an hour—and that was the last I saw of it."

"Good." Amin turned to the Jinja yardmaster. "Now, you did not see this train."

"No, Your Excellency." A fast study, this Jinja yardmaster had needed only once to hear how the president was properly addressed by his entourage.

"You are a man who sees things," Amin suggested. "This train could not have gone through Jinja while you were having a piss in the men's room."

"Your Excellency, I didn't relieve myself at all, Your Excellency, in that hour. And the stationmaster was with me as well. Your Excellency, I swear by my life, that train did not go through Jinja."

"Your life. Yes," Amin said, brooding at the man, seeing the shock in his eyes.

A member of the entourage said, "Your Excellency, there are seven stations after Jinja to Luzira. Every one has been called; none has seen the train."

Another member of the entourage said, "Your Excellency, we have checked with Kakira and Luzinga on the Mbulamuti northern branch from Jinja. The train did not go up that way."

"It couldn't have, Your Excellency," the yardmaster said, "without switching through my yards. I would have seen it."

"You bicycled," Amin said, brooding, beginning to hate this smart fellow and all this "Excellency"-ing. "This train went through Iganga. It did not appear at Jinja. It can go nowhere but on the track, so it stands to reason it must be *on the track between Iganga and Jinja*! But you bicycled."

"Yes, Your Excellency."

"Yes, Your Excellency!" Amin mimicked, beginning to give himself over to the pleasure of losing his temper. "Yes, Your Excellency! You saw no train, no accident, no evidence, nothing!"

The yardmaster, now too frightened to reply at all, stood helplessly staring at Amin, and in the silence they all heard the sound: *chuff*. And again: *chuff*. Looking up, away from the miserable yardmaster, Amin saw a locomotive through the station window, slowly easing past. "It's there!" he cried.

"No, Your Excel—"

But Amin had forgotten the yardmaster. Pushing through his entourage, he stepped out onto the sunny platform, where the curious spectators, mostly children, fled in all directions. Big, heavy, glowering, triumphant, jaw sticking out, Amin stepped forward, put his hands on his hips, and glared in sudden bewilderment.

It wasn't the train. It was just a locomotive and tender, and in any case it was pointing the wrong way: *from* Jinja. It was a 29 Class, just like the missing *Arusha*. This one was numbered 2938 and named *Samia*.

The entourage and the much more reluctant railwaymen came out onto the platform. The Jinja yardmaster said, "Your Excellency, I had this engine sent from Jinja to help us study the track."

"Very good," Amin said grudgingly. The man rubbed him the wrong way, that was all. Like all those doctors, professors, lawyers; all those Baganda, Langi, Acholi; all those smooth bastards who thought they were better than the poor Kakwa soldier Idi Amin.

The engineer of *Samia* had climbed down out of the cab, and now he reported to Amin in great excitement, "Oh, Mr. President, there was *nothing*! Not a sign, not a trace!"

"The coffee," Amin said, as though to himself. Slowly he nodded. "My little Baron," he said, while his entourage looked at one another in confusion. "That's what he's up to, he's stealing my coffee. But how is he doing it?"

Everyone waited respectfully while Amin thought. It would be hours before Chase was brought back from the Rwanda border; by then his scheme, whatever it was, might already be accomplished. Even now, in some unimaginable way, the coffee train could be on some track—some unknown, other, mysterious, incomprehensible, mind-bending track—steaming away out of the country.

"No!" Amin cried, punching the air with his big fist. "They won't do it! You," he said, pointing at *Samia*'s engineer, "turn that thing around."

The engineer looked dumbstruck. The Jinja yardmaster said, "Your Excellency, there's no turntable here. But the train can run just as well backward."

"Then we run it backward," Amin decided. "Come along," he said, shooing the engineer in front of himself. "They're stealing my coffee. We must find them and stop them."

*　*　*

They ran it backward. They traveled slowly, and Amin stood up on top of the tender, arms akimbo, glaring every which way, looking for signs of where the train had gone and how it had been done.

(If he'd come through half an hour earlier, standing that high atop the tender, he would probably have seen over the hedge the last two cars of his missing train, but by the time *Samia* passed that place four cars had been dumped into the gorge, the rest of the train had rolled forward among the trees and shrubbery, and there was nothing to be seen.)

Here and there dirt roads crossed the track, some abandoned, some still in use. None showed the slightest indication of any odd activity lately. An antismuggling helicopter was visible at one point, way to the south over the lake, and Amin thought for one mad instant of the train's being spirited away by helicopters. But *thirty* helicopters, dangling thirty railway cars, not to mention however many helicopters it would take to lift one of these extremely heavy steam engines? And no one anywhere to see it happening? Not even the Israelis could pull off such a thing.

As Jinja appeared dead ahead with no train in sight, Amin yelled, "Stop! Go back again, go back! It's somewhere, it's here somewhere, the clue is somewhere!"

Three members of his entourage were crowded into the cab with the engineer and the fireman. The others had piled into the automobiles to drive along the highway paralleling the rail line, occasionally visible when road and track ran close together. Now, with a great deal of fuss the engine was reversed again, to run frontward, and the automobiling entourage also reversed.

Nothing, nothing, and still nothing. When they traveled in this direction, smoke and steam made it impossible to ride atop the tender, so Amin crowded down into the cab with the rest, where he couldn't look at both sides of the track at the same time. The frustration, the overcrowding, the blindness on one side; all combined to make him finally yell, "Stop! Stop *here!*"

They stopped. Amin, with his belief in witchcraft and spirits, was now convinced something from another world had given him this sign, had told him where and when to stop. (The coffee train, however, had been removed from the track three miles farther on.)

What was the clue? What was the thing that made this spot call out to him? Amin tramped up and down the track in front of the sporadically coughing locomotive, glaring at the rails, the spikes, the joint plates, the sleepers, the gravel bed, the narrow dirt trails on both sides, the encroaching jungle growth.

Frustration built and built, and at last he stopped and stamped one booted foot hard on a sleeper. That was good, but not good enough. "I want my coffee!" he bellowed into the empty air. Jumping up high, he crashed *both* booted feet onto the sleeper; that was better. Doing it again, jumping up and down, waving his clenched fists over his head, Idi Amin roared, "I want my train! *I want my coffee! I want my traaaaaaaiiiiiiiiiinnnnnnnnnn!!!!!*"

53

Mazar Balim owned radios. Any number of radios: shortwave, commercial band, two-way, any kind you might want. He sold them at retail in his three stores, in Kisumu and Kericho and Kakamega. He sold them at wholesale out of his five-eighths-blue warehouse buildings on Kisiani Street. And he did not understand why it had not been possible to demand that Bathar take a radio with him.

Oh, he knew the reasons; the traceability of radio signals and all that. But when he paced the rooms of his two buildings, unable to sit still in his office, and when he passed the carton after carton of radios on his storage shelves, it bothered him horribly. It was *terrible* that he couldn't reach out to one of these wonderful machines, made in Taiwan or Hong Kong, that he couldn't switch it on and have Bathar right there, Bathar's voice reaffirming that he was alive and well, although in Uganda.

If at least Isaac were still here, Balim would have someone to talk with about his anxieties, he wouldn't have to keep them buried inside. Isaac would be sympathetic, sensible, reassuring. Except, of course, that the sensible, reassuring Isaac was now gadding about Uganda himself, playing at pirate, swashbuckling deep within the borders of a nation where, for him in particular, discovery meant death.

As it did for Bathar. An Asian. A smuggler. A man already expelled from Uganda once.

Perhaps I should let him go to London. Perhaps Africa is no good at all for Asians, no accommodation ever will take place. But that was a hard thought for Balim to accept. Prowling his merchant domain, frightened for his boy, brooding about the past and the future, Balim still felt the weight of his own father upon his shoulders.

Mazar Balim had been raised in the abolute knowledge that he would one day take over the family business. There had been no option, nor any reason to think of an option. He had tried to instill the same feelings in Bathar, but something had changed, some aura in the air had shifted, and none of today's generation was so unthinkingly secure as he had been about the future or about the continuation of family business.

The common reference to the Asians as the Jews of Africa was perhaps after all too glib. There were certainly similarities enough: the outsiders who retained their own customs and languages and religions; the shopkeepers and bankers, harbingers of the middle class, bringing with them civilization and usury, hated for their knowledge and success and difference. But in Europe and America it had finally been possible for the Jew to assimilate if he wanted to, or at most times and places to retain his difference if he preferred. Though anti-Semitism certainly existed, the Nazi experience was seen as an aberration, whereas in Africa the expulsion of the Ugandan Asians had been hailed by politicians of the surrounding black countries as a template for their own futures.

If Bathar were in London, the firm of Balim & Son would eventually cease to exist.

If Bathar were murdered in Uganda, the firm of Balim & Son would certainly cease to exist.

At least in London they won't kill him. So long as he stays out of the East End.

If my boy comes back alive, God, I promise I will let him do what he wants with his life.

Late in the afternoon a stockroom worker approached, hesitantly, unused to dealing directly with the owner. "Master," he said, "men in the office."

Balim frowned, his mind still full of thoughts of expulsion and pogrom. "Men in the office?" And Isaac not here, Frank not here, Lew Brady not here! Reluctant to confront them, these men in his office, he asked, "How dressed?"

"Northern clothes, master."

Suits; somewhat reassuring. Possibly merely salesmen. "What people?"

"Bantu, master."

Black; could be good, could be bad. Government functionaries, seeking a bribe? "How many?"

"Two, master."

So at least physical violence was unlikely. "Thank you," Balim said, with more careful courtesy than he usually showed his employees, and hurried away to the offices, where he found the two men at their ease in Isaac's room. How empty the place looked; how vulnerable Balim felt; how secure and comfortable these black men were, seated and smiling in their own country.

They rose, almost identical men of the civil service mode, a bit rumpled as was considered the appropriate way to express their independence from the European culture that had engulfed them. One had a thick moustache, the other black-framed eyeglasses. Both carried soft leather document cases under their left arms.

The moustached one stepped forward, smiling. "Mazar Balim?"

"I am Balim. In what way may I serve you?"

"I am Charles Obuong," the moustached man said, not offering to shake hands, using his right hand instead to indicate his companion. "And this is Godfrey Magon. We are with the Ministry of Commerce and Industry, just up from Nairobi."

"Import Control Department," Godfrey Magon added. They both spoke in correct academic English.

A bribe, then; on what pretext? "I do hope I may be of assistance."

"Oh, we think that quite possible," Charles Obuong said. "We are here to discuss with you this shipment of coffee you are anticipating."

Shock froze Balim, but none showed on the surface. Polite but puzzled, he said, "Coffee?"

Godfrey Magon smiled, his eyes twinkling behind his glasses. "From Uganda," he said.

"I'm afraid you have me at a disadvantage," Balim said. He had begun to perspire fiercely under the arms. He accepted the belief that Africans have a keener sense of smell, so he pressed his arms tightly to his body to keep them from getting a whiff of his fear. They know! he thought. They know everything!

"It would be better," Charles Obuong said, "if we could dispense with the first several hours of denials and evasions."

"You see," Godfrey Magon explained, his manner almost kindly, "we believe someone else plans to steal the coffee before it reaches Kenya."

"With violence," Charles Obuong said.

Balim by now had given up trying not to look shocked and fearful. "With violence?"

Charles Obuong nodded, smiling as though he quite enjoyed the anticipation of violence. "Oh, I'm afraid so," he said.

"Unfortunately," Godfrey Magon said, "our investigator was murdered by one of your people before he had completed his investigation."

"Oh, no, surely not!"

"I'm afraid so," Godfrey Magon said, but not as though he intended to make a major issue of it. "None of us can understand," he said, "why your chap wanted to murder a simple boneman."

"Boneman?" Balim shook his head; innocence always left him at a loss. "I know nothing of this," he said.

Charles Obuong waved a deprecating hand. "That is beside the point, for the moment. The concern for now is our desire that this coffee should come to Kenya."

Balim stared. "Oh, yes?"

Both men beamed at him. Godfrey Magon said, "Have you not heard of balance of payments? Of the difficulties of such small nations as ours in avoiding trade deficits? Of the terrible prices we are paying for the importation of oil?"

"Uganda plants," Charles Obuong said. "Kenya harvests. *So* good for our trade deficit. You are a patriot, Mr. Balim."

"Perhaps," Godfrey Magon said, "we would be more comfortable if we continued this chat in your private office."

54

When he heard Kekka's voice, Chase felt a moment of utter black despair. Amin, that cunning cunning bastard. Of all the crooks and incompetents in Kampala, by God he'd chosen the one who'd give Chase the most trouble. Could Kekka be outfoxed? Could he be bribed? Chase remembered, vividly, all those sessions in the State Research Bureau, and he knew he absolutely had to get out of this. Some way, any way. Somehow, between here and Kampala, he must either escape or die.

They had tied him with many ropes, his arms twisted painfully behind him, his knees bent and one rope looped first around his ankles and then around his neck, so that if he tried to straighten he would choke himself. But not to death, unfortunately; at the instant of unconsciousness, his legs would relax, the pressure on his throat would ease, and he would live some more.

The only faint hope he could retain was based on the lucky chance that he apparently had no broken bones. Those bastards had tried enthusiastically enough, but for all their pummeling and kicking they seemed merely to have given him a lot of bruises and scrapes. So long as he was not physically impaired, there was still some faint chance he could get himself out of this mess.

How many hours had he been lying here in the stench and heat inside this mud hut, the packed ground painful under his bruised body? The corner of the outside world he could see through the angle of the low doorway was still in daylight, though the shadows were lengthening. And now one of the shadows was Kekka's, and he could hear Kekka's voice giving orders, and two soldiers came in to grab Chase by the ankles and the belt and drag him outside, not caring whether they choked him or not.

Kekka stood in front of the hut, spraddle-legged in the dirt, hands on hips, staring with those cold eyes at Chase on the ground. With him was that damned fat border guard, and angry-looking Ulu and Walter, and a platoon of uniformed soldiers. In the background was a camouflage-painted armored car, dusty from the road.

I'm honored, Chase thought ironically. They're taking no chances with Baron Chase.

Kekka said, "So, Captain. They tell me you speak Swahili after all."

It was too late to deny it. His voice horribly hoarse—it was so important not to seem weak now, or afraid—he croaked in Swahili, "Ali. Let me talk with you, friend."

"I don't like your accent," Kekka said.

"Ali, I have something for you."

"And I," Kekka said, opening his trousers, "have something for you."

Chase squeezed his eyes shut, clamped his mouth tight, and felt the spray of warm urine rove over his face and hair, while the soldiers giggled together. When at last it stopped, Chase kept his eyes closed but called, "Ali, *motakaa*." *Automobile*. Then, hoping Kekka would know the English but none of the others would, he added, low and intense, "Money!"

A kick in the stomach knocked the wind out of him and bounced open his eyes. He stared up at Kekka's contempt. "If you speak again, in that miserable accent," Kekka said, "I shall have my men shit on you."

Something something some way out some hope somewhere some way not finished not finished not finished like *this*. The silent Chase stared, panting like a long-distance runner.

"Put him in the car," Kekka said, and turned away.

The soldiers picked him up, not gently, and carried him toward the armored car. To one side the Mercedes stood silent, all doors open. These fools here had run it all afternoon, crowding in for the air conditioning, until they'd used up the gasoline. Tens of thousands of dollars were in the panels of those open-sagging doors. There *had* to be a way to buy safety with that much. "Ali!" Chase called, not caring what he risked. "The Benz! Don't leave the Benz!"

There was no reaction at all, not even a kick. They threw him on the metal floor in back; then eight soldiers climbed in with him, four on the bench on each side, all using his body as a footrest and a target for when they had to spit. Kekka and the driver rode up front. The car jolted forward, leaving the Mercedes behind.

* * *

"Money?"

Chase, in fear and exhaustion, had lost consciousness for some time, until he heard that English word whispered in his ear. Then he opened his eyes to the semidark of twilight, no movement, and an armored car empty except for himself and the young avid-eyed soldier leaning over him. "Where—" Chase asked, and had to clear his throat and swallow.

"They've gone to eat," the soldier said in Swahili. "I made sure to be left as guard. General Kekka had one of his headaches; he required food. You know General Kekka's headaches?"

Chase nodded. He was still trying to work saliva into his parched mouth and throat.

"Sometimes," the soldier said, "General Kekka kills with his headaches."

Chase waited, watching the young soldier's eyes.

"This is Mbarara," the soldier said, keeping his voice low, just for Chase. "Not far yet. I heard you say 'money.' I know what that is. *Fedha.*"

"That's right," Chase whispered. Here's my man! he thought. Here's my man! Here's my man!

"In the automobile," the soldier said, his eyes gleaming not only with cupidity but also with his own cleverness. "That's what you meant! Money in the automobile!"

"Yes! If you—"

"How much?"

Chase thought. "You know who I am," he whispered, not yet trusting his voice. "You know I would not run away with a *little* money."

"Yes. Yes. How much?"

"Enough for two. One million British pounds, and *four* gold bars from Zaire."

The soldier's eyes bulged in his head; saliva reflected from his teeth. "We go there!" he whispered in shrill excitement. "You show me where you hide all this!"

"Yes, yes, just untie—"

But the man was gone. Rearing up as best he could, the neck rope biting into his throat, Chase stared and listened, and couldn't understand what was happening until all at once the armored car's engine started, the vehicle jolted backward, stopped, jolted forward, swung around in a tight U-turn, and went bouncing out some bumpy driveway to the road.

The bastard! The dirty dirty dirty bastard! As the armored car tore south, jouncing and swaying on the unrepaired road, Chase bitterly saw the soldier's plan: he would bring Chase back to the border, torture him until he got his hands on the hidden loot in the Mercedes, then murder Chase, bribe his way across the border, and enter Rwanda a rich man.

No. No. Fighting his ropes, fighting gravity, fighting the thuds and crashes as the armored car plowed from pothole to pothole, fighting his own battered weary body, Chase squirmed to the rear of the car. With his shoulders, with his forehead, he forced himself around into a position on knees and shoulders; then, at a particularly vicious jounce, he propelled himself upward so that he knelt sitting on his haunches with his back against the tailgate.

Outside, the road swept away at a dizzying pace under the armored car. Mbarara was less than fifty miles north of the border, and the soldier was clearly trying to get there and across before the alarm went out.

Still, as the road moved up into the hills there were more and more curves, and the soldier would eventually either have to slow down or crash. Chase waited, battered by the armored car's gyrations, his balance unsteady, and finally the armored car nosed up and turned into a sharp uphill curve. As it slowed, Chase *pushed* down with his legs, *heaved* himself up, flung himself backward. For one dreadful moment he hung there, the small of his back teetering on the tailgate, his feet stretched to their maximum, the rope grinding deep into his neck. Then the armored car once more jounced, and shrugged him off.

Strapped, swaddled, out of control, Chase fell heavily onto his head and ceased to struggle.

* * *

Jouncing. It was a dream, Chase thought, bile in his mouth. A dream of escape, nothing more. He moved his horribly aching body, and it was without ropes! And he was sitting on, propped up on, something soft, something that gave with the bumps.

His eyes flew open, staring for a dislocated instant without recognition at the nighttime road seen through a truck windshield. "AAAH!" he cried, and threw his hands forward onto the dashboard for support.

"You're awake, poor man," the driver said, in English.

"Stop! God, stop!"

The driver pulled off the road and stopped, and Chase fumbled open his door, fell out onto the ground, and vomited until he was down to dry heaves. Beside him, the man who'd been driving the truck knelt and consoled him, brushing his shoulder with a solacing palm. And when Chase finished, the man gave him a cloth to wipe his face. "I'm sorry I have no water for you," he said. "But it's not far to Mbarara."

Mbarara! Again! Chase looked up, and saw the turned-around collar; a minister. "You saved me," he said.

"The government doesn't like me to be out," the minister said, "so I visit my parishioners at night. You were set upon and robbed?"

"Yes. They took my car."

"You are very fortunate they didn't take your life," the minister said, helping Chase to his feet. "In Mbarara, we can get you medical assistance. And of course police."

"Of course. Thank you."

Chase permitted the minister to help him back up onto the passenger seat of the small battered pickup truck. His foot hit two metal tire irons on the floor, clanking them together.

"Such a messy car," the minister said, reaching forward. "I'll move those."

"No, no, that's all right."

The minister shut the door and walked around the front of the truck while Chase reached down for one of the metal bars. It was too bad this Good Samaritan story had to end on such a sour note, but Chase had need of this truck and couldn't afford the alarm to be raised.

It was no good trying to go back for the Mercedes; he had to cut his losses on that one. There was only one exit route left: back the other way, eastward, through Kampala and Jinja. He had to reach the coffee thieves before they emptied the train and started away across the lake.

The minister opened the driver's door. "Lucky I came along," he said.

55

Through the afternoon and into the night the transfer of the coffee went on. It took half an hour to load a group of four trucks, and nearly an hour for the trucks to drive down to the lake. With the work force at the lake half the size of that at the depot, it took another hour to unload each group of trucks onto the rafts, spread the tarpaulins on top, then moor each raft in the calm water just off-shore.

There was of course no way to hide these loaded rafts from the air, but the few planes and helicopters that passed overhead before nightfall paid them no attention. Those aircraft belonged to Uganda's antismuggling patrol and had been called in from duty over the lake to help look for the missing train. They saw the tarpaulin-covered rafts in the bay but ignored them. They could be floating there for any of a hundred reasons, ranging from fishing to oil exploration to archaeology, and certainly could have nothing to do with a stolen train.

The first batch of trucks to reach the lake was no more than half unloaded when the second arrived, and as the first quartet finished and started back up the access road the third came into view. Frank returned to the depot with the first group, leaving Charlie and a crony of his to remount the rest of the outboard motors. Their trucks squeezed by the downward-traveling fourth group halfway back, and arrived at the depot, just before six o'clock, in time to help finish loading the fifth and final batch of trucks.

Twelve freight cars had been tossed into the gorge by now, in three clusters of four, and each jettisoning had been the occasion for another round of self-congratulation and beer. Frank found the work force, including Lew and Young Mr. Balim and Isaac—who had been replaced as sentry by a workman who'd fallen off the back of a truck with a sack in his arms and landed under it—all feeling very chipper and optimistic indeed. "Have a beer, Frank," said Isaac. Isaac!

Frank took the beer, but gave them all a look of disapproval. "When we get drunk is afterward," he said.

Lew came smiling over to say, "Take it easy, Frank. We're moving the stuff. And there's a kick here, you don't know about it yet, there's something . . . Just wait for it."

Frank knew Lew Brady to be a solid reliable professional, if a trifle young. But now, peering into Lew's eyes, he saw a glittering spark that surprised him, a rashness he hadn't realized was there. He said, "Lew? What is it?"

"Just wait for that truck there."

He meant the truck Isaac had borrowed from the Ugandan Army a few days ago. Lighter and smaller than the other trucks, it was being used now to take the last coffee from the four freight cars currently being unloaded; eight or ten tons in all.

Frank swigged his beer and watched the men work, and even though it seemed to him their attitude was somehow frivolous, he had to admit they were doing the job, moving quickly and smoothly. And when that lone truck was filled and starting on its way—the driver had been the loser in a brisk short-straw contest—Frank got to see what drug it was that had made them all so high.

It was danger. As an ex-railwayman uncoupled the four empty cars, the thirty workmen all clambered up their sides, some climbing onto the roofs, some hanging on the ladders, the rest going inside the big open doors, all yelling and hurrahing, laughing and waving their beer bottles around.

Frank looked for Lew, to ask him what this was all about, but Lew was scrambling up onto the roof of the lead car. Young Mr. Balim was grinning in the doorway of the third car, taking deep swigs from his beer bottle.

Frank found himself almost alone on the ground, with Isaac. "Isaac," he said, "what the hell *is* this?"

"Boys will be boys," Isaac said. "That was Lew's explanation."

"Sounds like one of Charlie's."

The grinning ex-railwayman between the cars yelled and waved his arms to indicate the coupler was unfastened. The grinning ex-railwayman atop the fifth car waved and nodded to indicate his car's brake was securely on. And the grinning ex-railwayman on the first car drained his beer bottle and tossed it ahead of the car into the gorge. Then, with a grand gesture, he spun the wheel to release the brake. And nothing happened.

So why was everybody cheering? Frank looked, and the thirty men on and in and hanging from the cars were all whooping and cavorting and leaping and dancing around, stomping their feet like crazy people in the Middle Ages trying to frighten away plague.

"It's been building from the start," Isaac said, at Frank's elbow. "It's bigger and more ridiculous every time. God knows where it will lead."

The vibration. Now Frank saw what those clowns were up to; the vibration of their dancing and carrying on was overcoming inertia, starting the empty cars forward on the slight slope, sliding every damn one of those idiots toward the cliff!

"Jesus H. *Christ*, Lew!"

The men on top of the lead car were running now, Lew among them, leaping across the space to the next car. The ones riding below jumped out the open doorways on both sides, while the ones hanging onto the ladders simply dropped off and fell to the ground or on top of one another, laughing and kicking their legs.

There was some sort of contest taking place up on the roofs. The idea seemed to be to wait until the car you were on was actually falling, its front wheels already in space, before leaping to the next car back. The first car had already gone into the gorge; the second was going; the whole mass was accelerating. There wasn't room on the narrow roofs for everyone who wanted to play chicken; from the second car roof a half dozen men dove sideways at the last possible instant, rolling on the edge of the cliff, legs dangling, hands scrabbling for holds in the scrub.

"Holy leaping *shit!*"

And Lew was up there with those assholes; he was in the middle of it; he was a fucking ringleader. Always on the front car, he was never the first nor the last to jump back to the next, but invariably timed his move just before the last-second rush. Frank thought, I'm too old for this, by Christ. I *am* gonna retire.

"Frank!"

It was Young Mr. Balim calling. Frank watched in horror, thinking of what he would have to say to the old man, while Young Mr. Balim in the third car waved and grinned and waited until what *had* to be too long before pirouetting out of the car, beer bottle held high, and crumpling all in a heap next to the edge. Frank stopped breathing, and Young Mr. Balim uncurled and crawled quickly forward to look over the lip and watch his car fall.

Frank breathed. "Isaac," he said. "Isaac, how can you let them *do* this?"

Isaac's expression was doleful, but still good-humored. "How can you not?" he asked.

With a concerted cheer, and with bodies hurtling in all directions, the fourth car sailed out over the edge and into eternity. Amid the whooping and the hollering, Frank and Isaac stood unsmiling and alone, like a couple of preachers in a cowtown on a Saturday night.

Lew came over, grin and bottle both intact, bottle half-full, clothing spotted with dirt and twigs. "Whadaya say, Frank?"

"I say, if you aren't drunk you're fucking crazy."

"Then I'm fucking crazy, Frank." Lew lifted his bottle in a toast and swigged half the remainder.

"What makes you so goddam cheerful?"

"I'll tell you, Frank," Lew said, and pointed with his free hand. "You see that sign?"

"Ellen's Road. I'm sorry I put the fucker up."

"Don't be." Lew turned to give his happy grin to the remaining cars of the train, sliding down now into position for the next four to be unloaded, then looked back at Frank. "I've been with these guys all day," he said. "Every time I look up I see that sign and I wonder what went wrong, and then I look around at what I'm doing, shlepping coffee sacks, and I wonder why I'm so happy."

"Beer," Frank said.

"Maybe." Lew was plainly cheerful enough to agree with anything: that the world is flat, that the end justifies the means, that this is the Pepsi Generation, just any damn thing at all. "What I think it is," he went on, "more than the beer, I think I've figured out who I am."

"An asshole," Frank said. "Trying to be a dead asshole."

"Maybe that, too. But something more." Within Lew's merry madness, seriousness lurked. He said, "You know, Ellen isn't a one-man woman any more than I'm a one-woman man. I'm not gonna put on a tie and go down to the office, and she's not gonna stay home and sort the laundry. We're absolutely perfect for each other, and it's a great relief to me to know that."

"I'm glad for you."

"Thank you, Frank. Why Ellen and I are so perfect for one another is because we're so alike. *And* because neither of us wants the other one to be anybody but who we are."

"And who the fuck are you?" Frank asked, feeling more sour by the minute.

"I'll tell you who I am." Lew was really very excited. He said, "It came to me in a revelation, this afternoon. That sign, this train, that cliff. I've accepted my destiny, Frank. I'm the hero!"

Frank stared at him. "You're the *what?*"

"The hero. That's what I was born to be. And that's why I can go up on top of those cars and take a couple chances." The bastard had the effrontery to pat Frank *on the cheek*. "The hero doesn't get killed," he explained.

PART SIX

56

It was with the next group of cars that the first man went over. He'd made an error of judgment, that's all; it was a simple mistake and therefore hilarious. "Ai! Ai!" the others all shouted in shocked delight, and crowded to the edge of the cliff to watch their comrade drop.

"*Jee*-sus!" Lew cried, but he couldn't take it seriously either, and stared down the cliff face as though it was some silent two-reeler comedy he were watching instead of the death of a man. The cars fell, the man stood on the last roof gaping upward, and the last thing he saw in this world was three dozen men laughing at him. Then the cars hit the bay, the water boiled over full of slashing strips and shards of wood, and when the surface settled there was nothing on it at all.

The men at the cliff edge laughed till they staggered; they held their sides from laughing; they mimed for one another the round-eyed round-mouthed look of astonishment on that fellow's face when he'd scrambled to the end of the fourth car's roof only to find nothing beyond it but a widening carpet of air. But Lew lost the comedy of the thing the instant it was over, and when he turned and saw the expression on Isaac's face he was sorry he'd ever been amused at all. Stepping quickly from the edge, he strode over to solemn Isaac and said, "It's getting out of control."

He'd made such a comment only because he wanted Isaac to think he was a responsible individual and not one of the people laughing, but Isaac shook his head and corrected him. "No, it's *been* out of control. This will calm them for a while."

The workmen were drifting back from the cliff, undoubtedly remembering it was beer time, but they still mugged and mimed and expressed their pleasure at the unanticipated spectacle. Watching them, Lew said, "Are you sure?"

"They'll have an hour to think about it," Isaac said as Young Mr. Balim strolled over to join them. "Next time they'll remember, and they'll all be a little more careful."

"I thought," Young Mr. Balim said rather tentatively, "I might go up to the road, relieve the man on watch there."

Isaac frowned. "Why?"

"Because he's probably asleep." Young Mr. Balim smiled wistfully. "Also, I don't think I like the entertainment here."

Lew said, "Isaac says it won't happen again."

"Well, there's a great lesson in it," Young Mr. Balim said, "which I don't need repeated."

"What's that?"

"That it's dangerous to play hero," Young Mr. Balim said, "if you aren't one."

The echo of his earlier braggadocio remark to Frank made Lew uncomfortable, which made him aggressive. "How do you *know?*" he demanded. "How do you know if you're a hero?"

Young Mr. Balim shrugged. "You survive," he said.

*   *   *

Isaac had been both right and wrong about what would happen next. When the sixth group of freight cars was dropped off the cliff, the men were much more careful; barely half rode the cars, and those who did were much brisker about jumping to the ground. Nevertheless, a man died.

Lew didn't ride this time, but stayed on the ground as a good example. It had become evening, already dark under the trees, with bars and tunnels of pink light angling down through the open spaces. Lew watched the empty cars against the pink sky, rolling away, and when he saw the motionless man on the last roof, he cried, "Not again!"

But it was again. The man was short and chunky, with very heavy shoulders, who before this had been noticeable only because he was one of the very few workmen who wore a hat; a kind of tattered baseball cap, with no team designation. Now he stood on the freight-car roof, facing the cliff, both hands pressed to his heart as if he were a character in a Victorian novel, and leaned forward slightly, as though impatient to be gone.

There was no laughter. A few voices tried to raise a cheer, but it didn't take, and in silence everybody watched the madman ride his freight car down through the empty pink air, never changing his posture, not even when his hat blew off. And when the great black mouth of the water opened for him, showing its white-foam teeth, a general sigh went up, quickly dissipating in the trees.

The men were silent as they turned away, their faces inward-looking, and though everybody was fairly full of beer there was none of the usual roughhousing during the break before returning to work. Friends of the departed man explained that he had been unhappy in love; when this word reached Lew he said, "Shit, so am I! That's no reason!"

Isaac was the one who'd told him. Spreading his hands, he said, "It seemed like a reason to him."

* * *

Lew left for the lake with the next group of trucks, taking with him the engineer and fireman they'd hijacked with the train. Those two, having sworn they wouldn't try to escape, had much earlier been given their parole and had sort of been hanging around ever since, drinking beer with the boys and generally having a good old time. However, when they saw Lew make preparations to depart, they both came over and said they would like please to come along to Kenya. Lew shook his head at them. "What for? You aren't in trouble. When we're gone, you just go back and tell the truth."

"Well, mister," the fireman said, "sometimes in Uganda the truth is not so important."

"It was our train," the engineer said. "They might be very angry, and they would want someone to blame, and perhaps they would blame us."

"We like Kenya," the fireman said. "It's a very much better country completely."

"I have cousins there," the engineer said. "You say that? 'Cousins'?"

"Sure."

"We used to like very much when the railway went to Kenya," the fireman said. "We still have friends on the railway there."

"We get jobs," the engineer said, "and tell *everybody* the story about this train."

"They will buy us beer," the fireman said, and laughed.

"We will never have to buy our own beer again ever completely," the engineer said, and they both laughed.

"Then climb into the truck," Lew told them, and went over to tell Isaac he was off, adding, "When you leave, don't forget Young Mr. Balim up by the road."

"Oh, I won't." Isaac smiled in the near-darkness. "Can you imagine returning to Mr. Balim without his son?"

"No," Lew said, and left.

He probably should have stayed, but he just didn't want to anymore. The fun was going out of it. Night was falling, the lugging of coffee sacks was merely manual labor, the repetition of falling freight cars (with or without human sacrifices) had begun to pall, and he kept being given uncomfortable things to think about. First, that his idea of himself as hero might merely be self-aggrandizement; and second, that he didn't love Ellen enough to jump off a cliff because of her. It was enough to bring anybody down.

ELLEN'S ROAD said the sign on the way out. "Shit," said Lew.

57

Young Mr. Balim had been made very uneasy by the falling men. He himself was a man who had never known firm ground beneath his feet, so these reminders of how easily he too could drop away and cease to exist, never to matter again, never having mattered in the first place, troubled him and gave him a nervous sensitivity to his own frailty, surrounded by dangers. He tramped back and forth at the level crossing where the access road humped over the track, trying in the physical movements to reassure himself of his own reality, but the thud of his feet sounded hollow in the night, his determined movements the empty gesture of a substanceless shadow.

For who was he anyway but a half-solid ghost, with little more existence than the insects that whined and buzzed around him? He was a ghost of the British imperial era, which had brought both his grandfathers from India to work on this very railroad, leaving behind both the railroad and the men, like a half loaf of bread and a shopping list abandoned on the kitchen counter after the family has moved. Beyond that he was a ghost of Uganda; in this nation of his birth he was under a death sentence for the simple crime of having lived. And he was the ghost of his father's dream of security and continuity; there was no security, and this age was the enemy of continuity. Every man stands on the freight-car roof. We fall and fall, our feet planted on the solid surface, and the only question is how long before we hit.

Lights. It was fully dark now, and lights were suddenly winking at him through the trees from farther up the hill. At first he thought it was lanterns carried by people clambering their way through the undergrowth, but as they came closer he realized they were headlights. Some sort of vehicle was jouncing very slowly down the access road.

Who? The headlights were yellow, as though the battery were poor, but it could still be police; or Army. Particularly considering those trucks Isaac had borrowed.

As the yellow light touched him, Young Mr. Balim slid away from the level crossing into the tangle of trees and brush just downhill from the track. Nothing showed behind those slow-moving bouncing headlights. A faintly coughing engine could be indistinctly heard. Crouched down low, Young Mr. Balim watched and waited as the headlights reached the crossing, angled upward for the hump . . . and stopped.

Young Mr. Balim waited, staring. The yellow lights gleamed dimly on the upper branches of trees and the engine continued its weak cough, but nothing at all happened. The vehicle refused to move.

The wait was interminable. From feeling himself an almost incorporeal ghost, Young Mr. Balim now found himself too real by half; his crouched position was becoming distinctly uncomfortable, with shooting pains in his knees and calves, a growing ache in his neck, a heavy muscular cramp spreading across his back. When he could stand it no more, when he was certain ten minutes had gone by—ninety seconds had passed—he shifted position, but then immediately moved again, brush crackling around him.

Why had his father permitted him to come along on this expedition?

Mazar Balim was supposed to be the strong one, so much stronger and more self-assured than his son; why had he allowed Bathar to browbeat him into giving way? And what was Bathar's own nonsense of derring-do, of wresting some wonderful new fantasy life from the jaws of danger? He had come here as though to an initiation, a long-delayed ritual of manhood, never thinking he might fail and fall and not have mattered. Those two men who had gone over the cliff; neither of them had known their stories would end like that when they left Kenya yesterday.

He could wait no longer. He had to move, take the chance, go see for himself what was happening up there. Maybe after all it was nothing more than a couple using this abandoned road for a lover's lane.

Still, do couples on lovers' lanes keep their headlights burning? With great caution Young Mr. Balim worked his way through the brush, flitted quickly across the track at a point ten feet east of the crossing, and paused again amid the hedges on the other side.

From this angle, behind and to the left of the vehicle, he could see it silhouetted against the yellow light. It was an old small pickup truck, battered and dark. He couldn't make out who was in the cab.

Slowly, slowly, inching forward, he stalked the truck. The frail cough of the engine reassured him, suggesting there was no great strength here to contend against. In a last little nearly silent dash he reached the left rear corner of the truck and paused, his hand on the fender, feeling it vibrate from the wheezing engine.

Faint light reflected back from the tree branches. In that illumination, as he was about to move forward along the side of the truck, Young Mr. Balim saw a person lying on his side in the open truckbed. Asleep? Curious, he leaned down closer, saw the black face and the white clerical collar, smelled the caked blood before seeing it all over the man's head, recognized that he was looking at a corpse, heard a faint sound behind himself, spun round in terror, and saw the swinging tire iron for less than a second before it smashed into the side of his skull.

58

Chase tossed the tire iron away onto the ground, stepped over the fallen sentry, and went forward to switch off the truck's engine and lights; they had finished their work. Then, while his eyes grew used to the dark, he went back to the sentry, searched him, and was both surprised and annoyed to find the man had no weapons.

What sort of operation was Frank running here? An unarmed sentry was a real snag in Chase's plans. He himself had been stripped of weapons back at the Rwanda border, and of course the minister, former owner of this truck, had not been carrying any guns. Chase's primary purpose in luring this fellow forward had been to rearm himself at the sentry's expense.

All right; it wasn't the end of the world. Chase looked up at the velvet-gray sky, down at the black undergrowth. His eyes had adjusted as much as they would. Leaving the truck, he stepped over the level crossing, moving slowly, his body still very stiff from his time as a captive.

There were no more sentries posted. Chase moved down the old road in the dark, senses alert, reaching out with eyes and ears into the forest. He felt the change underfoot when he reached that part of the road which had just recently been mashed down by heavy trucks; reversing himself, he found the side road and moved slowly along it, hearing a confusion of faint noises ahead.

He almost walked directly into the side of the engine shed, not seeing it under the roof of tree branches. Circling, he saw vague illumination ahead, and took a moment to figure out what it was.

Of the coffee train, it appeared that only four freight cars were left, standing in a patient row on the old tracks like cows waiting to be milked. Or already being milked; a large Army truck was backed up against the side loading door of each. Kerosene lanterns in the cars gave illumination and tarpaulins thrown over the narrow space between freight-car roof and truck top guarded against that illumination's being spotted from the air. Hollowly echoing sounds came out to Chase in the still night: feet tramping back and forth, mutters of conversation, thuds of coffee sacks being dropped into place.

A weapon, Chase thought. I have to have a weapon.

The truck cabs were empty. He searched them, but the glove compartments, the map racks, the underseat spaces were all devoid of guns. Frank will be armed, Chase told himself. I'd better have a gun in my hand when I meet him.

A man jumped from one of the freight cars, feet thumping the ground. He walked a bit away from the trucks, then stopped to relieve himself. Chase waited till he was done, then came up behind him, gripped his head and neck between his forearms, and whispered in his ear in Swahili, "If you make a sound, I shall break your neck."

The man's body tensed, but with fear rather than intended action. He froze there, his hands out as though he were falling forward, and Chase whispered, "Where is Frank Lanigan?"

"Gone—" The man faltered, his voice scratchy and hoarse. "Gone to the lake." He spoke with a soft Luo accent.

"The lake. What about Brady?"

"I don't— Who?"

Chase gave him a little squeeze, for being stupid. "The other white man!"

"The lake!"

"Quiet!"

"Gone to— You hurt my neck."

"I can do worse," Chase told him. "Both white men gone to the lake?" That didn't seem sensible.

"Yes."

"Who's in charge?"

"Mr. Otera."

Otera. Balim's office manager. A picture came into Chase's mind of Otera putting on the Army uniform in that Jinja attorney's office. Not a difficult opponent. "Where is he?"

"The farthest wagon."

"Who else is with him?"

"People working." The man sounded surprised at the question.

"Bosses," Chase explained, again squeezing the man's neck. "What other bosses?"

"None here. Young Mr. Balim up by the road."

So that had been Balim's son up there, crashing around in the woods. Smiling, Chase said, "Thank you," broke the man's neck, and went over to the farthest freight car, where he stood in the darkness beside the truck and called, in imitation of that man's Luo accent, "Mr. Otera!"

He had to call the name twice before Otera appeared, pushing aside the hanging end of tarpaulin, squinting, unable to see much in the dark after the lantern light. "Yes?"

"Something for you to see, Mr. Otera."

"What is it?"

"Oh, you must come see, sir."

Reluctantly, ungracefully, Otera clambered down out of the freight car and came forward. He was wearing the shirt and trousers of the Army uniform, but not the jacket. "What is it? I don't see any— Oh!"

Chase lunged forward, left hand closing around Otera's neck, right hand grabbing his shirtfront and yanking him in close. "Not a sound!" he whispered, reverting back to English. "You'd be dead in one flick." His sudden movement had fired up inside his body all those pains that had been so slowly subsiding, none of which showed on his face.

Otera gaped at him, wide-eyed above Chase's clenching hand. "Chase!" he whispered in blank astonishment.

"Where's your uniform? The jacket."

"It's over—" Otera started, gesturing toward the engine shed, then too late tried to call the gesture back.

"That's right," Chase said, smiling at him. Sure of his man, he switched his grip from throat to upper arm, and pulled Otera along toward the shed. "There was a nice Sam Browne belt with that uniform, and a nice holster, and a nice pistol."

"Chase—" Otera said, but then couldn't seem to think of anything more to say, as he was propelled through the darkness.

Amiably enough, Chase said, "If I wanted to kill you, you'd be dead by now. I've been through a lot today, and I'll be more comfortable when I'm armed."

Otera, with a new worry, said, "Are they after you?"

"Not here. Don't worry," Chase told him in utter sincerity, "I won't spoil this operation. Not for anything."

The jacket and belt lay on the remaining mound of old rails, on the far side of the shed. Chase, to give warmth and support to his battered body, slipped the coat on, pleased that it was a bit snug. He cinched the belt tight, then snapped open the holster flap and slid the pistol out into his hand. Strength flowed from the cold metal. Otera's herbivore eyes watched him in the dark. Holding the pistol casually at his side, Chase said, "Let's go back." At Otera's sigh of long-held breath, Chase laughed. "I said I wouldn't kill you."

As they walked back, Chase said, "How much more is there to do?"

"These are the last trucks."

"Good. We can ride down to the lake together."

There was a bit more light near the trucks, and in it Otera frowned at Chase in bewilderment and dislike. "If you're in trouble," he said, "if all you want is to come with us to Kenya, you didn't have to attack me, and arm yourself, and all this business."

"We all have our methods, Watson," Chase said. He made a shooing gesture with the hand holding the revolver. "Go along, go along."

Otera turned away, and Chase went to rest himself in the nearest truck cab. But the map light didn't work, so he went on to the next, where the small narrow glow under the dashboard permitted him to study the weapon with which he'd armed himself.

It was a good one, though old. An English semiautomatic revolver, a Webley-Fosbery chambered in .455 caliber, it was one of the few pistols ever made which used the recoil of the last shot to cock the hammer and rotate the cylinder for the next. It couldn't be fired as rapidly as a full automatic, but it had a solid reliable heft to it.

Holding the gun down under the map light, Chase broke open the cylinder and looked in. For a moment he just gazed in silence, then he laughed at the joke. There wasn't a bullet in it.

59

Balim rode in the back of the Mercedes with the government man called Charles Obuong. The other one, Godfrey Magon, rode up front with the chauffeur; between them, out beyond the windshield, Balim could see if he wished the rural roads of Nyanza province, illuminated by the powerful white headlights of the Mercedes; what he could not see, unfortunately, was into the minds of Charles Obuong and Godfrey Magon.

Their manner with him was unfailingly polite and friendly though with the inevitable edge of power and mockery. And they had been quite open, freely repeating to him what they already knew of the smuggling, which was a *lot*. And even beyond what they knew, they also modestly claimed to have been of logistical help along the way. It was their office, they said, which had expedited the permissions and development-fund loans for the Port Victoria hotel. They had assisted Isaac in his purchase of false identity papers. They had even made lumber available when in the ordinary course of events he might still be waiting for the planks they'd used in making the rafts. They had in effect been Balim's partners all along, and they didn't even seem to mind it very much that their "investigator" had apparently been murdered by someone connected with Balim.

Was all this true? But if it were not true, how would they know so many details, and how did it happen that the assemblage of matériel *had* been so unusually smooth and effortless? And if it was indeed the truth, including their claim of a plot to resteal the coffee "with violence," then all that mattered now was that *Bathar* was in danger. Bathar, the only son of Mazar Balim.

Which was why Balim had immediately and sincerely offered his fullest cooperation, telling Magon and Obuong what little they hadn't already known, which was mostly the timetable: when the coffee would be hijacked, when it would be brought to Port Victoria. "It's happening right now," Balim had told them, and they'd been pleased at the news; a good dinner had been given Balim at a local hotel at their expense, and when they'd come out afterward the Mercedes and the truckload of soldiers were already waiting. And now they were running through the night over the washboard roads, the Mercedes in the lead, the truck following in their dust.

The Nzoia ferry did not run at night. They had to take the wider sweep through Sio, through tiny villages without electricity, down long dirt roads hemmed in by fresh growth after the long rains. Riding along in silence beside Obuong, Balim had leisure in which to grow used to his worry about Bathar, and to think about more mundane items, such as what these two government men were really up to. Was it all as selfless and official as it appeared? How unlikely.

Treading with care, Balim began his exploration into the question of motive as indirectly as possible. Breaking the long silence, "Uganda," he said to Obuong, "has been a troublesome neighbor for years."

"Oh, very troublesome," Obuong agreed. Smiling, he said, "That's why we were so pleased at your initiative."

"Yes, you called me a patriot."

Obuong found that amusing. "I did?"

"Yes, when we first met in my office." Balim made himself as small and round and inoffensive and harmless as possible. "I knew you meant it ironically," he said, the slightest hint of self-pity in his voice.

Politeness barely covering the mockery, Obuong said, "I hope I didn't hurt your feelings."

"Not at all." Balim sighed, accepting the calumnies of this world on his bowed shoulders. "But it did make me wonder," he went on, "what you thought our motive was in taking this coffee."

"Money," Obuong said, promptly and simply and emphatically.

"Only money?"

"Please don't misunderstand me, Mr. Balim," Obuong said. "I am not myself anti-Asian. Some of my best friends in Nairobi are Asian."

Balim nodded, accepting these bona fides.

"But I don't think it's unfair to say," Obuong went on, "that it is well known that patriotism is not an emotion known to Asians. Their interests—perfectly legitimate interests—lie elsewhere. Money, merchandising. Art. Learning. At times, religion. And they are very good family people."

"Patriotism," Balim gently pointed out, "is the love of one's country. *Unrequited* love of one's country is a passion difficult to maintain."

"There have undoubtedly been injustices committed against the Asians," Obuong said, in the manner of a person utterly uninterested in discussing such injustices. "But please let me reassure you. If profit *was* a consideration at all—in addition to the love you bear your adopted country, of course—you still have something to look forward to. Not as much, of course."

"Of course," Balim said.

"There will be various taxes to be paid, import duties and so on. Due to your . . . patriotism . . . I should think certain normal fines and seizures of goods would be waived in this case."

"Good of you," Balim murmured.

"Then, of course, the Jhosis have really far too small a plantation to handle all that coffee. We can make arrangements for particular other growers who could assist."

"I see," Balim said. He was smiling. The familiar whiff of corruption, so long missing from his relationship with these two, was at last a comforting presence in his nostrils. Politics, trade, graft, and the general opposition to Idi Amin; all had come together to make this unlikely partnership.

"Almost there," Godfrey Magon said from the front seat, and Balim looked out past him at the sharply defined world snared in their headlights.

At night Port Victoria ceased almost entirely to exist. One or two lights flickered deep in the interior of the shops around the grassy market square, but the little stucco-faced houses lining the dirt road down the long, steep slopes to the lake were black and silent, humped together in the darkness like natural growths, unpopulated hillocks.

At the bottom of the hill, near the shoreline, was the unfinished hotel. The two men Frank had left here to guard the building supplies were tending a smoky orange fire in a large oil drum. "A beacon," Godfrey Magon pointed out, "to guide our heroes home."

60

Isaac drove the first truck, with Chase in the passenger seat beside him fondling the pistol. Their headlights were taped down to mere slits, producing something not much stronger than candlelight, a faint amber glow barely bright enough to distinguish the road from the surrounding woods. Only the lead truck used headlights at all, each of the other three navigating by the red taillights of the truck ahead.

From time to time Chase tried to make small talk—"What are you going to do with all the money?" "Do you like your new life as a swashbuckler?" "What ministry were you with in Uganda?"—but Isaac refused to answer. He hated this creature beside him; he had to grip tightly to the steering wheel to keep himself from a useless suicidal attack against the man.

Bathar. Painful scenes played in his head, of himself telling Mr. Balim that Bathar was dead; and of course he must be the one to break the news. Frank lacked the sensitivity, and all the rest were strangers.

That's why he has the gun, Isaac thought, why he wasn't calm until he had a gun in his hand. It's because his viciousness makes him hurt people, he can't stop hurting people, and he needs protection against the rage and hatred he inspires.

The gun had been prominent in Chase's hand when Isaac had come over to the truck cab, back at the depot, to say, "All loaded. I just have to send someone up to get Young Mr. Balim."

"No need for that," Chase had answered, sitting in the cab, smiling at him in that lazy-cat way of his. "I already met him on the way down."

Isaac had stared, unwilling to believe. "What did you—?"

"You don't have to worry about him anymore," Chase had said, stroking the gun. "Get in, let's go."

For the next hour Isaac could think about that, all the way down the long road to the lake. Fresh pale scars winked from the tree branches, mementos of earlier trucks. The close-lying darkness to either side seemed peopled, teeming with watchful silent life; but none of it so dangerous or so evil as Chase.

It seemed to Isaac finally that they must have crossed into some other plane of reality where there was no lake, no farther terminus at all; there was nothing but the road and a permanent condition in which he drove endlessly through unrelieved darkness with this self-satisfied monster at his side. But then he saw a figure in the dimness ahead, standing between the ruts, and recognized that shambling posture immediately as belonging to no one else but Charlie. Of course it was; Charlie stood grinning, a long shaggy piece of sugar-cane sticking out of his mouth like a financier's cigar.

Charlie waved for Isaac to follow, then scampered on ahead, a manic figure, some ramshackle wood sprite with no redeeming social qualities. The previous trucks, empty and dark, were pulled barely off the road on both sides, leaving a narrow high-walled alley for Isaac to negotiate.

Chase said, "Why, it's a major operation."

It was. In near-darkness two trucks were being unloaded onto two rafts. The swarming lines of men, with their heavy sacks of coffee, looked like agitated ants forced to move their nest. Isaac braked to a stop, cutting the engine, and in the sudden silence he could hear beneath the muted sounds of the loading a disturbed plash of water against the rafts.

Frank strode up from the edge of the unseen lake, looking big and mean and bad-tempered; his boss expression. Lew followed, glancing quickly this way and that, looking for rips in the fabric. Sounding wistful, Chase said, "I could hit them both from here."

Isaac turned to look at the man, who was gazing through the windshield, smiling faintly. If he lifts the gun, Isaac thought, I'll stop him. I'll kill him if I can.

Chase met Isaac's eyes. Seeming both surprised and amused, he said, "I'm not *going* to, Otera." He made that shooing gesture with the gun. "Climb out. I'll follow you."

Isaac opened the door and clambered down to the ground. Chase followed through the same opening, so Isaac moved a few steps away. Frank, before coming up to them, was already calling out orders: "Get your men down to the lake, Isaac, let's finish this, it's too fucking dark to work."

"He has a gun," Isaac said quietly, and stepped farther away to the side as Chase shut the truck door and revealed himself, smiling in the faint light, holding the gun casually but prominently at his side.

Then it got very quiet inside their little circle. Below, on planks over the roiled mud of the shore, the workmen continued to load the rafts. Above, in the narrow corridor between the empty trucks, the men who'd just ridden down from the depot were jumping out onto the ground, demonic in the red glow of the taillights as they stretched their stiff muscles and made quiet conversation together. Here around the lead truck there was silence, with Chase beside the door in his torn trousers and the uniform coat and belt, the pistol gleaming in his hand. Isaac stood away from him to the side, Frank farther away toward the lake, Lew just beyond Frank. Charlie watched in childlike interest at the periphery of the light.

"Surprise," Chase said.

Frank said, "What's this all about?"

Lew took a step to his left, but with sudden harshness Chase gestured with the gun, saying, "Don't go anywhere, friend."

Frank, already angry, said, "Chase, what are you fucking around at?"

"A little trouble at the office," Chase told him, his good humor returning. "I had to leave."

Isaac said, "He killed Bathar."

Frank stared at Isaac, as though blaming the messenger. "He did what?"

"I hit him with a tire iron," Chase said, as though it were an unimportant detail. "He might be dead, he might be alive. What difference does it make?"

Speaking to Isaac as though Chase weren't there, Frank said, "Did you see it?"

"No. Bathar was on watch, up by the crossing. This man wouldn't let me send anyone for him."

Frank thought about it, then came to a conclusion. "Okay," he said, and walked toward Chase.

Chase had been lounging at his ease, shoulder against the shut truck door, but now he stood up straight, flashing the gun again, saying, "Frank, take it easy."

Slogging forward, workmanlike, Frank said, "How many times can you pop me with that little thing? I'll still take your fucking head off." Behind him, Lew had also started forward, moving to Frank's right. Isaac watched, openmouthed. He wanted to yell, to make them stop, but he couldn't think what the words would be. And Chase seemed just as astonished. "Frank!" he shouted. "Don't make me do it!" But Frank just walked forward, at the end reaching out for Chase's head.

Which was when Chase reversed the gun and tried to use the butt as a club. But Frank held his forearm, twisted the gun out of his hand, and tossed it dismissively to Lew. Then he started hitting.

Chase was big, but Frank was bigger, and he now went at Chase the way he drove the Land-Rover, the way he pushed his employees, the way he did everything in life, wading straight in.

"He's alive!" Chase cried, arms up to defend himself. "It's true, it's true, he's alive!"

But Frank didn't hear, or didn't care, or didn't believe. His elbows pumped out and back and up and down, his thick head was thrust out, his feet were planted like oak trees, and rather than box his way past Chase's defensive arms he pounded his way through them, crowding Chase against the side of the truck and hitting his arms and shoulders till they grew too battered and weary to lift anymore, then going to work on the man's torso instead, pausing once with his big palm against Chase's chest, saying, "I'm saving your head for dessert," then pounding his torso some more. The workmen who'd just come down from the depot gathered around to watch and admire.

"Frank," Lew said. He spoke quietly enough, but something odd in his tone attracted Frank's attention, and he at once stopped, took a step back, and as Chase sagged down onto the truck's running board Frank turned and said, "What's up?"

Lew had come over to stand near Isaac, who saw that he was holding the gun open so Frank could see the cylinder. Isaac saw it, too, as Lew said, "It's empty, Frank."

Frank gave an angry bark of laughter, as though saying it didn't matter, but when he turned back to Chase he no longer seemed so determined to beat him to death. "So, you simple bastard," he said. "You've got nothing in your pecker at all."

Chase didn't speak. His breath was short and ragged and loud; he hugged himself as though afraid he might be broken somewhere inside. He stared at the ground at Frank's feet, waiting for whatever would happen next.

Lew handed the pistol to Isaac and walked forward. While Isaac held the broken-open thing in both hands, not knowing what to do with it, surprised by the weight of it, Lew stopped beside Frank and said, "Chase. Talk to me about Young Mr. Balim."

"I hit him." His voice was flat and weary and uninflected.

"Where? With what?"

"Side of the head. Tire iron."

Isaac walked over to join them, the gun in his palms like a gift. Lew continued his catechism. "Check his pulse afterward?"

"No."

"Do anything else to him?"

"Searched him."

"Do you think he's alive, or do you think he's dead?"

Chase lifted his weary head, showing a flash of his old arrogance and contempt. "I didn't think about it. I didn't care."

Isaac said, "Why wouldn't you let me send people to get him?"

"What difference does it make?" Chase, who had suffered the beating in stoic silence, seemed pushed beyond endurance by the interrogation. "You're all dead, anyway," he said.

Frank jumped on that. "Who says? What's going on, Chase?"

But Chase lowered his head, his expression obstinate. Whatever he had meant, it was clear he would not explain any further. Frank glanced toward the lake, then back at Chase. "You got a double cross in mind? That would be your style, wouldn't it, you son of a bitch. I *told* Balim about you."

Isaac said, "And now we'll have to tell him about Bathar."

Lew said, "Frank, I'll go up and get him."

"Don't be stupid," Frank said.

"It's not stupid. What if he's alive? He isn't ready for Uganda, Frank, believe me. Think about it; they find him, they find the depot, they start to twist him."

"He'll talk," Frank said.

But Lew brushed that aside. "He'll talk the first ten seconds. But they won't stop, Frank. I know these bastards now. Chase! If Young Mr. Balim's still alive, and your pals find him, what then?"

Chase didn't lift his head. "They'll play him for a month," he said tonelessly.

"If ever there was a mouse in the land of cats," Lew said, "it's Young Mr. Balim."

"Wait a minute," Frank said, and turned to bellow, *"Charlie!"*

"Right here," said Charlie, who was.

"Take seven or eight guys," Frank told him, gesturing at Chase, "and tie this fellow up with a lot of rope. I don't want him comfortable, see what I mean?"

"Oh, sure," Charlie said, grinning.

"And put a gag in his mouth. A dirty gag. Use your shirt."

Charlie giggled, and called in Swahili to the men standing around, several of whom came forward in anticipatory pleasure. Meanwhile, Frank turned back to Lew and Isaac, saying, "Come on over here."

They walked a bit away, farther from the light, where Frank frowned at Lew, shook his head, and said, "You're talking about two hours, up and back. Minimum. We'll be out of here in less than an hour. And if Chase really is up to something, we can't hang around. In fact, we can't hang around, anyway."

Isaac said, "Frank, think of Mr. Balim."

"I *am* thinking of Mr. Balim. I'm thinking of every fucking body."

"I won't come back," Lew said. "Listen, Frank, whether he's alive or dead I'll get back a different route."

"There are no different routes," Frank told him. "We stole their fucking coffee crop, remember? They'll have that border shut like a nunnery in the Hundred Years' War."

"Ellen," Lew said.

Nobody understood him. Isaac, thinking Lew had forgotten in the press of the moment, said, "Lew, Ellen isn't with us anymore."

"Sure she is," Lew said. "She's at Entebbe."

Isaac gaped at him, too astonished to speak. Frank said it for them both: "Entebbe? You're gonna escape from Uganda through *Entebbe?*"

"I wouldn't be the first," Lew said, grinning. "Frank, get a message to her. You can do it, you're her former employer back in Nairobi. The message is, an old friend of hers from Alaska, a guy named Val Dietz, he's in Africa passing through, he says he'll be in Entebbe sometime the next twenty-four hours, he sure hopes he can stop by and say hello, buy her a drink."

Isaac, feeling very uncomfortable, said, "Lew, you shouldn't be the one to do this."

"I'm the only one who can," Lew said.

His expression sour, Frank said, "Still the fucking hero, huh?"

"Always and forever, Frank." Lew was already backing away, grinning, in a hurry to be off. "Remember the message."

Isaac said, "Val Dietz, from Alaska."

Frank said, "Where'd that name come from?"

"She'll understand it." Pointing at Isaac, Lew said, "Twenty-four hours."

"I'll remember," Isaac promised.

Lew turned and trotted away toward the empty trucks. Watching him, Frank muttered, "Ellen's gonna blame *me*."

61

He couldn't believe the pain in his head. It wasn't fair to hurt like this; no matter how much he'd had to drink, no matter how late he'd stayed up, it just wasn't fair. If the head was going to explode, why didn't it go ahead and explode and be done with it? Why go on torturing him, hurting so much he couldn't even get comfortable, the mattress was so hard and lumpy and—

Mattress? Lord, Lord, he wasn't even in bed, he was on the ground somewhere, he'd never made it home, he even had all his clothes on, his shoes—

Tentatively he opened one eye, saw nothing, and felt increased pain in his skull. Lifting a slow-moving shaking hand, he rested the palm consolingly against his throbbing brow, and the horror he touched there made him *shriek*! He sat bolt-upright, and stared in blank terror at the blackness all around him.

"My God. My God." He had no idea Who exactly his God was, only that in moments of distress he felt the presence of some potentially benign Figure gazing placidly and with some amused interest over the rim of Heaven and down upon poor little foolish Bathar.

Blood. Caked blood and torn flesh and a great throbbing pounding bruise. And blackness all around; nothing discernible except just beside him this dark small truck. Truck. Corpse in it. Yellow lights, engine coughing, noise behind him, turn, incredibly *fast* flash of metal.

Remembering everything—God, are you watching? I'm in *Uganda*, God—Bathar used the truck to drag himself to his feet. His nerves were all unstrung; he could barely stand; his stomach was roiled; stars and planets spun and imploded in the periphery of his vision. He leaned on the little pickup truck, gasping, waiting for the symptoms to go away, and they didn't even let up.

But he couldn't stay here. He had to get back to the depot, warn them. "There's a crazy person out here; he hits without warning, for no reason at all. Just a crazy person."

But was he? And *who* was he? And why do such a terrible thing?

Bathar pushed himself away from the support of the truck, not because he was ready to stand on his own but because he was driven by a sense of urgency. He had to report to Isaac right away, tell him what had happened.

He tottered over the level crossing, struggling to regain control of his legs, and thought he was doing well enough until he came down to the rocky, uneven, root-hampered roadway, where he promptly fell, breaking his fall painfully with his forearms. He rested awhile on the cool damp ground, but then again made it to his feet and proceeded in a wary half-crouch, hands splayed out to the sides.

He did fine until, just before Ellen's Road, he fell over the moped. Frank had ridden it up here at the very beginning, to get the first truck, and the thing had been shoved out of the way after that, its usefulness finished. When Bathar fell over it, he got a handlebar in the stomach that winded him and forced him to lie quietly on the ground for another little space of time. Then, sighing, hoping God was watching and admiring these strenuous efforts, he made it to his feet once more, found Ellen's Road, worked his way slowly in to the depot, and everybody was gone. Nothing was left but the last four freight cars, stripped of their cargo.

How could that be? How long had he been unconscious? He stared upward at the sky but saw no indications of dawn. Why had no one come looking for him? And where *were* they all?

Gone. They left Uganda. Left *Uganda*.

"Oh, my," Bathar murmured, his own voice a comforting friend in this unpopulated blackness. "Oh, God, am I in trouble."

Hurry after them? But how long had they been gone? He'd left his watch at home—ah, the lovely mahogany dresser in his lovely dark cozy comfortable room at home—his watch at home on the dresser top with his wallet, his little gold bracelet, his gold money clip, all his civilized fripperies, because he'd been going off on an adventure. An adventure!

The rest of them—Isaac and Frank and Lew and all of them—they surely must be out on the lake by now, safely away from Uganda. It had taken him so long to get down here from the level crossing, and they'd already been gone when he'd started or he would have heard and seen the trucks. Long gone. Marooning him, all alone, in this evil place.

He couldn't think why they would have done it, but at the moment he didn't even much care. Later—if there *was* a later—he would give himself over to rage and paranoia and self-pity, but at the moment he was too nervous for that. He had to move, he had to keep in motion or he would break down completely. Terrified, knowing or believing that his very mind was at risk, that if he stopped moving he would have a nervous breakdown and just sit under some tree somewhere gibbering until they came to take him away, knowing or believing that movement was at least therapy if not otherwise useful, he turned about and tottered away from the depot, back out Ellen's Road.

He found the moped by falling over it again, but this time he switched on its headlight, and the sudden appearance of the world out of blank nothingness was comforting.

Which way? He looked up and down the access road. Down was the lake, but how could they still be there? It would be a dangerous waste of time; he'd simply have to turn around and come back the twenty miles—with who knew how much gas left—and back again past the depot, which by then the Ugandan authorities might very well have found.

The other way? Up at the head of the access road was the main highway; east on that highway was the Kenyan border. People slipped across that border all the time.

Bathar mounted the moped, started the sputtering nasal engine, took a deep breath to calm his nerves, gripped the handlebars to keep his hands from shaking, and drove slowly and waveringly away, uphill.

62

Every person who came into the office, every report that was made, every caller on the telephone, only made Amin's rage deeper and more implacable. His big body in the heavy chair behind the desk became increasingly still as the afternoon blended into night, his shoulders sloping, his weight pressed solidly onto the chair, his Army-booted feet planted squarely on the floor. Only his hands and eyes moved, the eyes shifting left and right like gun turrets in search of enemies, his hands touching and investigating one another, the blind fingers of his right hand studying the fingers of his left.

The train was gone; that was the long and short of it. Coffee worth three million pounds U.K. had been stolen, and the whole train carrying it had been stolen, and no one could find the slightest trace of it or hint as to where it had gone.

There were theories, naturally, hundreds of theories. The frightened men around Amin spurted theories as if they were Sten guns jammed in firing position; they laid down barrages of theories as covering fire to hide their lack of facts.

There was the theory that perhaps the thieves had also stolen the wagon ferry from Jinja terminal, the large ferry that carried railway cars across the lake to Mwanza in Tanzania, but apart from the fact that the wagon ferry could carry no more than eight cars—and the missing train, apart from its locomotive, had contained *thirty-three* cars—there was also the fact that the ferry hadn't been stolen but was still in service.

There was also the theory that the train had actually gone through the Jinja yards after all, with the collusion of the railway employees, and had been diverted onto the northbound branch line toward Mbulamuti. But the entire eighty-some miles of the Mbulamuti branch, with all its spurs, had been searched on the ground and by air to no effect. And the Jinja yardmaster and stationmaster had been tortured for several hours without once changing their stories.

In an alternate theory, the train had never turned west at Tororo at all, but had been spirited across the border there into Kenya. However, extensive questioning with torture of railway employees at Tororo had turned up nothing, nor had torture changed the story of the Iganga stationmaster, who continued to swear that the coffee train had gone through Iganga heading west and had not returned.

All the helicopters of the antismuggling patrol had been brought in from their quadrants over the lake to roam the air instead over the railway line, without finding a thing. The Ugandan Air Force had scrambled, and jets had flashed and swooped here and there through the sky, to no effect. With the arrival of full night, all air activity was stopped, as being pointless.

The people who came into Amin's presence to tell him all these things were very reluctant to enter the room and even more reluctant to say what they had to say. But Amin was too angry at the missing train to pay attention to fear in the eyes and voices of his underlings. (He was used to a certain amount of that, anyway.) He asked the occasional question in his slow heavy voice, he made the occasional contemptuous dismissal of this or that crackpot theory, but for the most part he merely sat there like the Minotaur in its maze, waiting for food. In this case, the food would be the people responsible for the missing train.

And the missing Chase. Ali Kekka had failed on that, even on that very simple task; bring Chase back to Kampala. He had disappeared again, he *and* the train.

On one item everyone including Amin was in accord: the train had to be *someplace*. But that didn't help much. On the other hand, it did mean they would go on searching; sooner or later the train—and the explanation for its disappearance—would have to be found. It was impossible that the mystery would remain unsolved.

Which brought up a potentially hopeful road of inquiry. The railway was relatively modern, the Nile bridge at Jinja not having been completed until 1931; a mere forty-six years ago. Surely there were men still alive who had worked on that part of the road, and who would remember if there had ever been a previous line, or a no-longer-used branch, or anything at all off the main track that could have accommodated the train. A search was under way for such ex-employees, hampered by the fact that record maintenance had not been a high priority in Uganda in recent years.

Night fell, but Amin did not move. Sandwiches and beer were brought him, which he ate at the desk, masticating slowly, rolling his jaws as though chewing the arms and heads of the guilty parties. The phone rang as he was finishing, and it was an Air Force colonel at Entebbe reporting that all aircraft were now down for the night but would be serviced and refueled and ready to take off again at dawn. A man from the Uganda Coffee Commission came reluctantly into the office, stood quivering before the desk, and reported that the cargo-plane crews waiting at Entebbe and Sir Denis Lambsmith of the International Coffee Board had all been told that the coffee train had broken down east of Jinja but was being repaired now and would arrive at Kampala sometime tomorrow.

Amin looked at the man. "We got to find it first," he said.

The Coffee Commission man was a reader, a bit better educated than the soldiers Amin preferred around himself. He said, "We must remember what the great English detective Sherlock Holmes, advises. 'Eliminate the impossible,' he always said, 'and whatever is left, however improbable, is the answer.' "

"Sherlock Holmes, huh?" Amin brooded at the Coffee Commission man, not quite annoyed enough to have him tortured and killed. "Eliminate the impossible, huh?" Holding up his left hand, fingers spread, he ticked off the points. "A train can't go without tracks. A train is too big to hide. A train can't disappear. The train disappeared. There's your impossibles." He pointed a finger like a battering ram at the unfortunate Coffee Commission man. "Now you tell me," Amin said. "Tell me now. What do we got left?"

63

The ten rafts moved out of Macdonald Bay in a long straggling line, slow and unwieldy, their motors straining and groaning against the weight. Each raft, twenty feet square, was loaded twelve feet high, the coffee sacks covered with the gray tarpaulins, four or five men riding on top of each. Frank stood atop the lead raft, with Chase trussed up to one side and Charlie jabbering away with two other Bantu boys back by the steering stick.

It was a dark night, the quarter-moon giving very little illumination. Looking back, Frank could barely make out the next two rafts in the line, wallowing along on the placid lake like waterlogged suitcases from some wrecked liner. It had taken three hours to come here from Port Victoria, but it would be more like six hours going back.

From time to time Chase kicked up a fuss, apparently having something he very much wanted to say, but every time he thrashed around and made those growling noises behind the filthy gag, either Frank or Charlie cuffed him into silence again. However, Frank had continued to brood about that earlier hint of Chase's, the suggestion that he'd double-crossed them in some way that could mean trouble ahead, so after they'd come out of the bay and completed the long slow broad turn from south to east around Bwagwe Point, Frank stomped over the tarpaulin-covered sacks to where Chase was lying, all wound around with rope like a fly being saved by a spider for a meal later on. Hunkering down beside the man, rapping a knuckle on his temple to get his attention, Frank said, "I'm gonna take that gag off now. You got something to say, say it. But don't do any shouting or I'll make you sorry."

Chase nodded, eager and anxious. He was already trying to say something, behind the gag. "Wait a minute," Frank told him while he struggled with Charlie's knot. Then, when he finally got the gag off, all Chase could do at first was cough and spit and clear his throat. Frank waited, and at last Chase said hoarsely, "Will you make a deal?"

"With you?" Frank laughed without humor.

"If we don't deal," Chase insisted, lying there, twisting his head to look up at Frank, "you're certainly dead, and I'm probably dead."

"Tell me about it, Chase," Frank said. "What did you cook up for us?"

"Do we deal?" Urgently, pressing hard, limbs straining against the ropes, Chase said, "There's money in it, Frank, there's plenty of money in it. We can *both* retire."

"Tell me your story."

But still Chase hesitated. "Will you deal? Will you come in with me? Can I trust you?"

Frank laughed at him. "Look where you are," he said. "If I want, I can just roll you off the edge here. Plop, you're all gone. Baron Chase gone forever. Fish food. You want to *deal*? Tell me the story or shut your face."

Chase thought about it for a while, obviously unhappy. The side of his face looked raw where it had rubbed against the tarpaulin. Taking a deep breath, shaking his head, he said, "I've got to, Frank. You're my only hope."

"Tough," Frank commented.

"I sold the coffee," Chase said.

Frank frowned. "Sold it? *This* coffee? Who to?"

"That doesn't matter," Chase said. "A man in Switzerland. You've never heard of him."

"Why would he buy coffee from *you*, Chase?"

Chase rested his head against the lumpy tarpaulin. Sounding more tired, he said, "He's part of the combine buying the coffee. Buying it originally. I told him I had knowledge the coffee wouldn't make it out of the country, he and his people were going to lose out. But I might be able to find him some other coffee. The price has gone up, anyway; he can charge the Brazilians more for it if it isn't the same coffee anymore. He cuts his losses and I—we—make a very nice profit."

"He went for this?"

"He told me, if his coffee disappeared, if I had substitute coffee, we had a deal."

"Another convent child," Frank said. "What's your arrangement?"

"I deliver to his people in Dar."

Dar es Salaam, capital of Tanzania, was a major port on the Indian Ocean, second only to Mombasa in tonnage of cargo. But it was more than a thousand miles from here. Frank said, "How do you get it there?"

"By train from Mwanza."

Mwanza. Just as Kisumu was Kenya's principal port on the lake, Mwanza was Tanzania's, down at the southern tip, the extreme far end of the lake, well over two hundred miles away. Frank said, "These rafts can't make it to Mwanza."

"I know that." Again Chase hesitated, making it clear that now he was coming to the crunch. Inching cautiously into it, he said, "There's an Asian called Hassanali."

"I've heard of him," Frank agreed. "These are his engines. He had some police trouble."

"I arranged his police trouble," Chase said, not without pride.

"Why?"

"He owns a cargo ship called the *Angel*; it operates out of Kisumu."

"I know the *Angel*," Frank said. "Huge motherfuckin ship for this lake, but we don't use him. He's a crook, worse than the railway. But why make trouble for Hassanali?"

"He wouldn't deal, but Captain Usoga, who runs the *Angel*, he would."

Frank looked forward at the empty lake. It was very dark out there, except for the tiny glints of moonlight on wavelets. "You've got the *Angel* out there in front of us," Frank said. "To hijack us."

"Yes."

"They'll have armed men aboard," Frank said, turning to look back toward the other rafts. "They'll just steam by and pick us off."

"Not if we deal," Chase said. "Not if I call out to Captain Usoga, tell him who I am. He needs me alive to get his money."

Frank studied the trussed-up man with some surprise, almost with admiration. "You're a *pirate*, Chase," he said. "Do you know that? You're a goddam *pirate*."

Chase had no comment.

"All right." Frank brooded, looking forward. "Where do they figure to hit us?"

"I don't know."

"You're a liar, but it doesn't matter. *I* know. The only sensible place is the narrows between Matale Point and Sigulu Island."

"Frank!" Chase said, struggling against his ropes. "You can't out-run them! Frank, you're not just killing yourself, you're killing *me!*"

"Be quiet now," Frank told him. "I'm thinking."

Standing, Frank pondered a minute, then turned away and headed toward Charlie and the others back by the steering stick. Chase called something after him, which Frank ignored. Reaching the three Bantu, he said, "Charlie, old son, I'm gonna take you into my confidence."

"Oh, nice!" Charlie said. Moonlight reflected from his bright eyes and white teeth and wet chin.

"D'ja ever hear of pirates, Charlie?"

"Oh, yes," Charlie said. "Even so, in the cinema. Swing on ropes. Swords."

"You got it. And that's what's out in front of us. Except no swords. Guns."

Charlie looked around at their raft. He was a quick study. "Bad completely," he said.

"I figure," Frank told him, "they're waiting for us off Sigulu Island. Where it's narrow there, between the island and the shore."

"Oh, sure," Charlie said, happy in agreement. "Ambush. Very good."

"Good for them, not good for us." Gesturing at the other two Bantu, who were watching and listening and not picking up one English word in ten, Frank said, "Can either of these boys swim?"

"Oh, excellently. They're Luo, all Luo swim."

The Bantu smiled when they heard their tribe's name. Frank smiled back at them, then said, "Charlie, I want one of them to swim back to the next raft, and then to the one after that, and the one after that, and all the way to the last one, where Isaac is. Okay?"

"Much swimming," Charlie suggested.

"Then he treads water," Frank said impatiently, "he waits for the raft to catch up. Every raft, he gives them the message. There's pirates ahead, we should pull up closer together, we're going around the other side of Sigulu Island."

"Much longer way," Charlie pointed out.

"Can't be helped. Tell him."

So Charlie picked one of the Bantu and started to tell him the story in that goddam Swahili. While he was still at it, Chase started calling and yelling. "Tell it to him right, so he remembers," Frank warned the jabbering Charlie, and stomped across the coffee sacks to kick Chase in the head. "Speak when you're spoken to," he said.

64

By the light of his pencil flash, Lew studied the dead minister in the bed of the pickup truck. He'd been hit very hard on the head, more than once, and had bled considerably in his transit to a better world. Smears of blood on the metal suggested the assault had probably taken place elsewhere, then the body was thrown in the back and driven here.

Lew turned in a slow circle, playing the narrow beam of light on the road, the tracks, the surrounding trees and undergrowth. There was simply no sign of Young Mr. Balim. Either he was alive and had gone away, or he was dead and some animal had taken the body for dinner. But if the latter, wouldn't there be drag marks, some indication? There was nothing; only the rattletrap old black pickup parked just shy of the tracks, facing downhill, driver's door open, and in its bed a dead man in clerical garb.

Driver's door open, but no interior light showing. Lew went over to the cab, sat sideways in the driver's seat, found the small bulb in its translucent plastic pocket, and clipped it back in its socket. Weak light gleamed. Lew unclipped the bulb again and stood beside the open door.

He saw now the way Chase had done it. Drive down the access road, stop here; Young Mr. Balim would be down there across the tracks, unable to see anything past the headlights. Then, leaving those lights on as a lure, Chase had slipped out of the pickup—no interior light to give him away—and waited for Young Mr. Balim to come investigate. There should be some sign of it.

Lew bent low to the ground, moving the light in small slow arcs, starting beside the open door and working his way toward the back. It was just beside the rear wheel that he found the bloodstain, still soft to the touch. There wasn't much of it, and the ground nearby didn't seem particularly disturbed. Alive, then.

Straightening, he flicked off the pencil flash and waited for his eyes to readjust to darkness, his left hand resting on the pickup's rusty side panel. Young Mr. Balim had regained consciousness and had wandered off. Where? Though the keys were in the pickup, he hadn't taken it, neither to chase down to the lake after the rest of them nor to flee in the opposite direction. Had he wandered off and then passed out again?

In addition to everything else, Lew was beginning to feel the weight of time. It was nearly ten o'clock; the train had been hijacked nine hours ago. Sooner or later the Ugandan authorities must find this old depot, on some ancient map or mentioned in some old annual report. *Maintenance Depot Number 4—Iganga.* When they learned of its existence they would come here in strength, and they wouldn't wait for daylight to do it.

"If I were Bathar," Lew muttered to himself, aloud in the darkness, "what would I do?"

Go to the depot. Then run, taking the pickup. But he *hadn't* taken the pickup.

Still, the depot would be first. Maybe that's where he passed out again, or where he just sat down in a funk and abandoned hope.

Lew had left the Army truck just below the level crossing. Now he went back to it, swung aboard, started the engine, switched on the lights, and backed down as far as Ellen's Road. Then he angled around, turning the wheel as energetically as Frank at his worst, and drove in.

But Bathar wasn't there. The four last freight cars stood patiently on the spur track, waiting to be the major item of evidence in the coming investigation. Empty beer bottles littered the landscape as though all the softball teams in Chicago had come here together for a picnic. Small animals scuttled away from the light, disturbed from picking through the leftover bits of food. When Lew shut off the engine and stood out on the running board to listen, he could hear the water at the bottom of the cliff gnawing at the rocky shore of Thruston Bay. "Bathar!" he called, four times, once in each cardinal direction, but there was no answer.

Driving back out Ellen's Road, he went more slowly, studying the undergrowth to left and right. At the access road he stopped again and called Bathar's name, then turned uphill and went back up to the railway line.

"He's gone, that's all." Wandering in the woods, or trying to make it across Uganda to the border on foot, or unconscious somewhere not far from here, or after all dead.

Lew put Young Mr. Balim out of his mind. He had wasted his time coming back here, had accomplished nothing but to strand himself. Having jumped over the cliff, it was now time to figure out how not to fall.

Young Mr. Balim had chosen not to take the pickup, but Lew would prefer it to the Army truck, which at the moment might call too much attention to itself. Leaving its headlights on to operate by, he crossed the tracks on foot, opened the pickup's hood, and smeared his face and hands with black engine grease. Then he dragged the dead man out onto the ground and rolled him away from the road, cleaning the grease from his palms on the back of the man's coat.

The pickup's engine was reluctant to awaken; it kept coughing and going back to sleep, like a drunk in a doorway. But Lew was patient with it, like a Salvation Army girl, and at last the coughs became continuous, the engine came completely awake, and when Lew let out the clutch, it actually went to work.

He turned around on the level crossing, then headed uphill to the main road, the springless wheels bouncing and pounding on the washboard surface. At the verge of route A109, two lanes of empty silent blacktop in the darkness, he hesitated for just a second.

This was where they'd grabbed him, right here. The memory of the State Research Bureau returned, strong and vivid, every stench, every evil sight of it. He couldn't go back there; he *dared not* go back there. They would remember him as clearly as he remembered them, and he knew this time what they would do. They would begin by damaging one or both of his legs, to keep him from going anywhere. They might also remove some of his fingers or possibly just cut off both his hands. Then they'd be ready to begin.

His body ached in anticipation. His wrists burned, feeling the blade. "Damn Bathar," he muttered.

No. It's damn Chase, or possibly damn everybody. Or just damn himself for volunteering, for not being able to ignore the image of Mr. Balim hearing the news. It was to avoid being there when Mr. Balim was told that had made him come back into the horror.

"I could be on the raft," he muttered, "halfway home." He fought the floor-shift lever into first gear, let out the clutch, and drove out onto A109, turning left, west, toward Jinja and Kampala. "Halfway home," he repeated.

65

"Rest," Isaac said.

The dripping man, exhausted, nodded and let his body sag back onto the tarpaulin-covered coffee sacks, while Isaac walked back to the man working the steering stick to tell him the change in direction. The other two men on this raft squatted beside the weary messenger, staring at him with wide eyes. Pirates!

Isaac didn't use that melodramatic word. "We're changing our route," he told the steersman. "There may be a ship by Matale Point meaning to steal the coffee from us. So we'll go around the other side of Sigulu."

"Much longer," the steersman said.

"But safer," Isaac told him. "If that ship is really there."

The steersman was truculent. "You should have given us all guns," he said.

"Oh, it's better if we don't have to fight. Try to keep up close to the raft ahead."

"We should have guns out here," the steersman insisted.

"Nothing to do about that now," Isaac told him, and went away forward, not wanting any more of that conversation. Nor did he intend to be baited into repeating Lew's reasons for not arming these amateurs. He himself was an amateur, and he had no doubt but that Lew had been right.

The messenger still sprawled on his back, gazing up at the quarter-moon, his chest heaving. Over the last hour he had nine times dived into the water, swum from one raft to the next, clambered up the twelve-foot wall of sacks, and repeated Frank Lanigan's message; then, after a brief rest, he had dived again. By the fifth time he had become very tired, and others had offered to carry the message the rest of the way, but he had refused. Like most of the men, he lived in fear of Frank Lanigan—which Frank, who knew only Charlie's cheekiness, would have been astonished and a bit abashed to know—and *he* was the one to whom Frank Lanigan had entrusted this commission. He would delegate it to no one, but would finish the job himself. He had, too, though he'd come close to drowning on the final two laps, and was now so worn he couldn't even return Isaac's encouraging smile.

"Sigulu," said one of the other men, and pointed ahead and to the left.

Isaac squinted but couldn't yet see it. Despite the quarter-moon, despite the almost cloudless sky filled with high small white pinpricks of stars, it was a very dark night, the lake a deep black velvet, its softness obscuring all outlines. The coast of Uganda had disappeared behind them almost the instant they'd quitted Macdonald Bay, and ever since they might just as well have been in the middle of the Atlantic Ocean or traveling on some fuzzy black cloud between the planets.

The man who had pointed at Sigulu Island said, "Are there really pirates, Mr. Otera?"

"Well, there are certainly thieves in this world," Isaac said, smiling, trying to make a joke of it to reassure the man. "We just stole a train. When you do that sort of thing on the water, they call you a pirate."

The other man said, "You can't steal a train on the water."

The first man gave him a pitying look. "How can a person be so stupid?" he asked.

A wheezing sound distracted them all. It was the messenger, too exhausted to laugh, laughing. That made the others laugh, and when they'd stopped they were all friends again. "I see the island now," Isaac said.

It was a low shape ahead of them. The next raft forward was already angling to the right to go around the island's blunt end. By day, you would be able to see the coasts of both Uganda and Kenya from here, but now nothing was visible but that furry back humped up out of the water.

Isaac went aft to sit near the steersman and watch Sigulu Island move slowly past. The island was a good ten miles long, and at their current rate would probably be there on the left for nearly an hour.

Half an hour after they'd first spotted Sigulu Island, the steersman said in a strangely hushed voice, "Mr. Otera."

"Yes?"

"There's something behind us, Mr. Otera."

A chill ran down Isaac's spine. At first he didn't even think of the pirates. Being out here alone on the water, emptiness all about, and then the odd wording of the steersman—"There's *something* behind us"—made Isaac think first of ghosts, or lake monsters, supernatural and incomprehensible. But when he turned about, the hairs rising up on the nape of his neck, that black shape he saw bearing down on them, running without lights, cutting a harsh white V of foam through the water, was nothing otherworldly at all, except in name. It was the *Angel*, tired of waiting, seeking them in the open water of the lake. And finding them.

The *Angel*, originally named *Kikuyu*, had been built under commission to the Marine Services Division of the Kenya & Uganda Railway in 1925, and until the *Victoria* was finished in 1959 she was the largest ship on the lake. Two hundred thirty-seven feet long, with a beam of thirty-seven feet, she had a cargo capacity of eleven hundred tons. But she possessed almost no passenger space, and the railway found her wastefully large, so in 1963 they sold her to a private company. She had had four owners and three names by now and was showing signs of her final decline: rust, persistent leaks, rotted hoses, and uncertain engines. But she was still big, and when traveling empty she was still fast, and she came steaming onto the rafts like Juggernaut, high-sided, black, inexorable.

"Down!" Isaac screamed. "The pirates!" And he flattened himself face down on the tarpaulin.

White light bathed him: a searchlight from the ship's prow. Not looking up, Isaac folded his hands over his head, crushed his nose down into the rough gray canvas, and prayed for invisibility.

The stuttering sound was so diminished by the great emptiness of the lake that he didn't at first realize it was a machine gun, strafing them. Screams mingled with the stutter, and the flat crack of rifle fire joined in.

They're not giving us a chance! Isaac thought, as though they were all playing some game with rules. Terrified, believing himself already dead, he pressed lower and lower onto the lumpy sacks of coffee beans. A wasp stung the back of his left leg, and he whimpered into the canvas.

The machine gunner had a problem. He was firing down on the rafts from a greater height, and was under orders to avoid shooting up the cargo as much as possible. The men who lay flat made extremely difficult targets, but those who sat up or paused to shout or ran to the edge to jump were simple hits. Those who actually did jump overboard were picked off in the water by the riflemen, guided by the smaller spotlights.

When the white glare flicked away from Isaac he lifted his staring eyes and saw the *Angel* already passing the next raft, pinning it in the beam of the searchlights, the guns chattering and cracking.

On this raft, the steersman and one passenger were simply gone, leaving Isaac and the messenger and one other man. Isaac scrambled to them on all fours, crying, "Are you hurt? Are you hurt?"

Neither had been hit, though both were as panicky as Isaac himself, who had a three-inch gash burned in the fat of his upper leg. Teeth chattering, the messenger said, "What do we do? They'll come back!"

"Swim to Sigulu," Isaac said. "It's our only chance."

Shocked, the other man said, "Sigulu is in Uganda! Mr. Otera, tomorrow—!"

"God help us then," Isaac said. "But if we stay here now, they'll kill us sure."

The messenger cried, "Look! Look!"

The *Angel*, hurrying past the third raft, was suddenly veering off, no longer shooting, steering toward the open lake. Beyond her was a confusion of movement, other lights, the crackle of other guns. While Isaac stared, trying to sort out what he was seeing, there came the authoritative *phoom* of a small naval gun, a flash of muzzle fire, and a great spout of water burst up beside the turning *Angel*.

"More pirates!" the messenger screamed, and dropped to his knees. "Oh, Mother Mary! Oh, Mother Mary, gaze upon your little child!"

The naval gun barked again, this time the waterspout springing up behind the *Angel*. Isaac could see more clearly now, and could make out that two ships were in pursuit of the pirates. Small lean fast cutters, they were painted white and festooned with lights. First one fired its gun, then the other.

The fourth shot caught the *Angel* high on her port side, behind the bridge. Smoke at once billowed up, as though it had been preexisting, imprisoned inside there, and an instant later orange flames peeked through the new breach in the hull.

The two pursuing ships flanked the *Angel*, repeatedly firing, closing the distance, the guns achieving a practice-range accuracy. Holes and smoke and flame transformed the *Angel* into a writhing stage set of disaster on the placid lake. Twisting figures showed against the orange flames as they fell or leaped into the water.

While one of the white ships remained close to the *Angel*, continuing while she died to harry her with shot, the other veered away in a great sweeping circle that brought it at last behind the line of rafts. As it came forward, Isaac saw the flag whipping at its fantail: three horizontal stripes, black and red and green, separated by narrow white bands, and with crossed spears and a Masai shield in the center. The flag of Kenya. The Kenyan Navy. "We've been rescued," Isaac whispered. His breath was a painful rasp in his throat.

The rescuers slowed beside the raft, bathing it with their own searchlight. "Smugglers," said a bullhorned voice. "You are under arrest. You will proceed with us to landfall at Port Victoria."

"Thank you, Mother Mary," the messenger said.

But the other man was indignant. As the Navy ship went on to deliver its message to the other rafts he glared after it, hands on hips. "This is Uganda territory!" he announced. "They can't arrest *us*!"

"You must tell them that," Isaac said, "after we are very safe."

66

Patricia's small house on Nakasero Hill was, like Patricia herself, neat and modern and beautifully adorned, and yet impersonal. But Patricia felt herself to be no longer impersonal—Denis had made that change in her—so she could move from this house, which she had loved, without regret.

She had never brought Denis here before, possibly because of an unconscious fear that the house would reveal too much about her true self, but now it was merely a discarded shell, the cocoon of her former person. When she brought him here now, the intent was to be self-revelatory, to show him the emptiness he had filled, the reason for her gratitude.

And also, of course, this was to have been their last night in Kampala. The plan had been that Denis would finish his business with the coffee shipment out of Entebbe sometime today, they would spend tonight here in Patricia's house, and tomorrow they would fly away forever. But now that the train had broken down there was a very annoying delay; of no longer than one day, certainly, but annoying nevertheless.

Patricia had planned the menu and the evening with great care. Her cook was a Ugandan woman who had spent years in the employ of a wealthy Ugandan Asian family. Those people had taken her with them on their frequent vacations to Europe and had sent her to various cooking courses in France and Switzerland. She was now a culinary artist of sensitivity and skill, who cast a knowing yet still loving eye over the raw materials available to her in Uganda, adapting her sophisticated knowledge to the local fare.

She and Patricia had planned tonight's dinner together, through the cook's tears. (She was staying behind in Uganda, with her family; Patricia had given her a farewell bonus that had made her heart stop for just a second. They were truly fond of one another.)

The cook, as her final act in Patricia's employ, served the meal. Patricia and Denis sat in the small dining room beside the window looking out onto her garden, which was illuminated by small amber spotlights hidden under the eaves; smiling, Patricia said, "This is who we are now."

Denis poured the gentle Pouilly-Fuissé, and they toasted themselves. Then dinner began, with African avocados, plump and sweet and buttery, with a crayfish filling. The same wine took them through a course of grilled lakefish, the tastes delicate and evanescent, hiding in the firm nonoily meat.

The main course was a lamb curry with many sweet and spicy condiments, and lentils, and string beans as small and thin as a cat's whiskers, and to go with it a clear Château Montrose Médoc. Dessert was various fruits—mangoes, different kinds of melon, passion fruit, pineapple—with a homemade sorbet, and accompanied by a light dry Zeltinger Moselle.

They lingered for hours over the meal, now alone in the house, and at its end they made love, gently and without urgency.

Later, they went through the house selecting what Patricia would take with her and what leave behind. There were small objects, beautiful in themselves, which she no longer wanted because of the circumstances of their acquisition. She found herself explaining these rejections, and they became a kind of autobiography and confession, an emptying out of the past. Denis stood with her, holding the small things in his hands, listening to her stories, accepting them, erasing them from existence, giving her absolution with his nod and his smile.

The knock at the door, shortly before midnight, was only a minor annoyance and interruption—a servant returning for some forgotten possession, something like that—until Patricia opened it and the four State Research Bureau men came in, angry-looking with their beetle-browed glares, foolish but menacing in their nylon shirts and platform shoes and flare-bottomed pants. "Patricia Kamin," one of them said.

"You know me," Patricia answered, and they did. And she knew all four of them, if only by sight. And although she didn't understand yet what the trouble was, she knew at once it was very serious.

But her first fear was for Denis, who came into the living room holding in his hand a piece of ivory carved to the shape of a rose,

with a bit of stem and two very sharp thorns. "May we help you?"
he asked, looking coldly at the four men, doing that British thing of
showing anger by becoming very correct and polite.

The men ignored him. One of them said to Patricia, "You come
with us."

"She most certainly will not," Denis said, stepping boldly forward.
"Just what do you—"

"Denis!" She was terrified for him; he clearly didn't understand
the thinness of this ice. "Don't, Denis."

"I know about this country, Patricia," he told her. "I'm certainly
not going to let you go off with these—"

Two of the men approached to take her arms. Then it moved very
quickly. Denis, saying something else, tried to intervene; the man
who had spoken to her reached out to push Denis away; Denis lifted
the hand with the ivory carving in it; the man grabbed the carving
out of his hand, then cried out and dropped it on the floor; he stared
in horror at the blood dots in his palm where the thorns had stabbed
him. "Poison!" he cried. "You poisoned me!"

"No!" Patricia screamed, and would have thrown herself between
them but the other two men gripped her arms tightly; and the man
who thought he was poisoned pulled a small pistol from his hip pocket
and shot Denis three times in the face.

They then spent five minutes there, twisting Patricia's arms and
pulling her hair to make her tell them the name of the poison and its
antidote. "No poison," she kept saying over and over, not caring what
they did or what happened. Whenever they released her head she
looked again at poor Denis sprawled on the floor. He had never believed
how bad they were. He had never been willing to know just how bad
human beings can be, and the unwillingness had finally killed him.

After five minutes, when the man with the cuts realized he was
feeling no symptoms, he gave up the idea that he'd been poisoned.
"Bring her along," he said. "That man. Making fun of me." He went
over to kick the body to relieve his feelings, then followed Patricia
and the others out of the house.

67

When the two government officials took the radio equipment out of the trunk of the Mercedes and set it up on the car's hood, Balim was at first baffled. They'd already brought a truckload of soldiers with them to Port Victoria, these same soldiers now sprawled at their ease over the grassy slope between the hotel and the shore; who was left for these so-very-civil civil servants to get in touch with?

Someone. Godfrey Magon picked up the microphone and called a lot of letters and numbers into it, over and over, with maddening patience and to no effect at all, till abruptly the radio spoke in a snarling voice so distorted by static and a poor speaker system that Balim couldn't understand a word of what was said. Apparently, though, Godfrey Magon could; he replied in rapid sentences, quick questions that were answered with the same loud brusque incomprehensibility. Finally satisfied, Magon put down the microphone, lit a cigar, and leaned against the Mercedes's fender to gaze with benign self-complacence at the dark lake.

Meanwhile, Charles Obuong was admiring the hotel in the flickering light of the smoky oil-drum fire. "Good workmanship," he told Balim. "I'm glad to see you took it seriously and not merely as a diversion."

"I'm a businessman," Balim answered. That was a point he wanted in the forefront of Obuong's mind. He missed Isaac acutely; this was precisely the sort of person Isaac always handled.

"You are a very good businessman," Obuong said. "I don't doubt that, not at all." Nodding at the unfinished hotel, he said, "Do you know what I foresee for this place?"

Balim foresaw nothing further than a sale at a modest profit to some retired Britisher or German who desired, on a small nest egg, to play African innkeeper. "I am eager to know," he said.

"Here in Kenya," Obuong began, in the style of a cocktail-party bore with a set piece to deliver, "we are creating a traditional civilization. That is, a civilization based on a growing middle class. Not socialism, not Tanzania's collective farms"—said with some disdain—"nor the feudal states of most of black Africa, with their widening gulf between the rich few and the poor many. No; here in Kenya we are replicating, in less than a hundred years, the entire history of Europe."

"Interesting," Balim said politely.

Obuong smiled at him in the firelight. "More than interesting for *you*, Mr. Balim. Vital for you. The Asian must accommodate himself to Kenya if he wishes to survive here. So he must know what Kenya is, and what it is not."

Balim said, "Mr. Obuong, can it be that you are friendly in spirit toward me?"

Obuong's smile almost became a laugh, but then was replaced by earnestness. "Your former land," he said, "is a very unhappy one. If the same sort of thing were to happen here, I personally would live in fear all the minutes of my life. I would be exposed because of my governmental position, and my success, and my education. A contented middle-class Kenya is necessary to my peace of mind."

Admiringly Balim said, "Very few people, of any rank or color, have thought it through quite that clearly."

"Whatever my personal opinions may be," Obuong said, "and I will admit to you privately that I have my ambivalences, nevertheless I know that a Kenyan middle class must be heterogeneous. We need the Asian shopkeepers; we need the white farmers; we even need the Arabs from the coast."

Smiling, Balim said, "Even?"

"Some of my ambivalence," Obuong said, and shrugged. "I can get along with all sorts, if I must, to have a peaceful and comfortable life. Which brings me back, Mr. Balim, to this fine hotel of yours."

"Ah, yes, my hotel."

"Our tourist industry is still supported almost completely by the northern whites," Obuong said, "but, as you know, those people will never come *here*."

"One can hope," Balim murmured.

"An intelligent businessman does not live on hope. We both know, Mr. Balim, this will never be a place for foreign whites to visit, despite the lake, the harbor, the potential. But what of our *own* middle class, eh? On my holiday, shall I go to Treetops to be stared at by the Swedes and Americans as though I were one of the exotic animals at the water hole? Where is *my* tourist spot, Mr. Balim?"

"*Very* interesting," Balim said, this time meaning it.

"The growing middle class," Obuong said, nodding at the hotel. "That's the hope of the future for your hotel, Mr. Balim, as it is my personal hope for my personal future. Do not sell the hotel when this is all over. Do not throw it away." Lowering his voice, turning his shoulder against his partner, Magon, over by the car, he said, "We can talk again, a little later. A few months from now."

In Balim's mind the flower opened. A partnership with Obuong, government influence, links to the Ministry of Tourism and Wildlife, improved roads, subsidiary businesses . . . I must buy a great deal more land here, Balim thought, knowing that Obuong was thinking the same thing. But I must buy through fronts, natives, not with the name Balim attached. Isaac can—

"Look!"

It was Magon. When Balim turned, Magon was standing beside the Mercedes, pointing out at the lake. "Ah, now," Obuong said, awed, below his breath.

Far out on the lake, flames were leaping up, smoky and orange; an imitation of their oil-drum fire on a massive scale. "Bathar!" Balim called, and ran heavily down to the water's edge, where he stood staring at the oblong bowl of flame against the black night. Sounds of guns and explosions came faintly over the water.

Obuong had immediately shouted something at Magon, who grabbed up the microphone and called into it, his voice merely excited. Obuong, meanwhile, came down to stand beside Balim and say, "Your son is with them?"

"Yes."

"I'm surprised. I hadn't thought—"

The abruptness with which Obuong cut off the sentence made Balim turn to give him a bitter smile. "You hadn't thought Asians took their own risks, did their own dirty work. He wouldn't be there if it were up to me. Bathar is already heterogeneous, part of your middle class. Shopkeepers know better than to *look for* adventure."

"That's no raft burning," Obuong said, "it's a ship. Come along; we'll find out what's happening."

They went over together to the Mercedes, where the radio was responding to Magon's questions. But Balim still found the radio voice unintelligible and was grateful when Magon translated: "A ship attacked the rafts. We have interceded."

"In whose waters?" Obuong wanted to know.

Balim had his own more urgent question. While Magon relayed Obuong's query through the radio, Balim said, "*Who* has interceded?"

"We have," Obuong said. "The Navy. We put two patrol boats out there to make sure nothing went wrong." With a limpid smile, he added, "Such as the rafts deciding to make for a different landfall."

Magon said, "They're in Ugandan waters, but there was no choice. It's the *Angel*, out of Kisumu. It was firing on the rafts."

Balim touched the cool flank of the Mercedes for support. I'm a businessman, I shouldn't be involved in these things, nor should Bathar. Let him go to London. There, the middle class has won.

The radio continued to snarl, and Magon continued to translate: "They have attacked the *Angel* and sunk her."

The distant sounds of firing still continued. Obuong, sounding angry, said, "She isn't sunk, we can see her burning."

"She's as good as sunk," Magon said. "There were no survivors." He shrugged with the microphone. "Let them play."

Obuong, grim-faced, caught Balim looking at him and managed a small smile. "I hate disorder," he said. "Excessive force. I am no friend of chaos."

"But chaos has many friends in Africa, still," Balim said, looking out at the burning ship.

68

Pistol in his right hand, Lew slipped into the dim church, which was lit only by three candles on the altar at the far end. Three old women dressed in white knelt in front pews, praying. A young man in a black cassock and large round eyeglasses crossed the altar and disappeared through a low door at the side. The silence of the church was accented by the sibilant whispers of the praying women.

Driving through Bugembe in the old pickup truck, just a few miles before Jinja, seeing the town's name on the road sign, Lew had remembered Bishop Michael Kibudu from the dreadful holding cell in the State Research Bureau. Evangelical Baptist Mission; he'd spoken with pride of his church in Bugembe. But that had been only a passing memory, unimportant until Lew had driven into Jinja and had seen the police check at the bridge.

He must cross the Nile to get to Entebbe. If one bridge at Jinja was blocked, the other would also be. The next nearest bridge was forty miles north at Mbulamuti, and why wouldn't that also be blocked? A white face blackened with grease would not get him through a police check; that was why he had turned around and come back to Bugembe. There was nowhere else to go for help.

He felt terribly exposed as he walked down the center aisle to the altar, right hand holding the pistol under his shirt, but none of the women looked up from their exhortations. Stepping over the rail, Lew went through the low door into a small sacristy, whose wooden walls were covered with hung vestments. The young clergyman was at a rolltop desk in the corner, copying numbers from a hymnal by the light of a kerosene lamp. He lifted his head to stare at Lew, his eyes startled behind the large glasses. "It's all right," Lew told him, fast and low, as he closed the door. "I'm a friend of Bishop Kibudu."

The clergyman got to his feet. His manner, though frightened, was alert and suspicious. "You know the bishop? May I ask from where?"

"The State Research Bureau. We were in a cell there together."

Astonishment replaced apprehension. "*You're* the white man? The bishop was certain you had died. We remember you in our prayers."

"Not a bad idea," Lew said.

"The bishop will be delighted," the clergyman said, clasping his hands together in front of himself like a much older man.

It was Lew's turn to be astonished. "*He's* alive?" He brought his hand out empty from under his shirt.

"Oh, yes, our bishop has come back to us. Are the police after you?"

Lew grinned. "The police, the Army; you name it."

"Wait here," the clergyman said, and went out through a door in the opposite wall.

It was only after the clergyman had gone that it occurred to Lew that he'd taken the man on faith, with no particular reason to do so. Why would Kibudu be alive? Why wouldn't this curate, or whatever he was, to save his own skin, be calling the police right now? I should have gone with him, Lew thought, his hand reaching again for the comfort of the pistol under his shirt.

But it actually was Bishop Kibudu who next came in through that door, beaming from ear to ear, rolling forward, arms outstretched for a bear hug, crying, "God is wonderful, God is good! You have lifted my spirits!"

"And you mine," Lew said, grinning back, permitting himself to be crushed in the bishop's surprisingly strong embrace. Then they stood at arm's length to study each other, and Lew was happy to see that only a few small scars around the bishop's eyes remained as visible reminders of his time at the State Research Bureau. Cleaned up, horn-rim glasses perched on his broad nose, he looked more a scholar than a bishop, and not at all like a broken victim in a foul dungeon.

He himself, he knew, was not that presentable. The bishop laughed at his appearance, saying, "That's not much of a disguise, that dirt on your face."

"I've been driving; I didn't want anyone to notice a white face going by. Bishop, how did you get out of there?"

"An attorney in Jinja named Byagwa," the bishop said. "Sometimes he can help in religious cases. Fortunately, mine was one of the problems in which his persistence finally bore fruit. But what of you?"

The young clergyman had also come in and shut the door, and now stood smiling to one side, hands clasped in front of himself. Lew said, "A friend of mine in Kenya managed to get through to somebody in the government here. They convinced the Research Bureau it was all a mistake."

"You were very fortunate indeed," the bishop said blandly. "Oh, by the way," he said, gesturing at the young priest, "this is my assistant, Father Njuguna."

Lew and Father Njuguna smiled and nodded at one another. Bishop Kibudu watched Lew's face, his manner still smiling and friendly. "Your popping up again," he said, "suggests that you weren't entirely candid with me last time."

"I don't think I will be this time either," Lew admitted, and shrugged. "I'm involved in a little something. Nothing you could endorse, but you wouldn't oppose it, either. We're giving Idi Amin one in the eye, in a small way. Not an important way, but every little bit helps."

"It has been said," the bishop commented, "that you can tell a man by the quality of his enemies. That's all I need to know about you."

"Thank you."

"You need help. I hope it's something within my grasp to do."

"I'm trying to get out of the country," Lew said, and grinned again, adding, "For obvious reasons."

The bishop nodded.

"I have a way out," Lew went on, "if I can get to Entebbe. But the Nile bridge is blocked. If I can get across it, I'll be all right."

"Is that all?" the bishop asked. "You simply want to get across the Nile?"

"Yes, please."

"Nothing could be simpler," the bishop said. "Come along."

* * *

In the church basement, by the light of another kerosene lantern, the bishop showed Lew his coffin. "You will be very comfortable in it, I assure you," he said.

"I don't particularly *want* to be comfortable in it," Lew told him.

Earnest young Father Njuguna said, in complete seriousness, "You'll be the first to use it."

Lew laughed. "That's good to know. Just so I'm not the last."

Bishop Kibudu said, "We shall paint your face and hands with colors that would make a grown man faint, suggestive of various terrible diseases. We shall put a little piece of very strong cheese in the coffin with you. I myself will drive our hearse, and Father Njuguna will drive your own vehicle. In no time at all, you will be on the other side of the Nile." Grinning like Mr. Pickwick, he made a clerical joke: "That's not the Jordan, mind you. The Nile."

Lew said, "Bishop, I can't tell you how much I appreciate this."

"But it's nothing," the bishop protested. "It's so very little a thing, a brief drive to Jinja and back. Are you sure there's nothing more we can do? Drive you on to Entebbe?"

"No, no, I'll be fine once I'm across that bridge. I don't want to make fresh trouble for you."

"Man is born to trouble as the sparks fly upward," the bishop quoted. "And never more so than in Uganda. May your path be easy from here on."

"Thank you."

"And may you," the bishop said, "find no employment for that pistol under your shirt."

69

Landing being such a delicate operation, Frank handled it himself, running the raft aground with such violence that the man standing at the front of the pile of sacks fell off into the shallow water and sat up muddy and sputtering. "Shit," Frank commented, pulled the rope that shut down the outboard motors, and looked at Port Victoria.

It had become practically a metropolis. An Army truck to one side apparently contained a generator, to feed a pair of floodlights in which the smoky oil-drum fire looked neurotic and useless. Kenyan Army troops lolled on the ground at their ease, an official Mercedes-Benz was parked in the center of things, a pair of government civil-service types waited with their fat-cat smiles firmly in place, and here came Mr. Balim down to the water's edge, calling across, "Frank! Where's Bathar?"

"Shit," Frank said again. "Be right there!" he called, then turned to Charlie, saying, "You might as well untie Chase now. He isn't going anywhere." And to Chase he said, "I'm now going to have a talk with Balim Senior. Any message, you son of a bitch?"

But Chase had nothing to say. He looked toward the lights and people in expressionless silence.

Frank climbed down the wall of sacks, waded through the shallow water to the shore, and said, "Mr. Balim, Lew went back to get him."

Shock made Balim look like a round-headed hand puppet. "Back? Back where?"

"Your old pal Chase joined the party." Frank was aware of the civil-service types coming this way, and hurried through his story. "He bushwacked Young—your son, up at the depot. Knocked him out and left him there. Lew volunteered to go back and get him."

"In *Uganda*? They're both in Uganda?" Balim stared across the water as though he could see them. "How will they—? What will they do?"

"Get to Ellen at Entebbe. That's Lew's idea." As the government men arrived, Frank said, "Lew's very good, Mr. Balim. He'll get out. But to help him, I've got to get to a phone as soon as I can."

One of the government men, blandly smiling, said, "Is there a problem?"

"Nothing serious," Frank told him. "Listen, I just got here, I'm kind of confused. Okay if I talk to my boss privately a minute?"

One of them started to frown, but the other one smiled and said, "But of course. You'd be Mr. Lanigan? Take all the time you need, Mr. Lanigan."

While the government men went back over to the Mercedes, talking quietly together, and the second raft bunked quietly ashore beside the first, Frank led Balim upslope and off to one side, saying, "Fill me in. What's going on here?"

"The Kenyan government knew what we were doing," Balim told him. "They could have stopped us, but they let it happen for their own reasons."

"They don't like Amin, either."

"That would be one of the reasons, I suppose." Balim glanced away toward the lake, clearly still distracted by thoughts of his son; but then he called himself back, saying, "There's also money. Less for us, some for those fellows and their friends."

"Very cute," Frank said. "We do all the heavy work, they get all the gravy."

"The very definition of a government," Balim suggested. "Who were those people attacking you out there?"

"More hanky-panky from Chase. He set us up to be hijacked."

"I should never have done business with that man," Balim said. "And please don't say 'I told you so.' "

"I'm biting my tongue."

Balim frowned. "But what's he doing now?"

Frank turned to look over at the Mercedes, where Chase, looking like the beachcomber in a Maugham story, was in confidential conversation with the two government men, both of whom seemed quite interested. Frank said, "Selling some windows and orphans, I suppose."

Quietly Balim murmured, "Frank. If Bathar does not come back, would you do me a great service? Would you kill that Baron Chase?"

"My pleasure," Frank said. "I don't know why I never did it before."

70

There were no telephones in the transient aircrews' quarters at Entebbe. When the word came just before midnight that there was a phone call for her in the lobby, Ellen was seated on her bed reading an Agatha Christie, and was not yet far enough into it to realize she'd read it before. She frowned at the knock on the door, calling out, "What is it?"

"Telephone, missus." It was the night floorman, who insisted for some reason on calling Ellen "missus."

Telephone? Unless it was somebody from Coast Global to say they were washing the whole operation—which was not a bad idea—Ellen couldn't think who might call her here. "Be right out," she answered, reluctantly put down the paperback, and slipped into her shoes.

The coffee train, of course, had not arrived. The official story was that the train had broken down the other side of Jinja, which was even possibly the truth, but Ellen in her secret smiling heart knew they'd pulled it off. Lew and Frank and all of them, they'd really done it; they'd slipped into Uganda, knocked off that blessed train, and skinned back out again with all that coffee. More power to them. Tomorrow, or the next day, or whenever she finally got out of Uganda, she might make a phone call of her own, a nice circumspect call of congratulations on a job well done.

In the meantime, her own job wasn't getting done at all. There were confusions about payment, there were conflicting orders as to whether or not the other coffee that actually had arrived via truck from west-central Uganda should be loaded onto the planes, and nobody seemed to know who was in charge or what was supposed to happen. Three of the planes had been loaded, not including Ellen's, and two of them had taken off, the pilot of one saying to Ellen before departure, "If they won't pay us, we'll sell their coffee ourselves." Anarchy was becoming the rule of the day. Perhaps the Ugandans had also figured that out, because the third full plane was barred from taking off, and the other five members of the fleet continued to stand empty.

The phones were across from the check-in desk, in small booths with windowed doors. "Number three," the night clerk said, and Ellen went into booth number three, picked up the receiver, and said, "Hello?"

The first voice she heard belonged to a male operator, who wanted to know if she was absolutely and for certain no-fooling Ellen Gillespie. Once she'd convinced him she was, there followed a silence so long she was about to give up and return to Agatha Christie, when all at once Frank's voice came roaring into her ear: "—from a hole in the ground!"

"Frank?" She believed it, but she didn't believe it. "Frank, is that you?"

"Ellen? By Christ, have I got through at last?"

She thought, He's going to say something awful about Lew. "Frank? What's going on?"

"Lemme give you the message quick," he said, "before these assholes fuck up again. An old pal of yours from Alaska was just in town, looking for you."

That made no sense, no sense at all. "Who?"

"Fella named Val, uh, dammit, Val—"

Then she got it. "Deez?"

"Dietz! That's it, Val Dietz."

"What did old Val have to say for himself?" Ellen asked, wondering why Lew would use such a roundabout way to get in touch with her. Did he think she was mad at him or something?

"He's gone on to Uganda now," Frank said, being as casual as a fanfare of trumpets.

"Uganda? He's *here?*"

"Right. He says he hopes to get to Entebbe sometime in the next twenty-four hours, maybe he can buy you a drink."

"I'd—" She gripped the receiver with both hands, turning her back on the glass door. "I'd be delighted. I hope he shows up."

"Oh, he's a reliable fellow," Frank said. "Nice to talk with you, Ellen."

"You, too, Frank."

She hung up, but stayed in the booth half a minute until she had her emotions and her facial expressions under control. The coffee had been stolen. Frank was apparently okay. Lew was still in Uganda. He was trying to make his way here. "Oh, my God," she whispered, and took a deep breath, and went out of the booth to the lobby, where she saw the night clerk avidly watching something going on outside.

The view out the glass front doors was across an empty parking lot toward the main terminal building. Signs just before the parking lot pointed toward the botanical garden and zoo down on the lakeshore. In the parking lot, under a floodlight on a tall pole, four black men were wrestling with a white man.

Lew! she thought, but as she stepped closer to the lobby doors she recognized the white man as the middle-aged American pilot named Mike. He ran Uganda Skytours; he had brought her here just the other day. Yes, and he'd brought Lew back to Kisumu that time.

And now they were beating him very severely, those four garishly dressed men. Ellen turned to see if the night clerk were phoning the police, but he had turned away and was busily filing a lot of small cards in a metal drawer. She faced front again, to see two black Toyotas pull up to the struggling man, and realized she was watching the secret police make an arrest. The men, with Mike, all piled into the two cars and were driven rapidly away.

Ellen went over to the desk. "You saw that," she said.

"Oh, you don't want to see things in Uganda," he told her, not looking up from his filing. "No, no, nothing to see around here."

Ellen shook her head. "But . . . why did they do it? He isn't anything bad, he's just a pilot."

He sneaked her a quick look. "You know him?"

"He flew me here."

The night clerk studied his filing. "Many young pilots back," he said, as though he weren't talking to her at all. "Air Force pilots, come home, thrown out of America." Slamming the little file drawer in a satisfied manner, he nodded and said, "Uganda Skytours. New owner for that plane tomorrow. Good night." And he went through into the inner office, shutting the door behind himself.

71

Patricia, crammed into the backseat of the Toyota between two of her captors, slowly rose through the warm comfortable gelatin layers of shock toward the knife-edge pain of reality. Reluctantly she drifted up to that spinning, hopeless, fast-moving world in which she no longer wanted to struggle to stay alive.

But the habit of life, the habit of struggle, was too ingrained. Despite herself, the external world's signals were still being received; she became aware that they were not on their way to the State Research Bureau but were traveling east instead on Jinja Road. Why was that? She didn't want to ask the question, she didn't want to have to think, but her mind insisted, it kept turning the problem over, and even offered a theoretical solution: Whoever did this doesn't want me where I can reach my friends. They're taking me to Jinja Barracks.

A vision of men came unbidden into her mind, a room filled with men all smiling at her in a horrible way. They cared nothing about her wit, her elegance; they coveted her beauty only to mangle and destroy it. In the vision they moved closer.

The future was unbearable, but so was the past. Memory plucked at her, the memory of Denis falling dead, taking away with him into that nothingness the brightest and happiest future she had ever known. Leaving her with this instead: abasement, degradation, horror, and at long last death.

The men in the car were talking about her, laughing and telling one another what the soldiers at Jinja Barracks would do to her. Of course she had the strength to hate, but what good was that? There would be no revenge, no escape. She was now nothing but a trinket for boys to play with and break. Let me die, she asked herself, pleading with that active brain to stop its fussing, turn itself off, rescue her the only way that was left.

Could I try to escape, so they'd shoot and kill me?

The man on her right roughly stroked her thigh. "We ought to take some of this ourselves," he said. "Before they mess it up at Jinja."

The driver laughed, agreeing. "She won't look so good tomorrow."

"Stop somewhere," the man on her right said, gripping her leg.

"When we're out of the city," the driver said.

Let me die. Please.

72

They did open the coffin. Lew hadn't believed they would, but they did. They took one look at him, and one whiff of him, and slammed the lid so hard it bounced. He heard them jabbering away out there at Bishop Kibudu, and then came the solid *thunk* of the hearse's side door being slammed. Lew breathed a sigh of relief, forgetting about the cheese, and then had to hold his breath till the nausea became less acute.

It had been too nice a dinner to throw up, particularly while flat on one's back in a coffin at a police checkpoint on the Nile. Lew swallowed, and held his breath again, and counted slowly in his mind. When I get to five hundred, he promised himself, I'll surrender to the police.

The dinner had been at Bishop Kibudu's insistence. He simply wouldn't permit Lew to cross his path like this without a celebration. Father Njuguna was sent out into the lanes and byways of Bugembe, returning with a couple-dozen parishioners, evenly divided between men and women, and many of them carrying something for the feast. Chicken three different ways, two sorts of stew, a rice and vegetable dish that seemed both Oriental and wonderful, other vegetables, fruits, even some local cheese.

Cheese. The same sort with which he now shared this stuffy box, but several years younger.

The celebration had taken place in the church basement, near Lew's coffin. A lot of beer had been brought along, but he drank sparingly of that. The beer he'd downed all day at the depot had mostly worn off by now, which was just as well.

All in all, it was a very nice celebration, even if rather hurried. Hymns were sung, other rescues and deliverances from Ugandan officialdom were recounted, and one of the men present gave a progress report on the new church, which was not actually a church at all but a small concrete-block storehouse behind a furniture factory. Idi Amin's religious persecutions had reached the level where it was dangerous to attend Christian services, so this church here, of which Bishop Kibudu was so proud, would remain at least for now a symbolic empty shell; within the month the bishop and his congregation would have transferred to their new secret quarters at the furniture factory. "There are many secret churches now," one of the few English-speaking parishioners explained to Lew. "It is the only way, in Uganda, we can keep in touch with God."

After the meal and the singing, Lew was fitted for his coffin. His legs and torso were wrapped around in a white sheet, and then three of the men lifted him up and laid him ever so gently on the pink quilting; which turned out to be a lot thinner than it looked and which was tacked onto extremely hard and uncomfortable wood. (The customary occupant, of course, wouldn't be expected to complain.)

Four or five of the women then set about painting his face and hands, using lipsticks and soot from the kerosene lanterns and left-over sauce from one of the chicken dishes and various other things he didn't want described too clearly. They all had a wonderful time with the project, laughing and telling each other jokes in Swahili, clapping their hands at particularly grotesque accomplishments, and generally having great fun at his expense.

Somebody offered to find a mirror so Lew could see the transformation for himself, but he said no. He could see what his hands looked like, which was precisely like the hands in the final painting of Dorian Gray in that old movie, and that was enough for him. "I'll have to live with this face the rest of my life," he told them. "I don't want too many scary memories associated with it."

At the end, the bishop gave Lew two items: a two-foot-long stick, for propping up the coffin lid so he could get air on the journey, and a small lumpy package wrapped in aluminum foil. "That's the cheese," the bishop said, handing it to him as though it were radioactive. "Don't open it before we get there." A horridness seemed to hover around the little package, a tiny but virulent little demon, perhaps the assistant devil in charge of all the world's tooth decay. Lew put it down gently on the quilt beside his left hip, propped the lid open with the stick, folded his hands, and was carried in his coffin up the stairs from the basement and out to the waiting hearse, a battered old vehicle of the same vintage as his pickup, and lacking glass in its back window.

Hushed good-byes were combined with hushed giggles, and the last he saw of Bishop Kibudu's flock, the men were waving and the women were blowing kisses and they were all laughing. The bishop drove, Father Njuguna presumably followed in the pickup—in what strange ways it had gone from minister to minister—and soon they had left Bugembe behind.

The partition between the driver's compartment and the business space contained a sliding panel, which the bishop left open, but there seemed very little to say beyond Lew's expressions of gratitude and the bishop's assurances that it was nothing at all. "You have a wonderful congregation," Lew said.

"Magnificent people. They keep me going."

Lew suspected it was the other way around, but he didn't say so.

The little foil-wrapped package was making its presence felt; or smelt. The bottom of the bottommost cistern in Calcutta; an elephant graveyard on a hot day; the interior of a freezer after a three-week power failure; those were some of the images that came into Lew's mind as the hints and tendrils came into his nose, and the damn thing wasn't even open yet.

"This is Jinja," the bishop said. "Not much longer now."

"I'm set." Though he wasn't, really; it suddenly occurred to him that the winding sheet effectively separated him from the pistol under his shirt. Had that been deliberate on the bishop's part? Well, if things went wrong up ahead, a pistol wouldn't help much anyway.

"Bridge ahead," the bishop announced. "Open the package now, and close your lid."

"Right."

Lew opened the package, and his nostrils slammed shut. His hair curled, his lungs became corrugated, his tongue died, his teeth shriveled and went back up into his gums. The skin under his eyes turned to leather. His ears fell off.

Close the lid? With himself in here with *that*? Turning his head away, hoping in vain for fresh air, Lew gulped in a full breath, tucked the reeking package in against his left leg under a fold of the winding sheet, removed the propping stick and slid it under his right leg, closed his eyes like a proper dead person, and lowered the lid.

Yug.

Then, after an eternity, they opened the lid, which gave him at least a memory of fresh air, but with great alacrity they slammed it shut again, and down inside there Lew began counting. At five hundred he would turn himself in. . . .

Two forty-seven . . . two forty-eight . . . The hearse started slowly to move, but Lew continued to count, and had reached two sixty-one when the bishop's voice came faintly through the lid: "All right, now."

"Nggaaaaaahhh!" Lew flung back the lid, sat up, grabbed the little package, and hurled it through the glassless rear window.

Laughing, the bishop said, "If any pedestrian saw you sit up like that, he must have fainted."

"The cheese'll bring him around," Lew said unsympathetically.

*   *   *

Farewells were said in the darkness behind a closed general store in Njery, the first little town on the west side of the Nile, less than two miles from the bridge. Fortunately, it seemed that the winding cloth had absorbed most of the cheese odor; unfortunately, it was the only thing he could use to wipe the death mask from his face. "I explained you were a plague victim," the bishop said, while Lew cleaned himself up. "And that we'd had to wait two weeks for official permission to bury you."

Father Njuguna, standing to one side, smiling, hands clasped before him, said, "The life of an adventurer must be a very interesting one."

"I don't know," Lew said. "Not if traveling with that dead cheese was a high point." Then he shook hands with both men, thanked them again for their help, and asked them to repeat his thanks to their parishioners. The bishop said, "May God bring us together again, under less exciting circumstances."

"Amen." Lew held the bishop's hand in both of his. "I'd say 'God bless you,' but why would He take my word for it? Besides, it's clear He already has. May Uganda get healthy enough to deserve you. Good-bye."

*   *   *

On the outskirts of Kampala, a golf course lay beside the road on the right. Lew, driving properly in the left lane, the time well after

midnight, the road very sparsely dotted with other traffic and completely free of pedestrians, glanced across at the golf course, the smooth
curling fairways, the triangular flags limp on their poles at the greens,
the swimming pool-shaped sand traps, and it surprised him to realize
that of course there must be people in Kampala who used that golf
course, who came out in the sunlight, well fed, well dressed, blessed
with leisure time and money, and spent a pleasant afternoon knocking
the little white ball around the course. In any society, no matter how
repressive, how terrible, how awful the things done, there are always
those people who remain untouched, who live their comfortable easy
lives in the middle of horror and death, as though absolutely nothing
untoward is going on.

Lew was startled from his reverie by an astonishing sight in his
headlights: across the way, a black Toyota was stopped at the verge,
headlights off but running lights on. Several men—three or four
men—were wrestling with a slender attractive well-dressed girl; all
were African. Seeing Lew's lights, they grabbed the girl up bodily
and ran away with her, out onto the golf course.

It wasn't his business. He couldn't even be sure who were the good
guys and who the bad. He had troubles enough of his own. He yanked
the pickup across the road, trying to find those running figures in his
dim headlights, failed, and finally slammed to a stop in front of their
car.

A Toyota. License plate starting with UVS. In his lights the men
had been garishly dressed. They and their car were exactly like the
men and the car when he'd been arrested.

Lew slapped off the pickup's lights, jumped out onto the ground,
unlimbered the pistol from under his shirt, and trotted off into the
darkness.

It was easy to follow them; the girl was screaming bloody murder.
The rolling land in this blackness was a little tricky underfoot, but
he didn't have a lot of fighting girl to contend with and could make
better time than they could.

Had they heard him coming, or could they see him against the
dim light from the roadway? One of them was suddenly standing in
front of him, looking very severe, absolutely secure in his power and
authority, barking something in Swahili that was probably along the
lines of mind-your-own-business.

Hardly slackening stride, Lew lifted his gun hand in a fascist salute. The man stared, following the pistol upward, and Lew kicked him in the crotch, then gun-butted him on the back of the head as he doubled over. One down.

They had stopped up ahead, on one of the greens. Lew trotted forward; the girl screamed; there came the sound of repeated slapping. "Let her go!" he yelled, and fired a shot in the air.

Astonishment. Silence. Even the girl was silent, but when he came closer he could see her alone on the green near the flag, on her knees; struggling groggily to rise, she only fell over.

Lew reached her, went down on one knee, and said, "Miss? Do you speak English?"

"I don't speak anything anymore," she answered, gasping, face down on the cropped grass, voice bitter.

"I've got wheels over there. Can you—"

A shot rang out. Lew dropped flat beside her. "They don't give up easy," he said.

"Get away from here," she told him. Her face, when she turned toward him, was beautiful, but ravaged by strain. "Don't buy trouble, don't—"

"Hush," he told her. "Let me listen."

"They'll kill you. They'll kill you right here."

"Hush!"

She hushed. He lifted his head to listen, looking left and right. Just beside them, the flag lazily moving in a slight breeze read *16*. Looking at it, he laughed out loud.

A pair of shots were fired, apparently at the sound of his laughter. The girl stared at him as though he were crazy. "That's what I've been needing," he explained, gesturing at the flag.

She shook her head. Apparently she didn't know whether she was more afraid of the Research Bureau men or of her rescuer. "I don't know what you mean."

"The flag. All through this deal something's been missing, and that's it. Now I know what I'm fighting for. Green sixteen."

She worked hard at being cool, but her voice trembled. "Mister," she said, "terrible things have happened to me tonight. Don't make fun."

Out there in the darkness, voices shouted to one another. "I'm sorry," Lew said. "I've been under a certain amount of pressure myself. Now, those boys may attack. Or they may just try to stay between us and the road. On the other hand, *I* want to get behind them so I can finish them off, because their vehicle is a lot better than mine. Do you know why I'm telling you this?"

"No."

"Because I'm going to need your help. I can see you're bright and quick-witted, so even though you've been through a lot, it would help if you could avoid hysteria."

She was considerably calmer already. "I thought you were the hysteric," she said.

"That's just my outgoing personality. Now, what you do, you lie here and talk to me. Can you do deep voices?"

Sounding like a girl foghorn, she said, "Like this?"

"Use it sparingly. See, I'm going out there and deal with those fellows, and in the meantime you stay here and hold a conversation."

"So they'll think you're still here. I get it."

"Right. See you soon."

He started away, but she said, "Wait a minute! What if they come *here*?"

"Holler."

"Oh. Sure."

Lew crawled down over the edge of the green onto the shaggier grass of the fairway. Another shot sounded from out there, followed by an angry yell from another direction. Lew wriggled rapidly along the ground on elbows and belly and knees, while behind him the girl said, "If you don't mind a question, how long ago did you escape from the mental home?" Foghorn voice: "Just today." Own voice: "And is it true you've been running President Amin's foreign policy all these years?" Foghorn voice: "No, he does that himself."

The men up ahead were arguing. Without knowing the language, Lew could still guess that one faction wanted to rush the sixteenth green right now, while the other faction wanted to wait until dawn, or possibly send for reinforcements, or whatever.

They were undisciplined and poorly trained. They kept jumping up and moving around, shouting to one another, silhouetting themselves against the running lights of their own car in the background. Lew crawled around their right flank, came up behind his first choice, took his knife out of its sheath in his boot, waited till the man finished yelling a sentence about something or other, and then put him away. A search revealed two handguns but no car keys.

On his way to number two, Lew came across the fellow he'd hit at the beginning, who was just sitting up, rubbing his head, and thinking about taking part. Lew dispatched him and crawled on.

The next man was even more active than the first, probably more nervous. In the distant blackness the girl continued her inane conversation. Lew approached his man, knife in right hand and pistol in left. The fellow turned, saw him, and at once attacked, shrieking and swinging his pistol barrel at Lew's head.

Lew stepped inside the swing, drove the knife up and across, and stepped out of the way to let the man fall. Then he went on to the last one, who was calling questions, getting no answers, and becoming too nervous.

Far too nervous. Before Lew could reach him, he made a dash for the car. Discarding the knife, Lew dropped to prone position on the fairway, arms stretched out in front of himself, left hand palm up on the stubby grass, pistol butt cradled in that palm, right hand holding the grip, finger squeezing back gently on the trigger as he sighted on those Toyota lights. Sooner or later, his man would cross them.

He did. Lew fired twice, and the man dropped.

He was tough to find in the dark, but it was worth the search, since he was the one with the keys. Pocketing them, putting the pistol away in his hip pocket and the wiped-clean knife back into his boot, Lew permitted the girl's voice to lead him back to the sixteenth green. As he neared her, he said, "It's okay, we're alone now."

She gasped, clutching her throat, then made out who it was and said, "They're *gone?* They ran away?"

"They're dead."

"Thank you," she said. She was suddenly fierce. "Thank you thank you thank you. I hope you made them hurt a *lot*."

Worried, he knelt beside her, touching her shoulder, feeling her vibrate like an overstrained machine. "Take it easy," he said. "They're gone now. It's over."

"They killed the man I was going to marry."

"I'm sorry. I'm very sorry."

She folded herself against him, becoming less tense. Was she going to cry? No. "I can't tell you," she said, breath warm through his shirt against his chest. "I'm back from the dead, from the worse-than-dead. They were taking me to Jinja Barracks."

"Through green sixteen?"

"They wanted me for themselves first. They wanted me while I was still fresh."

"Oh. Yes, I suppose so."

She lifted her head, and when her cheek brushed his jaw he was surprised to feel dampness. So there had been a tear—two at the most. This was no Amarda. "You saved me," she whispered.

"Triple A is here to help."

"Don't joke," she murmured, her lips moving lightly against his. Not again. "Miss—"

"Patricia," she said and kissed him, and he couldn't not hold her, he had to be aware how alive she was, how good she felt.

This is impossible, he thought. This is ridiculous, I'm on my way back to Ellen, there's dead bodies around here like lawn statues, this can't be happening.

But it was. After earthquakes people fall into one another's arms; after ship sinkings, disastrous fires, pitched battles, the survivors reach for one another; after the dragon is slain, the damsel rewards the knight; after the danger, life surges.

She lowered her head to his shoulder. "I know it's awful," she whispered, then looked up again, half erotic and half defiant. "I can't help it. Terrible things happened, I don't know how I can feel this way, but I do. I was in Hell, there was no hope, and now I'm back, and I need something warm and friendly inside me."

"I'm Lew," he said.

73

"You understand, Mr. Chase," said the smarter one, Obuong, "we can make no commitment now. There will still have to be a very close investigation."

Chase understood a lot more than that. "I welcome an investigation," he said, smiling his self-confidence. "All I hope for is the opportunity to be of service, to prove my worth to the government and people of Kenya."

They stood in a close triumvirate beside the Mercedes, Chase and Charles Obuong and Godfrey Magon. Along the shore four rafts were now moored, their eighty feet of width using up all the available coastline space. The fifth and sixth rafts were even now being lashed to the lakeward edges of the first and second by a squad of soldiers. The remaining soldiers continued to sprawl on the ground, accompanied by a growing number of Balim's bewildered workmen, who didn't yet know if they were under arrest. Frank had been given permission to go off in a truck to the general store to make his important phone call, and Balim himself paced nervously back and forth in front of his unfinished hotel, gazing out at the lake, even though he knew his son wasn't out there.

As for Chase, he had snatched—he was even now snatching—victory from the jaws of defeat. The most incredible day of his life this had been, ranging all over southern Uganda and now to Kenya, twice captured and in presumably hopeless circumstances, twice surviving to land on his feet. His Mercedes was gone, with the wealth hidden in its door panels. The *Angel* had failed in its mission about as thoroughly as it was possible to fail. Chase had been bound, beaten, pissed on, insulted, robbed, and betrayed; and yet at the end he would finish on top.

And why not? How could these tame bureaucrats resist a man who'd spent his life playing such minor officials as though they were toy drums? He spoke to them with assurance, insinuatingly, letting them know he shared with them the bureaucrat's outlook and language. Also, he was a modestly famous man in East Africa; he had accompanied Amin here and there as a high-level official, he had been photographed with popes and presidents and prime ministers. Past troubles in another land had no importance here. It was true that Obuong and Magon were seeing him now in an unfortunate state, but his name and manner and background simply had to override his dirty face and torn clothes. They were minor civil servants, and he was the sort to whom they had learned in infancy to bend the knee; how could they hold back against him?

Without actually acknowledging any connection between himself and the *Angel's* attempted piracy, he had led them to realize that if he'd been prepared to take charge of so much coffee he surely already had a customer for it. A customer at a good price, who would not be fussy about documentation.

He could bring these people together with Grossbarger. In fact, he would be delighted to.

They would also be delighted, of course, since their own shares would be proportionately higher, though Obuong did demur briefly, wondering about Balim, mentioning his name in an indecisive way. But Chase shrugged that off, saying, "The Asian? I'm not sure where he fits into this, if at all. He never owned the coffee. In fact, he's never even had physical possession of it."

"Still," Obuong said, "still, Mr. Chase, one does feel a certain moral obligation."

Meaning that to cut Balim out completely might have repercussions, might give Balim no reason not to make trouble. "If you want to be generous," Chase said, admiring Obuong's nobility with his smile, "I suppose some sort of emolument could be given to the Asian, to cover his expenses and so on. What should we call it? A finder's fee?"

Magon laughed, but Obuong gave the phrase serious consideration. "Perhaps tax credits on other transactions would be a better way to do it," he suggested. "It would associate him not so clearly with *this* coffee."

"Very good," Chase said, and all at once realized it wasn't the missing son that Balim was thinking about while staring out over the lake, it was Isaac Otera. Balim had to know he was being squeezed out of the deal, that it was happening here and now, but what could he do about it? He didn't dare challenge Chase directly, not an Asian challenge a white man like Chase in this black country, no matter what Chase might or might not have done to him in the past. Frank Lanigan would be useless in a situation like this. Otera, Balim's antibureaucrat, was the only one who might have been able to join this conversation and salvage something for his employer beyond a few vague tax credits. But Frank in his wisdom had placed Otera on the last raft; it would be half an hour at least before that raft reached shore, and by then it would be far too late.

In fact, the best thing for Chase to do at this moment, to cement the new alliance, was to leave these two alone to plot against him. Such plotting would of course presuppose the existence of the alliance, which would confirm it in their minds. He was confident there was little they could think of to do that would harm him. Also, his moving away now—opening the field, as it were, to Balim and Otera—would merely serve to underline his self-assurance. "I know you have other things to do," he said. "I've taken up too much of your time."

"No, no," Obuong said, "you've been very helpful."

"I hoped I could be. And tomorrow, after I've cleaned up, rested, had a good wash in a hotel, I'm sure we'll all want to talk again."

Obuong smiled. "We surely will," he said.

Chase strolled away. Behind him, Magon excitedly began in Swahili, "He's in no position to—"

There wasn't even any necessity to eavesdrop, though it was nice to reflect that here he was in a new nation where all his secrets were intact.

There was a thick-trunked tree over near the smoldering oil-drum fire; Chase walked over there, sat down, and made himself more or less comfortable with his back against the tree, where he could look out over the lake and watch the rafts slowly arrive. Beside the Mercedes, Obuong and Magon murmured passionately together.

All that coffee, Chase thought, looking at the great wall of sacks, eighty feet long and twelve feet high. All in all, he was rather pleased at what he had wrought. All that coffee. All that money.

It's pleasant to be a winner.

74

"I'm going for a walk," Ellen replied, three different times. First she replied it to the night clerk, as she passed once more through the lobby. "Very late at night," he suggested. "Insomnia," she explained, and pushed through the glass doors to the outside world before he could say anything more.

Twenty minutes later, she replied it to the guard down by the planes parked beside the taxiway, who challenged her with a great deal of suspicion and perhaps even fright, though he was the one clutching the submachine gun. "No walk by planes," he insisted, staring at her round-eyed. Pointing past him, she said, "Don't be silly, I *fly* that plane. I can certainly walk around it." He became uncertain, but clung to sureties: "No fly tonight." She agreed: "No fly tonight. Walk tonight." Then, hoping she looked a lot cooler than she felt, she simply stepped around him and went for a stroll among the planes, and he gave her no more trouble.

Not quite an hour after that, she replied it to the pleasant overweight girl who ran the empty coffee shop. "You be careful," the girl told her, "and don't go far away." "No, I won't," Ellen promised, fortified by her two cups of coffee, and went back out.

The late-night air was as humid as ever, but with a chill in it off the lake. Turning the collar of her Burberry up, putting her hands in the pockets, Ellen strolled along through pockets of light and shadow, moving this time toward the main entrance from the highway.

The problem was, Frank had said twenty-four hours and that was just nonsense. If Lew was going to make it here at all, it would have to be before daylight; after that, a lone wanted white man wouldn't be able to move an inch without discovery. And tomorrow night would be too late; Ellen couldn't possibly refuse to leave with her plane.

So it was tonight that Lew had to get here, and the main questions were: How would he arrive, and how would he make contact? Poor Agatha Christie had had no hope of attracting Ellen's attention after that phone call; she'd tried to read, but her eyes failed to focus on the page. And when she came to the conclusion there would be no way for Lew to signal her in this room—the night clerk received and listened to all calls coming into this building—she put the Christie down, shrugged into her Burberry, and went out to answer three times the question "Where are you going?"

The two extremes of her walk were the main entrance and the runways. If Lew came boldly in via the main road, as she fully expected him to do, they would meet right here along the road and could make their plans. If his presence in Uganda were known, if he were being hunted, he might choose a less visible route, in which case he would surely head for the planes, and she would meet him there.

In the meantime, the wait was equal parts tension and boredom. Entebbe, which was perhaps the most underutilized commercial airport in the world by day, became an absolute desert of inactivity by night. The coffee shop was kept open very late, as though in deliberate defiance of reality, and here and there a slow-moving janitor cleaned, and the occasional soldier or sentry passed, but that was it. And for all Ellen knew, she would walk back and forth in this empty airport another six or seven hours, until well after sunup; for all she knew, she would walk here uselessly. Lew might not appear at all.

What would she do if daylight came, and no Lew? Thoughts of borrowing a car; but to drive where? She had no idea where he was, what had happened to strand him when the others left, what condition he was in. Either he had some sort of vehicle or he would certainly steal one. Either the Ugandan authorities were searching for him or they didn't know he was in their territory. Either—

He's a soldier, she reminded herself. He's trained to survive in bad situations. He even trains others. He'll get here.

At the traffic circle—the road signs, inspired by Uganda's British former owners, called it a *roundabout*, a word Ellen thought very well described the night she was having—she turned about and strolled slowly again toward the low stucco-faced buildings of the airport. The few sharp lights and the low pale flat-roofed buildings made her think of prisons or prisoner-of-war camps.

A car came purring toward her from the roundabout. She glanced back, hoping against hope, stepping off the blacktop onto the packed-dirt verge, and when the black car slowed she had a moment of absolute assurance, was already smiling when she saw it wasn't Lew at the wheel after all but a woman. A very attractive black woman, under thirty, quite elegant. If it weren't for the strain lines around her eyes and mouth, she would be absolutely beautiful. But she wasn't Lew.

Idly, Ellen wondered what such a person could possibly want at this airport at this hour. Surely she wasn't the graveyard-shift countergirl in the coffee shop. There were no passenger planes scheduled, either in or out. Could she be a hooker? If so, for whom?

The car having stopped beside her, the woman smiled out her open window, saying, "Excuse me. Could you direct me to the transient aircrews' quarters?"

"Of course," Ellen said, and did so, pointing, and the woman thanked her and drove off, the black car humming to itself, in no apparent hurry.

So she *was* a hooker, summoned by one of the pilots. Ellen was surprised, not because this looked like a "good girl" or anything like that, but because as a hooker she would be far more expensive than most pilots would be willing to pay.

Ellen walked. Ahead, the car's brakelights flashed on, and it came to an abrupt stop. Then the white backup lights gleamed, and the car backed hurriedly toward her, whining, weaving from side to side. Now what?

Again the car halted beside her. Ellen looked in, frowning, and behind the beautiful black woman, up from the floor in back, reared the smiling, sheepish face of Lew. Ellen stared from his smile to the woman's—very knowing eyes, that woman had—and back at Lew. "I might have known," she said.

* * *

Wishing her flight bag were full of rocks, Ellen flung it out her room window at Lew's head, twelve feet below. He caught it, the bastard, waved to her, and scampered away into the darkness. I really ought to leave him here, she thought. The man's incorrigible.

At the same time, she was trying to be fair. In the car, in a dark corner of a parking lot, they had described everything to her—well, perhaps everything—and it wasn't his fault that Patricia Kamin had needed rescuing just as he was driving by. Nevertheless, she rebelled at the inevitability of it, and was annoyed by the knowledge that Lew Brady would *always* find some beautiful woman who needed to be rescued, whether from the hopelessness of life like Amarda or from physical assault like Patricia. The calls for help would just keep coming, and one thing you could say for Lew: he would always get it up.

Well, he never rescued *me*, she thought as she left her room and headed for the lobby, and she was surprised at how comforting she found that idea. It was true. She had often wanted him, but she had never needed him, and that made a difference. There was some comfort at least in the reflection that their relationship was a break with tradition.

In fact, come to think of it, *she* was the one rescuing *him*. Take that, Lew Brady.

The night clerk was astonished by her. "Out again? You need your sleep."

"I'm a copilot," Ellen told him. "I'll sleep tomorrow in the plane."

He laughed politely, and out she went, turning once more toward the parked planes.

It was very hard this time to maintain a strolling pace. She reached the taxiway, and her old friend the insecure guard passed by, and she gave him a big smile. He was getting used to her; he actually flickered a frightened smile of his own in response. She moved on, ambling, hands in pockets, smelling the night air fragrant from the exotic specimens in the botanical garden, and when she reached the Uganda Skytours plane there was no one at all in sight.

Poor Mike. He had known it was coming, some sort of bad ending was coming, but he was tied to his property. The authorities would have let him and his wife leave Uganda at any time, but not with the plane. He could fly the plane out, but not with his wife aboard. He had tried to keep everything, hoping for the best, and in the end he had lost it all, including himself. But how do you know for certain that moment when your way of life has become a sinking ship that must be abandoned? Jews in Hitler's Germany; intellectuals in Stalin's Russia; Christians in Amin's Uganda. People were imprisoned most securely by who they had chosen to become.

Ellen unclipped the three mooring ropes, and opened the Cessna's only door, on its left side. Climbing up into the pilot's seat, leaving the door ajar, she touched the controls in the dark, reacquainting herself with a breed of plane she hadn't flown in about three years.

How long would it take the engines to turn over? Ellen remembered Mike's boast—"I keep her gassed up and ready to go"—as though the plane were a lucky talisman, as though his attentions to it were a kind of offertory to the gods to guarantee his safety. Would that attitude have included careful engine maintenance? It would be ignominious to be caught on the ground here by her friend the nervous guard as she fruitlessly ground the starter, over and over.

It would be worse than ignominious. Much worse.

Were Lew and his doxy in position yet? (Ellen didn't feel like being fair. On the other hand, Lew's reason for being here in the first place was certainly a credit to him. Already safe, he'd come back in a vain attempt to find the missing Bathar, not wanting to have to face Mr. Balim without the boy. Poor Mr. Balim. And poor Bathar, come to that. And very noble and heroic of Lew, which Ellen found very irritating to have to admit.)

She sat there, touching the controls, until she realized she was merely stalling, she was reluctant to make that step beyond the point of no return. All right; taking a deep breath, she punched her thumb to the left starter.

Good Mike. That engine turned over at once, and a few seconds later so did the right. Easing off on the ground brake, she rolled forward onto the taxiway, swung left, and trundled rapidly toward the nearest north-south runway. Tonight's breeze was slight and fitful, but its general trend was from the lake, south of here.

They were supposed to be waiting in the bushes along the right side here, near the chain link fence. Her engines would already have alerted whatever sentries were nearby; she flicked on her landing lights, and in the white glare she saw Lew running over the coarse grass from the shrubbery, Ellen's flight bag clutched in his right hand, pulling Patricia Kamin along with his left. They're holding hands; isn't that nice.

They had to run across the taxiway in front of the plane to get to the door. Ellen stopped, moved to the right into the other seat, and folded down the pilot's seatback so they could climb aboard. They'd both have to ride in back, which Ellen didn't much care for, but the only way to get Lew into the front seat beside her would be to deplane, let him board, then clamber back in herself, which would take too long.

The woman came in first, out of breath but smiling, gasping, "Thank you."

"Please don't mention it," Ellen said. "I'll get the door, Lew."

"Right." He stopped his contortions, trying to board the plane and shut the door behind himself at the same time, cleared her seat, and thumped into the other space in back. Ellen flipped the seat up, got again behind the wheel, and accelerated.

"They're shooting at us back there," Lew said conversationally. "I can see the flashes."

Why did I have to meet this man? Shoulders hunched, Ellen steered the plane to the beginning of the runway, braked hard, turned hard, and accelerated before she was really set. The earphones hanging from a hook in front of her squawked away, but she paid no attention. Glancing to her left, she saw headlights—two pairs of headlights—racing toward her across the grass, bouncing on the uneven terrain.

Leaning forward near her head, his voice a bit more urgent, Lew said, "They're trying to cut us off, Ellen."

"I see them."

The plane had its own speed, its own system, its own way of doing things. She must simply roll forward, accelerating, watch the tarmac flash by under her wheels, and wait for the plane to be ready to lift.

A British-style jeep was over there on the grass to her left, running at a very long angle to the plane, almost parallel but not quite, as though the driver intended to meet them just this side of infinity. Quick bright spots of light from the interior of the jeep must be the flashes Lew had been talking about; they're shooting at us!

It was hard to hold the wheel steady, hard not to pull back too soon or too much. A botched takeoff, leaving them on the ground with too little runway left, would be the end. They would get no second chance.

Patricia Kamin said something Ellen didn't catch, her voice uneven with tension. Good, Ellen thought, she's more scared than I am. "No," Lew answered her, "I think they're probably shooting at the wheels. It's what I'd do."

The plane lifted fractionally; its tires still ran on the tarmac but carried less weight. "Come on," Ellen whispered, remembering how far Mike had had to run this plane to get it airborne. "Come on, come on."

The wheels, still spinning, lost contact with the ground. Turning lazily, they skimmed along just above the surface of the runway, two fat black doughnuts riding so low a two-by-four couldn't have been slipped in beneath them. Ellen, every muscle tense in her arms and chest and neck and back, drew the wheel minutely toward herself, and the plane, though still looking at the ground, inched higher into the air.

The end of the runway was ahead. The jeep, having lost the race, veered sharply to get onto the runway and chase from behind. The plane nosed up, like a sleepy horse finished with its oats; it seemed to see the sky, to take a sudden interest, at last to understand. Wings out, nose rising, tail canted at a jaunty angle, the plane soared up over the end of the runway, over the scrub, over the muddy coast, over water glinting with shattered reflections of the quarter-moon.

Ellen switched off every light except the small green ones illuminating the control panel. She'd never flown in such darkness before. The altitude meter read three hundred feet; angling downward, she banked sharply to the left.

Lew said, "Ellen? You're going back?"

"I can't get any control-tower guidance," she told him. "They're sure to scramble other planes after us. Out over the lake we'd simply get lost, so I'm going down on the deck so their radar can't see me, find that highway that goes to Kenya, and run along beside it."

"Oh, that's good," Lew said. "That's terrific."

"Thank you."

He was leaning forward again, his right hand on her right shoulder. Sincerity dripping from his voice, he said, "I really appreciate this, Ellen. I want you to know that."

She shrugged, bouncing his hand off. "I'd do it for anybody," she said. She was really very angry.

75

Charlie waited for Mguu to do it, but Mguu just stomped around in his usual style, being angry and accomplishing nothing. Charlie waited for Isaac to order somebody to do it, or for Mr. Balim to hire somebody to do it, but Isaac was spending all his time in fruitless frustrating conversation with the two slippery government men from Nairobi, while Mr. Balim remained seated on the chair of concrete blocks and planks that Charlie had made for him, sighing and gazing unhappily out at the lake.

Mr. Balim was sad about his son. Wasn't that reason enough to do it?

This Baron Chase from Uganda was a very bad man. He sat there against that dead tree, smiling, happy about himself, but he was a very bad man who had done many bad things. He was the one who had sent the ship to murder them and rob from them. And now he was stealing the coffee again, with the help of those government men from Nairobi.

But that wasn't the reason. The reason was that this man Chase had robbed Mr. Balim of his son. He had made Mr. Balim unhappy in a way that no robbery of money or power could do. He had stolen the light from Mr. Balim's eyes. Charlie could see it, if none of the others could; and Charlie loved Mr. Balim above all human beings; and that was why.

He walked over to where Baron Chase was seated, and bent over him as though solicitously, in a posture he knew Chase would like to see. "Sir?" he said.

Chase glanced up with casual recognition. "Yes?"

"Look," Charlie said, and withdrew from his sleeve the long narrow extremely sharp blade. As Chase opened his mouth, his hands beginning to move, Charlie inserted the blade between the man's ribs and pressed it home, directly through the heart.

It hit Chase like a drug. First there came the rush, the jolt, the shock; his eyes bulged, his neck muscles tensed, his hands curved like talons, his feet kicked out. Then the drug took hold; his eyes lost their luster, his mouth sagged open, his hands lay peacefully at his sides. The drug was death.

Charlie watched the death rise like mist, until it covered Chase to the eyes, and above the eyes. Then he drew out the blade and slipped it back under his sleeve. The heart was not beating, so there was almost no blood. Charlie strolled away into the darkness behind the floodlights.

76

Lew wished Patricia wouldn't persist in holding his hand. He understood she was only doing it because she was frightened; he was certain Ellen couldn't see it; and under the circumstances he wasn't likely to become aroused by it; still, he wished she wouldn't do it.

He also wished Ellen would get over her mad. But more than anything else, he wished he'd been able to find Bathar. (Since the poor guy was probably dead by now, or soon would be, he deserved his own name, not that dismissive *Young Mr. Balim.*)

"Here they come again," Ellen said.

Patricia squeezed Lew's hand even tighter as he said, "Where?"

"Ten o'clock high."

Leaning forward, ducking low so he could look up past Ellen's left ear, Lew was just in time to watch the two jets flash across the black sky from left to right, blazing with noise and light and speed and their own significance. For the last fifteen minutes these two had been skating back and forth up there, like kids who didn't realize they were late for supper. At first Lew had been convinced they would spot the Cessna with no trouble and would simply shell them into abrupt oblivion—the golden-red instant fireball would be beautiful against the night sky, too bad he wouldn't be around to see it—but as the jets kept flashing back and forth, nervous hunting dogs who had lost the scent, he realized their very speed and power worked against them. A poky little Cessna, running without lights, skimming the treetops just south of the A109, was beneath the range of their vision.

Which didn't mean they couldn't get lucky. Ellen was doing her best to avoid all ground lights, but the jets' angle of view constantly changed; if one of those pilots looked in just the right place at just the right time, and if he saw a little black object pass between himself and some streetlamp or lit-up house, he'd be on them in a second.

"I wish they'd give up," Ellen said, echoing Lew's own thoughts.

"They don't dare," Patricia said. "Amin would slice them to pieces. They'll stay up until we're found or they run out of gas."

"I'd rather you lied to me," Ellen said.

"I'd prefer it myself," Patricia answered, and squeezed Lew's hand again, this time suggestively.

Uh-oh. Lew had been on enough cliff edges for one day. Gently but firmly, he removed his hand and grasped his other elbow with it. So she put her hand on his thigh.

Ellen said, "Do you see them?"

"What, the jets? No."

"Not out this side," Patricia said.

"I've got to cross the road," Ellen explained. "Jinja's up ahead, I don't want to go over the lake, they'd be able to spot us there against the water."

"They're not around," Lew assured her. He didn't mention, because of course both women already knew, that the jets tended to arrive very fast, without advance warning.

"Now or never," Ellen said. She'd already been barely a hundred feet in the air, and now she banked sharply to the left and dropped even lower. Lew could see a kerosene-lit living room through a curtainless window in a roadside house as they flitted by. The man reading a book on the sofa was just lifting his head at the engine noise; then they were past.

Jinja had seemed quite dark when he had driven through it, first in the pickup and then in the coffin, but from the sky it was a blaze of light; particularly if you were trying to avoid light. Ellen kept angling farther and farther north, and then to complicate matters Jinja

Airport was dead ahead, so she had to turn westward again, back toward Kampala, flying low over the little villages, dirt roads, small isolated lights.

"There they are!" Patricia cried, her hand convulsively clutching Lew's thigh. "Over on the— Over there!" She was making herself angry and panicky by being unable to describe simply and quickly where the jets were. "To the *right*! *Up!*"

"Three o'clock high," Lew said, ducking down to look for them out Patricia's window. Realizing he was putting his head in her lap, he immediately sat up again.

"I hate this," Ellen said. She throttled back, and Lew felt that roller-coaster feeling in his stomach when the Cessna slowed and dropped another twenty feet.

"Oh, my God," Patricia said, and simply came over and wrapped her arms around Lew and his seat back both. He had no choice but to hold her.

Ellen said, "How tall do the trees grow around here, Miss Kamin?"

"Patricia. Call me Patricia."

"All ri— Where *are* you?" Because of course Patricia's voice had come from directly behind Ellen, where Lew was supposed to be sitting.

Patricia clung to Lew, staring around. "Are they gone?"

"Yes," Ellen said. "Lew?"

"Here," said Lew.

Returning to her own side of the plane, Patricia said, "I'm sorry. They just scare me, I can't help it. I don't know about trees, but I think they must grow taller than this."

"After Jinja we'll be all right," Lew said. "There aren't any more big towns till Tororo, right at the border."

"I can hardly wait," Ellen commented, swinging the Cessna around through the north to an easterly direction again.

Patricia gave Lew a shaky smile, her face mysterious in the faint green light from the instrument panel, her dark skin gleaming with a sensually metallic look, as though she were the alien beauty in a science-fiction movie. "I am sorry," she said. "I'm under control now."

In the Toyota, on the way to Entebbe, he had told her what he and Ellen were to each other, so he knew she now meant she wouldn't make any more trouble. "It's all right," he assured her. "We're all a little tense."

"There's the Nile," Ellen said.

"So just relax," Lew continued, patting Patricia's hand, "and listen to our tour guide."

"Oh, shut up," Ellen said, but she sounded a bit less bad-tempered.

Brightly lighted Jinja lay away to their right. Ahead, to the east, the darkness seemed unbroken, but there would be plenty of lights to greet them along the way.

For fifteen minutes they droned eastward, Jinja dropping away behind, the A109 angling north to meet them, the little towns passing with their dim half-hidden lights. Their only route to safety, just as though they were an earthbound automobile, was that narrow line of highway down there. Anyone going to Kenya tonight, by air or by land, would follow that road.

As they hummed along, dark in the dark sky, Lew explained to Patricia the clock method for describing where one had seen another plane in the sky, and once they saw far above them the light and flame trails of a multi-engine jet streaming northward above the planet, but that sighting of the two fighter jets while Ellen had been skirting Jinja Airport remained their last appearance. "Maybe," Lew said, voicing a thought he'd been silent about for five minutes, "maybe their search area only extends as far east as Jinja."

"I was thinking that," Ellen told him. "I was afraid to say it."

"So was I. Let's see if I brought us bad luck."

But another five minutes went by without the jets' return, and finally they did all begin to relax and to believe they would get away with it. They were past Iganga, past Bugiri, over a hundred miles from Entebbe, with less than forty miles to the Kenyan border. Ellen, increasingly confident that they were alone in this part of the sky, was flying much closer to the highway, an unlit faintly paler ribbon across the black chest of the world. An occasional car appeared down there, moving at less than half their hundred twenty miles an hour.

"That looks like the flashes," Patricia said.

Lew, his long day ending, had been half-asleep. He sat up, blinking. "What?"

"The flashes, when they were shooting at us at the airport," Patricia explained. "That looks like the same thing. What would make that?"

She was pointing out her window, down toward the road. Leaning over, his arm against her breast, he looked down and at first saw only an automobile, a Peugeot, speeding along down there, traveling east as they were. They were already ahead of it, and pulling away. But then he saw the flashes at the side windows and said, "They're shooting, that's why."

But what were they shooting at? Ahead of the Peugeot, visible in its headlights, being steadily overtaken, was someone on a small motorcycle, a narrow figure hunched over the handlebars, about to be shot or run down, his motorcycle or moped slower than the—

Moped. Lew stared. "That's Bathar!"

"What?" Ellen dipped the right wing for a better look, dumping Lew more firmly into Patricia's lap. "My God!" Ellen cried, "they're killing him!"

"Jesus! Bathar!" Lew picked himself out of Patricia's lap and held onto the back of Ellen's seat. "I completely forgot that goddam moped!"

Ellen was swinging left, away from the road. She said, "Lew, do you have a gun?"

"Of course."

"The window flap by my elbow here. It opens. But not yet, wait'll I throttle back."

Ellen's left turn segued into a long arc to the right, finishing with her over the road, facing the other way, the Peugeot and moped just ahead, rushing toward them. She throttled back, dropping low, the wheels no more than twenty feet above the road. Lew, arm sticking out the top-hinged window flap, fired three shots as they and the car passed one another, but to no effect. "No good," he said. "I can't see, I can't aim. Run parallel, let me broadside them."

"They've stopped," Patricia said, looking back.

So they had, apparently startled by the sudden appearance of a plane shooting at them. But as Ellen swung around for another attack, they started up again, tearing down the highway. "Good," Ellen said. "The faster they go, the easier it'll be to pace them."

They came in on the car's right, flying low, Ellen slowing to match the car's ninety miles an hour. This time she held the flap up and out with her elbow while Lew crouched against her seat back, holding the pistol in a two-handed grip, bracing it by pressing his knuckles against the door panel just under the window, the barrel sticking out through the opening. The driver was on this side, clearly visible, staring at the plane, his eyes huge white circles in his dark face, making a toy target. A passenger in the seat behind him was firing wildly in the general direction of the plane.

Lew's first shot went nowhere in particular, but his second made that target face disappear, like something in a shooting gallery. The car slued and careened, turned sharply right, went over on its side, rolled completely over twice, and landed bone-jarringly on its wheels, smoking. Ellen lifted them higher, and looking back Lew saw the first flames, and two men staggering out onto the pavement.

Ahead, Bathar and the moped still ran, not looking back, not slackening pace. Ellen accelerated to overtake him, while Patricia said, "Who is that?"

"A friend of ours. My employer's son. We thought he was dead."

"He almost was."

They flew over the speeding Bathar, then Ellen brought the Cessna down onto the highway for a very bumpy and scary landing, the fuselage fishtailing the whole time. Once they'd stopped, Ellen opened the door, leaned out, looked back, and said, "Where is he?"

Lew went through the contortions necessary to get past Ellen's seatback and stick his head out the doorway. The road back there was dark and empty. "He's hiding," Lew said. "He's hiding from *us*. Let me out, I'll go get him."

"We can't stay here forever," Ellen pointed out, climbing down so he could get out. "Sooner or later, there'll be traffic."

"Yes, ma'am." Taking a few steps back behind the plane, Lew cupped his hands around his mouth and yelled, *"Bathar!"* No response. He yelled it again, then muttered something, and went jogging away down the middle of the road. He counted fifty paces, then stopped and yelled, *"God damn it*, BATHAR!"

A distant unbelieving voice said, "What?"

"Bathar, it's Lew! Come on!"

A shadow separated itself from the roadside darkness some distance away. "Lew? Honest to God?"

"No, I'm lying. Come *on*, Bathar!" Lew gestured mightily for Bathar to come on, then turned and jogged back toward the plane.

Behind him, the moped sounded its nasal sputter. It rapidly approached, passed the jogging Lew, and as he reached the plane, Bathar was off the moped and embracing Ellen with great vigor. "Say, there," Lew said.

Bathar, grinning from ear to ear, released Ellen, then immediately grabbed her again and kissed her smiling mouth. Then he truly did release her, turned, and enthusiastically shook Lew's hand in both of his, saying, "I can't believe it. I thought this was a dead Paki, Lew, I really thought that, I really did."

"Let's get in the *plane*," Ellen said.

"Right," Lew said. He started forward, but Ellen put up a hand to stop him, saying, "Oh, no, you don't. You ride up front with me."

"Oh, sure."

"Get in, Bathar. Step there, and there."

"Very good." Bathar hoisted himself up, climbed into the plane, and was heard to say, "Well, hello."

Patricia's grin sounded clearly in her voice: "Hello, yourself."

Lew went next, working his way over to the front passenger seat, and then Ellen climbed aboard and at once started them rolling down the potholed road.

"By golly, here comes a car," Lew said, seeing the headlights appear around a curve far ahead.

"I hope he has sense enough to get out of the way." Ellen switched on the Cessna's landing lights so the oncoming driver would at least know what was out in front of him.

He wasn't a particularly intelligent driver. First he flashed his high beams; whether requesting this airplane to get out of his way or objecting to the brightness of its single forward floodlight, it was impossible to guess. Then he just kept coming, for the longest while. In the backseat, Bathar and Patricia were oblivious, engaged in mutual introductions. "Ellen," Lew said, "what if he doesn't stop?"

"Guess," Ellen said.

But the clown finally did stop, and in fact he steered himself off the road, which was just as well, because the Cessna needed more road before it could struggle back into the air. The verge dipped down here, which was also good; the Cessna's speeding left wing swept by just over the roof of the car while its driver gaped idiotically at them.

Sometime later, they became airborne at last, and Ellen switched off all the lights. Then Bathar told them his story.

"I was trying to get to the border, but I had to hide every time a car came along. I was still groggy, and once when I was hiding I just fell asleep. Then I woke up and started again, and people came out of a little hotel by the road and saw me and chased me. Because I'm an Asian, I guess."

Lew swiveled around to grin at him, saying, "Well, did you have fun?"

"I guess I did, really," Bathar said, "so long as I survived."

"And will you go to London now?"

"Oh, absolutely. In all the bad moments, I kept telling myself, 'There's London at the end of this.' "

Patricia said, "You're going to London?"

"Yes, indeed."

"I thought I might go back there, too," she said. "I have cousins in Fulham."

"A nice neighborhood, Fulham," Bathar suggested. "Near to Chelsea and all. I used to live in Bayswater with the other wogs, but I didn't much like it."

"My cousins could put you up," Patricia offered, "until you find your own place."

"Why, thank you. Would they be putting you up, too?"

"Oh, yes," she said. "Until I find my own place."

The conversation in the backseat continued, Patricia and Bathar not at all hiding their mutual pleasure of discovery. In front, Ellen silently drove. Unbuttoning his shirt, Lew pulled out the long triangular pennant, dark green with the orange numbers on it, that he'd been wearing wrapped around his chest. *16.*

Looking at him, Ellen said, "What's that?"

"My flag. My guidon, standard, pennant. I'll have to get it a new pole."

"What's it for?"

"It came from the golf course where Patricia was having that trouble."

"So it's a souvenir."

"Well, no. Not exactly." Holding the flag up, studying it in the dim control-panel light, he said, "At first, when I saw it, I thought it was a good joke. That's why I took it. But now I think it really *is* my flag."

"Because you'll be forever sixteen?"

"Maybe so," he said, grinning at her. "But for another reason, too. I've been in so many armies, fought so many times under so many different flags. This time there wasn't a flag at all, there were no noble ideals, there wasn't even a cause beyond money. But I bet I did more good today, more real good in the world, than I've ever done in my life before." He waved the flag. "I'm going to keep this to remind me not to get too serious about other people's flags."

"You mean you won't hire out as a merc anymore?"

"I don't know. I'm not sure what I could do instead." He shrugged. "Grow up, maybe, though I'd rather not. I'll have to think about it. What about you? Still going back to the States?"

She gave a little sigh and shook her head, as though in long-suffering irritation. "Oh, I suppose not," she said. "You get in too much trouble when I'm not around. Besides, I'd like to see what kind of knight you'll be, following that flag."

Lew smiled, reaching out to touch her shoulder. "I'll be good," he said.

"Okay," she said.

EPILOGUE

Idi Amin slept, and dreamed. He dreamed that he rode on a white cloud over Lake Victoria, and the lake was steaming. All the lake had turned into coffee, hot steaming coffee, and bobbing on that lake of coffee were the severed heads of all his enemies. Hundreds of heads, thousands, millions of heads floating and nodding on that great lake of coffee, extending to the horizon in every direction, steam rising up past the dead nostrils and the eyes held open with staples.

It was a good dream, very pleasant and comforting. In his dream, on the cloud, sailing above them all, Idi Amin smiled.

AFTERWORD

Idi Amin, unfortunately, is real. So are or were his cronies (Major Farouk Minawa, Colonel Muammar al-Gaddafi) and his victims (Mrs. Dora Bloch, Archbishop Janani Luwum).

Africa is real, sort of. Uganda is real. The railroad, the town of Jinja, the State Research Bureau building, all the stage sets are real.

The 1977 failure of the Brazilian coffee crop and the resultant rise in worldwide coffee prices are real. The long-established practice of smuggling coffee out of Uganda, which reached some kind of manic peak in 1977, is real.

So much for reality.

The specific coffee-smuggling operation described in this novel—though similar events did take place—is an invention. The characters connected with that operation, every last one of them, are fictional, without specific real-world counterparts.